BRENDA MINTON

His Little Cowgirl

&

A Cowboy's Heart

HARLEQUIN® LOVE INSPIRED® CLASSICS

Recycling programs for this product may not exist in your area.

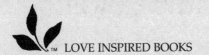

LOVE INSPIRED BOOKS

ISBN-13: 978-0-373-65168-9

HIS LITTLE COWGIRL AND A COWBOY'S HEART
Copyright © 2014 by Harlequin Books S.A.

The publisher acknowledges the copyright holder of the individual works as follows:

HIS LITTLE COWGIRL
Copyright © 2008 by Brenda Minton

A COWBOY'S HEART
Copyright © 2009 by Brenda Minton

www.Harlequin.com

Printed in U.S.A.

CONTENTS

Books by Brenda Minton

Love Inspired

BRENDA MINTON

started creating stories to entertain herself during hour-long rides on the school bus. In high school she wrote romance novels to entertain her friends. The dream grew and so did her aspirations to become an author. She started with notebooks, handwritten manuscripts and characters that refused to go away until their stories were told. Eventually she put away the pen and paper and got down to business with the computer. The journey took a few years, with some encouragement and rejection along the way—as well as a lot of stubbornness on her part. In 2006 her dream to write for Love Inspired Books came true. Brenda lives in the rural Ozarks with her husband, three kids and an abundance of cats and dogs. She enjoys a chaotic life that she wouldn't trade for anything—except, on occasion, a beach house in Texas. You can stop by and visit at her website, www.brendaminton.net.

HIS LITTLE COWGIRL

And ye be kind one to another,
tenderhearted, forgiving one another,
even as God for Christ's sake hath forgiven you.
—*Ephesians* 4:32

This book is dedicated to

Doug, for always supporting me in my dreams,
and to my kids for allowing me to be the
"crazy mom." Dream big and never give up.

To all of my family and friends who have kept me
going forward when I wanted to quit.

To Janet Benrey and Melissa Endlich,
for everything they do and have done for me.

To Janet McCoy of McCoy Ranches, for taking the
time to answer my questions about bull riders and
bull riding. (Mistakes I've made are of course my
own.) To bull riders like Cord McCoy, who are an
inspiration and a role model to young people, and
who leave their own footprints of faith.

To the readers for reading.

To God for all of the blessings.

Chapter One

Bailey stuck her hands into the hot, soapy water and began to scrub the dishes she'd put off washing until after lunch, wishing for the umpteenth time that the dishwasher still worked. Her father had helped for a few minutes, until his legs had grown weak and he'd taken himself to the living room and his favorite recliner to watch *Oprah*.

The throaty snore she heard through the doorway told her that he'd fallen asleep. She didn't mind; it was sleep that he needed these days. At least when he was sleeping, he wasn't worrying.

Oprah's voice drifted into the kitchen, borne on the gentle breeze that blew through the house. "So tell me, Suzanne, how much did you pay for your home in Malibu?"

Bailey strained to listen. "Three million, a bargain." Audience laughter.

Bailey shook her head and scrubbed harder. Three million for a house. What couldn't she do with three million dollars? She looked out her window above the sink, at the farm shimmering in the late-afternoon sun. It looked as tired as her dad. A good eye could see that things were falling apart. The fences were sagging and the last windstorm had done a number on the barn roof. Not to mention her truck, which was on its last leg, and tires.... Three million dollars. That would help pay the mortgage. Well, of course, with three million dollars in the bank, there wouldn't be a mortgage.

She was doing well if she made the mortgage payment each month. The tips she earned as a waitress put shoes on her daughter's feet—one pair at a time—and cutting a few more cows from the herd would pay the property taxes. Life in the Ozarks was far removed from Hollywood.

A little cutting back, a lot of prayer and making it through another day with her dad still in her life. That was how it went in the real world. At least in her world.

Bailey squeezed her eyes shut. She opened them when she heard a distant rattle and the rapid-fire bark of her blue heeler. Her mind turned, wondering who it could be. She wasn't expecting anyone, and it sounded like whoever it was, they were pulling a trailer.

She squeezed the water out of the dishrag, tossed it on the counter and walked out the back door. If she didn't catch the dog now, the person paying them a surprise visit would have a hole in his pant's leg and a bad attitude to go with it. Bailey was holding on to faith by a string; she didn't need someone's bad day to rub off on her.

A shiny, red extended-cab truck pulling an RV rumbled to a stop. Blue, her five-year-old blue heeler, stood in the middle of the yard. The yard that really needed to be mowed before it became a hayfield.

But Bailey stopped herself there and reached for the dog's collar. She had a list of things that needed to be done. All of those things dimmed in comparison with the bigger problem she saw stepping out of the truck and into her life.

The hair on the back of Blue's neck was standing on end. Teeth bared, the dog strained against her hold on his collar. For a brief, really brief, moment, she considered letting go.

Six years had passed since she'd seen Cody Jacobs face-to-face. Six years since she'd spent a summer working on a ranch in Wyoming. Six years since she'd tried so hard to tell him she was pregnant. Six years since she'd given up because he wouldn't answer her phone calls.

Now he was here. Now, when there were so many other worries to work through. She looked up to see if God would send her a sign, a parting of the clouds or some other gigantic miracle. Instead she felt a soft whisper of peace. If only it hadn't gotten tangled with dread and a good dose of anger as her day went suddenly south.

Cody walked across the lawn, looking for all the world like he belonged on her farm. He was suntanned, wore faded Wranglers, and a soft, cotton T-shirt stretched across his broad shoulders. He was smiling like he hadn't a care in the world.

Every time she had imagined this moment, she'd thought what she'd say. She'd be strong, send him packing, show him she was in control and that he couldn't hurt her again.

Not once had she been breathless or speechless. Not once in her imagination had she thought that she'd remember how his laughter sounded on a quiet summer night in Wyoming, or how his hand had felt on hers. She had told herself that she'd only remember him saying goodbye and how he laughed when she told him she loved him.

All of her imaginings melted like a snowman in July when faced with the genuine article—Cody Jacobs walking toward her. Now what in the world was she going to do about that? What was she going to do about the little girl inside the house, and the truth that she'd kept from him? All of her good intentions—wanting to protect her daughter from someone whose lifestyle had seemed unfit for a child—seemed irrelevant at the moment.

Cody Jacobs was about to learn he had a daughter. She hadn't wanted it to happen like this. Meg knew who her daddy was. Bailey had wanted to confront Cody in her own way, when the time seemed right.

Not today.

Blue yanked at the collar and jerked her forward a few feet, a warning that her visitor had entered the imaginary danger zone of the dog. Bailey flexed her fingers and wished she wasn't leaning forward the way she was.

"Bailey, you're looking good."

Her foot she was looking good. She was wearing the same faded jeans and stained T-shirt she'd worn while working in the garden.

"Thanks, Cody."

Still smiling, he held his hand out to Blue. The dog suddenly forgot that the man was the enemy. Pulling free from her grasp, the animal belly crawled to Cody. Bailey stood, stretching the kink from her back. Her gaze connected with Cody's, really connected for the first time since he'd gotten out of the truck.

Up close and in person he was still about the prettiest man she'd ever seen. Like the average bull rider, he wasn't tall, just a few inches taller than her five feet five inches. He still had lean, boyish looks and long eyelashes that could make a girl swoon—if she were the swooning type. Bailey wasn't, not anymore.

"How've you been?" He closed the gap between them, his hand still being licked by Blue.

"I'm fine." Most days she really was. "What are you doing in Missouri?"

She knew the answer. She was a convenient stop on the highway to Springfield, just thirty miles north. The town was hosting a pro bull-riding event, and Cody was in line for the world title this year.

"I wanted to talk to you."

"Okay, talk."

Looking suddenly unsure, he took off his bent-out-of-shape, straw cowboy hat and shoved his fingers through black hair, which was straight and a little too long. When he looked at her, with his stormy blue-gray eyes, she thought of Meg and how she didn't want Cody to learn the truth without any warning.

Her heart shuddered at the thought. With a quick glance over her shoulder, she breathed a sigh of relief. Meg was taking a nap on the couch. That gave Bailey a few minutes to decide the best course of action.

"Bailey, I'm here to say I'm sorry." Cody shrugged and said, "I guess this is part of a man turned thirty and realizing he's wasted a lot of years and hurt a lot of people."

"I'm not sure what to say." The words of his apology were much as she had imagined them to be, but in her dreams they made more sense. In real life his words didn't bring instant healing.

"You don't really have to say anything. This is something I have to do. I…" He cleared his throat and brought his gaze up to meet hers. "I joined AA and part of the process is making amends for the things I've done. I know that when I drove away from Bar A Ranch, I hurt you."

"So is this about wanting forgiveness, or are you truly sorry?"

She needed more than words because words were easy enough to say. Words promised forever and something special on a summer night.

Words said *I'm sorry* and even *I forgive*.

Cody worried the hat in his hands, keeping his head down and his gaze on his dusty boots. When he looked up, his eyes were clear, his jaw set and determined. She had seen that look on his face before, normally with a camera focused in tightly as he gave the nod and the bull he was set to ride busted from the gate for an eight-second ride that always seemed to last eight minutes.

"This is about me needing forgiveness, and it is also about being truly sorry."

It was her turn to look up, to search for something in his gaze, in those eyes that reminded her of a summer storm on the horizon. He meant it, or at least she thought he did. She nodded and took a step back.

"Okay, you're forgiven."

"You mean it?"

Did she mean it? She closed her eyes, wanting him to be gone, wanting to walk back into the house to a sink full of dishes and chores waiting to be done. Those were the things that made sense to her these days.

What also made sense was Meg, and the life they had here, the life they had built for themselves in spite of everything. Bailey had paced the floor alone when her daughter had been colicky. Bailey, alone, had held Meg tightly when a bad dream woke her in the middle of the night.

Cody hadn't been there, not even for that stormy night when Bailey's dad had driven her to the hospital.

Her conscience poked at her, telling her that he couldn't apologize for the things he didn't know. Cody couldn't apologize for leaving her to raise a child alone, not when he'd never known about that child. They'd both made mistakes. He didn't know it, but they both had apologies to make.

"I forgave you a long time ago." She smiled, feeling the heat of the August sun on her head and back.

"That means a lot to me, Bailey. I want a fresh start, and I didn't want to make that start thinking about you and what happened."

What happened—the way he said it made it sound simple and easy to forget. It wasn't easy to forget a decision that made a person feel like she'd let down not only herself, but everyone who counted on her. Even God.

Maybe Cody was finally starting to understand.

"That's good, Cody. I hope that this is the change

you need." She paused, unsure of how to proceed. She should tell him about Meg. Before he left she should let him know what she had tried to tell him the last time she saw him.

The screen door thudded softly behind her. Bailey lifted her gaze to his, fearing the truth and the look on Cody's face. He stared past her, his eyes narrowing against the bright sunshine. As his gaze lingered, Bailey knew that the time for truth had arrived.

It had never happened this way in her dreams.

"Mommy."

Cody stared at the little girl standing on the porch. He tried to catch his breath, but the weight on his chest pushed down, forcing air from his lungs as his heart hammered against his ribs. He stared into a tiny heart-shaped face he'd never seen before, and yet, and yet, the face seemed so familiar.

The little girl had Bailey's straight blond hair. She had a rosebud mouth, just like her mom's. His gaze stopped at her eyes. It was there that he discovered the truth and he knew that Bailey had apologies of her own to give.

Six years of traveling, riding bulls and putting money in the bank for a place of his own, a place he wouldn't let his own dad buy for him, and it came down to this. It came down to a child with stormy-blue eyes wearing jean shorts, a T-shirt and pink cowboy boots.

Cody felt a huge dose of regret because while he'd been having the time of his life, Bailey had been here raising his daughter alone.

With a million questions and plenty of accusations racing through his mind, he switched his attention back to Bailey. She twisted away from him but not quickly enough for him to miss the streak of red creeping up her neck.

Cowgirls couldn't lie.

"Go inside, Meg," Bailey said.

"But I need a drink."

"Get a juice box out of the fridge. I'll be in soon."

"Who is he?" The little girl crossed her tanned arms and gave him the look that said she was the only law in town and he was trespassing. He wanted to smile but he couldn't. Not yet.

"He's someone I used to know."

The little girl nodded and walked back into the house, the screen door slamming behind her. Bailey waited until her daughter, his daughter, too, was out of sight before facing him.

"It looks like I'm not the only one who needs to apologize," he whispered, not really sure if he could say the words aloud.

He had a daughter. He was six months sober, living in an RV, and he had a daughter.

He was on step 9, and it seemed that Bailey had a Step 9 of her own. Making amends.

"I tried to tell you." She looked away, the breeze blowing her hair around her face. He remembered the feel of her hair, like soft silk and feathers.

He remembered that being with her had made him believe in himself. For a few short months he had believed he could be something better than his own father had been. Now he couldn't find that feeling, not with anger boiling to the surface.

"You didn't try very hard."

"The day you left the ranch, I told you that I loved you and that we needed to talk. You laughed and walked away because, and I quote, *'Cowgirls always think they're in love.'*"

As she faced him with his own stupid actions, it was his turn to look away. He focused on the same tree-covered hill her gaze had shot to moments ago. Without really trying, he remembered that day. He remembered getting in his truck and driving away, with her running out of the barn trying to stop him.

He remembered thinking that if he didn't get away, he would drown in her. More memories returned, along with the knowledge that he had wanted to lose himself in that feeling. That had scared him more than anything. At twenty-five he'd been too afraid of love to take a chance. He'd been afraid of failure.

Now he had a daughter. He was in the middle of a program that included not starting new relationships, and this one had to be taken care of. He had a little girl. He needed to wrap his mind around that fact and what it meant, not just for the moment but for the rest of his life.

"I should have listened to you." He ran his hand through his hair and shoved his hat back in place. "But you could have told me. You've had six years of opportunities to tell me."

"I left messages for you to call me. After a while I gave up. Wouldn't you?" She crossed her arms, staring him down with brown eyes that at one time were warmer than cocoa on a winter day. "You were running so fast, Cody. You didn't want to hear what I had to tell you because you were afraid it would be about love and forever."

"You should have told me."

"And have you believing that I was trying to trap you? The day you left Wyoming you made it pretty clear to me that you weren't looking for 'forever' with anyone."

He needed to sit down. He didn't want to think about how much he needed a drink. Six months sober, and he wasn't going to end his sobriety like this.

"Bailey, don't throw my words back in my face. That was six years ago. I've learned a lot, and I've been through a lot." He shook his head and took a step back from her.

"Keep your voice down."

"And on top of that you want me to be calm about this?"

"I'm sorry."

He remembered her at twenty-two. She had dreamed of being a famous horse trainer with a ranch and a few kids. He'd been running from those kinds of women, the kind who dreamed of forever.

"I won't keep you from seeing her." She made it sound like the offer of the century.

"Of course."

"In case you're wondering, she knows that you're her dad. I haven't kept that from her. But you're not on her birth certificate."

"Did you ever stop to think that maybe she needed to see me?"

"When would she have seen you? Maybe once or twice a year as you drove on through? Or on TV with a pretty girl on your arm."

"Is that how you portrayed me to her?"

She sighed and shook her head.

Of course she wouldn't do that. He knew that much about her. Bailey was kind. She had faith, and he'd taken advantage of her innocence. That had haunted him for years. Her tears had haunted him, too, and her regret.

"I told her that someday she could meet you."

"That's great, Bailey." He took a step back. "I have a daughter and you were going to let me meet her *someday*?"

"What did you expect from me, Cody?"

"Bailey, I don't know the right answer to that. I just know that I have a daughter and she's five years old. Don't ask me to make sense of this or tell you how I would have reacted a few years ago. I'm a different person today."

"Older and wiser?"

"Something like that."

He couldn't adjust with Bailey staring at him with soft brown eyes and a guilty flush staining her cheeks. He had to get away from her because he didn't know if he should hug her or throttle her.

"I need to think."

She shrugged as if it didn't matter. But he could tell that it did. It mattered to him, too.

And he had honestly thought he'd be able to stop by, say his apologies and leave. He'd been surprised on more counts than one. He'd been surprised with a daughter, and surprised that Bailey Cross still had the ability to undo him.

"I have to ride in Springfield tonight." He walked to his truck, followed by the tongue-wagging blue heeler. He turned when he realized that Bailey was right behind him. "I'm leaving my RV here so that you'll know I'm coming back. I'm not a twenty-five-year-old kid now, Bailey. I don't run."

"I'm sure you don't."

"Maybe I shouldn't even go to Springfield."

"I think you should go, Cody. You can call and we'll talk this out." She took a few steps toward him, and he hadn't counted on the rush of feelings and memories that returned. "I know you can't miss this ride. I know you're at the top of the point standings."

"Bailey, some things are more important than eight seconds on a bull. Family is more important."

"I know that. But I also know what this world title means to you."

"I'm coming back," Cody said. "Tonight."

He leaned to unhitch the RV from the back of his truck, aware that she stood next to him, her hands shoved into the front pockets of her jeans.

"Fine, you can come back and we'll talk." Bailey backed up a step, as if wanting that distance between them. "We'll work something out."

"Work something out?" He shoved the tongue of the trailer off the hitch and turned to face her. "You make it sound like we're disputing over a property line and not a little girl with eyes like mine."

"Cody, I am sorry."

He shook his head and raised his hand to wave off her words. Instead of staying to argue, he got into his truck and pulled away. When he glanced into his rearview mirror she was walking across the lawn to the farmhouse where she'd grown up.

And inside that house was a little girl he should have known about, a little girl who needed to know her daddy. He wasn't going to walk away this time. Bailey Cross would have to find a way to deal with that.

Bailey stopped on the back porch, lingering for a long moment in the breeze created by the overhead ceiling fan. Inside the house her dad and daughter were waiting.

Driving down the road was the man who had given her that child and broken her heart. Her head was spinning like the blades on the ceiling fan.

She'd forgiven him. She had really thought she'd forgotten. Instead it all returned in a heady flash of memory, including remnants of the pain she'd felt when he'd left her in Wyoming.

After Meg's birth she had done what she'd been taught—she'd pulled herself up by her bootstraps and moved on. As a single mother coping with lonely nights and an uncertain future, she hadn't had time for wallowing in her mistakes.

How was she going to deal with Cody Jacobs? Worse, how was she going to deal with the fact that having him back in her life had turned her emotions inside out?

And then came fear. Would he take Meg away from her? Would his knowing about their daughter mean that holidays and summer vacations would be spent apart? How would she cope with sharing Meg?

Bailey stopped the downward spiral of thoughts. She wouldn't be sharing Meg with a stranger. Cody was Meg's dad. He had rights.

That assurance didn't make her feel any better.

She leaned against the side of the house, waiting

for the world to right itself before crossing the threshold to face her dad. The dog lumbered up the steps and belly crawled across the porch. Bailey reached down and Blue nuzzled her hand as if the dog knew she needed to be comforted.

"Thanks, girl."

When she walked into the kitchen, her dad was there, waiting for her. Bailey pulled a pitcher of tea out of the fridge and pretended that nothing had happened. Not that she'd get away with pretending. Her dad had probably heard the entire conversation through the open window.

"Who were you talking to?" Jerry Cross was leaning on the counter, his afternoon meds in his hand. His skin had lost the healthy farmer's tan he'd always worn. Now he just looked old and gray. And he wasn't old.

Every time Bailey looked at him and saw him wasting away in front of her, she wanted to cry. She wanted to explain to God that it wasn't fair. She had lost her mom when she was ten. Now she was losing her dad.

And Cody Jacobs's RV was parked in her driveway.

"It was…" She turned to see if her daughter was in the room.

"She's watching that goofy cartoon she likes."

"That was Cody Jacobs."

"Humph."

"He came to apologize."

"I guess he got more than he bargained for." He coughed, the moment of breathlessness lasting longer than a week ago and leaving him weak enough that he had to sit at the kitchen table. "His RV is still here."

"He says he's coming back."

Her dad looked almost pleased. "Good for him."

"Good for him? Dad, this isn't good for me. It isn't good for Meg."

"Maybe it's good for me." He wiped a large, work-worn hand across his face. "Maybe I need this, Bailey. Maybe I need to know that he's here for you."

"He showed up to apologize. That doesn't put him in my life. I don't want him in my life. I don't want to be his girl of the week. Isn't that what the announcers on the sports channel call the women who hang on to his arm?"

"We've both noticed a change in him since that bull trampled him last winter." Once broad shoulders shrugged. "People change."

Bailey couldn't agree more. She had changed. At twenty-two she had gone to Wyoming for a summer work program, starry-eyed and thinking that all cowboys were heroes. She had come home four months later, pregnant and brokenhearted.

It had taken her more than a year to forgive herself and move on. She had struggled with the truth, that God's grace was sufficient. She had grown and learned how to stand on her own two feet without dreams of a man rescuing her.

Now she had a dad and a little girl who needed her. She had a farm with a second mortgage, back taxes seriously in arrears and medical bills piling up in a basket on the coffee table. She had horses that needed to be fed.

"Dad, I have to get to work. You have to let me be an adult and take care of this myself."

Moisture shimmered in her dad's brown eyes. "I know you can take care of things, Bailey. I only wish I could help you more."

She hugged him tightly, her heart breaking because of his continued weight loss.

"Don't worry, Dad. We have peace, remember?"

"Peace." He nodded as he whispered the word.

Bailey walked to the back door. "I need to walk to the back pasture to check on that cow that didn't come up this afternoon. Can you keep an eye on Meg?"

"I'll watch her." He swallowed his pills before continuing. "He has a right to know his daughter."

"I know."

She knew, but she didn't quite know how to deal with it, not yet. Cody now knew about Meg. It had to happen sooner or later. She wouldn't have been able to remain out of the rodeo circuit forever. Avoiding Cody had meant avoiding people who could send horses her way for training.

Maybe God had meant for it to happen this way, with Cody driving into her life when she had the least amount of energy to fight? And maybe, just maybe, he would meet Meg and then leave town.

Chapter Two

Bulls bellowed and snorted, the sound combining with the steady hum of the crowd and the banter of cowboys, medical staff and stock contractors. Cody leaned against the wall in a corner of the area that was almost quiet.

"What's up with you?"

"Bradshaw, I didn't know you were here." Cody smiled at the guy who had been a friend for years. Rivalry had come between them a few times. And for a while Jason Bradshaw's faith had driven a huge wedge between them.

Cody hadn't known what to do when his friend "found religion" two years earlier. They had gone from being drinking buddies to strangers, both wanting different things out of life.

The rift had grown until the day seven months earlier when Cody had woken up in a hospital, unsure of who he was or where he was. Later he had watched tapes of the fall. The wreck of the season, they called it. He had been twisted in the bull rope, dangling from the side of a fifteen-hundred-pound animal. When Cody came loose, the bull twisted and the two butted heads with a force that had given him a huge concussion and some loss of memory.

Jason said it must have knocked some sense into him, because the Sunday after his release from the hospital Cody gave in to the urge to attend the church service the bull riders held each week. He had stood next to his friend, hearing a message his grandfather had tried to tell him when he had been too young to understand. Later on in life he had thought he didn't need it.

That Sunday he knew he needed it. He knew that he needed to be forgiven. He needed the promise contained in those words, and he needed a fresh start.

He had never dreamed his second chance would lead him to Gibson, Missouri, and a little girl named Meg.

"You look like you got hit by a semitruck." Jason nudged Cody's side, gaining his attention.

"Something like that."

"Did you see Bailey?"

Cody moved to the side to see why the crowd was roaring. He watched a young rider make it to eight seconds and then some. The kids on tour were going great guns with enthusiasm and bodies that weren't being kept mobile with cortisone injections, Ace bandages and a diet of ibuprofen.

"Remember what that felt like?" Jason laughed and watched as the kid on the bull jumped off, landing on his feet and running out of the arena without a limp.

"Vaguely." He remembered what yesterday felt like, when he knew who he was and that his life was all about winning the bull-riding championship and walking away with a seven-figure check. Now his goals were as scrambled as his insides.

"I found out today that I'm a dad. I have a five-year-old daughter named Meg."

Jason took off his hat and ran a hand through short red hair, his eyes widening as he leaned back against the wall. His being speechless didn't happen often. Cody was sort of glad his friend reacted with stunned silence. His surprise validated Cody's own feelings of disbelief.

"Wow."

"Is that all you have to say?"

Jason laughed and shrugged his shoulders. "Congratulations?"

"Thanks. I think."

"What are you going to do?"

"Well, if Bailey was seventeen and madly in love with me, I'd do the right thing and marry her. Right now she's about twenty-eight, and I'm pretty sure she hates me. So that leaves the little girl. I might have a chance with her, but I'm not sure."

His daughter, a sprite with her mother's perky nose, heart-shaped face and flaxen hair. Cowgirls were hard to beat. They were tough as nails and soft as down. Until you made them mad. Bailey was definitely mad. She had a right to be, but that didn't help Cody.

He had a daughter. It was still sinking in. Thinking back, he remembered the luminous look in Bailey's eyes when she said she loved him, and then the tears when he teased her about cowgirls always thinking they were in love. Finally there were the frantic phone calls that lasted five or six months after she left Wyoming. It all made sense now.

He looked down, shaking his head at the tumble of thoughts rolling through his mind. He had missed out on five years. Without knowing it, he had become his own dad.

"Cody, don't beat yourself up for something you didn't know about."

"If I had called her back, I would have known. Instead I went on my merry way, thinking she just wanted to cry and try to drag me back into her life." He fastened the Kevlar vest that bull riders wore for protection and tried to concentrate on the ride about to take place. "I should have known Bailey better than to think that about her."

"You know, I think you only ran because you were so stinking in love with her." Jason laughed as he said the words, his loud outburst drawing the quick glances of a dozen men in the area.

"Do you think you could announce it to the whole world?"

"Sorry, but I think they're going to find out sooner or later."

Cody pulled off his hat and ran shaking fingers through his hair. "I could use a…"

"Friend to pray with?" Jason smiled as he replaced the word with something that wouldn't undo six months of sobriety.

"Yes, prayer." His new way of dealing with stress. "I have a daughter, Jason. What in the world am I going to do with her?"

"Buy her a pony?"

"My dad bought me a pony."

Jason slapped him on the back. "Go back to Gibson, Missouri, and get to know your daughter. You've got enough money in the bank to last more than a few years, and a good herd of cattle down in Oklahoma. Maybe it's time to start using your nest egg to build a nest? You could even use that business degree of yours for something other than balancing a feed bill and tallying your earnings."

"What if I can't be a dad?" He didn't know how to be something he'd never had. That's why he'd run from girls looking for "forever."

"No one really knows how. I think you just learn as you go. It's probably a lot like bull riding, the more you work at it, the better you get."

Someone shouted Cody's name. He was up soon. He tipped his hat to Jason and told him he probably would lay off the tour after this event, at least for a few weeks, at least until he settled things with Bailey.

And he would give up ever being a world champion. His goal and his dream for more years than he could remember had been within his grasp, but one afternoon in Gibson, Missouri, had changed everything.

Five minutes later he was slipping onto the back of a bull named Outta Control. He hated that bull. It was part Mexican fighting bull and part insane. As he pulled his bull rope tight, wrapping it around his gloved hand, the bull jerked and snorted. The crazy animal obviously thought the eight seconds started before the gate opened.

Cody squeezed his knees against the animal's heaving sides and hunched forward, preparing for the moment that the gate would open. Foam and slobber slung around his face as the bull bellowed and shook his mammoth head.

"This is crazy." He muttered the words to no one in particular as he nodded his head and the gate flew open.

If he survived this ride, he was going back to Gibson, to his daughter and to Bailey. He would find a way to be a dad.

The fact that Cody's RV was still in the drive the next morning meant nothing to Bailey. The problem was, his truck was there to. That meant he'd survived his ride and returned.

She didn't know how to feel about Cody Jacobs keeping promises. Six years ago they'd been sitting around a campfire when he leaned over and whispered that he loved her. She had believed him. She had really thought they might have forever.

She wouldn't be so quick to believe, not this time. This time she would protect her heart, and she would protect her daughter. Changed or not, Cody was a bull rider, and the lure of the world title would drag him back to the circuit, probably sooner than later.

"He got in at around midnight. He was walking straight but a little stooped." Her dad had followed her to the porch. He pressed a cup of coffee into her hand.

"What were you doing up?"

"Praying, thinking and waiting to see if he'd come back." Jerry Cross smiled.

"Nice, Dad. It sort of makes me feel like you're plotting against me."

"Not at all, cupcake." He scooted past her and back to the kitchen. "Want me to feed this morning?"

"Nope, I'll do it. I have to face him sooner or later." She glanced over the rim of her cup and watched the dark RV. "You mind listening for Meg?"

"Honey, you know I don't. And you know I don't mind feeding."

"It's too hot. The humidity would…" Her heart ached with a word that used to be so easy.

"Don't cry on me, pumpkin. And the humidity isn't going to kill me." He winked before he walked away.

Bailey prayed again, the silent prayer that had become constant. *Please God, don't take my dad.* She knew what the doctors said, and she knew with her own eyes that he was failing fast. She didn't know what she'd do without him in her life.

She drained her cup of coffee and walked out the back door. The RV in the drive was still dark and silent. The barn wasn't. As she walked through the door, she heard music on the office radio and noises from the corral.

Cody turned and smiled when she walked out the open double doors on the far side of the barn. Her favorite mare was standing next to him, and he was running his hand over the animal's bulging side.

That mare and the foal growing inside of her were the future hope of Bailey's training and breeding program. If that little baby had half the class and durability of his daddy, the Rocking C would have a chance of surviving.

"Any day now." Cody spoke softly, either to her or to the mare. She and the mare both knew that it would be any day.

"What are you doing here?"

He glanced up, his hat shading his eyes. "I told you I'd be back. I'm in it for the long haul, Bailey."

"In what for the long haul?"

He shot her a disgusted look and sighed. "I'm a father. I might be coming into this a little late, but I want to be a part of Meg's life."

"So, you've gone from the guy who didn't want to be tied down to the guy who is in fatherhood for the long haul?"

"When confronted with his mistakes, a guy can make a lot of changes." He slid his hand down the mare's misty-gray neck, but his gaze connected with Bailey's. "I'm alive, and God gave me a second chance. I don't take that lightly."

"I see." But she didn't, not really.

Bailey walked back into the barn, knowing he followed. When she turned, she noticed that he wasn't following at a very fast pace. The limp and slightly stooped posture said a lot.

"Take a fall last night?"

He grinned and shrugged muscular shoulders. "Not so much of a fall as a brush-off. This is what one might call 'cowboy, meet gate—gate, meet cowboy.' The bull did the introductions."

"Anything broken?" Not that she cared.

"Just bruised."

"Good, then you should be able to hitch that RV back to your truck and leave today."

"Actually, no, I can't. Funny, I've never really had a reason to stick before, but I like Missouri and so this isn't such a bad thing. And the folks at the Hash-It-Out Diner all think you're real pretty and a good catch."

Bailey searched for something to throw at him, just about anything would work. She wanted to wipe that smug smile off his face. Especially when smug was accompanied by a wink and a dimpled smile.

"Cody, I don't need this. You don't understand what it's like here and how long it took me to rebuild my reputation after that summer in Wyoming."

He didn't understand about going to church six months pregnant, knowing God forgave, but people weren't as likely to let go of her mistake.

"I didn't tell them who I am, or that I'm Meg's dad." He turned on the water hose as he spoke. "I think most of them have gotten over it, Bailey. Except maybe Hazel. Hazel has a daughter in Springfield who is a schoolteacher and a real good girl."

Bailey groaned as she scooped out feed and emptied it into a bucket. Cody dragged the hose to the water trough just outside the back door. He left it and walked back inside.

"Yes, Maria is a good girl. I'll introduce the two of you." She managed a smile.

"Bailey, I was teasing." Smelling like soap and coffee, he walked next to her. "This isn't about us, or a relationship. This is about a child I didn't know that I had. I'm not proposing marriage, and I'm not trying to move in. I want the chance to know my daughter."

Bailey glanced in his direction before walking off with the bucket of grain and the scoop. She remembered that he had shown up for a purpose other than his daughter.

"Why did you come to apologize?"

"It's a long story."

"I have thirty minutes before I need to leave for work."

Cody took the bucket from her hand and started the job of dumping feed into the stalls. "You water, I'll feed. And they told me you work three days a week at the Hash-It-Out."

"Since Dad can't work, we do what we can to make ends meet." She didn't tell him that the ends rarely met. "So, about you and this big apology."

"Why can't your dad work?"

"He has cancer."

She couldn't tell him that her dad had only months to live. Saying it made it too real. And she couldn't make eye contact with Cody, not when she knew that his eyes would be soft with compassion.

"I'm sorry, Bailey."

"We're surviving."

"It can't be easy."

Cody poured the last scoop of grain into the feed bucket of a horse she'd been working with for a few weeks.

"It isn't easy." She turned the water off and then finally looked at him. "But we're doing our best."

"Of course you are." He sat down on an upturned bucket, absently rubbing his knee as he stared up at the wood plank ceiling overhead.

"Let's talk about you, Cody. What happened?"

"Bailey, I'm an alcoholic. I started AA about seven months ago. I've been sober for six months." He shrugged. "About five months ago I wrote out a list of people I had hurt, people that I needed to apologize to. You were at the top of the list."

"I see. And how did this all start?"

"Apologizing, or realizing that I needed to grow up and make changes in my life?"

He smiled a crooked, one-sided smile that exposed a dimple in his left cheek. Bailey hadn't forgotten that grin. She saw it every time Meg smiled at her. It reminded her of how it had felt to be special to someone like him. He had picked her wildflowers and taken her swimming in mountain lakes.

That moment in the sun had happened when her dad had been healthy and the farm had been prosperous. Their horses had been selling all across the country, and they'd had a good herd of Angus. Now she had five cows, two mares, no stallion and a few horses to train.

"What made you go to AA?"

"I turned thirty and realized I didn't have a home and that I had a lot of blank spots in my memory. I was getting on bulls drunk." He shrugged and half laughed. "I realized when I got trampled into the dirt back in Houston last winter."

"I saw you on TV the night it happened." She closed her eyes as the admission slipped out and then quickly covered her tracks. "I've always watched bull riding. Dad and I watch it together."

"Gotcha." He leaned back against the wall. "I guess one of the big reasons for changing was that I didn't want to waste the rest of my life."

"I'm glad you're doing better." It was all she could give him. She was glad he was sober and glad he was safe. "We'll work something out so that you can get to know Meg."

"Get to know her? Bailey, she's my daughter and I

want more than moments to 'get to know her.' I want to be a part of her life."

"You can, when you're in the area."

"I made a decision last night." He didn't smile as he said the words. "I'm not leaving."

"What does that mean?"

"It means I'm staying in Gibson, Missouri."

Bailey's heart pounded hard and she shoved her trembling hands into the front pockets of her jeans. Dust danced on beams of sun that shot through the open doors of the barn, and country music filtered from the office. She had been here so many times and yet never like this, never as unsure as she was at that moment.

"What about the tour? You're closer than ever to winning a world title."

She knew what that meant to him. She knew how hard it was for bull riders to walk away from the pursuit of that title.

"Some things are more important. And if I choose to go back, bull riding will always be there."

"You can't stay here."

"I'm going to park my RV under that big oak tree by your garage, and I am most certainly going to stay."

"This is my home, my property, and I beg to differ."

"And that's my little girl you've got in that house, so I think you'll get over it."

Bailey sat down on the bucket he'd vacated, her legs weak and trembling. She looked up, making eye contact with a man she didn't really know. He wasn't the guy she'd met in Wyoming, the one who'd said he didn't plan on ever having a family or being tied down to anyone. Back then she had thought finding the right woman to love would change him. Now she didn't want him changed and living on her farm.

She had to get control. "Fine you can stay for a week, and then we'll work something out."

"I'm not leaving, not until I decide to go."

"Cody, I don't have time to argue with you."

He shrugged, casually, but obviously determined. His mouth remained in a straight line, not smiling and not revealing that good-natured dimple.

"I've lost five years of my daughter's life, Bailey. I'm not losing another day. Don't take this personally, because I'm not trying to make it personal, but I'm not letting you call the shots. You're not going to keep my daughter from me."

Did it look that way to him? She hadn't meant for that to happen. She had really thought he didn't care, or wouldn't care. He was in this life for a good time. Those had been his words the day he walked away from her.

People did change. He wasn't the only one who needed to apologize.

"I'm sorry. I never meant to keep her from you." She glanced down at her watch and groaned. "I have to go to work."

"I'll be here when you get home."

Would he? She didn't know how to deal with that thought. Of him in her life, and in her daughter's life.

She had learned to rely on God and the knowledge that He would get her through whatever came her way. If she closed her eyes, she could think of a long list of *whatevers*. At the top of the list was losing her dad; then came being a single mom, and then the pile of bills that were growing as large as Mount Rushmore. God could get her through those things.

Now she had to worry about Cody and what his staying would mean. Would he try to gain custody of Meg, or visitation? Would he stay only long enough to prove that he had rights?

How would it feel if he walked away? She tried to tell herself that she wouldn't be hurt. This time it would be different because now the person who would be hurt was Meg.

Bailey wouldn't let that happen.

Chapter Three

Cody stood outside the barn and watched Bailey drive away, the old truck stirring up a cloud of dust as it sped down the rutted gravel drive. When he turned toward his RV, Jerry Cross was there. It had to happen sooner or later, that the father of the woman he'd gotten pregnant would want to take a piece out of his hide.

If someone ever hurt Meg that way, Cody would like to think he'd be there to do the same thing. It would help to start off on the right foot. "Hello, sir. I'm Cody Jacobs." Father of your grandchild.

"Are you staying?" Jerry sat down in the lawn chair that Cody had unfolded and stuck under the awning of the RV.

"Planning on it." Cody grabbed another chair out of the back of his truck and plopped it down next to Jerry's.

"Think she'll let you stay?"

"The way I see it, she doesn't really have a choice."

Jerry laughed at that, the sound low and rasping.

Cody glanced sideways, noticing the tinge of gray in Jerry's complexion. It couldn't be easy for Bailey, having her dad this sick and handling things on her own. The condition of the farm pretty much said it all. The barn needed repairs, the fence was sagging and the feed room was running on empty.

"I like you, Cody, and I hope you'll stick around. Let me give you some advice, though. Bailey isn't a kid anymore. She isn't going to be fooled. She's strong and she's independent. She takes care of this farm and she juggles the bills like a circus clown." Jerry's eyes misted over. "I worry that life is passing her by and she isn't squeezing any joy out of it for herself."

"I didn't mean to do that to her."

The older man shrugged shoulders that had once been broad. Cody couldn't imagine being in his shoes, knowing that life wouldn't last and that people he loved would be left behind.

"It wasn't all you, son. I have more than a little to do with the weight on her shoulders."

"Is there a way I can help?"

Jerry shook his head. "Nope. Others have offered. She's determined to paddle this sinking ship to shore. She thinks she can plug the holes and make it sail again."

"I've got money…"

Jerry's gnarled hand went up. "Save your breath and save your money. She won't take charity."

"It isn't charity. I'm the father of the little girl in that house."

"Then I guess you'd really better tread lightly."

Jerry stood, swaying lightly and balancing himself with the arm of the chair. Cody reached but withdrew his hand short of making contact. If it were him, would he want others reaching to hold him up, or would he want to be strong on his own? He thought that Jerry Cross wouldn't want a hand unless it was asked for.

That made him a lot like his daughter.

"I'm going in to check on the young'un. Holler if you need anything," Jerry said as he walked away.

The young'un. Cody sat in the chair and thought about the little girl. His daughter. For a long time he waited, thinking she might come out of the house. When she didn't, he went to the barn.

Thirty minutes and two clean stalls later, a tiny voice called his name. Cody swiped his arm across his brow and peered over the top of the stall he had been cleaning. Meg stood on tiptoes peeking up at him. He hid a grin because she was still wearing her nightgown and yet she'd pulled on those pink cowboy boots she'd been wearing the previous day.

"I have kittens." She chewed on gum and smiled.

"How many?"

"Four. Wanna see 'em?"

He wanted to see those kittens more than anything in the world. A myriad of emotions washed over him with that realization. He had never hugged his child. He hadn't held her or comforted her. He hadn't wiped away her tears when she cried. Five years he had missed out on loving this little girl with Bailey's sweet face and his blue eyes.

"I do wanna see 'em."

He opened the stall door and joined the little girl that barely reached his waist. Her hand came up, the gesture obvious. Cody's heart leaped into his throat as his fingers closed around hers.

In that instant he knew he'd follow her anywhere. He'd give his life for her. And if anyone ever did to her what he'd done to her mother…

Regret twisted his stomach into knots. He couldn't undo what he'd done to Bailey, but he could do something now. He could be a father. Or at least make his best attempt.

Doubt swirled with regret, making him wonder if he could. What if he couldn't? What if he turned out to be his own father?

"The kittens are in there." Meg pointed to a small corner of the barn where buckets and tools were stored. The area was dark and dusty, but a corner had been cleared out and straw put down for the new mother.

"How old are they?"

"One week. They don't even have their eyes yet."

Cody smiled and refrained from correcting her about the eyes. "I bet they love you."

She shook her head. "Not yet, 'cause I can't touch them or the momma kitten will hide them. She's afraid they'll get hurt."

"Momma cats are like that." He peeked into the corner and saw the mother cat and the four little ones.

"There's a yellow tabby, a gray, one black cat and a calico. I like calico cats best."

"I think I do, too." Little fingers held tightly to his, and at the same time it felt like they were wrapping around his heart.

Meg led him from the area. "We can't stay long or she'll be mad."

"We wouldn't want to make the momma mad."

"My mom is mad at you."

Cody had never been fond of amusement-park rides. He could handle eight seconds on the back of a bull, but that up-and-down roller-coaster feeling was one he couldn't hack. And this felt like a roller coaster.

"I'm sorry that she's mad at me, Meg. Sometimes adults need time to work things out."

He kneeled in front of his daughter. Her mouth worked her gum as she stared into his eyes. When she rested her hand on his cheek and nodded, his eyes burned and he had to blink away the film of moisture.

"I know you're my daddy." She nodded at that information. "My mom told me about your eyes when I was just a little kid."

"Meg Cross, you're about the sweetest girl in the world." And he hoped he wouldn't let her down.

As he was thinking of all the mistakes he could make, his daughter stepped close and wrapped her arms around his neck. Her head rested on his shoulder and he hugged her back.

He wouldn't let her down. He wouldn't let her grow up thinking that a dad was just the guy who sent the check each month. Whether he stayed in Gibson, or settled somewhere else, he would be a part of his daughter's life.

The alarmed bark of Blue ripped into the moment. Cody hurried from the barn with Meg holding tightly to his hand. He scanned the yard, past his RV to the house. He saw the dog near the back porch and next to him on the ground was the still form of Jerry Cross.

* * *

Bailey didn't feel like working. She felt like going home and being by herself. Not that she could be alone at home. And today would be worse because Cody would be there, wanting to talk.

Why in the world did he suddenly think they needed to talk things out? Had he been watching afternoon talk shows and learning about sharing feelings?

Or was it just a step in a program?

She sighed, knowing she wasn't being fair and that God wanted her to give Cody a chance because grace was about being forgiven. She knew all about grace.

"Why do you look like someone messed with your oatmeal?" asked Lacey Gould, her black hair streaked with red, as she walked up behind Bailey, who was starting a fresh pot of coffee. The two of them had been unlikely friends for four years. They didn't have secrets.

Lacey didn't know who Meg's dad was. That was something only God and Bailey's dad knew. That was Bailey's only secret from her friend.

"I don't even like oatmeal." Bailey poured herself a cup of coffee and reached for the salt shakers that needed to be refilled.

The Hash-It-Out had been busy nonstop for over an hour. Now the crowds had waned down to the regular group of farmers who gathered for mid-morning coffee and good-natured gossip.

Lacey grabbed the pepper shakers and started filling them.

"Rumor has it someone showed up yesterday

driving a new truck and pulling an RV. And another rumor states that the truck and RV are still in town."

"Rumor has it that the rumor mill in this town could grind enough wheat to feed a small country."

"Cute. That doesn't really make sense, but it is a little bit funny." Lacey pulled ten dollars from her pocket and slid it across the counter top. "You had a four-top leave this the day before yesterday."

Bailey knew better. She didn't reach for the money. Lacey had a bad habit of trying to help by lying. She was a new Christian and her heart was as big as Texas, even if she didn't always go about helping the right way.

"You keep it."

"It's yours."

Bailey shook her head. "Good try, sweetie, but I didn't have a four-top the other day."

Lacey shoved the money into the front pocket of Bailey's jeans. "Stop being a hero and let a friend help."

The phone rang. Bailey glanced toward the hostess station and watched Jill answer. The older woman nodded and then shot a worried glance in Bailey's direction, with her hand motioning for Bailey to join her.

"I'll be right back." Bailey touched Lacey's arm as she walked toward the hostess.

"Honey, that was someone named Cody, and he said he's taking your daddy to the hospital in Springfield."

The floor fell out from under her. Lacey was suddenly there, her hand on Bailey's. "Let me get someone to drive you."

"I can drive myself."

"No, you can't."

Bailey was already reaching for her purse. She managed a smile for the two women. "I can drive myself. Could you let Jolynn know that I had to leave?"

"Sure thing, sweetie, but are you sure you're okay to drive yourself?"

Bailey nodded as she walked away from Jill's question. At that moment she wasn't sure about much of anything.

In a daze she walked out the door and across the parking lot, barely noticing the heat and just registering that someone shouted hello. Numb, she felt so numb, and so cold.

It took her a few tries to get the truck started. She pumped the gas, praying hard that the stupid thing wouldn't let her down, not now. As the engine roared to life she whispered a quiet thank-you.

Springfield was a good thirty-minute drive, and of course she got behind every slow car on the road and always in a no-passing zone. Her heart raced and her hands were shaking. What if she didn't make it on time? What if this was the end? She couldn't think about losing her dad, not yet, not now when she needed him so much.

"What if he's gone and I don't get to say goodbye?" She whispered into the silent cab of the truck, blinking away the sting of tears.

She couldn't think of her dad not being in her life. He had always been there for her. He had been the one holding her hand when her mother died, and the one who drove her to the hospital when Meg was born.

Her dad had been the one who hadn't condemned

her for her mistake. He had loved her and shown mercy. He had insisted that everyone makes mistakes. Without those mistakes, why would a person need grace?

Those who are healthy aren't in need of a physician. In those months after she had returned from Wyoming, she had really come to understand the words Jesus had spoken and the wonderful healing of forgiveness.

Her dad had taught her to bait a hook, and to train a horse. He had taught her how to have faith, and to smile even when smiling wasn't easy.

"Please, God, don't take him from me now."

Roots, this all felt very much like putting down roots. Cody's mind swirled as he waited for Bailey to arrive.

In the last few years he hadn't stayed in one place longer than a month. He usually spent time between events parked at the farm of a friend where he kept his livestock.

With Bailey's dad sick and Meg in his arms, thoughts of leaving fled. He had never known how to stick. Now he didn't know how he could ever think of leaving.

He knew himself well enough to know that before long the lure of bull riding would tug on him. Between now and then he would pray, hoping that when the time came he would make the right choices.

He knew enough to know that there wouldn't be any easy answers.

The door of the E.R. swished open, bringing a gust of warm air from the outside. Cody shifted the sleeping child in his lap and turned. Bailey stood on the threshold of the door, keeping it from closing. She watched him with a look of careful calculation, her gaze drifting from his face to her daughter.

Their daughter.

He couldn't stand up to greet her, not with Meg curled like one of her kittens, snuggling against his chest. She felt good there, and he didn't want to let go.

Cody didn't want to hurt Bailey. It seemed a little too late for that. Her brown eyes shimmered with unshed tears, and if he could have held them both, he would have.

Bailey crossed to where he was sitting. She looked young, and alone. She looked more vulnerable than the twenty-two-year-old young woman he'd known in Wyoming.

"Is he…"

"He's alive." He answered the question she didn't have the heart to ask. "He had an episode with his breathing. They're running tests. That's all they'll tell me because I'm not family."

Bailey sat down next to him. "I don't know what I'll do without him."

"He isn't gone, Bailey."

She only nodded. Shifting, he pulled a hand free and reached to cover her arm. With a sigh she looked up, nodding as if she knew that he wanted to comfort her. Her lips were drawn in and her eyes melting with tears. The weight of the world was on her shoulders.

He wanted to take that weight from her. He wanted to ease the burden. He wanted to hold her. He moved his arm, circling her shoulders and drawing her close, ignoring the way she resisted, and then feeling when she chose to accept. Her shoulder moved and she leaned against him, crumbling into his side.

"I won't leave you alone." He whispered the words, unsure if she heard but feeling good about the promise.

Time to cowboy up, Cody. He could almost hear his grandfather say the words to a little boy who had fallen off his pony.

The door across from them opened. A doctor walked into the room, made a quick scan of the area and headed in their direction. He didn't look like a man about to give the worst news a family could hear. Cody breathed a sigh of relief.

"Ms. Cross, I'm Dr. Ashford. Your dad is resting now. We've given him something to help him sleep and moved him to the second floor. You should be able to take him home in a day or two." He reached for a chair and pulled it close to them. "I'm not going to lie—this isn't going to be an easy time, and it might be better if you let us send him to a skilled-care facility."

"I want him at home. He belongs at home." Her stubborn chin went up and Cody shot the doctor a warning look.

"The family always wants that, but you have to consider yourself. How are you going to take care of him? You work, you go to town, and he's there alone."

Bailey's eyes closed and she nodded. Her face paled and Cody knew what she was thinking. She was blaming herself for not being there when her dad collapsed. She was thinking of all the ways she'd let him down.

"Bailey, you aren't to blame for today. I was there. I shouldn't have left him alone."

"He isn't your responsibility—he's mine." She moved out of the circle of his arm. "I should have been there for him."

The doctor cleared his throat. "Neither of you are to blame. Ms. Cross, your father has cancer. He isn't going to get better. He's going to get worse. You have to accept that you aren't going to be able to give him the twenty-four-hour-a-day care that he needs."

"But I want him home now, while he can be at home."

"You have to think about..."

"He's my responsibility," Bailey insisted, cutting off the doctor's objections. This time her tone was firm enough to stir Meg.

"Bailey, you have two choices." Cody got her attention with that, and she glanced up at him. "You can either let me help or you can put your dad in a facility where he can be watched over while you're at work."

She shifted her gaze away, focusing on the windows that framed a hot August day and afternoon traffic. "I know. I just didn't want it to be this way. I wanted him to get better."

"He can't, Bailey, not on this earth. I know that isn't what you want to hear, but sometimes the way God heals is by bringing a person home to Him, to a new body and a new life."

Shock and then relief flooded her expression as tears pooled in her eyes and then started to flow. Cody shifted Meg and reached to pull Bailey back into his arms.

Her head tucked under his chin and her body

racked with grief, he held her close and let her cry. He wondered if she had cried at all before then, or if she had been so busy taking care of everyone else that she hadn't allowed herself to grieve.

He glanced up, making eye contact with the doctor, who was looking at his watch and starting to move. Bailey's sobs quieted and she leaned against his side. Meg had awoken and was touching her mother's face, her sweet little hands stroking Bailey's cheek.

How had he gotten himself into this? Last week he had been a guy with a new faith in God and in himself, trying to make changes and making amends. And now he was here, holding Bailey and knowing he couldn't leave.

Adjusting to the wild buck of a bull was easy compared with this. A bull went one direction, and a countermove on his part put him back in control, back in center. No such luck with this situation.

On a bull they would have called the situation, "getting pulled down in the well."

"Bailey, I won't let you go through this alone."

She moved from his embrace, as if his words were the catalyst she had needed to regain her strength. The strong Bailey was back, wiping away her tears with the back of her hand.

"I appreciate your offer to help, Cody. I really do, but I know that you have a life and places you have to be."

He shook his head at what she probably considered was a very logical statement. To him it meant that she still didn't expect him to stay. And it probably meant that she didn't want him in her life.

"Bailey, we'll talk about the future, but for now

I'm staying and I'm going to help you with your dad and with the farm."

He meant it, and she would have to learn that his word was good.

Chapter Four

Bailey looked out of the kitchen window and breathed in the cool morning breeze. She used to love lazy summer mornings, the kind that promised a warm day and not too much humidity. Two years ago she would have spent the morning doing chores and then packed a picnic to take to the lake.

This was a new day. Her dad was home from the hospital, but the doctor was certain they wouldn't have him for long. How did a person process that information?

By going on with life, as if nothing was wrong? Bailey was trying. She was making breakfast, thinking about work on her to-do list and planning for Meg's first day of school in two weeks.

School—that meant letting go of her little girl, and it meant school supplies and new clothes. In the middle of all of the *normal life* thoughts was the reality. Her dad was in bed, and Cody was living in an RV outside her back door.

How could she pretend life was normal?

Eggs sizzled in the pan on the stove, and the aroma of fresh coffee drifted through the room, mixing with the sweet smell of a freshly mown lawn. Bailey glanced out the window again, eyeing the mower still sitting next to the shed, and then her gaze shifted to the man who had done the mowing. He walked out of the barn, his hat pushed back to expose a sun-tanned face.

It should have felt good, seeing the work he'd done in the two days since her dad had come home from the hospital. Eggs frying and coffee brewing should have been normal things, signaling a normal morning on a working farm. Instead these were signs of her weakening attempts at keeping things under control. Make breakfast, do the laundry, dust the furniture, which would only get dusty again, the little things that signified life was still moving forward.

She reached into the cabinet for a plate and slid the eggs out of the skillet. A light rap on the back door and her back instinctively stiffened.

"It's open."

The screen door creaked and booted footsteps clicked on the linoleum. And then he was there, next to her, pouring himself a cup of coffee. Had she actually dreamed of this, wanted this to be her life—Cody in her kitchen, pouring a cup of coffee, sitting across from her eating breakfast?

If so, the dream had faded. Now she dreamed of other things, of making it, and of a stable full of other people's horses to be trained, and money in the bank. Romance was the last thing on her mind, especially when she hadn't even brushed her teeth this morning and her hair was in a scraggly ponytail.

It didn't help that he smelled good, like soap and leather. Maybe romance wasn't the last thing on her mind. This opened the door for other thoughts, the kind she quickly brushed away, reminders of his hand on her cheek and the way it had felt to be in his arms.

"Are you going to work today?" He turned and leaned against the counter, his legs crossed at the ankles and the cup of coffee lifted to his lips.

"I can't work." She answered his question as she flipped a couple of eggs and a few slices of bacon on the plate with already buttered toast.

"Can't work? Why?"

"Because my dad needs me here. I can't leave him alone with Meg." She handed him the plate.

Cody set his plate down on the counter. He turned to face her, his jaw muscle working. Bailey shifted her gaze from the storm brewing in his blue eyes. She picked up the dishrag and wiped crumbs from the toaster off the counter. A strong, tanned hand covered hers, stopping her efforts to distract herself. She slid her hand out from under his and looked up.

"I'm here, Bailey. I'm trying to help you."

"Why, why are you here now?"

"I want to be here." He sipped his coffee and then set the cup on the counter. "I know I can't stay forever, but I'm here and I want to help."

How many people had tried to help and had accepted her refusal, and her insistence that she could do it herself? How long had she been holding on to the reins, telling herself she could do it all, while everyone called her stubborn? It wasn't stubbornness; it was determination, and maybe a survival instinct she hadn't recognized until recently.

It was a mantra of sorts. Keep going, keep moving forward, don't slow down or you might not make it. She had become a horse with blinders, able to only focus on the job at hand. She didn't want to lose focus.

"I ordered supplies to fix that north fence." His carelessly tossed-out words jerked her back to the present.

"I didn't ask you to do that. I can't afford it right now."

"I'm paying for the materials."

"Cody, you have a career. You can't let go of your place standing." She let her gaze drift away from his. "And really, I don't expect you to foot the bill around here."

He mumbled under his breath and walked away from her.

"What about your breakfast?" she called out after his retreating back, noticing the dark perspiration triangle between his shoulders. He'd been up for a while, working.

"I don't think that cooking my breakfast is your problem." He turned at the door. "Bailey, you push me further than any woman ever has. On so many levels. Get in there and get ready for work. If you don't, I'll load you up and drive you myself."

And then he was gone. The sound of his retreating footsteps sent a shudder up her spine. When she glanced out the window, she saw him walk into his camper, the door banging shut behind him.

"Sis, you're going to have to let someone help—it might as well be Cody."

Bailey turned, fixing her gaze on her dad. He had hold of the back of a kitchen chair, his knuckles white with the effort. She turned back to the normal thing, fixing breakfast and pretending her dad would be around for another twenty years.

"I know, Dad. I know that I need help, we need help, but I don't know..."

"How to accept help." The chair scraped on the linoleum as he sat at the kitchen table, pushing aside yesterday's paper and a pile of mail. "You learned that stubbornness from me. Now let me teach you something new: Let someone help you out. It'll make the burden that much lighter."

He paused for a long time. Bailey turned with his plate and a cup of coffee. His head was buried in his hands, and his shoulders were slumped forward. Bailey put the plate down on the table and touched his arm. His hand, no longer steady, came up to rest on hers.

"Sis, it would make my burden lighter if you'd let him help."

And that was the way he shifted it, from her to him, no longer her problem. She knew he had planned it that way. He knew that she'd do it for him when she couldn't do it for herself. She leaned and kissed the top of his head.

"For you, Dad." But it wouldn't be easy, not when the long-forgotten memories of a Wyoming summer were starting to resurface, reminding her of what dreams of forever had felt like.

The light rap on the thin metal door of the RV announced her arrival. He had seen Bailey crossing the yard, her mouth moving as she talked to herself, more than likely about him and the unpleasant things she'd like to do or say.

He opened the door and motioned her in. She stood firm on the first step and didn't accept his offer. The hair that had been held in a ponytail was now free, blowing around her face, and the slightest hint of pink gloss shimmered on her lips.

"I'm going to work."

"Okay." He knew it couldn't be easy for her, letting go of pride and having him be the one who stepped in to help.

She shoved her hands into the front pockets of her jeans. "I need to show you his medication and how to give him the injections. Can you handle that?"

"Bailey, you know that I can." He'd given more shots than a lot of veterinarians. Growing up on a ranch, he'd doctored his own livestock. There hadn't always been a vet on duty, or one that could get to them fast enough.

"You'll have to make lunch. I won't be home until after two."

"I know that."

"Meg will need a nap."

"I can handle it."

She chewed on her bottom lip, her brown eyes luminous as she stared up at him. He reminded himself that he was here because he had a daughter, not because he meant to become a part of Bailey's life.

Other than that summer in Wyoming, he'd never really been a part of any woman's life. He hadn't allowed himself those forever kinds of entanglements. He wasn't about to find out he really was his father's son. But then, hadn't he already found that out? He had walked out on Bailey, and he hadn't been there for Meg.

Neither of his parents had really taught him about being there for a person, or about sticking in someone's life.

"Let me turn off my coffeepot and I'll be right over."

Bailey nodded and then she walked away. He watched her cross the lawn to the house, her shoulders too stiff and her head too high. He wondered if she was really that strong or if she was trying to convince herself. He thought the latter was probably the case.

Switching off the coffeepot and then the lights over the small kitchen, he walked out the door of the RV, ignoring the jangle of his cell phone. The ring tone was personalized and he knew that the caller was one of his corporate sponsors. They wanted to know when he'd be back on tour. He didn't have an answer.

Unfortunately he had their money and he had signed a contract. That meant he had certain obligations to fulfill. He needed to be seen, on tour, on television and wearing the logos of the corporations on his clothing.

There weren't any easy answers, and there was a whole lot of temptation trying to drag him back into a lifestyle he'd given up months ago. He wasn't about to go there. He was going on seven months of sobriety, and with God's help, he planned on making his sobriety last a lifetime.

When he walked into the house a few minutes later, Bailey was sitting at the kitchen table with a plastic container full of pills and individually wrapped needles.

"You don't have to worry, Bailey, I can do this."

She nodded, but she didn't have words. When was the last time she had really smiled, or even laughed? He sat down across from her, pushing aside those thoughts.

"Show me what to do."

She did. Her hands trembled as she explained about the pain meds and the pills. She explained that Meg wasn't allowed to drink soda, and that she should have milk with her lunch.

He felt as if he should be taking notes. Shots, cattle and fixing fences were easy; being this involved in someone's life was a whole new rodeo. He wasn't about to ask what five-year-old girls ate for lunch.

"I have to go. What I just showed you, I also wrote on that tablet." She nodded toward the legal pad on the table and stood, immediately shoving her hands into her front pockets. "If you have any problems…"

"We won't."

"If you do, call me. I can be home in ten minutes." She headed for the door. "Oh, if you get any calls about horses, I put an ad in the Springfield paper for training. My rates are in the ad, and no, I can't come down in price."

He followed her to the door. "I'll take messages."

"Cody, I appreciate this."

He shrugged, as if it didn't matter. "I'm here as long as you need me."

He waved as she got into the truck, and he tried to tell himself this would be easy. Staying would be easy. Helping would be easy. Rolling through his mind with the thoughts of staying were the other things he didn't want to think about, such as his place at the top of the bull-riding standings, his obligation to his sponsors and the herd of cattle he was building in Oklahoma.

Bailey parked behind the Hash-It-Out Diner, the only diner, café or restaurant in Gibson, Missouri. No one seemed to mind that the tiny town nestled in the Ozarks had a shortage of businesses. They had a grocery store and a restaurant; of course they had a feed store.

And they had churches. In a town with fewer than three hundred people, they had four churches—and every one of them was full on Sunday. So the town obviously had an abundance of faith.

If the people in Gibson needed more than their small town had to offer, they drove to Springfield. Simple as that. And on the upside, since Gibson didn't have a lot to offer, it didn't draw a lot of newcomers.

What Bailey loved was the sense of community and the love the people had for one another. Gossip might come easily to a small town, where people didn't have a lot to do, but so did generous hearts.

Not only that, how many people could say that on their way to work they passed by a grocery store with two horses hitched to the post out front? Bailey had waved at the two men out for a morning ride. She wished she could have gone along. She hadn't ridden for pleasure in more than a year. These days riding was training, and training helped pay a few bills.

As Bailey got out of the truck, she didn't lock the doors or even take the keys out. She did grab her purse. From across the street a friend she had gone to school with waved and called out her name, asking how Bailey's dad was doing.

Bailey smiled and nodded. She didn't have an answer about her dad, not today. She hurried down the sidewalk to the front door of the diner, opening it and shuddering at the clanging cowbell that had been hung to alert the waitresses to the arrival of new customers.

"We're expecting the ladies' group from the Community Church." Lacey tossed a work shirt in Bailey's direction as soon as she walked into the waitress station.

"Wonderful, quarter tips and plenty of refills on coffee."

Bailey loved the darlings of the Community Church, but she would have liked a few tables that left real tips, especially today. Real tips would have helped her to forget the call from the mortgage company, letting her know that she was behind—again.

"They specifically asked for you," Lacey informed her as she started toward the coffeemaker.

"Of course they did." They liked to tell her how much they loved her and how they were praying for her.

Bailey closed her eyes and grabbed hold of the cynical thoughts that were dragging her down a dead-end road. She told herself to count her blessings, like the song said. Count her blessings; see what God has done.

So she did. She counted her dad, still in her life. She counted Meg, whose morning hugs made everything better. She counted Lacey and her church family.

Cody's face flashed through her mind, as if God was trying to remind her of something. She squeezed her eyes tightly, but the mental image wouldn't fade. "Okay, God, thank You for Cody."

"What was that?" Lacey walked up behind her, carrying a full pot of coffee.

"Nothing." Bailey washed her hands and reached for the nearly empty ketchup bottles, wondering how they went through so much ketchup during the breakfast rush. Who used ketchup at breakfast?

"You mentioned Cody."

"I was thinking aloud."

"Okeydoke, then, I guess this isn't something you want to talk about."

"No, it isn't."

The bells on the front door clanged, signaling the arrival of customers. Saved by the bell, Bailey flashed Lacey a smile and hurried to the tables that had been set up for the Golden Girls Bible Study.

The ladies—there were ten of them today—were especially chipper and talkative. They were the same ladies Bailey had known all her life, in pastel and floral dresses, cheeks powdered and hair styled twice a week at Ruth's Beauty Shop. These women had been her teachers, librarians, neighbors and friends. These ladies had held a baby shower for her when others had been busy whispering behind their hands.

After bringing their food, Bailey hovered, listening to stories of grandchildren and bad-pet behavior. Every now and then one of the women would motion for her to take a plate or refill a coffee cup.

The diner had started to fill up, and Bailey slipped away to take the orders of her other customers, but she hurried back to the Golden Girls when they motioned for her.

Mrs. Lawrence, once the town librarian, reached for Bailey's hand after the meal and Bible study were over. Her cool fingers wrapped around Bailey's, and she wouldn't let go. Her eyes filled with tears and she shook her head.

"Honey, I've been thinking about you and your daddy and praying for you night and day. You feel like family, I've known you all so long."

Bailey leaned in and hugged the woman. "Thank you, Mrs. Lawrence. We appreciate your prayers."

The other women started to add their condolences. Bailey's eyes filled with tears as she listened to stories about her dad and even her mom when they were young kids.

Bessie Johnston laughed as she reached for her empty cup of coffee and then shot Bailey a hinting look. Bailey hurried to fill the cup.

"You all probably remember this as well as I," Bessie started, "but one of my favorite memories of Jerry Cross is the pie he stole from my windowsill."

Anna Brown was nodding her head so vehemently that Bailey was afraid the woman would lose the pins that held her nest of gray hair in place.

"Yes, I remember. It was Jerry and that Gordon boy. They were out riding horses and causing no end of trouble. They'd just ridden through the clean laundry hanging on my line when they headed toward your place."

"They rode through my hen yard," Jean Forester added. "My hens were scattered in all directions."

"They rode right through my yard, past the window, and they grabbed that apple pie that I'd put on the sill to cool." Bessie chuckled as she told the rest of the story. "I was frying chicken for supper and when I turned around, the pie was gone and those boys was riding as fast as they could down that dirt road."

Jean Forester sighed, "Oh, honey, those were really the good ole days. Remember, we thought those boys was bad. But they weren't bad—they were just boys."

"I remember that when my Eddie got killed after that tractor rolled—" Elsbeth Jenkins wiped her eyes with a handkerchief she pulled out of her sleeve "—it was Jerry that took care of our place for nearly a month. He'd feed his animals and then he'd come and feed ours. And here I've been, sitting at my house wishing I could do the same."

Bailey had been a bystander, listening to the memories unfold as the women of the Golden Girls Bible Study relived a past that Bailey hadn't known about. She took back her mean thoughts about quarter tips and silently asked God to forgive her for her cynicism.

"I'm really glad you all came in today. I'm glad you shared your stories."

"Sweetie, we came to do more than share stories." Mrs. Lawrence reached for her hand again. "Honey, we came to share our hearts. We know that we're not the best tippers in the world, and yet you always give us the best service. You always smile and ask how we're doing, even when you're going through so much."

"I don't mind." Hadn't she minded earlier? Her heart ached.

"Well, we're right sorry about the trouble you all are having and we want to help. So here's our tip, for today's service and for the past when you've been so good to us." Elsbeth Jenkins pushed an envelope into

Bailey's hand. "Don't argue with us, Bailey Cross. We're being faithful to God, and if you don't take this, you'll steal our blessing."

Bailey nodded, but her throat tightened, restricting words. Her sweet ladies took turns standing and hugging her and then they gathered their purses and left. And at each of their plates was the customary two quarters that they always tipped.

Without looking in the envelope, Bailey shoved it into her pocket and started to clear the table. Lacey was nowhere to be found as Bailey headed toward the kitchen with the tub of dirty dishes and sloshing glasses of ice water.

"Wasn't that the sweetest thing?" Lacey walked out of the employee's restroom, her eyes red and tearstains on her cheeks.

"It was sweet." It was God showing her something about the people in her life. And it was God showing her something about who He was in her life.

Bailey set the tub of dishes down for Joey, the teenager who came in every afternoon for cleanup. Jolynn and Harry, the owners of Hash-It-Out, had a soft spot for anyone in need and hired nearly anyone who asked for a job.

"I wish I could have grown up somewhere like this."

Lacey had that wistful look on her face again, the one she wore when she thought about the idyllic life of her dreams. That life included growing up on a farm, not in the city—watching her parents fight until the fighting ended with the two going in separate directions and sixteen-year-old Lacey left to her own devices.

Bailey knew that Lacey was saving her tips and working two jobs to buy a place of her own. She wanted a few acres, "bottle calves" and chickens. And she had an absurd dream about finding a cowboy of her own.

"I wish you could have grown up here, too." Bailey hugged her friend. "But if you had grown up here, you wouldn't be you. And I really like you."

"Oh, honey, you're going to make me cry all over again."

"It's true, Lacey. You're unique because of where you came from and what God has done in your life. I know it wasn't easy to get here, but there's a reason for all of it."

Lacey's smile melted. "Don't forget that, Bailey. There's a reason for all of this. There's a reason for what those ladies did for you today. And you might as well accept that the church is having a fund-raiser to help cover some of your dad's medication."

"I know, Lacey. And I am thankful." Bailey walked away, she was thankful, and she knew God had a plan.

It made her wonder if there was a reason for Cody in her life, just when she needed him. He had showed up for one reason, thinking it was for himself that he had to see her.

God had had another plan. Bailey wanted to count that as a blessing, but she didn't know how. Instead it felt like a big test she hadn't studied for.

Chapter Five

Cody stood in the center of the kitchen, trying to come up with the correct expression of parental authority for his young daughter. The problem was, he was struggling not to laugh.

Standing in front of him, her hands with pink painted nails resting on her hips, she looked like the one in charge. Today she was wearing a yellow sundress with her pink boots. Those boots obviously meant a lot to her.

Snapping back into control, he gave her a long look, hoping he could read the truth, or lack of truth, in her stormy-blue eyes. With her lips pursed and her nose wrinkled in disbelief, she looked a lot like Bailey, and she had him nearly convinced she would never try to con him.

"Honest, she said we could have ice cream for lunch."

She had been trying to convince him of this for a good fifteen minutes. He was a novice at parenting, but he was sure a mother who said no to soda probably didn't say yes to ice cream for lunch. He was almost thirty-one years old, he had to be smarter than a five-year-old.

"I tell you what, we'll call your mom at work and ask her about the ice cream."

"I think that would be a bad idea. She doesn't like to be bothered at work." She fidgeted and squirmed, trying hard, it seemed, to avoid looking at him.

"Meg, I really think we need to be honest here. I think your mom would want you to have soup or a sandwich, and maybe ice cream for dessert. If you're honest with me, we'll do something fun later."

Bribery had to be a part of parenting. If it wasn't, well, he could always claim that he didn't know better. It seemed to be working. Meg swayed, swishing her yellow dress back and forth as she worked her mouth and eyed him with deep suspicion.

"Okay, she didn't say ice cream for lunch. But she did buy some chocolate kind with bunnies in it. It has chocolate bunnies."

"Well, I can see how that would be better than a sandwich, but it also wouldn't be too good for us. Now I need for you to be a big girl and help me figure out where everything is. You can be my helper."

She gave him another one of those disbelieving looks and sighed. "You really don't know much about being a dad, do you?"

A five-year-old had figured him out. She had put into words all of his fears and the reason he ran from Bailey in the first place. And he was already doing what his dad had taught him to do, bribing a kid.

He hitched his jeans at the knee and squatted in front of her. She was holding tight to a stuffed bunny that Jerry had bought her two years ago on her birth-day. She told Cody that when she woke up. It was then that he had counted the Christmases and birth-days he'd missed. Thinking about it had left a huge hole inside him.

"You're right, Meg, I don't know a lot about being a dad. But I'm going to do my best. And when I do something wrong, I want you to tell me. And I prom-ise I'll listen." He twirled one of her blond pigtails around his finger and she smiled. "And the other thing I can't do is offer you something for being good."

Her mouth dropped at that bit of information. "But it's okay. It's like giving me 'lowances if you buy me something. Especially something like a pony. Or a pet monkey."

A chuckle worked its way up and he had to laugh. "A pet monkey?"

She nodded like it made perfectly good sense to her, and then she leaned closer. "I heard that mon-keys are a lot like babies, and that would be almost like a brother or sister."

They were definitely two to nothing, and he was on the losing team.

"Tell you what, we'll think about a stuffed mon-key but no bribes. I want you to be good because you are good. And when I buy you something, it'll be be-cause I love you."

"Okay, and then we can have ice cream."

Cody stood up, his knees creaking a protest. It was moments like that—when his joints creaked or when he could barely get out of bed in the morn-ing—when he realized that his career as a bull rider was almost over. He had almost made it to the world championship.

Now, with Meg staring up at him, wasn't the time to dwell on what could have been.

"How about fried bologna for lunch?" He tossed the suggestion over his shoulder as he looked in the fridge.

"Ewww, that would be gross."

He looked behind him and the expression on her face matched the disgusted tone of her voice. "You don't like fried bologna?"

"No, I don't think so. I do like oatmeal."

"Oatmeal for lunch." It seemed reasonable. "What do you like on your oatmeal?"

"She's trying to pull one over on you, Cody," Jerry's voice from the hall interrupted the lunch discussion. Cody waited until the older man walked around the corner into the kitchen before responding.

"So, no oatmeal and no fried bologna?" He shifted his gaze from Jerry to Meg. "Any other suggestion, Meghan?"

"That *isn't* my name." She glared and he knew he was losing ground quickly.

"Sorry, I didn't know." He had felt less pain at the mercy of a fifteen-hundred-pound bull. Gut-stomped didn't begin to describe this moment in his life. He didn't know Meg's complete name, he didn't know the exact date of her birthday and he didn't know what to feed her for lunch.

"We'll have grilled cheese." Jerry made it sound like an easy decision.

Cody shot the older man a look and a smile of appreciation. Jerry winked and sat down at the table, pulling his granddaughter close.

"And Meg Alice is going to eat her sandwich and then take a nap." Jerry kissed her cheek and she smiled again.

Jerry knew how to be a dad.

The clock on the dash of the truck read 2:45. It had never kept accurate time, so Bailey knew it was closer to three as she pulled to a stop next to the barn and killed the engine. The truck rattled and shuddered a few times after she turned the key.

That couldn't be a good sign.

She glanced toward the house. It appeared to be in one piece, which was more than she felt. Today had been one that seemed to rip her into little pieces of emotional baggage. The Golden Girls had done a number on her, leaving a patch of vulnerability that she hadn't been able to overcome—not even with the sundae covered in hot fudge that Lacey had made her for lunch.

Now she had to go into the house and deal with Cody. To make it even worse, her head ached and she was exhausted. Maybe she could sit in the truck for an hour or so and no one would notice.

No, she couldn't do that. She had dinner to cook and chores that needed to be done. Her gaze carried across the two-acre lawn and landed on the weed-infested garden, which she'd thought was such a good idea in early spring. Her weeding job last week hadn't done a bit of good.

It had given them plenty of tomatoes and quite a few zucchini. Now it was a wonderland for Japanese beetles. The leaves on the green beans were gnawed away, leaving lacy skeletons of green. All in all, gardening was not her thing.

Her gaze shifted to the barn and the mare that was close to foaling. Peaceful, the mare, was the only animal she had left that was broke. Bailey longed to go for a long ride, to put all of her worries aside, if just for thirty minutes.

And she wanted to go inside and find a list of numbers, people who had called and were interested in her horse-training services. The two horses she had would be gone in a month. And then what? That extra thousand dollars a month meant a lot to her family.

Speaking of money. She pulled the envelope of money from her purse. It held enough cash to buy groceries, pay the electric bill and buy school clothes for Meg. Bailey closed her eyes and whispered a soft "Thank You" into the cab of the truck.

She opened her eyes after the brief prayer and looked out the window. Blue had spotted her. The dog trotted across the yard and sat down outside the truck, waiting patiently for some kind of command. Bailey pushed the truck door open and hopped down to the ground. Blue waited, her hind end wagging a nonexistent tail.

"Come on, girl, let's go in the house." The invitation was all the blue heeler needed. She jumped up and started running in circles. The dog wanted cattle to herd; so did Bailey.

The quiet drone of voices reached Bailey as she walked across the porch. Cody's voice and her dad's, blending as they discussed the farm.

"I keep telling her to sell off some of the land."

Jerry Cross's voice was weaker than it had been a few days ago.

Bailey thought about his idea to sell, an idea she'd been ignoring for a few months now. It would make him feel better, knowing she had that money. It would make her feel as if she was selling her birthright.

"Maybe we could find another way." Cody shuffled papers. Bailey waited, wondering what they were looking at and what papers Cody had in his hands.

"We've used up all the other ways." Jerry spoke quietly and then continued, "Maybe if you offered to buy a portion of it?"

"I don't think that would be the right move."

Of course he didn't. And Bailey knew why. Having that land, not that she wanted him to have it, would put him in their lives permanently. Cody Jacobs didn't want forever.

"It seems like the only move that makes sense," Jerry answered, sounding about as low on faith as she had ever heard. She didn't want that for him.

Bailey wanted her dad to have peace and to know they were going to survive. And it seemed as if only one thing could give him that peace. She didn't know if she could do that. She didn't know if she could sell her family farm.

She walked into the house, tossing her purse on the counter as she made her way into the living room. The two of them were sitting on the couch, the farm records on the coffee table in front of them. They looked up when she walked in, both with guilty expressions on their faces.

Cody's gaze locked with hers and held. Her dad looked away. Bailey waited, hoping they would offer an explanation. Cody's hands were on the pile of bills, the ledger where she kept records was open in front of him.

They were pushing her out, taking over and making decisions. And she hadn't been involved. Her thin thread of control was being snipped and she was dangling.

"Did you two manage to sell the farm while I was at work?"

"Bailey, we're only trying to come up with solutions. Better to sell and hold on to the house than to have the bank auction it off." Her dad leaned forward, pointing to the pile of bills she'd been trying to juggle paying.

That brought to mind a picture of herself in the center of the room, tossing envelopes into the air, trying to catch them all, and watching them fall all around her. She would never be able to run away and join the circus.

"Did we get any calls from the ad?" She pointed that question in Cody's direction.

"Only one."

Her faith was bottoming out and needed a serious refill. "I need to check on my mare."

As Bailey walked out the back door, her gaze flitted to her purse. How quickly she had forgotten the blessing that had been handed her that day. Maybe it wouldn't solve every problem, but that envelope of money would give her breathing room. She really needed to breathe.

Her mare was standing in a far corner of the corral, her head down and her sides heaving. It wouldn't be long. Or it might be forever. It would take longer if the mare knew she had an audience. Bailey walked into the shadowy barn, feeling more at peace in that quiet place with the scent of horses, hay and cedar shavings.

Alone, she felt the presence of God and that still, small voice that told her heart to trust Him. There wouldn't be big answers or great miracles, she was sure of that, but she was also sure of the peace and the strength He gave her to climb the mountains in the path she had to take.

How could she sell her family farm? She leaned against the rough oak of the doorway to watch the corral and the restless mare. She had called the horse Peaceful because from the day the mare had been born, she had been so calm, so sweet natured.

Trust. It wasn't easy to trust with something as huge as selling the farm. She prayed that God would help her make the right decision. And she would tell her dad she was considering it. She would do that for him, so that he could have peace.

Soft footsteps on the hard-packed dirt floor alerted her to Cody's presence. She knew it had to be him. The steps were sure and steady, accompanied by the light rattle of spurs on his boots. He'd told her yesterday that he was going to ride a few bulls today. He needed to keep in shape.

His hand touched her shoulder, his fingers lightly massaging. Bailey froze with him at her back, her breath catching as he leaned closer, his forehead touching the back of her head, resting lightly as his hands moved to her arms.

"I know I can't make it better, but I do want to help." He whispered the words.

Somehow she shook herself loose from old memories that his touch evoked. Instead, she remembered minutes earlier and his easy offer to buy her family farm and then she remembered him, six years ago, walking away from something he thought would tie him down.

"This is helping? I can't rely on temporary fixes and on someone who will only be here as long as it is comfortable to stay."

"I'm here because I want to be here."

Bailey nodded; she didn't know what to say. She could tell him that she knew he wanted to be there. As much as she wanted to deny it, and as much as she wanted to think he was looking for a way out, she could see determination in his eyes. He planned on being in their lives. She also knew how much he wanted that world title. If she could have made the words come out, she would have told him she understood, and she wanted it for him, too.

Words wouldn't come, because her heart wanted something more. She wanted to lean into him and let him hold her for a while. She wanted to stop being strong, just for a few minutes. And no one but Cody made her feel as if she could let her guard down that way.

"Bailey?" He pulled her around to face him, and she let him hold her close because for that moment that was what she wanted.

How long had it been since she'd let herself have something she wanted?

The silent tears rolling down Bailey's cheeks were his undoing. He had come here a week ago to make amends and then to move on with his life, and here he was, holding on to something he couldn't have.

He could count the reasons why this wouldn't work. First and foremost, he was just learning to trust himself to be a person who could be counted on. Second, he had a commitment to sobriety, to wait a year before building new relationships.

Somehow he didn't think his daughter counted in that. That was a relationship that had to be built now.

"Bailey, don't—" He stopped himself from telling her not to cry. Instead he gathered her into his arms and held her close. She didn't fall apart the way he expected. No sobs shook her shoulders.

He lifted her chin with his finger and looked into her eyes, wishing he could know if she felt the soft connection he felt.

"Cody, I…"

If she meant to resist, he didn't know. For a fleeting second he didn't care. Bailey was in his arms and the memories were returning, reminding him of a time when someone had made him feel worthy. Bailey made him feel that way, in a way that no other woman ever had. He didn't understand it, didn't want to figure it out; he just wanted to hold her close and feel that way again—like someone who could be counted on.

He leaned and her lips parted in a silent acceptance. The moment had all of the innocence of a first kiss, soft and tentative, more miraculous than the first breath of spring on a winter's day. Her arms moved to the back of his neck, holding him close, and he felt her rise on tiptoes to bring them closer.

After a long moment he pulled back, moving out of the circle of her arms and swiping his hand through his hair. That had definitely felt like something. She looked like a woman who didn't want to feel something, and he knew she had.

Maybe she had more sense than he did.

"We can't do this," she whispered as she backed away. "I can't let myself go there, Cody, not with Dad and Meg."

"I know." He couldn't tell her about "no relationships" for another five months. A kiss didn't really mean a relationship.

He touched her cheek, letting his fingers rest on the softness, and then he moved, knowing they both needed distance. "I know we can't, and I know we shouldn't. I'm sure not sorry that I did."

But she was sorry and that said it all. She had regret written all over her face, just like six years ago. He didn't want to be the person she constantly regretted letting into her life.

Instead he had to do something he might regret.

"Bailey, I want to buy that hundred-thirty acres. That'll leave you twenty-five and the house."

"I don't want to sell it to you."

"I'm not going to take control of your life."

"It isn't you, Cody. I don't want to sell it, period. And I especially don't want you to buy it just to bail us out." She turned away from him, back in the direction of the laboring mare. A long sigh and her shoulders slumped. "I know that I might have to sell, and I'm going to tell Dad that, because he needs to hear it."

"Let me loan you money." It made perfect sense to him.

"I can't. I don't want to borrow and have one more debt I have to worry about repaying."

"It isn't going to go away, Bailey. Ignoring it all isn't going to make it disappear."

"You think that I don't know that?" She turned again, facing him with eyes bright with tears and frustration. "You've been here a week and you think you know all there is to know about me, my dad and our situation."

"No, Bailey, I'm aware that I don't know it all. The one thing I do know is that you're too stubborn and too full of pride for your own good."

He walked away, leaving her to deal with her issues because he had plenty of his own to work through. He had to figure out how he was going to get himself out of this mess and back in control of his own life.

As he got into his truck, his gaze shifted to the house and the little girl sitting in a lawn chair on the back porch with a big calico cat on her lap and a sleeping blue heeler at her feet. She waved her hand and smiled, the ice-cream argument obviously forgotten.

Her smile was an arrow to his heart, reminding him of why he had stayed in Gibson. He had a daughter and his life was no longer about himself and what he wanted.

From the cavernous recesses of the barn, Bailey watched Cody drive away. She let go of the breath she'd been holding and the warm mush inside her belly—aftereffects of the kiss.

She definitely couldn't linger on the memory of that moment in his arms. Instead she walked back outside to check on the mare.

The mare wasn't going anywhere. She had paced, heaved and then settled in the shade of the barn. Bailey rubbed Peaceful's gray neck and leaned close to inhale the scent of the animal.

"I'll be back in half an hour, sweetie. Please have that baby so I don't have to call the vet."

As she walked across the yard, Bailey saw Meg sitting on the porch with her cat and Blue. The frown on her daughter's face issued a warning.

"Hey, Meggie, how was your nap?"

Meg stood up, dusting cat hair off her yellow sundress. "It was a long nap."

"Maybe the two of us should have an ice-cream cone?"

"Maybe." Meg's eyes narrowed and then watered. "I'm sorry, Mommy, I didn't mean to lie, but I wanted those chocolate bunnies."

Okay, this wasn't the wonderful bonding moment Bailey had counted on. She pulled her daughter close and hugged her, enjoying the feel of having her near. And then she felt another dose of regret. When was the last time she'd spent a real day with her daughter? When was the last time they'd had fun?

"Meg, we should go to the creek and wade. Maybe we could take a picnic for later, for our supper?"

Meg sniffled. "Even though I lied?"

"What did you lie about?" Bailey sat down on the edge of the porch and pulled her daughter down next to her.

"I told Da—Cody that I could have ice cream for lunch."

"Did he believe you?"

Meg shook her head. Bailey moved onto the bigger issue, the one she would rather not deal with.

"Meg, do you want to call him Dad?"

Meg nodded and held tight to the cat that had crawled back on her lap. "I think he makes a pretty good dad, even if he doesn't get me a pet monkey."

Bailey almost asked about the monkey, but she was afraid she didn't want to hear the explanation. Monkeys, lies about ice cream and Cody being Daddy seemed to be enough for one day.

"Let me check on Grandpa and then we'll drive to the creek. Can you get the fishing poles for us?"

Meg nodded and then she was off and running. Bailey stood and walked into the house. Her dad was still in his recliner in the living room, a glass of iced tea on the table next to him.

"Dad?"

He shifted and turned to face her, the oxygen tube saying more than words about his condition. Bailey mentally pulled herself together and smiled strongly for his sake.

"Dad, I'll put out feelers for selling the hundred acres."

"I'm glad, sis, real glad. And don't be so quick to turn down Cody's offer."

"I'll pray about it."

"I know you will." He leaned back, his eyes closing. "Did I hear you telling Meg you'd take her to the creek?"

Bailey sat down on the arm of the sofa. "Yes. Do you want me to take the truck so you can go with us?"

The way they used to, before he got so bad.

"No, not this time. Maybe in a day or two, when it's cooler."

Bailey nodded, pretending that they both believed he would go fishing again. She stood and leaned to kiss his cheek. "Maybe on Sunday after church?"

"That's a good idea. We can take a picnic."

"I'm taking the walkie-talkie, Dad. And yours is here on the table if you need me."

"I'm just going to watch *Oprah*. You two have fun." He opened his eyes. "Bailey, have fun for Meg's sake. She needs to be a little girl, and you need to be her momma."

Bailey touched his arm as she left the room, his words still hanging in the air around her. Had she let Meg down? He hadn't said that, hadn't even implied it, but now she had to think about the lack of time and attention her little girl had gotten.

She took a few minutes to fill a backpack with junk food and bottled water, and then she walked out the door, smiling for her daughter's sake and determined to make this a good time for the two of them. But as they crossed the yard to the truck, the part of her that was still her daddy's little girl wanted to go back into the house and beg him to hang on, to not let go.

Instead she helped Meg into the truck and then tossed the backpack and poles into the back. They were going fishing and they were going to have fun. They were going to laugh.

"Mom, is Grandpa going to be okay?" Meg leaned out the truck window, her blue eyes more like Cody's than ever before.

"He's going to be okay, today." Bailey stepped

close and put a hand on each of her daughter's cheeks and kissed her brow. "But you know that he's going to go to heaven, right?"

Meg nodded. "I know, but I've been praying that Jesus will change His mind."

Meg scooted across to the passenger side of the truck as Bailey opened the door and climbed in. She smiled at her daughter as she turned the key in the ignition.

"Me, too, Meg. Me, too." She remembered almost a little too late to pull herself up by the bootstraps. Meg brought her back to firm footing. "But we have to be willing to accept that God's plans and ours aren't always the same. We have to be willing to let Grandpa go. And we have to know that we aren't going to be alone. God isn't going to forget us. We have to trust that He'll get us through."

"And God brought my daddy to help." Meg said it so brightly, as if it was one of the smartest ideas God had ever had.

Bailey smiled. "Yes, honey, God brought your dad."

And even if she didn't want to see the wisdom of God's plan, and as much as she fought the truth, it felt good to lean on someone.

Chapter Six

Cody leaned against the fence at Jack Brown's place and watched a young bull run past the chute for the second time. The bull had won two out of three rounds against Cody. The last ride had lasted only three seconds.

To make himself feel better, Cody decided to blame his inability to last eight seconds on Bailey. He didn't know if he should blame it on the disagreement over the land, or the way his mind had gotten stuck on the way she felt in his arms.

"He'd make a good bull for you to start with, Cody. I've had him in a few smaller events and he knows what to do. He comes out of the gate spinning."

A good spinning bull that threw in a few bucks and some quick direction changes was exactly what Cody wanted. He would need something to do when he retired from bull riding. And the way things were going, retirement would come sooner than he planned.

"I like him, Jack. He's out of some good bucking stock, and you've done a good job raising him."

"He's a bull you could take all the way to the world finals." Jack leaned on the opposite side of the fence, not on the same side as the bull, like Cody. Jack loved the sport, but he had never been a bull rider.

"He's definitely the bull I could go places with. And the sport is growing fast."

"Always good to be in on the ground floor. Or as close to the ground as you can get." Jack had been chewing on a long blade of grass. He tossed it now and whistled, waving for his son to move the bull out of the pen. "I want to show you those geldings that I need to have trained. Are you sure she can do the job?"

"Loan me a trailer and I'll take them with me this evening."

"Are you going to stay in Missouri long? I watched on TV the other night, and they were talking about your absence and some speculation that you'll lose the world title over this."

Cody shrugged and let his gaze drift over the two-hundred-acre ranch, a good-size place for this part of the country where grass was more plentiful and could graze more head of livestock per acre than out West.

He really liked Jack's farm, with its white vinyl fences and the clean lines of the brick ranch house a short distance away. It was the kind of setup that made a guy dream about having a place of his own.

"I heard that Jerry Cross isn't doing very well." Jack reached over the fence to run his hand down the neck of a buckskin gelding that his son had turned into the corral after the bull had finally been penned up.

"He's holding his own."

"And his daughter?"

"Running the show and as strong as that old oak tree out there." Cody reached for the halter of the buckskin as a deep red bay trotted up to the fence. "I like this guy."

"He's for sale."

Cody laughed. "Everything's for sale, isn't it, Jack?"

Jack shrugged at that. "Just about everything. Did you want to ride that bull again?"

Cody shook his head. "I don't think my body would take another throw like the last one."

He'd be paying for that toss for a few days, and then some. He could already feel his joints stiffening and a tight catch in his back. It didn't help that the bull had turned on him, ramming him with horns that had been cut but still did the job.

"Bull riding is a young man's sport."

"Yes, and they're getting younger every year." Raising a few bulls, maybe some horses, was looking better all the time.

"Take the horses with you. If you decide to buy the buckskin, let me know." Jack unlatched the gate and Cody walked through, holding the rail for support.

"I'll take the buckskin, Jack. I'll pay you for him now, and I'll take them both to be trained."

And he'd deal with Bailey's anger. But he had to do something. He'd seen the worry furrowing her brow when she realized there had only been one call on the ad. She needed the income and he could provide it.

Cody's phone rang as he walked toward his truck. He frowned at the caller ID with Chuck Colson's name, and this time he answered. Chuck owned a

huge farm-supply business, and it wouldn't do Cody
any good to ignore the man who helped pay his bills.

"Cody, I've been trying to reach you." Chuck's
voice was deceptively good-natured. "How are you?"

Sober, Cody wanted to reply. He knew Chuck's
concern was genuine, but it was about more than
Cody's well-being; it was about the name *Colson
Farm Supply* that was stitched onto almost every bit
of clothing Cody wore into the arena.

"I'm fine, Chuck. I just bought myself a nice buckskin gelding."

"Cody, we need you on tour."

Cody opened the door of his truck and slid behind the wheel, holding the phone with his chin and
shoulder. "I know, and I'll be back. Next weekend in
Chicago. I'll fly in on Thursday."

"Good, I'm glad to hear that. We'd like to have
you stop by the dealership in that area and sign some
photographs."

"I'll be there, Chuck."

Long pause. Cody waited for the question that had
to come. He knew that Chuck would be straight up;
he wouldn't beat around the bush.

"Are you sober, Cody?"

Cody started his truck as he ruminated over that
question and how offensive it could have been. It
would have been nice to have trust from the people
who knew him. But trust had to be earned. He was
on the path to earning it but obviously wasn't there
yet. He hadn't proven himself.

"I'm sober. I'm helping a friend whose dad is sick."

"Good, I'm glad to hear that. Cody, you know if
you need anything…"

"I'd call you, Chuck. And I appreciate that offer."

"Next week, then?"

Yes, next week. He would have to fly out, leaving Bailey, Meg and Jerry behind. Three weeks ago they hadn't been a part of his life. Now he didn't know how to walk out on them.

He told himself he wasn't walking out. He had a career. He had responsibilities, other people who were counting on him. He was three months away from finally being a world champion.

Bailey watched from the creek bank as Meg splashed near the water's edge, grabbing at minnows that swam past her feet. They had tried fishing, but fishing meant staying out of the water. That was hard to do on a warm summer afternoon, especially for a five-year-old.

"I wish I could have more picnics down here." Meg sat down on the grassy slope near the creek. She moved her hands through the water and then leaned to look at her reflection. "I really do look like him."

She whispered the words as if it was the most miraculous thing of her young life. Maybe it was. Maybe it was a connection that Bailey hadn't realized her daughter needed.

"Yes, honey, you look like him." Bailey opened the backpack and pulled out cupcakes and bottled water. "How about a snack?"

"It might ruin my supper."

"It might, but we don't do this very often, so I think it will be okay."

Meg scrambled up and climbed onto Bailey's lap. "I love you, Mommy." She giggled and wiggled, wrapping wet and slightly muddy arms around Bailey's neck.

"You little rat, you." Bailey kissed Meg's cheeks until a real belly laugh rolled out. "I love you, Meg."

"I love you, too."

"Hey, what does it take to get in on this party?" Cody's voice carried from a short distance away. Blue barked a greeting, not a warning, to the man walking toward them.

"Sorry, this party is by invitation only." Bailey smiled to let him know she was teasing. His grin flashed in return.

"Did you catch any fish?" He pulled a second lawn chair from the back of the truck and opened it next to Bailey's. At close range she noticed the bruise on his jaw.

"Good practice session?"

He shrugged and touched his face. "Yeah, wonderful. I bought a bull."

"You bought a bull?"

"I figured if I couldn't ride him, I should probably own him."

"And is this wonder bull the reason you're walking like a ninety-year-old man?"

"He might have had something to do with it." He shifted and pulled Meg onto his lap. "What about fishing?"

Meg, the little traitor, leaned closely and whispered in his ear, "Mommy doesn't like to touch the worms."

Cody laughed and Meg laughed with him, their heads touching and their smiles matching. "I always knew your mom was a silly ole girl."

"She's not silly—she's just scared." Meg shivered and then laughed again.

"Let me see that pole. I can't ride a mean old bull, but I bet I can handle an earthworm."

Meg handed him the pole and the container of worms. "Do you think we can catch a fish?"

"Now *that* I'm not going to promise. I haven't been fishing in a long, long time." He hooked the worm and cast the line, letting the worm settle to the bottom and then pulled Meg down next to him on the grass bank. Father and daughter. Bailey's heart clenched at the scene.

This is what it feels like to be a family. The thought took her by surprise.

"Do you have another bottle of water?" His question shook her loose from dangerous thoughts that felt like remnants from the past.

Bailey dug into the pack and pulled out a bottle. She unscrewed the cap and handed it to him. He took it with a smile that somehow made everything seem okay.

"Do you want a sandwich?" Bailey reached for the small red cooler that held their meal. "I made soup for Dad before we headed down here. We're having a picnic."

"Do you mind if I join you? I don't want to barge in on something."

Bailey watched him, sitting next to Meg on the creek bank, helping her hold a fishing pole. She shook her head at the question. He wasn't barging in; he was fitting in. The last felt more dangerous than the first.

"We have plenty."

She made their sandwiches. Cody and Meg ate

theirs sitting on the creek bank, the pole resting between them. He told her stories about growing up out West. She told him about the tooth she'd just lost.

The valley grew cool as the sun set behind the hill, leaving the creek and their fishing spot in the shadows of early evening. Pink spread across the horizon, and cicadas began their nightly song. Bailey wanted it to last forever. Every night should be like that one, with Meg laughing and Cody being her dad.

Bailey shooed the thought away because she knew it couldn't happen, and told herself she didn't really want it to, anyway. She had never wanted Cody trapped in her life, against his will.

"You have a foal." Cody's words came out of nowhere as he and Meg were reeling in the fishing pole for the last time.

"I have what!" Bailey jumped up, grabbing her lawn chair and the backpack. "And you're just now telling me?"

He glanced at Meg and then back to Bailey. She got his meaning and she stopped herself, taking a deep breath as she let go of the moment of panic.

"I have a foal." She said it calmly and he smiled, standing up with Meg still in his arms.

"A little gray filly."

"You shoulda told us," Meg whispered into his ear.

"Yes, I should have, but we were having a lot of fun. And the foal is fine. I stayed with the mare, made sure the little girl was eating and I gave her the shot."

"She's okay?" Bailey grabbed both lawn chairs. "They're both okay?"

"They're both okay." He limped to her side, still

holding Meg. "Come on, you're not going to believe what else is up there."

"What's up there?" Bailey had a sick feeling as she considered all of the things it could be, and what she didn't want it to be.

A foreclosure notice was at the top of the list.

"I can't tell you—it's a surprise."

"I don't like surprises."

He pushed his hat back and sent an accusing look in her direction. "Neither do I."

Blue jumped in the back of the truck. Meg hurried to the tailgate, as if she thought Bailey wouldn't notice that she was about to climb in the back.

"Where do you think you're going?"

Bailey held her hands out to her daughter, an order to climb down. Normally compliant, Meg this time shot a look at Cody.

"I'll drive slow. She can ride with Blue." Cody stepped in, his face—smooth planes and whiskered cheeks—hidden in the shadows of his hat, but their gazes connected.

Her traitorous mind remembered the firmness of his lips and the way his hands had felt on her back. She gave herself a mental shake and tried to find a way to take back control—of the situation and her daughter.

"She'll be safe, Bailey." Cody's voice was soft, as soft as the southern breeze that slid through the valley.

Bailey caved, and caving was something she had worked hard against since that summer in Wyoming. Cody smiled, as if he knew that he was the common denominator that equaled her weakness.

She wouldn't let him take over. But Meg was looking at her, wanting so much to be a child with two parents.

"Drive slow, and Meg, sit down on the bottom of the truck bed." Bailey kissed her daughter's cheek.

"I'm proud of you." Cody winked and then opened the driver's side door.

Cody slid behind the wheel of her truck as Bailey climbed into the passenger seat. She glanced over her shoulder to make sure Meg was sitting up near the cab, on the bed of the truck and not on a wheel well. She reminded herself that it was a five-minute drive going less than five miles per hour.

She reminded herself that she had to be strong. She changed the subject.

"Did you check on Dad?"

"He's fine." Cody started the truck and started up the rutted trail toward the house. His hand slid across to hers, his fingers wrapping loosely, but the connection feeling like a strong bond. "Bailey, I don't know when my daughter's birthday is."

The air evaporated from the truck. Bailey rolled the window down and fought back a wave of nausea as that one question bombarded her, making her really think about what she'd done. Her father was the most important person in her life, and she had almost kept Meg from having one of her own.

She could say it was to protect her daughter from someone who might not be a fit parent, but now it looked as if she had been trying to protect herself from someone who didn't want her in his life the way she had wanted, forever.

"March twentieth," she whispered. "Cody, I'm really sorry. I should have told you."

"It's water under the bridge."

"That water can't be brought back. It's five years the two of you have lost."

"We'll manage." He shifted into low gear as they neared the open gate. "I have to leave next week."

Just like that, he undid all of the good thoughts.

"Okay."

"That's all you're going to say?"

"I didn't expect you to stay forever."

He stopped the truck in front of the barn. Bailey looked in the side mirror, watching as Meg and Blue jumped out of the back of the truck and ran to the fence of the corral. The mare was standing with the new foal, the baby still wobbly, but her dark tail wagged as she nursed.

"I have commitments." He was still trying to explain. She tried to listen, but her mind was doing an instant replay of the guy who had said cowgirls always believe they're in love.

Her tumbling thoughts came to a sudden, screeching halt when her gaze landed on the two horses in the front corral and then moved on to the seldom used round pen.

"Why is there a bull in my round pen?" She grabbed the door handle and gave the door a shove with her shoulder. "And where did the horses come from?"

As she walked toward the horses, she heard the jangle of Cody's spurs. She glanced over her shoulder, shooting him a questioning look, which he ignored. The horses, two geldings, trotted up to the fence. The animals moved side by side, and she made a good guess that they were used to being together. He'd brought them from the same place.

The bull had to go. She couldn't have that rangy animal getting loose and getting in the field with her Angus cows.

"Cody?" She reached out and the buckskin gelding, with his almost dappled yellow coat and black mane and tail, nudged at her hand, his velvety soft lips moving along her fingers for a treat that didn't exist.

"Jack Brown wanted to know if you had time to train a couple of horses. And the bull is on his way to join my herd in Oklahoma. Willow Michaels is picking him up next week on her way through Missouri."

"Gotcha." And she despised the odd emotion twisting at her heart and feeling a lot like jealousy. Willow Michaels was the most beautiful woman Bailey had ever seen. She was tall, slender and had honey-blond hair that hung to her waist. And her friends called her Will. Like having a man's name detracted from her appeal. Bailey knew this all secondhand from interviews she'd seen on TV.

"You don't mind, do you?" Cody hitched up his jeans and lifted his foot to rest on the bottom rail of the corral. "I won't be here to help load him."

"I know you won't. I can handle it."

"Will is a great person. If you haven't met her, you'll love her."

"I've seen her on TV, and I believe the consensus is that everyone loves Will."

"Because she's a nice person."

Bailey nodded but she wouldn't say another word, not with her eyes turning from brown to green and

Cody staring at her with a silly grin that added depth to his dimples.

She absolutely was not jealous of Willow Michaels. She turned away from the barn, forgetting to say goodbye until she was nearly to the corral, where Peaceful was nuzzling her new foal. It was too late, then. She glanced over her shoulder and saw Cody talking to Meg. They were petting the buckskin and her daughter was giggling.

Next week he would be gone. They would deal with that when it happened, not today when Meg was laughing like a five-year-old ought to laugh.

The thud of the barn door was Cody's first warning that Bailey had noticed the work he'd done that morning. He hadn't known what else to do. It was Saturday, the feed store was open only until noon, leaving a limited window of opportunity to get something accomplished. They had needed grain and fencing for the back fence or Jack Brown's horses would be out and running down the highway.

Next to him, Meg moved, drawing him back to the picnic table under the shade of the oak tree next to his RV. The laptop in front of him had switched to the screen saver, and his daughter was antsy. He turned his attention back to the business of shopping, knowing that Bailey was heading their way.

"Do you think she's going to be mad?" He asked his daughter as she sipped on the chocolate milk he'd poured for her.

"Pretty sure." Meg peeked back over her shoulder. "Yep, she's mad."

"At me, remember that, not at you."

"Okay." Meg pointed to a dress and he clicked the option to send the size and style to his shopping cart.

The virtual shopping cart full of clothing was a pretty good feeling. It felt almost as good as the two horses in the corral. Bailey might be upset with him, but he'd watched last night when she went out to work the animals, starting them in a circular pattern on the lunge line, and then brushing them until they had nearly followed her to the house for more attention. At least she wasn't sorry to have the horses to train.

He wasn't about to tell her the buckskin was his, or maybe he would give it to Meg. A shadow fell over the picnic table.

"What are you up to now?" She sat down across from him. Her smile softened the words. For a moment, he thought about being in her life like this forever.

"Meg and I are shopping."

"For?"

"School clothes," Meg answered, her tone chipper. He would have picked a different tactic. He might have tried a quieter, less enthusiastic approach.

"That's great, sweetie."

Surprised, he looked up, making eye contact with the woman across from him. She didn't look angry. Her eyes were soft, focusing on her daughter.

"We're almost done. Time to check out." Cody pointed for his daughter to hit the correct button as he pulled his wallet out of his back pocket. "Your dad told me about the BBQ fund-raiser at the church tomorrow night."

He typed in his credit card number as he waited for Bailey to answer. When he looked up, she was staring off into the distance. He cleared his throat to get her attention. When she turned, her attention fell first on her daughter and then on him.

"Meg, why don't you go check on the kittens? Their eyes are open and they're starting to crawl around the feed room."

Meg was off and running before another word could be said. It made Cody wonder if she had sensed her mother's mood and wanted to escape, or if she really was that excited about the kittens.

He picked up the insulated carafe of coffee and one of the disposable cups out of the bag. When he set the cup in front of her, she nodded and he filled it. That went well, so he moved on, hoping to persuade her that his help was something she could accept.

Maybe she thought help from him meant ties, or owing him something?

"I wanted to get some things done around here before I left. I hope you didn't mind."

She shook her head, the light breeze catching the feathery strands of her hair. When she looked up, her brown eyes were dark with emotion.

"I don't mind. I've given up minding." She breathed in and let it out in a sigh, a light shake of her head shifting blond hair off her shoulders. "I appreciate your help, Cody."

"Then what's wrong?"

"Meg loves you, and I love her. I don't want her to be hurt. I know how close you are to the world title, and I know how much it means to you...."

He lifted his hand to stop her. "You obviously know how much everything means to me, and yet you don't know how much Meg means to me."

"Cody, I'm sorry."

He closed his laptop and stood up. "I'm sure you are, but you have to trust me. You didn't let me finish what I was trying to tell you yesterday."

"Okay, finish. You were telling me that you're leaving. That's when I saw the bull and the horses."

Cody leaned, resting his hands on the top of the table, and forcing her to make eye contact. "I'm coming back."

She nodded but looked away, which answered his trust question. Could he blame her?

"Okay, you're coming back."

"And right now, I give up. I can't convince you and I'm not going to argue. I'm going to work on that back fence, which is something I *can* fix." He grabbed the work gloves he'd dropped on the picnic table and the bottle of water he'd taken out of the freezer.

As he pulled on the gloves, he remembered telling her that he'd call that summer after Wyoming. And after he left, he hadn't. Not because he hadn't wanted to, but because he'd been afraid to hear her voice, and afraid of what she'd make him feel. He didn't want her to know that.

While he'd been distracted by the past, she had stood and she faced him now, a cowgirl in faded denim and a pink T-shirt, her blond hair framing her face.

"I'll help."

"No, I'd like to do this alone. You should spend time with your daughter, and with your dad."

"Now you're telling me how to be a mom?"

He couldn't win this one. "No, I'm telling you that

I can take care of this and you should take care of more important things."

What he couldn't tell her was how he needed distance from her to get his thoughts straight. He couldn't leave at the first of the week with Bailey on his mind. He couldn't ride bulls distracted by thoughts of strawberry lip gloss and brown eyes that looked into his heart. What he could do was work on the farm, and tomorrow he would attend a fund-raiser for Jerry.

Chapter Seven

The four of them rode to town in Cody's truck. Bailey felt her heart grab as they pulled into the parking lot of the small church at the edge of Gibson, the church that Bailey had attended since her birth.

The building had been added onto and now boasted the traditional white-sided sanctuary with a bell tower, and at the back was a brick addition that housed classrooms. Old and new blended together, making everyone happy. Most of the time.

Bailey had new thoughts today, thoughts about the coming weeks and months, and about attending church without her dad. And today, attending with Cody, who had been seen, but no one really knew who he was.

Or maybe some had guessed.

Since she'd come home from Wyoming, she had dealt with the embarrassment and the shame of what had happened with Cody. In time the gossip had waned, people had moved on with their lives and with new gossip. Bailey had resumed her roll in the church as someone respected and loved. Meg had been welcomed with loving arms.

Now it was all back, the past had become present.

As Bailey walked next to her dad, Meg holding his other hand and Cody behind them, it was obvious that the rumor mill was working round the clock. A few people stared, and there were carefully averted glances that were less noticeable.

Heat crawled up her cheeks and she slowed her pace.

"What's up, pumpkin?" Her dad's hand tightened on hers. He stopped to take a breath, and she tried to ignore the ashen gray of his complexion. She couldn't, not anymore. And for him she would accept help. The money earned tonight was for him.

"Nothing's up, Dad. I thought maybe you'd like to rest."

"I'm fine. And don't try to fool me. You know I can tell a fib from a thousand feet away."

She leaned against his shoulder and sighed. "Yes, you've always known how to read me."

"Don't let it get to you."

Cody moved closer. Bailey tried to smile at him, but once again he was the reason she felt like hiding. Not that she could blame it all on him. She'd been a partner in that moment six years ago.

"I see Pastor John, I'm going to head that direction and to that lawn chair he's a pointing to." Jerry pulled free, kissing her on the cheek before he walked away.

Bailey let him go, aching to help him but not wanting to point out his weakness. He walked with slow, determined steps, stopping occasionally to rest. When he finally reached Pastor John and the promised seat, Bailey allowed herself to look away.

"Mom, I'm going, okay?" Meg jumped up and down next to her. "I'm going to swing with Katy."

Bailey nodded.

Meg was off and running. Bailey watched as her daughter ran to the swings and a group of children who were calling for her to join them. At least Meg didn't feel it. She was five and hadn't felt the sting of gossip.

Only once had she come home from a friend's house, crying because a little girl at the birthday party had teased her because she didn't have a daddy.

"What's up?" Cody stood next to her, his hair still damp from a shower. He smelled like an Irish spring and cinnamon gum.

"Nothing's up."

"You're acting a lot like that dog of yours when she skirts around the hooves of the horses trying to keep from getting stepped on. Is there something that I don't know about?"

"I'm sorry, Cody, but I can't face this again."

"Face what?"

"Gossip."

She glanced around the picnic area, an acre of grass, swings and tables. She didn't have to look far to see small crowds looking her way, their lips moving. Of course they could have been talking about how she was holding up. Or maybe they were only trying to figure out where she'd come up with a man.

"So, we tell them that I'm Meg's dad. End of story."

She laughed at his innocence. "Oh, come on, you should know better than that. That will only be the beginning of the story. And from the way people are looking at us, the story started before we got here."

"Do you want me to leave?"

Did she? What did he mean by leave? What she wanted was for him to be gone, taking remnants of her past with him. She glanced in the direction of Meg and knew that the past was always with her. And as much as she regretted her mistake, she didn't regret her daughter.

For Meg, she had to allow Cody into their lives. No, she didn't want him gone. She couldn't lie to herself and say that it was all about wanting him in Meg's life.

"Sometimes I don't know what I want."

He laughed, "That makes two of us. I don't know what you want, either. And so, if you don't mind, I'm going to join your dad and Pastor John. I've met him at the diner, and he seems like my kind of guy. He knows that people aren't perfect."

"Cody, I know that, too. And I don't expect you to be perfect. I don't know if you understand that this is more than I can deal with right now. My focus, as you pointed out yesterday, needs to be on Dad and Meg. But with you next to me..."

"Good to know you can't think or focus when I'm around." He bent his head and for a moment she thought he might kiss her. "I'll give you space to think."

Bailey nodded and watched him walk away, Wranglers, a red plaid shirt open with a T-shirt underneath, and the casual swagger of a cowboy. She remembered a little too late that Willow had recently been seen on his arm. Willow, who always looked perfect. Willow, who would be showing up in a few days.

"What's got you working yourself over, talking under your breath like a crazy woman?"

Bailey smiled at Lacey, relieved to have an ally.

"Where've you been?"

"Making my rounds. I walked from the Hash-It-Out. You know that the kids from the agriculture class auctioned themselves off a bit ago, and the money is for your dad. A few of the people who bid are volunteering the kids to work at your place."

"I didn't know." Her heart squeezed at that bit of kindness when just minutes ago she had been worried about what people were saying behind her back.

"It's true. That should make you happy, sweetie. So why do you look so blue?" Lacey wrapped a comforting arm around her and squeezed Bailey's shoulder. "Is that cowboy messing up your oatmeal again?"

He stood next to her dad, the red of the shirt a stark contrast to his dark skin and black hair. He had a can of soda, and someone had given him a plate of food. Pastor John pointed to an empty chair and Cody sat down.

"He isn't bothering me." Not really.

"Okay. You know, people are always going to talk, Bay. Remember how they wore out the topic of my hair when I dyed it black and got the red streaks?" Lacey's smile disappeared. "And you have a man that they don't know living out at your place."

"I questioned the black-and-red hair myself. But it looks good." Bailey laughed. "And they had more fun with the nose ring."

"Cowboy in an RV," Lacey reminded.

"I know."

"So, set people straight or send that cowboy on down the road."

"He's Meg's dad."

Silence. Lacey looked from Cody to Meg, and then back to Bailey. For some reason, Bailey had assumed her friend would guess, or at least have a clue. The stunned silence meant she hadn't thought of the connection.

"I didn't know." Lacey stared in Cody's direction. "I mean, I knew he was someone from your past. But now that you mention it, Meg has his eyes. And you've got a serious problem, because I bet you thought you were over him."

"I am over him. And he won't be here much longer. He stopped to talk and…"

"He stayed. And that's what broke brother Bill's balloon."

"What?" Bailey could never follow a conversation with Lacey. And that reminded her, hadn't she just been considering Lacey an ally?

"Sorry, I think that was a kid's picture book I read one time. A whole set of calamities, and it all ends with one little balloon getting busted. Anyway, it would probably be good if he went on down the road, because then people could let it rest."

"There's nothing to talk about."

"There will be once they figure out he's Meg's daddy."

Bailey ran a hand over her face and shook her head. She didn't need this. She didn't need another problem to solve. And the problem at hand had tossed his plate in the trash barrel and was walking in her direction.

"Well, I hate to skip out on you, but I think they want me to serve pie." Lacey patted Bailey's shoulder as she backed away. "Love ya, sweetie."

"It feels like love." Bailey called out to Lacey, who was laughing as she walked away.

"Small-town life is always a joy, isn't it?" He hooked his arm through hers. "Would you like to do the cakewalk?"

Bailey glanced in the direction of the parking lot, where a circle had been taped off and music was playing as a crowd went around the circle, stepping from numbered square to numbered square.

"The cakewalk would be great. I could use some chocolate." And she didn't even pull her arm loose from his.

"What are we going to do about the talk?" he asked.

"Maybe you should do the right thing and marry me." She regretted the joke immediately. "I'm sorry, that was supposed to be funny."

"I almost laughed." He did chuckle and Bailey sighed.

"I'm sorry, Cody."

"No, I am. I'll be back in a week and I'll move the RV. If I'm gone, they won't have a reason to talk."

In a week he would leave. She should feel relieved. If she thought about it for a few minutes, she was positive relief would surface.

Cody heard the deep sigh and felt Bailey move a step away from him. He would move his RV. That should give her peace of mind, not cause a buildup of tension. He tugged her close and she relented, her shoulder touching his.

"I'm not ashamed of my daughter, Bailey. I want people to know that I'm her father. I understand if you're not ready to tell everyone."

In answer, she shrugged.

Silence hung between them. He looked down and saw that her eyes were on Meg, running across the large lawn, holding the hand of another little girl. The two girls were heading toward the crowd that had gathered on the parking lot where they were holding the cakewalk. Cody, with Bailey at his side, continued to move in the same direction.

A local band had set up on a flatbed trailer, and a country gospel song, a little heavy on the guitar, covered the other noises. The fund-raiser for Jerry had turned into a festive gathering of friends and neighbors, all with the same goal—to help one of their own.

Cody hadn't felt that sense of community until he joined the pro bull-riding tour. And then when he first went to the church services with Jason and some of the other riders.

Those guys had become his first real family following the loss of his grandfather, when he was just a kid a little older than Meg.

Bailey pulled him to a stop fifty feet short of reaching Meg. He saw her gaze dart quickly to her daughter and then back to him.

"Cody, I don't mind if people learn who you are. Meg needs you in her life. She shouldn't have to be the little girl without a daddy."

"No, she shouldn't be that little girl." He wanted

her to have everything, including him, in her life. He wanted to be there for her when she needed him. "I don't want to make things difficult for you."

"How bad could it get? The worst was when I came home that summer. This is just leftovers."

"Sometimes leftovers are the hardest to swallow. Especially if it wasn't that great the first time around." He moved his hand to hers and felt her fingers clasping his.

"I can handle it, Cody. I just don't want it to hurt Meg."

"We won't let it."

They reached the crowd at the edge of the parking lot. A line had already formed for the cakewalk on the pavement. He dug into his pocket for money that he handed to a teenager.

"Three of us."

The girl tried to hand him his change, but he shook his head. This was for Jerry and Bailey's peace of mind. And it was for himself, to ease the guilt he felt each time he thought of her carrying a burden that had been partly his.

It didn't sit well, the fact that—like his dad—he was trying to buy an easy conscience. He shuffled those thoughts away as he led Bailey forward.

"You're going to do the cakewalk?" Bailey laughed as he stepped onto the square and pulled her to the one in front of him. From across the circle Meg squealed and ran toward them. Her arms came up and Cody grabbed her and lifted her to his shoulders.

The teenager in the center of the circle hit Play on an ancient cassette player, and praise music, tinny sounding and unable to compete with the band, started to play. As the music continued and they walked around the circle, Cody knew that this was what family felt like. He could even see that this was how a family looked.

As they walked to the wavering music, he glanced around, noticing with envy the way fathers walked with their children or stood in line to shoot baskets for prizes. Those men seemed to know and understand the role of fatherhood and what was expected of them.

Bailey, Meg and he were three pieces but not a whole. He didn't know that he could make them anything different.

"Cody, the music stopped." Bailey pushed him back as he nearly ran over her.

"Sorry, I wasn't paying attention." Longing for something he had never had, never thought he wanted, inched into his heart.

"I know, you stepped on my heel." She smiled, a teasing smile.

The teenage girl called a number. His number. Bailey pulled him in the direction of a table of cakes. His first cakewalk and he'd won. On his shoulders, Meg bounced and laughed. He lifted her off his shoulders when they reached the table.

"Which one do you want?" he asked his daughter.

Meg was already reaching for one with pink icing. It matched her cowboy boots, worn today with a denim skirt and a pink T-shirt.

"We'll take that one." He pointed and the woman behind the table handed over the cake. He tried to pretend he didn't notice the gleam in her eyes as she looked from him to Bailey to Meg.

"We should go check on Dad." Bailey shifted away

from the table, and away from him. Her cheeks were stained with pink and her eyes bright with tears.

She probably wanted him gone. He wasn't ready to leave.

After a Monday that somehow turned into the stereotype of what Mondays were supposed to be, and not in a good way, Bailey walked onto the back porch that evening for the quiet she'd been craving since the picnic the previous day. With her dad and Meg both in bed, this was her time.

Velvety darkness and sultry air blanketed the countryside, and millions of stars twinkled in the inky-black sky. As Bailey sat down with her glass of iced tea, she sighed with relief, feeling totally cut off from the world. That's exactly what she wanted to feel at that moment.

As she sat curled up in a cushioned patio chair, cocooned by the dark night and country silence, she didn't relax. She didn't find the peace she had sought. Instead her mind replayed an earlier conversation with Pastor John, when he had called to tell her that the gossip would fade and that the people who mattered knew the truth—that Cody was living on the property to help out.

On the whisper of a soft breeze a quiet thought returned, a reminder of grace, and forgiveness. The words had been her father's when she had gone to him in tears to tell him she was pregnant.

This, too, shall pass, her dad had said. And the words meant the same today as they did then. This, too, would pass, and soon Cody would be gone. But not really. This new Cody, the grown-up version, didn't appear to be ready to walk away from his daughter.

And that meant she would now have to learn to deal with him in her life on a permanent basis. In her life, but not. More like he was visiting her life, hanging out on the periphery. The most important thing was that he made a real move into Meg's life.

Sort of. If she was trying to fool herself, she could believe it was all about Meg and Cody, and that her own heart had nothing to do with it.

As her mind cleared, her attention wandered and her gaze went with it, in the direction of Cody's RV. The lights in the living area glowed soft yellow through the closed curtains and a faint melody drifted across the lawn.

Forget Cody. She closed her eyes, intending to make good on that. Meg started school next week. Bailey sighed and leaned back in her chair. That was one more thing she wasn't ready to deal with, her little girl going to school.

The door of the RV clicked. She opened her eyes as a shaft of light split the darkness of the yard. Cody stood in the doorway, not yet realizing that she was watching. He slid a hand through his hair and glanced around, obviously upset about his own life and his own problems.

It couldn't have been easy for him. He'd come here to do the right thing; she had to give him that. And look what he'd landed in the middle of. He suddenly had a family, and she knew that family was the last thing Cody wanted. What she didn't know was why.

He stepped down from the RV, pushing the door closed behind him. Blue jumped up from her place on the porch and trotted across the lawn to join him. That's when he saw her. He cocked his head and stared into the dark, and then he raised his hand in greeting and headed in her direction.

Her heart did a loud ka-thump in her chest, almost like the first time she'd seen him back in Wyoming, with eyes that sparkled and a mischievous grin that tied her heart in knots.

So much for the peaceful country night.

Did he know that people paid for noise machines that imitated nights like this, with the sound of the creek in the distance, the chirrup of the cicadas and occasional call of the whippoorwill?

She had the peaceful noises, and she'd been seeking a peaceful feeling to go with them. She and God had almost cleared up a few misunderstandings, and she'd even started to deal with the check from the church, which had felt a lot like charity.

Her dad had reminded her that of the three—faith, hope and charity—charity was the greatest. And how many people could say that enough people loved them to give the way the people of Gibson had given to them?

Cody looked like a man seeking peace, too.

He looked plain drawn out, the mischievous grin no longer in place. He stepped onto the porch and then hesitated, as if he wasn't sure of his place in her world. She couldn't help him with that.

"May I sit down?"

"Of course you may."

He smiled at that, his grin one-sided and landing in her heart. "Really?"

Really? She nodded and motioned for him to sit.

Cody sat down in the chair next to hers, sighing as he settled, stretching his legs in front of him. He had changed into khaki shorts and a white button-down shirt. She wondered where her cowboy had gone.

Blue nudged his hand and he rubbed her ears. When he didn't say anything, Bailey leaned back to relax. Sort of.

But who could really relax with that man sitting next to them. A woman made of stone, maybe. Bailey wanted to be that woman, but she wasn't. She was older, wiser, but still a woman.

"I'm sorry that I have to leave tomorrow."

And that's what broke brother Bill's balloon. Or something like that. Anyway, it was enough to shake her loose from the soft enchantment of a summer night.

"I know that. And I know that Willow will be here in a couple of days to get the bull."

He tilted his head and glanced in her direction. "Bailey, I'm sorry if it feels like I'm running out on you."

This all felt strangely familiar. Hadn't she heard the same thing six years ago?

"You aren't running out on me. You have a life and a career. You have a chance to win something you've dreamed of for as long as I've known you. Or when I knew you."

Another sigh and he tipped his head back. Her gaze followed his to the slow-spinning blades on the overhead fan.

"The world title suddenly doesn't seem so important."

"Don't regret, Cody. You can't get this back."

"There's always another year." He leaned forward, his arms resting on his knees.

Bailey's hand hovered above his back, and she thought about regret and moments you can't take back. Things that couldn't be undone. She moved her hand back to the armrest of her chair.

"There's more to this, isn't there?" Her question brought him back into her presence.

He leaned back again. Blue, at his side, nudged him for attention and his hand settled on her neck.

"I'm just struggling. I didn't think I would. I thought I would quit drinking, go to an AA meeting or two, pray and be suddenly cured."

And she hadn't realized her question would bring such an honest answer. She didn't have time to form an answer; Cody turned toward her, his smile hesitant.

"So much for being in each other's lives, huh?" He brought his left leg up to cross it over his knee, grimacing with the motion. "I'm an alcoholic. I can't undo that or make the facts different. I can't go back and be the person you wanted me to be six years ago. I'm working hard to be the person I want to be."

She shook her head, still praying for wisdom and knowing that God had answers that she didn't. "I'm not asking that from you. We're here today, and we are who we are. Now we have to find the answers for the situation we're in."

"This last seven months or so has been one continuous string of events that I hadn't expected."

"Like learning that you have a daughter?" She thought about it now, what that must have done to someone who was trying to build a new life. "I keep saying I'm sorry, and that isn't going to fix anything. I hope you do know that I mean it."

"I know you are, and I forgive you. I'm still working on forgiving myself."

"It isn't easy—I know from experience. But I also know that God's forgiveness is complete. He doesn't hold on to our past, using it to taunt us or make us feel guilty." She rested her hand on his arm, wondering why that contact with him made her breathe deeper and feel a little calmer. "And the struggle with alcohol isn't going to go away, not overnight, and maybe not ever."

He nodded, his eyes closing. "I know. Right now I feel a lot like Jesus must have felt when He had been in the wilderness for forty days and was being tempted by the enemy."

"He promised He wouldn't give us more than we can handle." She moved her hand from his. "But the key to that is that we aren't supposed to try and handle it alone. We have to lean on Him."

"I'm not sure what I was thinking back in Wyoming."

"What do you mean?"

"I shouldn't have walked away from you. I didn't realize then that women like you don't come along every day."

Bailey's insides quaked as his words registered. When she didn't respond, he reached for her hand and she felt strong fingers wrapping around hers. Men like Cody didn't come along every day, either. She wanted to tell him that, but she couldn't let herself move that far into his life, not yet.

Keeping it about Meg made it easier to deal with

him in her life. But hiding behind a five-year-old wasn't really fair.

"Cody, you're stronger than you think. And the way you've stayed here with us. I want you to know that it means a lot to me. You could have left but you didn't."

"Thank you, Bailey." He leaned toward her, still holding her hand, and his lips grazed hers. "Thank you."

"I need to go to bed. I have to work tomorrow." She stood, and he released her hand.

"I'm sorry, I shouldn't have done that."

"I can't go back, Cody."

"That isn't where I'm planning on going." He stood next to her. "I'm only planning to move forward from this point."

"I have so many things to deal with right now." In football she thought they would call this a fumble; she really felt like she was fumbling. She slid past him to the door. "Take care of yourself."

"You, too."

And she walked away from him, when walking away was the last thing she wanted to do. What she wanted, he couldn't give. He couldn't tell her what the future held or where he would be next month, or even next year.

Chapter Eight

Cody pulled up in front of the store, next to Bailey's truck. He needed a few things for the trip. He didn't know if he needed them badly enough to face Bailey after last night. And then again, he wasn't a coward.

He walked into the store, which had probably been a fixture in Gibson since the early 1900s. It still boasted a wood facade, hardwood floors and only four aisles. It smelled like produce, lemon oil and pine cleaner.

Mr. Hastings, the owner, smiled from behind the meat counter, and Mrs. Hastings scurried toward him, wiping her hands on the apron she always wore. Her smile was huge and her eyes were twinkling. Cody suddenly wished he had driven on by and waited until he had gotten to Springfield for the things he needed. Springfield had stores where a person could shop with anonymity.

"Why, Cody Jacobs, we're so pleased to hear the news."

He wondered what news, and he wondered where

Bailey had gone to. A giggle from the aisle with canned vegetables and baking supplies answered his question. Whatever was about to go down, Bailey obviously thought it was pretty amusing.

He had a feeling he wouldn't.

"Mrs. Hastings, what news would that be?"

She laughed and patted his arm like she'd known him forever. "Why, honey, we heard about the wedding. We're all so tickled that you're going to do the right thing and marry our little Bailey."

Marry Bailey? He opened his mouth to reply but he couldn't. Marry Bailey? He heard her laughing now. Mrs. Hastings heard it, too, and her smile grew.

"Well, now, I forgot she came in a bit ago. I bet you're looking for her."

"Actually, I…"

"Bailey, come on out—your man is here." Mrs. Hastings gave him a look. From the meat counter, Mr. Hastings, obviously sympathetic to Cody's plight, coughed and cleared his throat. Mrs. Hastings ignored him. "Now, I want the two of you to know that we're going to throw you a wonderful reception at our place on the river."

"Mrs. Hastings, there…"

"Don't argue." She smiled, as if she knew he was trying to set her straight, and she wasn't going to hear it. "Oh, there's Bailey."

Yes, there was Bailey. She pushed a cart around the corner, and his heart tripped all over itself as if maybe she was the one. Blond hair and the face of an angel—what guy wouldn't look at her and feel the same way?

"Cody, I didn't know you were going to be here. Honey."

He couldn't believe she was playing along with this. Had he entered some strange dimension where Bailey played practical jokes? Or had the whole town gone crazy. What if they kept him here, forcing him to marry the woman he'd done wrong?

It could happen. He'd seen movies like that.

"Bailey. I knew you were gone. I thought you were at work."

"No, I'm staying at home with Dad today and tomorrow. After that a few of the women from the church are going to pitch in and help."

"I'll be back as soon as I can. Maybe next Sunday night, if I can fly out that soon."

"No hurry, we'll be fine." She had pushed her cart to the one register and was piling her groceries on the counter.

Cody held his debit card out to Mrs. Hastings. She laughed and didn't take it.

"We don't take plastic, just checks and cash, the way it was intended to be," she explained.

Intended to be? He didn't even want an explanation for that.

Bailey pulled her checkbook out of her purse and shot him a sweet smile. Okay, this was definitely some parallel universe. Shouldn't she be furious about the rumor that they were getting married?

He started to get a little itchy on the inside, like an allergic reaction he'd once had to walnuts. What if Bailey was in on the conspiracy?

What if it was something like the town of Stepford? They were going to clone him and turn him into a good man, the kind who knew how to be a father and a husband. The kind who never made mistakes.

Bailey paid for her groceries, and he picked up two of the paper bags to carry out for her. She followed with the last. As they walked out the door, she growled.

Now *that* was the Bailey he knew.

"What in the world is going on?" He set the bags on the floorboard of the truck and closed the door. Bailey stood next to him, her eyes squeezed shut but a tiny smile quivering on her lips.

"I'm not sure, but I'm going to get to the bottom of it. Seems someone at the picnic overheard us talking about getting married."

"Wasn't that a joke?" He had thought it was, when she said he should do the right thing and marry her.

"It was a joke. Do you really think I want you to marry me?"

She didn't have to stomp all over his ego and act as if it was the last thing she wanted. "No, I didn't think you were serious."

"Someone did and the entire town knows, and they're planning our wedding."

Now what? He leaned against the truck, not caring about the dust or what people driving by would think. "Should we get married?"

She hit him on the arm. "That is the last thing on my mind at this point. Especially to someone who so obviously doesn't want to be married. I want to marry someone who loves me and wants to be with me forever. Remember, cowgirls always think they're in love. Well, we also think it should be forever."

He rubbed the back of his neck and thought about

how much easier it was to get stomped by a bull than to deal with an angry female. There were similarities between the two. Both could attack from behind and when you least expected it. Both could be perfectly docile one minute and out for blood the next.

Both seemed to have it out for cowboys.

"You know, Bailey, contrary to popular belief, cowboys feel the same way about love and forever. In our case, there's a little girl involved, and I want to do what is best for her."

"I'm not sure what the answer is to that. I've been trying to do the best thing for her for about six years."

"Well, you're going to have to cut me some slack if I don't have your parenting experience. Remember, I just found out that I'm a dad."

He caught a movement in the window of the store and groaned. Could it get any worse?

"What?" Bailey was looking at him, her back to the store.

"We're being watched. They think either it's a lover's spat or we're talking about wedding plans."

"It's neither, and I'm tempted to go tell them that."

"I wouldn't. Let it die down. When people don't get their invitations, they'll figure it out."

"When your RV is gone, they'll figure it out."

Her big eyes were full of hurt, fresh or from the past, he wasn't sure which. He didn't know how to make things right.

"Bailey, give me a chance to think this through. Give me a chance to do the right thing."

She nodded and turned away from him. He couldn't let her go like that. He couldn't let her walk away with anger between them.

He reached for her hand and pulled her back to him. Before either of them could react or think it through, he leaned, brushing his lips across hers. He lingered in the kiss for just a minute, the way he'd wanted to do last night.

For that minute he wanted to stay forever.

Bailey pulled back, her eyes wide with shock and anger.

"That wasn't the right thing to do, Cody."

"It felt like it in the moment." He brushed the back of his hand across her silky cheek. "See you in a week."

She walked away angrily and he let her go, because he was pretty sure her anger was just an act. And he knew that he had been sober for only seven months and needed a few more under his belt before he pursued a relationship.

The buckskin quivered as Bailey slid the saddle onto his back, but he didn't buck or sidestep. That was the way she had planned it. In the four days after Cody had left, she'd worked with the horses when she could.

She'd taken it easy with the buckskin, getting him used to her touch, to her leaning on his back and to the smell of the leather. And the creak of the saddle. She had learned that lesson a few years earlier, when she'd dealt with a horse that had been terrific until the saddle creaked under her weight.

She never would have thought about that sound being the undoing of a horse. Now she thought about it each time a storm hovered on the horizon and her bones ached, a remnant of the fall she'd taken.

The buckskin was a baby and leaned against her as the saddle settled onto his back. He wanted to be comforted during this strange new process.

"Big Baby, that should be your name. I think I'll recommend that when they come to get you." She rubbed his neck and whispered that if she could, she would keep him.

"Mommy, look at the big trailer."

Bailey pivoted and the horse shied, sending the saddle to the ground and further scaring him. He jumped away from her, jerking the leather reins from her hands.

"Easy, fella." she reached for the reins and the horse moved again, his eyes rolling wildly.

Meg ran across the yard, her pigtails flapping. That didn't help. The horse turned to see what the new danger was and his hoof came down on Bailey's heel. She bit down on the scream and blinked furiously to clear her vision. The truck and cattle hauler had rumbled to a stop a short distance from the corral.

"Mom, are you okay?" Meg whispered in a loud voice from outside the pen.

"I'm fine, honey, just a little sore." Nothing broken, just bruised. She hoped. She couldn't be hurt, not with her dad needing her, and Meg needing her.

Her eyes watered again, this time not from pain. And walking toward her was the most magnificent woman Bailey had ever seen. Willow Michaels, taller and more beautiful in person.

And with a smile that had to be genuine. Now why didn't that make Bailey like her? Why did it add depth to the stab of jealousy?

Because nice women were hard to resent. Because

it was only on Monday that Cody had said cowboys wanted love and forever, too. And Willow looked like the type of woman who would make a man think about forever.

"Bailey Cross?" Willow's voice was husky and oddly toned.

Bailey hobbled across the arena, still leading the traumatized horse. She nodded in answer to Willow's question.

"Yes, I'm Bailey. You must be Willow."

Willow's hand went to her ear, just a flick and then she smiled again. "I am. Cody asked me to pick up a bull."

Bailey shifted her gaze in the direction of the bull. "There he is—the troublemaker."

"I'm sorry?"

"The bull, that's him."

Willow touched her arm. "I'm sorry, you'll have to look at me when you speak. The wind is carrying your words, and I can't hear you."

Bailey turned and Willow slid her hair back, allowing a small peek at the hearing aid hidden by the long tresses of blond. With that knowledge, Bailey suddenly didn't ache to be rid of Willow Michaels. She hadn't expected that, not when her first reaction had been jealousy. Jealous because Willow had a truck that didn't look like it was more scrap metal than anything else, and jealous because Willow smiled like smiling was easy.

"Of course, I'll speak up." Bailey added a smile of her own. "Would you like a glass of iced tea before we load the bull?"

"That would be lovely." Willow didn't talk like

someone who had grown up in the country, or around farm animals. She sounded like someone used to tea served in china cups, not in plastic tumblers with ice.

Meg circled them, staring openly at the tall blond who towered over her mother. She took hold of Willow's hand and Willow leaned toward her.

"Do you know my dad?"

"I do know your dad. He's a friend."

The oddly unsettling pinch of jealousy returned, but Bailey swept it away, reminding herself that Willow was kind and obviously had a story. A woman as elegant as Willow, one who hauled bulls around the country, had to have a story.

"He likes my mom." Meg smiled sweetly, sashaying away before Bailey could get hold of her.

"I'm sorry, this is all new to her." Bailey hurried to explain. "She and Cody just met."

"I know—he told me." Willow looked down at Bailey's foot. "Are you okay?"

Okay? Did she mean okay with the fact that Cody had shared their story with this woman. She couldn't answer that because she didn't think she was okay. But Willow pointed to her foot, clearing up the misunderstanding.

"The buckskin shied and stepped on me. It's just a bruise." It couldn't be more than that, because working tomorrow wasn't optional.

And from there her thoughts spiraled to stacks of bills and repeated calls from the mortgage company. Her words for Cody came back to haunt her, that God wouldn't give them more than they could handle.

She hoped God knew she was holding tight to Him, and to faith.

As they walked through the back door of the house, greeted by still air and heat, Bailey's gaze traveled to her dad. He was at the table with a notebook and a calculator.

"Dad, I'll do that." Bailey covered his hand to stop him.

"I have to do something." He smiled up at her, his eyes less focused today and his skin papery and gray. His attention shifted to Willow. "Willow Michaels, nice to meet you."

Willow extended her hand to Jerry. "Nice to meet you, too."

Bailey poured three glasses of tea as Meg rummaged through the fridge for a juice box. The pink boots, a gift from an older woman at church, were getting small. How was she going to convince her daughter that some things had to be let go of?

She turned with the glasses of tea, and her heart sank as her gaze landed on her dad, remembering how he had looked just a few years earlier, before cancer. And she knew that her daughter wasn't the only one who had to learn that some things had to be let go of.

Bailey should have been an old pro by now. She had let go of her mom, Cody, and now her dad. She knew that she was going to have to let go of the farm.

After they drank their tea, Bailey and Willow walked back across the yard to the pen that had been the bull's home for the last week. Meg was in the house, sitting on her grandfather's lap watching the midday news.

"Life is never easy." Willow spoke as they neared the bull, the words so soft that Bailey had to strain to hear.

She wondered what in Willow's life had been difficult and then chastised herself for that thought. A beautiful face didn't guarantee that everything would be perfect.

"No, it isn't always easy." Bailey stopped at the gate to the pen. "Sometimes it is downright difficult."

Willow touched Bailey's shoulder. "Surviving makes our faith strong."

"You're very kind, Willow." Bailey thought she could even be friends with the other woman. "No wonder Cody thinks so much of you."

"He's just a friend." Willow smiled as she turned to walk away. "I'll back the trailer over here."

Bailey wanted to call out to Willow's retreating back that it didn't matter what Cody was to her. Really it didn't. After all, Bailey was used to letting go.

Cody shot through the air like a circus clown being ejected from a cannon. But he knew that the only net that would catch him was a hard dirt-packed arena floor, and no time to prepare for contact. On impact the thud of the ground knocked the air from his body and his head slammed backward.

And then darkness until the medic shouted his name.

"Cody, do you know where you are?" Dr. Charlotte Gaines, her black hair in a braid, spoke sharply. Sometimes he wondered why she had this job.

"I know who I am, and I know you don't like bull riders."

The crowd laughed because his words carried through the speakers. Dr. Gaines was wired for sound. The audience and the TV viewers liked that little extra insight.

"Cody, tell me where you are."

"Illinois," he mumbled as he tried to sit up, against the restraining hands of the doctor and her medic. A bullfighter, one of the guys who had saved his hide more than once, was laughing and mumbling that even on the ground, Cody was hitting on Dr. Gorgeous. He sat up, several pairs of hands holding his arms. "Did I get a reride?"

The bull hadn't spun; good bulls always spin. Instead he had made a straight line across the arena like a horse heading for the barn. At least Cody had lasted eight seconds. He distinctly remembered hearing the buzzer before his flying-monkey act.

And he remembered thinking about Meg, and how he wanted to be there for her, not part-time, not injured, but forever. And just as he hit the ground, he thought about Bailey lecturing him for taking chances.

Dr. Gaines didn't answer his question about a reride; instead, she ordered the medics to get him back to the exam room so she could get a better look at him.

Jason was at the gate when Cody walked through. Cody grabbed his friend's arm. "Did I get a reride?"

"Yes, you got your reride." Jason grabbed Cody's bull rope. "I'll get it ready for you."

Cody started to nod, but his head ached and he was seeing double. He swayed and Jason caught hold of his arm. Cody backed away, slipping free from the restraining hand of his friend.

"I'm fine."

"Of course you are." Jason shook his head and pushed the bull rope back into Cody's hand. "But I don't think you'll be riding."

"I'll ride." Cody let the medic lead him back to the exam room. Dr. Charlotte Gaines, small but straight as a rod, marched ahead of them.

The exam room was a makeshift emergency room, with everything the good doctor needed to examine her many patients each weekend. Two other bull riders were stretched out on cots, both with ice packs on various joints. Another was sitting on a chair, his foot up on a table but his gaze on the beautiful doctor.

"Sit." Dr. Gaines pointed and Cody did as she commanded.

She examined him, her frown growing with each minute that passed.

"I'm going to be fine."

"This time, Cody, but what about next time? How many concussions do you think you can take before the damage is permanent?"

He shrugged, because he wasn't an idiot and he knew the answer. He also knew she expected a little bit of a fight from him.

"But riding the reride bull could be the difference between winning this event or not." Cody knew she didn't care, but he reminded her anyway.

"Cody, you only get one brain and yours has taken more blows than is good."

"Oh, Dr. G, you say that to all the guys."

A slim smile slid across her lips and she shook her head. He had no feelings for her, other than those of a friend, but he did like to tease her, especially when he managed to produce one of her rare smiles.

"Fine, ride. I know I can't talk you out of it."

She slipped her stethoscope down and backed away from him. For a moment it wasn't her face that he saw, but Bailey's and then Meg's. That had to be the concussion.

"Did you know I'm a dad? Her name is Meg."

Her eyes softened with that maternal glimmer. "You have a daughter?"

"I met her for the first time a few weeks ago."

And he wasn't going to crack his skull and let her down. His days of taking chances were over.

"Congratulations." Charlotte Gaines patted his shoulder, the way she did when she was trying to distance herself. He knew her well enough to know that about her.

"Thanks. Now, if you'll let me have my walking papers, I'll let them know that I'm not taking the re-ride. Doctor's orders."

Because he had a daughter and he didn't want to let her down. He didn't want to put one more burden on Bailey. With everything else going on, she didn't need to hear that he was in the hospital, or worse.

Bailey pulled her truck past the gas pump and parked in front of the only convenience store in Gibson. It was packed, of course; on Sundays it was one of the few places open. With breath held—as if that would help—she eased out of her truck to keep from banging her door against the shiny paint of the Lexus parked next to her.

As her feet hit the ground, a sharp jab shot up her heel and she was reminded of the incident with Bucky the buckskin. She had named him because

Cody hadn't bothered to tell her what to call the poor animal. *Bucky* didn't take a lot of creativity, and it wasn't an "I'm attached to the animal" kind of name.

She hobbled into the store, her left shoe feeling a size smaller than it should. Being on her feet while she waited tables for the Sunday lunch crowd at the diner hadn't helped. The work she still had to do at home would make it worse.

At least Mary, one of the Golden Girls, was at the house with Bailey's dad and Meg. Pastor John had called a few days earlier and given her a list of volunteers that would be showing up this week. He had been right, again. Knowing someone was there to help had given her peace of mind.

Okay, at first it hadn't been peace of mind but instead a definite stubbornness and the remark that she could manage. Pastor John had reminded her that Christians were to serve one another and that she should let them put that act into practice.

Bailey smiled at a few people she knew in the store and made her way to the aisle of snack foods. Nothing like a nutritious meal to give her the energy she needed. Somehow she didn't think it would give her a boost. She was going on five hours of very interrupted sleep and the knowledge that her dad was failing fast.

"Bailey Cross, how are you?"

She turned at the familiar greeting and smiled at Chad Gardner. "Fine, Chad. How is Kate?"

"Still pregnant." He grinned like the father of a first child should, but the smile quickly faded. "Bailey, your dad called me about listing the farm, or at least the majority of the acreage."

Her heart jolted and for a few seconds she had to close her eyes to adjust. The fluorescent-lit convenience store, with neighbors walking the aisles, wasn't the place for this conversation, or the place for her to fall apart.

She had just wanted a package of cheese crackers. "I didn't know."

"That's why I wanted to talk to you." He moved her to the side as a few teenagers crowded through the aisle. "I thought you should be in on the decision."

Her dad had gone behind her back. With everything else, she didn't need that. She wasn't angry with him, just hurt. Hurt because he thought he needed to speak to Chad on his own. And hurt because she knew it had to be done.

"Thank you, Chad, I appreciate your telling me."

"I drew the papers up and I'll bring them out for the two of you to sign. Whenever is good for you, but you should understand that a property that size could take six months or longer."

He didn't have to explain what he meant by that. She could lose the farm before it could sell. She smiled, pretending that everything would be okay.

"It's okay, Chad, we'll be fine."

"I know you will." He patted her arm and walked away.

Bailey hobbled to the racks of snack crackers and beef jerky. The diner had been busy, and she hadn't taken time for lunch. Now her stomach was growling, and even crackers with fake cheese spread sounded good.

"You know, that isn't good for you."

Bailey jumped at the familiar voice whispering in

her ear as she reached for the package of six crackers. She turned, surprised by Cody's presence a day earlier than she had expected. And if she was honest, she was surprised he had even come back.

Really surprised.

"What are you doing here?"

"I have a daughter here."

Of course, a daughter. But that didn't eliminate the way her mood shifted to hopefulness, like a friend had shown up just in time.

"I saw the fall you took." And her heart had plummeted, seeing him on the ground for the second time in a year, watching as the medical staff rushed to his aid. "Are you okay?"

"A headache, but nothing a week or two off won't cure."

It would be another hit on his lead in the point standings. She knew how much those points meant. It meant the difference between winning a world championship, or not.

"What's the plan now?"

"Do you mean for bull riding?"

She continued on to the cooler section and opened the door to get a bottle of water. Cody reached around her and grabbed two, and then he looped his arm through hers. She wanted to tell him she didn't need his support, but it felt too good to object.

Maybe she should remind him about small-town rumors and how easily they got started? People had already figured out that he was Meg's dad.

"I meant, what are your plans for the future? Bull riding, when you plan to leave, and when do you want to set up a schedule for seeing Meg." It wasn't easy to bring up that last part about Meg, but it had to be said.

"I'm not leaving yet. And I don't want to talk about schedules to see my daughter. That makes it sound like I'm a visitor in her life."

"Fine, we won't talk schedules, but we can't avoid the facts. You had a life before you came here, a life that included a career and friends, and obviously a place you considered home."

"And now I have a daughter and responsibility. I'm going to figure it all out."

"Fine. But in the meantime…"

"Pastor John said the gossip is fading and that I should stay where I am. He's making sure everyone knows that the wedding is off."

"Oh, very funny." She couldn't help but smile. "So, your plans then?"

"I guess I'm leaving that up to you. I can't see moving the RV for a month or two and then moving it back to Oklahoma after the finals. I'd rather leave it where it is."

"That's fine; you can leave it."

"Why are you limping?" His hand reached for her arm and he pulled her to a gentle stop.

"Your buckskin—" she refused to admit she named the horse "—got spooked and stepped on me yesterday."

"Did you go to the doctor?"

No time, no money and she knew she didn't need to. "No, it's only a bruise."

"I'll look at it when we get home. And to make it up to you, let me buy you lunch."

"Lunch would be nice. What do you have in

mind?" It was that easy to take him up on his offer. "Of course, keep in mind that the diner is closed. That's why I'm buying crackers."

"Leave it to me."

"I'm frightened."

He led her to the front of the store and pointed at the warming tray of fried foods. "Anything you want, price is no object."

"Anything?"

He nodded and swept his arm in a grand gesture to display her choices. "Anything."

Bailey laughed until her eyes watered, maybe because it was funny or maybe because of the sudden wave of relief that she couldn't explain.

"You mean, I can have chicken strips, egg rolls, corn dogs and fries with Cajun seasoning? Or even a mini pizza, or those little tacos?"

Cody motioned for the cashier. "We need two orders of everything, because I am not a cheap date."

At the word *date,* Bailey lost her appetite.

Chapter Nine

How could he expect her to sit in one place, her foot up and packed in ice, while there was work to be done? Bailey fumed as she sat on the porch, the food from the convenience store on a plate and a glass of iced tea sitting on the table next to her.

From across the yard, Meg yelled. She had found the kittens that the mother cat had hidden. Meg didn't understand that hiding the babies was the way a mother protected her young.

"He's just trying to take care of you, sis." Her dad's voice was weak, and he hadn't touched a bite of the food on his plate.

"I know, Dad. But I can't let myself get used to him being here."

"I don't see why not."

"Because…" Because she didn't have a good reason. She smiled at her dad. "I'm stubborn, like my dad, and I don't like to depend on someone else."

Because Cody wouldn't stay. He couldn't. She knew that about him, that he had a hard time putting down roots. She knew now that it had something to do with his childhood.

What kind of child had he been? Had he been lonely and unloved? Had he been the kind of little boy who stayed in trouble?

She smiled at her dad, hoping to ease his concerns. He didn't smile back; he just moved his food around the plate and then set it down on the table.

Cody came out of the barn, his casual swagger as familiar to her as the blue of the sky. He headed in their direction, smiling as he got closer.

"How's the foot?" He leaned against the rail of the porch, his arms crossed over his chest and his dark hair damp from perspiration.

"Cold."

He laughed and kneeled next to her, moving the ice and touching her heel with his hand. "I don't think it's broken."

"I don't, either. Remember, that's why I wasn't worried."

"It is swollen."

"I was on my feet all day."

His hand, warm with a firm touch, rested on her ankle, and she moved to dislodge it. He leaned back on his heels and then stood, as if he suddenly couldn't handle the close contact, either.

The chair next to hers creaked. Bailey shifted her attention to her dad as he tried to stand. Cody moved to Jerry's side and wrapped an arm around his waist to help him to his feet.

"I think I need to sleep." Jerry smiled down at Bailey, and she told herself she couldn't cry. For him she had to smile.

"Okay, Dad. Ring the bell if you need anything." Harder than anything was the fact that Cody was taking over, and taking care of everyone.

"I'll be right back. Don't move," he ordered as they managed to get through the screen door side by side, her father and the father of her child.

Bailey's emotions were more bruised than her heel. She didn't think a person could put an ice pack on her heart. She did move the ice pack from her foot and dropped it onto the porch. Blue had joined her, and the dog licked the condensation off the plastic bag.

The screen door creaked open and Cody joined her again. His accusing gaze landed on her foot and then drifted to the dog and the ice pack.

"That's going to help." He sat down in the vacated seat next to hers.

"Blue was hot." Bailey focused on Meg in the yard with the kittens.

"School starts soon."

"It does."

"I'd like to be there, with the two of you."

"I don't mind." She didn't, but she did. She would have to share Meg's first day of school. She would have to face the public with Cody as Meg's father.

"If you don't want me there…"

"You should be there." Because he deserved to take part in one of Meg's *firsts,* and because he'd done so much for them.

"Your dad says he has an appointment tomorrow." Cody stretched and put his feet next to hers on the footstool.

Bailey bit down on her bottom lip and pretended it didn't bother her. "He needs new pain meds. I'm going to take off part of the morning to take him up to his doctor."

"I can take him."

Bailey moved her feet, dropping them to the floor of the porch. "I should do it."

"I'm here and I don't mind."

Bailey sighed and then nodded. "If you would, that would help."

She wondered if he knew how hard it was for her to let him in, not just him but anyone. She'd been used to doing things on her own for a long time.

Cody pulled up close to the house with Meg in the back of the truck sleeping and Jerry staring blankly out the window, a wet streak tracing down his cheek. The appointment for a new pain medication had turned into more than either of them had expected. It wouldn't be easy to talk to Bailey about what they had learned from the doctor.

He hadn't told Meg what the doctor had said, but he'd seen the worry in the little girl's eyes. To make it better, he did the only thing he knew how to do. He'd taken her shopping while the doctor ran tests on Jerry.

She would start school tomorrow. Hard to believe she was really old enough for that. She certainly didn't seem big enough. Or maybe he had a hard time thinking about letting go of someone he had just found.

He would have to deal with that because this farm, this steadiness, wasn't his life. Sooner or later, like every other time, he would get restless. He would feel the pull of bull riding, even if it did seem to be waning right at the moment. He would feel the urge to travel, even if for now his wandering feet seemed pretty content.

No matter what, he would always be there for Meg. He wouldn't let her down. He sighed at that, not wanting to be a weekend and summer-vacation dad.

"Ready to get out?" Cody turned to Jerry, who nodded. "Okay, let me help you."

"I can do it myself. You get the June bug into the house." Jerry glanced over his shoulder at his granddaughter. "Hard to believe she starts kindergarten tomorrow."

"I was just thinking the same thing."

Cody got out of the truck and opened the back door, reaching in to pull Meg out. She whimpered and curled against him, her face damp with perspiration and probably slobber. He smiled as she buried her face into his shoulder.

Man, she felt good in his arms. She made him feel strong and able to do anything. She made him feel like the hero he definitely wasn't. But it sure made him want to be one.

He walked through the house with her, perspiring in the warm air and feeling pretty good about having purchased the window air units in the back of his truck. Four of them. That should put a chill on this old farmhouse.

And the other thing in the back of his truck was a swing set for Meg.

Meg curled into her bed and he tucked her stuffed animal into her arms. She blinked a few times, smiled and drifted back off to sleep.

"I love you, sweet pea." He touched her cheek and

walked back to the living room, where Jerry was settling into his recliner with his oxygen.

The blinds over the windows were drawn to keep afternoon sun from baking the room, and the only light came drifting in from the kitchen window. Cody reached to turn on the lamp but Jerry's words stopped him.

"Not every day that a man finds out he has less than two weeks to make sure his life is in order." Jerry fumbled with the tube in his nose and closed his eyes. "I don't have too many regrets."

Cody did. That seemed to be the theme of the year.

"What can I do to help?" He sat on the armrest of the brown plaid sofa in the stifling heat of the living room. The ceiling fan barely circulated a breeze, and the TV remained quiet for once. "Other than put those air conditioners in?"

"Now that'll be real nice." Jerry reached for the TV remote but pulled his hand back. "There is something else you can do for me, Cody."

Cody waited, unsure of what would be asked and how he would handle the request. He knew it would be big. He knew, with the tightening of his insides, that the request would change his life.

"I'll help you in any way I can."

Jerry nodded. "I know you will. Cody, take care of my girls. There are plenty of people around here who will look out for them, but not many who can stand toe-to-toe with Bailey. She's headstrong and used to taking care of things."

"I know, but I don't know how much she'll let me do for her."

Jerry sucked in a few deep breaths before he continued.

"Don't let her get away with trying to do it all on her own. She needs you."

Cody moved from the arm of the sofa to the seat. He stared at the dark paneled wall and tried to think of ways to explain to Jerry that he was the last thing Bailey needed.

"I'm not the right person for that job. I look at you and what a good man you are, like you don't even have to think about the right thing to do. I don't know how to be the person who always makes the right choices. I'm struggling with even being a dad to Meg."

Jerry smiled and sort of laughed. "You aren't any different from me or any other dad that I know. We all struggle, hoping we're doing the right thing."

"It seems like I do the wrong thing a lot more than I do the right thing."

Jerry's eyes closed. "She needs you. If you bought the land, you'd have a place of your own and you could be here to watch Meg grow up."

"I'll be here for her."

Jerry drifted off as Cody sat on the couch wondering how in the world he was going to keep that promise but knowing he would have to.

After overhearing the conversation between her dad and Cody, Bailey walked off the porch mumbling to herself about her dad's interference and Cody making promises he wasn't going to keep. Promises she wouldn't hold him to. She didn't need a babysitter, or a cowboy in shining armor.

On her way to the barn she passed Cody's truck. In the back were four rectangular boxes and one long box. She stepped closer to read the labels and then she turned and stomped back to the house.

Cody was coming out the back door and he looked perfectly innocent. She knew better.

"What in the world is in the back of your truck?" She ignored his finger raised to his mouth. She wasn't being that loud. "It looks like you've been shopping."

"We stopped by Wal-Mart on our way home from the doctor's office. Meg needed new shoes." He took hold of her arm, and she let him lead her away from the house. "Bailey, we need to talk about your dad."

Not about what her dad had asked him. She knew that from the serious look on his face.

"What happened?"

She didn't want to have this conversation. The look on Cody's face, the softness in his eyes—she didn't want to hear. It was meant to be only a checkup today; that's why she hadn't gone. Her dad had needed new medications, and the doctor had wanted to see him first.

She should have gone. Guilt was tangling with dread like barn cats fighting in the hayloft, twisting and turning in her stomach.

Cody's hand gripped her arm as if he was afraid she might fall. She was afraid, too. Her head was swimming and the only thing keeping her upright was the man standing in front of her.

"The doctor said it could be less than two weeks."

Air conditioners and swings were no longer important. Conversations about Cody taking care of her meant nothing. Useless anger wouldn't solve any-thing.

Bailey covered her eyes with her hand and waited for the world to right itself, but that wasn't going to happen, not this time, not yet. She knew that eventually she would recover; she would move forward and life would return to some semblance of normal. But she also knew that in a matter of weeks there would be a hole, a vacancy where her dad's presence should have been.

A hand touched her arm and she moved her hand from her eyes to look up at Cody. Were those tears shimmering in his eyes? She would have taken a closer look, but he didn't give her a chance. His arms closed around her, and he pulled her close, holding her against his solid chest as sobs rolled through her body.

"I'll be here," Cody promised.

This time she didn't argue with him. She didn't have the strength to protest or to tell him she didn't expect him to stay forever. She wouldn't hold him to the promise he'd made to her dad.

Cody's cheek rested on the top of her head, and Bailey couldn't convince herself to pull free from his arms. Not yet. She wanted to melt into him, to soak up his strength and pretend for a few minutes that he was going to stay forever.

"Mom." Meg's happy shout ended the moment.

Bailey pulled back, wiping her eyes with the back of her hand and then lifting the neckline of her shirt to wipe away the mascara that would have smeared. Cody blocked Meg's view for those few seconds.

"Hey, kiddo, did you have a good day?" She leaned to hug her daughter, the gesture bringing to light the reason for her daughter's happy smile. "Are those new boots?"

Meg did a dance and then raised one foot for Bailey to see the brown boots with white flowers going up the outside of each. The boots were leather, expertly tooled and hadn't come from a discount store.

"Dad bought them for me because my pink ones were getting too small."

Bailey wanted to cry all over again. She wanted to cry because Meg was learning to let go, and because Cody had been able to do what Bailey had wanted to do. And he hadn't even had to think about it. He didn't have to count one penny or make one end meet another.

"And he said we could have the buckskin, that it can be my horse someday 'cause Dad bought it."

Cody groaned. At least he had the sense to do that.

Bailey didn't sigh, but she wanted to. She didn't tell her daughter that she couldn't have the boots, the swing set or the horse. She wouldn't punish Meg. Instead she gave Cody a look that if he didn't understand it, he'd better learn the language.

"That's wonderful, Meg." Bailey kissed her daughter on the top of the head. "Why don't you run inside and get yourself a Popsicle? I'm going to go feed the cows."

"I'll help you." Cody followed as she headed toward the barn.

"You've helped enough."

"Bailey, could you give me a chance to explain?"

Bailey grabbed the barn doors and jerked to swing them open; the door didn't budge. Cody moved the latch that he had hung and pulled. The door swung with ease.

"Everything is easy for you, isn't it, Cody? Being the hero is easy. Giving my daughter what I can't is easy. And walking away is easy."

Somewhere deep inside she knew she wasn't being reasonable. She didn't need the look from Cody to tell her that, or her own conscience to goad her into backing down. She knew, but she hurt so much she couldn't stop herself from saying the words.

"Will the gifts make you feel better when you leave? Like the dozen roses you sent me the day you left Wyoming? Like that would undo everything and make it okay. The only thing the gifts undo is the guilt you feel."

"I didn't buy Meg these gifts to make myself feel better." He followed her into the barn, just a step behind, and she could tell from his movements that he was angry.

She spun around, not wanting her back to him. "So, this isn't about what makes you feel better?"

He ran both hands through his hair and shook his head, his fingers still buried in the hair at the back of his head.

"I don't know, maybe it is." He looked away, giving her a clear view of his clenching jaw. "I haven't been here, Bailey. I've missed out on a lot, and I have a lot to make up for. You've had her the whole time. Give me a break if I haven't completely passed Parenting 101."

Give him a break. Forgive him. Admit that the anger with Cody was just easier than dealing with what he had told her about her dad. Bailey unlatched the feed-room door, pulling the string to switch on the light as she stepped into the dark. Mice scurried to hide and the room smelled like molasses and leather. She breathed in a moment, comforting herself with something familiar and unchanging.

"Bailey, I missed out on everything. I missed out on Meg's first smile, her first tooth and her first birthday."

"Yes, but now you're the hero, giving her everything that I've never been able to give her. You're making me feel like the one who has let her down."

"I didn't mean to make you feel that way."

"No, I know you didn't. But you have to understand how much I've wanted to give her and how hard it has been to raise her on my own. I had Dad, and he did his best. But the last few years have really been hard on us."

"I can't undo what I didn't know about."

More guilt. Her own this time. He didn't have a monopoly on that emotion.

"Neither of us can undo what has happened." She scooped grain into a bucket and he grabbed the handle. "We just have to try and be grown-ups from this point on."

"Can she keep the gifts I've given her, or do you want me to take them back?"

Bailey allowed herself to smile at that. "No, she can keep them. I really like the buckskin."

Cody walked out of the feed room with the bucket of grain. When they walked into the sunlit corral where the cows had come up to be fed, he stopped. Bailey came to a halt next to him, wondering what had happened. She looked at the black angus cows. They were all there, and all looked healthy.

"What?"

"Bailey, you act like it is all worked out—everyone is happy. I'm not. Sometimes I'm so mad at you, I want to shake you. Sometimes I want to leave and not look back." He shook his head. "I'm going to have to take a break and attend an AA meeting in Springfield. I'm not as able to handle this on my own as I thought."

He set the bucket down and walked away. She started to say something to stop him, but he raised a hand and kept going. As Bailey poured grain into the feed trough for the cows, she heard his truck start and then heard the crunch of gravel on the drive as he left.

Each time he left and then came back, it was as if he proved something to her. She wondered what it would feel like if he didn't come back.

And then her thoughts took a different turn as a solid truth sank in. Soon she would know how it felt for her dad to leave and not come back.

All of the anger melted. It hadn't really been about Cody, the past or his gifts to Meg. It all came down to her dad and not knowing how to deal with losing him.

Tears streaked down her face, wetting her lips with their saltiness as she broke apart a few flakes of hay for the cows and tossed it over the fence. Everyday chores, as if nothing was wrong. Her body shook as the reality of the doctor's forecast for her dad really hit home.

When she walked into the house, Jerry was waiting at the kitchen table for his afternoon meds. Meg was in the yard with Blue, throwing a ball for the dog who had no limits on her energy or capacity to play.

"Sis, your eyes are red." Her dad reached out and Bailey took hold of his hand. She swallowed a lump and then leaned down to hug him.

"I don't want to do this." She whispered into his thinning gray hair. "I don't want to talk about losing you."

"Life has seasons, Bailey—we both know that. This is my season to die and yours to mourn. But there will be a new season for us both. Yours is going to be full of hope and promise here, and mine is going to be in Glory."

He was still teaching her lessons on life. Bailey cried and his hand held her back, trembling as he pulled her close.

"I thought there would be another answer, Dad. I really thought God would answer my prayers."

"He's giving us peace to get through this." He pulled his hand back and Bailey sat down in the seat next to his. "He answered by bringing Cody, whether you see it as an answer or not."

"But I don't want to lose you."

His skin was gray and his mouth tight. Bailey knew he was in pain. He reached and covered her hand with his. "Let me go, Bailey. Don't pray to keep me here—pray for God to do His will."

And face the world without him in it? She wanted to tell him she couldn't do that, but she knew she could. She knew that her tears would be for her own loss, but that her dad would no longer be suffering. She'd been given time to adjust, and she knew she could make it.

She smiled to ease his fears for her. "We'll make it, Dad."

"I know you will. You're stronger than you think, Bailey."

She didn't feel strong.

Cody pulled his truck up to the RV, switched off the engine and then just sat. It was dark and the only light on in the house was the kitchen light. Blue was sleeping under the picnic table next to his RV. He'd seen her there when he pulled up, her eyes glowing red in the headlights of his truck. He had seen her tail thump a greeting, recognizing him as someone who belonged there.

Tonight he'd sat in a meeting with twenty other people who could admit they were tempted to drink. The group had consisted of a banker, a salesman, a housewife, a business owner, a doctor and a construction worker. Those were the ones he remembered. He hadn't felt so out of place, thinking he had to be the lowest of the low. All types of people struggled and made mistakes.

On the drive back to Gibson, he had prayed for help, for strength and for answers. He didn't know where to go from here. Back to Oklahoma, back on tour with the gold buckle in mind, or should he stay in Gibson?

He'd made Jerry Cross a promise to take care of things. He didn't really know how to do that or how far the promise went. He knew how to ride bulls. He had a degree in marketing and business. He knew how to live a temporary life without roots. He'd seen what roots could do to something. Roots could wrap around the wrong thing and strangle the life out of it.

But sometimes roots just dug down and gave life.

He closed his eyes, wondering if staying in Gibson would be good roots or bad. So far it felt good, but he also felt bruised. He felt like that vine that Jesus had talked about, being clipped and pruned. So the roots would go deeper and be stronger.

He opened his eyes and saw the shadow of Bailey as she walked across the kitchen. At one time he had wanted her to be his roots, what kept him strong. But she hadn't been. She'd just been the person who made him want to be strong. Fear had been the dominate emotion in Wyoming. Fear that he'd let her down. Fear that if he didn't get away, she would hold him in one place.

He felt it again, that fear of not being the one who could be strong for her. What if he slipped and fell off the wagon? Would four or five more months of sobriety, making it to that one-year anniversary, really prove anything?

Crossing the lawn a few minutes later, he hesitated, almost turning away from the house. Blue barked and Bailey walked out the back door. That took it out of his hands.

"Look what the cat dragged in." She smiled in the dark shadows of the porch, her hair in a ponytail with wisps of blond coming loose to frame her face.

"I saw that you were still up. I wanted to make a last-ditch attempt at apologizing."

"No, I should apologize." She joined him in the front yard. "I was hurt because you make it all seem so easy. You can give Meg what I can't. And you gave my dad the peace of mind I couldn't."

She had lost him. "What do you mean by that?"

"I heard you tell him you'd take care of us."

"What was I supposed to do? Did you want me to tell him that I'm walking and I'm not about to stay here and make sure you're okay?"

"I don't want you to lie to him. And I don't want you to think that I need you to take care of me. I'm letting you out of your promise."

"Okay, fine." He started to turn but she caught hold of his arm. Her hand was soft and tentative, like in his dreams.

"Cody, I didn't come out here to fight. I came because I have something for you."

"What?"

"Come inside—it's in the kitchen."

He followed her into the house, which was still too warm. Tomorrow he would get those air conditioners installed and put up the swing set for Meg. He had a long list of things that he would get done, tomorrow.

Tonight Bailey had a gift for him. She pointed to a photo album and a videotape on the table. "Those are for you."

He looked at her and then picked up the photo album. Page one, Bailey pregnant. The young woman in the picture smiled, but shame flickered in her dark eyes. She looked alone.

He hadn't been there for her. And now her dad expected him to be the one who wouldn't let her down. His track record wasn't very good.

"You were beautiful." He sat down at the table, and she sat down across from him. She was still beautiful. Her skin was sun-kissed and makeup-free. Her eyes were so warm he thought he'd melt if she looked into his heart.

She made him want to be the man of her dreams,

the man she had assumed he was all those years ago. He had made sure she knew better because he hadn't wanted her to count on him. He had counted on his dad; look how that had turned out.

"It was hard." Bailey leaned across the table to study the pictures he was looking at, bringing the fresh herbal scent of her shampoo with her. "I loved that baby growing inside me, and I struggled with shame and guilt."

"And my presence here brought that all back."

"In a way. People had forgotten, but you made them remember. You're Meg's dad and we're not married."

He flipped the page to study the pictures because he couldn't look at Bailey. Instead he looked at his daughter's first day of life. She was pink and wrinkled, with a bow in her one strand of hair. She was beautiful. He closed his eyes as it really hit home what he'd missed out on and what he couldn't get back. Through pictures he took a five-year trip, seeing the *firsts* in Meg's life.

"This is why I buy her gifts." He finally looked up. Bailey was watching him. "Because it's all I can give her. You gave her everything else, Bailey. You gave her the things that really matter. You gave her life. You gave her comfort and love. You walked the floors with her when she couldn't sleep."

"Then maybe we're even." Bailey shrugged as she stood up. "Do you want a glass of ice water?"

"No thanks. If you don't care, I'd like to take these back to the RV and spend some time looking at them."

"Of course you can. I went through all of my other

photo albums and made that one for you. It's yours to keep and to take with you."

Her unspoken words hit home. When he left, he would have something to take, something to help him remember his daughter. It made him feel like the loser on a game show, walking away with the consolation prize.

"Thank you." He pushed the screen door open, and she followed him out.

"Tomorrow is Meg's first day of school. I wanted to make sure you're planning to go with us."

The reminder caught him off guard. He stopped at the top step, Blue at his side and Bailey standing at the door. She was offering to make him a part of one of the *firsts* in his daughter's life.

"I would really like to be there." He walked off the porch. Standing in the yard, he turned to face her. "It means a lot to me, that you're willing to let me share in her life."

"I want you to stay in her life, Cody. She needs you there." She walked down the steps. "I know that you have to leave soon, but please don't be the dad who shows up just to buy gifts."

Don't be his own father. She didn't know about his dad.

"Bailey, I love my daughter and I'm going to be a real part of her life. I'm not going to buy her gifts to make up for not being here."

She shook her head and he knew that she was remembering the roses she got after he left the first time. He had given her a gift to make up for not being there. Standing there in the dark with Bailey a silhouette in the light from the porch, he remembered another summer night and the trust she'd given him.

"I'm sorry." He didn't know what else to say but he had to say more. "I'm sorry for walking away. I'm sorry for everything. Most of all, I'm sorry that you don't trust me."

"I'm trying."

He nodded, but he didn't have more words; he only knew that leftover feelings were emerging and Bailey stood in front of him, trying to trust. Tentative, he took a step closer, breathing in her clean scent and wondering how this one woman had the ability to undo everything he thought about himself.

When she reached up and touched his cheek, he closed his eyes and remembered how it felt to want to keep her in his life. He opened his eyes and looked for answers in hers. Leaning in, he looked for something more as he covered her mouth with his.

The kiss lasted moments, but it felt like a lifetime. And when she stepped away, he didn't know how to let her go.

"The roses were a bad idea, Bailey."

She pulled away, smiling. "Yes, the roses were a bad idea. Don't forget, tomorrow morning we take Meg to school."

She left him standing alone in the yard, clouds covering the moon and dampness in the air promising rain. He turned toward his RV, carrying the gifts she had given him. The photo album and the videotape weren't parting gifts. They felt more like an invitation for him to be a real part of his daughter's life.

And he wanted to believe the invitation extended to Bailey's life.

Chapter Ten

"Okay, smile one more time real big." Camera poised, Bailey caught another *first* for the photo album. Meg in one of her new outfits—a denim skirt, peasant blouse and the boots that Cody bought— standing next to her grandfather. It was her first day of school.

It was the first time a *first* included a picture of Cody and Meg together. It was the first time a *first* had been shared. Bailey felt as if she was on a tee-ter-totter, going up and down. Jealousy mingled with selfishness and some other feeling, something that re-sembled expectancy. A feeling of things to come. She couldn't handle that thought, not right now.

The entire morning had been a combination of rolling emotions and giggles from the little girl who couldn't believe she was finally going to school. The rolling emotions were Bailey's because she couldn't believe her daughter was big enough to go off by her-self and be gone all day.

"Shouldn't you all be going?" Jerry nodded in the

direction of the clock on the fireplace mantle. "Nearly eight now."

"Yes, we should go." But Bailey didn't want to. Her little girl was standing in front of her, one tooth missing and a smile that said life was better than a carnival. And the only thing Bailey could think of was that little baby she'd brought home from the hospital nearly six years ago.

That day she had been alone. Today Cody stood in the living room, not really a part of her life, and yet…

He was here. And he wasn't a kid anymore with a smile that said life was just for fun, without responsibility. This Cody had a smile that said he'd learned a lot in the last six years. He had laugh lines around his eyes and a hint of gray in his dark hair.

Smiling, he took the camera from Bailey's hand and set it down on the table. "Can't have her late on the first day."

Meg hugged her grandfather and then raced to the kitchen for her new backpack and lunch box. Both were pink with her favorite cartoon character on the front. Bailey followed slowly, not really giving into the excitement that everyone else seemed to feel.

Ten minutes later they pulled into the school parking lot with all of the other parents bringing their kids for the first day.

They looked like a family. A father, mother and daughter.

As they walked down the sidewalk with Meg in the middle holding each of their hands, Bailey tried to pretend the illusion was real. For Meg's sake.

The illusion was shattered as they entered the building and walked down the hall to Gladys Parker's kindergarten class.

Half the town of Gibson was at school that morning, and most of them were looking at Bailey, Cody and Meg. Bailey could imagine what they were thinking. Some knew who Cody was; others were putting it all together or making up some new rumor. Bailey didn't have to hear the words.

She knew all about curiosity. People needed something to talk about at supper because the same old gossip could get as stale as the bread at the convenience store. Bailey wished they'd find something other than her life. Maybe they could talk about how pretty Myrtle Lewis's flowers looked, or the color of the new fire truck.

Maybe they could discuss how a rooster could possibly get arrested for crowing and disturbing the peace. That little incident had happened a month ago, and it had to be more interesting than what was going on at the Cross farm.

Meg's steps had slowed and Bailey was able to concentrate on something other than the heat crawling up her neck and settling in her cheeks. Her daughter and the first day of school definitely took precedence over gossip.

When they reached the door of the kindergarten class, Bailey stopped, ignoring Cody's questioning looks. The minute they stepped over the threshold, a new phase of life started for Meg, and for herself.

"Are you ready for this?" She pulled Meg close and hugged her again, remembering the verses her dad had shared the other day about life's seasons.

It was Meg's time to grow and to take this new

step. And Bailey's time to let go. And she could do that. In a minute, after she held her daughter tightly and said a quick prayer over her that this day would be a good one.

"Bailey Cross, wasn't it just yesterday that I had you in this class?" Gladys Parker stood in the doorway, looking not much older than she had twenty-something years ago. "You were here my first year. My goodness, where did the time go?"

Bailey stood, pretending her throat wasn't tight and tears weren't burning her eyes. She could do this. She could smile and turn her daughter over to Mrs. Parker.

"I haven't lost one yet, Bailey." The teacher, hair still brown and only a few wrinkles around her eyes to show the passing of time, took Meg's hand, and Meg wasn't at all hesitant. She skipped into the room, waving goodbye as she ran to join the kids she already knew.

"Have a good day, Meg." But Meg wasn't paying attention. Bailey choked back a sob and the feeling that she was no longer needed. Of course Meg needed her.

"See you at three, Bailey." Mrs. Parker patted her arm and walked away, as if this happened every day. Bailey guessed it probably did. Anxious mothers, happy children taking new steps and teachers who had been through the process dozens of times.

"That was too easy." Bailey turned away from the room, trying not to think about how easy it was to have Cody's arm around her waist, walking her out of the school.

"Easy for Meg to let go, not so easy for her parents." Cody spoke in a voice almost as choked up as her own.

Parents, plural. Another *first*.

A few minutes later Cody stopped in front of the Hash-It-Out.

"Do you want me to pick you up this afternoon?"

Bailey reached for the door handle. "Lacey said she would take me to get Meg and bring me home."

"Good, then I'm going to work on your truck and get a few things done around the house."

They stared at each other, and Bailey was the first to move, to break the moment that had become too strange. Or maybe he hadn't felt it, felt that thread that connected them like they were a couple, like this mattered and meant something.

She pushed the door open and mumbled goodbye as she hopped to the pavement and hurried toward the front door of the diner, aware of the diesel rumble of Cody's truck as it rolled slowly away.

It all felt like someone else's life. Bailey knew it wouldn't last, this feeling of things coming together and being right. As she walked through the front door of the diner, the bell clanged and a few of the regulars—farmers in work clothes and worn leather boots—turned to smile. Lacey waved from the waitress station.

How could it feel like every other day when it wasn't? Today was Meg's first day of school, and yesterday she had learned that she would have her dad only for a few more days.

A farmer with a neighboring piece of land raised his coffee cup as she walked past. Bailey nodded and headed for the waitress station and a pot of coffee.

"First day of school. How exciting is that?" Lacey already had the coffee pot.

"Exciting? No, more like traumatic."

Lacey paused to talk. The farmer called out to her, but she waved him off and shook her head. "Didn't Meg want to go to school?"

Bailey laughed at her friend's genuine concern. "Meg wasn't the one traumatized, I was."

"I can see how it would be traumatic, having to go through all of that and then being dropped off at the front door by a gorgeous man."

"He's only here temporarily."

"He only stopped to talk. How long ago?"

Bailey took the coffee pot from Lacey. "Mr. Donaldson wants his coffee."

"Avoidance won't make it go away, Bay."

"Will it make you go away?"

Bailey's truck was a lost cause. Or at least it was by Cody's definition. He hadn't ever been much of a mechanic. He could do the basics, but this looked like an engine problem. And he knew that Bailey didn't have the money to have it rebuilt or replaced.

He could have it done for her. How well would that go over?

He dropped his tools into the toolbox and closed the lid. The mailman was pulling away from the mailbox, and Blue was barking at the side of the road. He would get the mail, fix Jerry some lunch and find something else to repair.

Maybe the swing set. He'd already put in the air conditioners. He could hear the hum and he knew the house would be cooling off.

As he walked down the drive to get the mail, Blue hurried to reach him. She bounced around, her bobbed tail wagging and her tongue lolling out one side of her mouth. Late summer heat beat down on Cody's head; obviously the dog didn't feel it.

"You crazy dog." He patted her head and she bounded ahead of him.

He grabbed the pile of envelopes out of the mailbox and headed back to the house. His mouth was dry and his mind had settled on those air conditioners and a glass of iced tea. And he'd try to think of something tempting for lunch. Maybe he could get Jerry to eat.

Probably not.

He entered the house through the back door. The kitchen was already a good ten degrees cooler than it had been. The lights were off and the only noise, other than the hum of the AC units, was the sound of the news on the TV in the living room. He poured himself a glass of tea and checked the contents of the fridge.

"That you, Cody?"

"It's me."

Cody walked into the living room and sat down on the sofa, the mail still in his hands. It wasn't his mail and wasn't his business. He glanced up, meeting the unfocused gaze of a man who had asked him to take care of things. No, more than things—he wanted Cody to take care of Bailey and Meg.

"What's wrong?"

"Another letter from the mortgage company." Cody held it out but Jerry shook his head.

"You read it."

"It isn't my business, Jerry. I don't think Bailey would want me to step this far into her life."

"I'm asking."

Cody pulled out his pocketknife and opened it, sliding the blade through the top of the envelope. He took the letter out, silently reading over it and then reading it to himself one last time. He sat back, trying to think of his next move.

"It's a foreclosure notice, isn't it?" Jerry closed his eyes as a tear slid down his cheek. "I never should have gotten that line of credit on this place. I just didn't know how to pay the medical bills."

"You did what you had to, Jerry. There's no shame in that." Cody looked over the letter again as he took a long drink of iced tea. "It's a final notice stating the amount you need to bring the loan back into good standing. I could pay this for you."

"And then we'd still have those payments to make. I appreciate the offer, Cody, but it would only be a temporary fix." Jerry closed his eyes and didn't open them when he continued. "The payment went up last year. We handled it until then."

"Then I'll buy the land. I've wanted a place of my own."

"I thought you were worried about making her mad."

"I want you to know she's taken care of. This is something I can do." Because he couldn't promise to be in Bailey's life and he was positive that's what Jerry really wanted.

"Do you know what it's listed for?" Jerry's voice was getting weaker.

"I do, and I'm willing to pay it all. We'll call Chad and I'll cut you a check today. We can get the closing done, we can notify the mortgage company and it will be taken care of. Bailey will have enough left over to set up the horse farm she's wanted, and she won't have to worry."

"It isn't about the money, Cody."

Lost, Cody leaned forward, not sure what he was meant to take away from Jerry's statement. Pain medication could do that to people, make them groggy and unable to connect sentences or thoughts.

"I'm sorry, Jerry, I don't understand."

Jerry didn't answer right away. They sat in silence, Jerry's eyes closed, and Cody waiting.

"Jerry?"

"I want more for my daughter than your money. She needs more. Meg needs more."

Cody got it.

"I know, Jerry, and I'm doing my best. I'm still learning." He scooted to the edge of the couch. "I didn't have a dad like you, someone who showed me the right way."

"You have a God who will, so stop looking for excuses."

Excuses? He could have argued; instead he let the words sink in, and he wondered if that was what his parents had become for him. They'd made mistakes so they were to blame for every wrong decision he made? He couldn't let that be his life. Not anymore. He had to make decisions based on what he believed was the right thing to do.

Bailey and Meg were a big factor in that.

Jerry fell asleep and Cody went to the kitchen to call the real-estate agent. His mind continued to whirl after the call and while he was sitting in the shade trying to put together his first swing set.

Swing sets, he realized, needed an assembly book for dummies. There were a few too many screws, there were too few parts, and nothing really seemed to match up. The directions in the box weren't written in English.

From time to time his gaze traveled to the hundred-thirty acres he'd agreed to buy. His land. He had worked for it, saved for it, and now he'd have it. At what cost? Surely more than the actual price he was paying.

Jerry was right. It wasn't all about the money. And it could no longer be about what Cody's own father had done wrong. It had to be about what he was going to do right.

At the end of the drive, right under the oak tree, was the biggest swing set Bailey had ever seen. From the backseat of Lacey's car, Meg was shouting and breathless from excitement. Her first day of school, and now this. Could life for a five-year-old get any better?

Bailey turned and smiled at her daughter. She should tell her to calm down, but it wouldn't do any good. Besides that, a swing set was a big deal to a little girl. Bailey remembered her own and how she had sat on the ground and watched her dad put it together.

Bailey's dad had been her hero. Looking at Meg, her blue eyes focused on Cody as if he could do no wrong, Bailey knew that a part of her daughter's heart now belonged to Cody.

She was okay with that. Really she was. Even if it did hurt a little. It felt worse than when she was a kid and her dad's cattle dog had licked off the best bite of her candy bar, which meant giving the greedy thing the entire treat.

"Can I swing now? Please, Mom?" The car had stopped and Meg was hurrying to unbuckle. "I don't have to have a snack."

Cody was attaching the slide, and the swings were already in place. He waved and smiled. Bailey smiled as Lacey chuckled. That earned her friend a look.

"But I brought you cheese fries from the diner." Bailey glanced in the backseat at her daughter. Meg's seat belt was off and she was reaching for the door handle.

"I can have cheese fries anytime."

"Okay, you can swing. But don't leave the yard." Bailey barely got the words out, and Meg was out of the car and running across the lawn.

"Sweet." Lacey smiled and said the word with a soft longing. "You've got something good going on here, Bailey. I know I've teased you a lot, but this is good."

"This is temporary, and I don't want Meg to be hurt."

"He isn't going to walk out of her life."

"Yeah, I know." She glanced at Lacey and saw understanding. "Want to come in?"

"Nope, I have a lot of yard work to catch up on. Call me if you need anything."

Bailey nodded and got out of the car. Warm summer air and the scent of drying grass greeted her. Cody smiled in her direction, a pleased look on his face. He was the hero. She could let him have his moment.

She walked across the yard to where Cody stood.

Meg was already swinging, her legs kicking to push the swing higher.

"I need iced tea and I have to check on Dad. Do you want anything, or are you going to stay out here?"

"I'll come in with you."

She didn't expect that, or the tight expression on his face as if something was wrong. "For a man who made a little girl's day, you look pretty serious."

He followed her up the steps to the porch and reached ahead of her to open the door. "We really need to talk."

"Hey, you put the AC units in. I bet you're my dad's hero, too."

"In more ways than one," he mumbled, making her think she might have misunderstood.

"What does that mean?" Bailey flipped on a light and opened the refrigerator door. "Get a couple of glasses down."

She turned with the pitcher of tea and saw a pile of papers on the table. Cody's gaze shifted away from her and the papers. He opened a cabinet and pulled out the glasses while she set the pitcher down and walked to the table.

"What is this?"

"Bailey, we had to do something."

Her chest ached and her hands trembled as she sifted through the paperwork. "No, Cody, you can't do this. A swing for a little girl is one thing, but this is my family farm."

"Bailey, we can't let them auction it off on the courthouse steps. You can't lose a farm that has been in your family for almost a hundred years."

"But I did lose it, didn't I? Now it's your farm."

"It isn't going to be sold to a developer who will divide it into five-acre parcels. And that is exactly who was hovering over it. Chad had received three calls already."

Bailey dropped onto a chair and buried her face in her hands. She couldn't deal with this. A part of her mind knew that it had to happen and that Cody had saved the land she loved so much. And part of her saw him as the person who could do everything she couldn't.

Maybe that was okay. Maybe it was good, to know that he had it and it wouldn't be lost.

His hand was on her shoulder, warm and strong. She didn't want to feel anything for a minute, not comforted, or relieved, or like the rug was about to be jerked out from under her. And she felt all of those things.

She wanted to thank God for providing an answer. And she wanted to ask Him why it had to be this answer.

"I'm sorry." Cody moved his hand and stepped away from her. "I wish I could do the right thing for once."

"Cody, you did the right thing. I'll deal with this."

"Is this about your pride? Do you realize how ridiculous that is? What is more important, you being in control or your dad having peace of mind?"

"Dad, of course. And this farm, knowing it will be here and that it won't be divided." She could say the words and even know that the words were the truth.

"Then why don't you relax and realize what this does for your life. You don't have to worry about how to make ends meet, they've been met and for a good long while."

Air-conditioning, her daughter on a swing set in the backyard and now a farm that was out of debt. She had the house and twenty-five acres to build a dream.

And Cody standing in her kitchen, confident that he had fixed everything. Except her truck. He hadn't been able to fix the beast.

"Bailey, it's done, so let it be."

He had taken care of them, just like he promised her dad. And it hit her just like that. His hands were clean. He'd done what her dad had asked, and now when he left, he wouldn't have a guilty conscience. He wouldn't even have to send her roses.

The thought of him walking away hurt more than anything. But she would let it be about the land because that was easier to deal with.

"Fine, it's done. Now why don't you go work on fixing your own life and leave mine alone for a while?"

Chapter Eleven

Fix his own life. Cody replayed Bailey's words over and over in the next few days. He had fixed fences, fixed her finances and made his daughter happy. In a way, he had been fixing his life. He'd at least been making himself feel better about things he'd done.

Maybe he'd just been fooling himself. The real fixing of his life had to do with the foundation: his parents. He hadn't talked to his mother in three years. She was living in Paris with her new husband. He had tried calling, but she was away for the next month. That was typical when he called.

His dad was in California. Cody opened his cell phone and dialed a number he hadn't dialed in a long time. When his dad answered, it took him a few seconds to adjust.

"Dad, it's Cody."

"Cody, I haven't heard from you in a while. What do you need?" Of course his dad would think it had to do with money or some other problem that needed to be solved.

That's what fathers did; they solved problems.

"I don't need anything. I wanted to call and touch base." He looked out the window at Bailey on the buckskin and Meg sitting on the grass with a black, orange and white kitten. She liked calico cats; so did he. "Dad, I have a daughter."

"You're married? Seems like that is something a father should know."

"I'm not married."

"Well, that explains why I haven't heard about this."

"She's five years old and I didn't know about her." As he said the words, he counted reasons his dad had for feeling ashamed. Maybe this call hadn't been a good idea. Maybe it had been the worst idea ever.

"Are you going to do the right thing?" Dalton Jacobs, neurosurgeon, *always* did the right thing.

Cody crushed down anger and resentment and searched for forgiveness, the real reason for this call. "I'm trying to do the right thing."

He was thirty years old and when he talked to his dad, he still felt like the seventeen-year-old kid who ran a car through the neighbor's fence. Back then doing the right thing had meant spending an afternoon repairing a fence.

"I'm glad to hear that. Listen, Cody, I have to go. Melinda is having a dinner party tonight, and I need to do something for her." Always for Melinda. "Next time you're in California, come by. I miss you."

Never those words before. Cody glanced out the window again, the tightness around his heart easing. "I'll be out there in a few months."

"Good. And, son, congratulations."

Cody hung up, but he felt better. He felt better knowing that he had talked to his dad, because a person never knew what tomorrow might bring. And he felt relieved because he had finally forgiven his dad for walking away.

He walked outside and across the yard to the corral, where Bailey was working the buckskin. She slid off and then remounted, leaning over the horse's neck to whisper to him. She loved the horse. And he felt a twinge of something sharp, like jealousy. Of a horse?

He watched as she worked the animal, first walking him around the arena, then a slow trot and then a controlled lope, with the horse leading with the right foot. It was easy to watch her ride. It was almost lyrical, woman and horse, fluid and one.

That jealousy thing stabbed at him again because she felt that oneness with a horse and yet she was barely talking to him.

Bailey slowed the horse to an easy walk and rode to the fence where he stood. Cody leaned on the top rail and waited. She slid to the ground with an easy grace and walked over to him. He remembered why he had been drawn to her in Wyoming.

Because she was the real deal. She was genuine and her smile felt like sunshine after a hard winter.

"I forgive you." She said it as if it was the natural progression of things, and he didn't quite know what she was talking about.

"Forgive me?"

She smiled. "The land. It isn't easy, being rescued. Especially when I've been working so hard to rescue us for the last few years. You made it seem like it was nothing. You made a call, wrote a check and tah-dah—problem solved."

"I didn't mean to do that to you." He reached for her hand and she gave it, her fingers lacing through his. "I called my dad."

"Okay."

Of course she didn't understand. He rarely shared his life with anyone. "I haven't talked to him in a while. I wanted him to know about Meg."

A range of emotions shifted across her face, like clouds playing across the sky. "It sounds like you and your dad have some things to work out."

"We have to work out the fact that he was never a part of my life. He walked out on us when I was eight years old."

"I didn't know."

"No, you didn't. But I'm telling you this because I want you to know that I'm not my dad and I'm not going to walk out on my daughter."

At that moment he realized how much he wanted her to believe that about him. If she could believe in him, he might be able to believe a little stronger in himself.

"I know you won't."

He drew her hand to his lips and held it there. "Thank you."

Bailey walked into the living room the next day, the day after learning that Cody had his own past and lessons on letting go. Her dad was sitting in his recliner, his eyes closed and his breathing shallow and raspy.

His eyes flickered and he turned to smile at her,

the gesture a weak attempt. Bailey wanted to hold on to him and keep him with her. She knew she couldn't.

"Dad, do you want to sit outside and watch Meg ride the buckskin?" She squatted next to his chair and covered his hand with hers.

In the last week she had watched him drifting away from her. She knew she couldn't bring him back. And she thought again about the conversation with Cody yesterday, when he had told her about his father, who hadn't really been a father.

Knowing this helped her to understand why Cody needed to do so much for Meg. She felt as if there were still missing pieces in the story of his life, things he had yet to share. Maybe he didn't want her to understand.

Her dad moved, bringing her back into his presence. He smiled at her, and for a moment she had hope. She sighed, knowing better than to let herself think he would get better.

"I'd like to sit outside." Her dad stood, wobbling as she slipped her arm around his waist, trying to pretend that it wasn't because he couldn't make it on his own.

They walked through the house, Jerry shuffling and Bailey keeping her steps small to match his. September had arrived and brought cooler weather. The fan on the porch made it almost too cool.

"Sit here, Dad, and I'll get you a pillow." She eased him into a chair.

"I don't need a pillow." His attention had already shifted to the corral and Meg. "I wanted it to be like this."

Bailey pulled the chain to turn off the fan and then sat down next to him. "Like what, Dad?"

"I wanted it to be a farm again, with horses and cattle and you not worrying about the future."

"It is a farm, Dad. We're going to make it."

She could have told him she still worried, just not over the finances. She worried about him not being there, and about Cody leaving and what that would do to Meg—and what it would do to herself.

At twenty-two she had felt something like love; maybe it had been a whisper or a promise of something that could have been special. Now, it felt different; it felt deeper, touching a different area of her heart. That frightened her because it also felt as if it could be gone tomorrow.

Laughter rippled across the lawn, Meg's childish tone and Cody's deeper one. Bailey watched as they rode double on the buckskin, not really liking that because the horse was young and sometimes flighty.

She had to trust Cody. He wouldn't do anything to hurt their daughter. That trust issue was becoming easier, but only because she was working on it.

"I sure love you, pumpkin." Jerry patted her arm.

"I love you, too, Daddy." She hadn't called him that in years. "Everything is going to be okay."

"I know it is." He smiled. "Don't be afraid to let Cody love you."

"Dad…"

"Honey, I know love when I see it, even if you don't."

She looked out at Cody and Meg, the little girl on the front and Cody behind her, his arms holding her secure. His arms made Bailey feel secure, too.

"I'm not afraid, Dad."

He nodded and closed his eyes. Bailey knew he needed to rest. He'd had a long night and he'd been in so much pain. She had wanted him to go to the hospital, but he'd argued that the hospital couldn't do anything.

Blue ambled up the steps and over to them. The dog nudged Jerry's leg and then his hand. Bailey turned her attention from her daughter to her father.

"Dad?" She touched his arm and then his neck as tingles of fear raced through her body. "Dad, wake up."

She heard Cody, knew he was running toward her. "Please, Dad, not yet."

It couldn't be time. She didn't want it to be now. She touched his neck, wanted there to be a pulse. When there wasn't, she started to tremble. She wanted to stop it all from happening. She prayed that God would change His mind.

Cody was there, holding her and Meg. Bailey couldn't move, not on her own, not away from her dad, because what if, what if he woke up, and what if this was all just a mistake?

"Bailey, we have to call the ambulance." Cody lifted Meg. "You have to come inside right now and take care of your daughter. She's the one who needs you."

Bailey nodded as she touched her dad's cheek. "Goodbye, Daddy."

She wasn't ready for him to be gone. She wasn't ready to be alone. But then, she wasn't. She felt Cody's hand on her back as he guided her into the house, Meg holding tightly to his neck. And she felt

God's presence, touching her heart and letting her know that He would never leave her or forsake her.

Meg reached for Bailey, wrapping her arms around Bailey's neck as Cody went in search of the phone. The two of them sat at the dining room table, holding each other as Cody made the calls. Bailey wanted to feel, but everything drifted and she felt only numbness, removed from the action.

"Bailey, you've made arrangements, right?" Cody squatted in front of her, his eyes damp from tears. Real cowboys did cry. She had seen her dad cry more than once.

"I have. The coroner knows." She leaned and he moved toward her, drawing her against his chest as he stood.

"Take care of Meg, and I'll take care of the rest."

"I have to call people."

He put the phone in front of her and then walked outside, out to where her dad had finally found peace. From the window she could see the ambulance coming down the drive, Blue running next to it. There were no lights, no siren. There wouldn't be a need for those things.

She closed her eyes and said a silent prayer of thanks, that God had allowed her dad to leave this earth knowing that they would be okay.

Next she prayed she'd make it without him. The hole where he used to be was already evident. Because he wasn't there to tell her everything would be okay.

To everything there is a season. A time for every purpose under heaven.

She closed her eyes and could almost hear her dad

telling her that life had seasons. You don't plant tomatoes in the winter, he had once told her, and you
don't prune in the summer. Every season has a purpose. God made it that way. Even the seasons of life.

"I don't want Grandpa to go." Meg whispered
through her sobs.

"Neither do I, sweetie, but we have to let him go."
Bailey hugged Meg to her as she dialed Lacey's number.

A time to be born, a time to die. A time to plant
and a time to pluck what is planted. A time to kill. A
time to heal. Her heart shook from within and tears
burned her eyes again as she allowed the words she'd
memorized as a kid to run through her mind.

A time to break down and a time to build up. A
time to weep and a time to laugh. A time to mourn
and a time to dance. A time to cast stones and a time
to gather stones. A time to embrace and a time to re-
frain from embracing.

She couldn't go further, not with the ache growing inside her like a huge wound that would never be
healed. A time to heal.

The hardest part, missing the person who was
gone, missing what he'd been in their lives and the
way he had kept hold of them, making everything
right. And he'd held on until he knew that they would
be taken care of.

The screen door creaked open. "Bailey, Pastor
John is here."

Bailey nodded over her daughter's silky blond
head. Her gaze connected with Cody's, and she remembered when he had been the empty hole in her

heart. Now he was in her life, filling up the empty places.

A time to gain and a time to lose. She didn't know which was which, and her heart ached with gain and loss, and the knowing that loss would happen again.

It hadn't taken long for the community of Gibson to arrive, filling every empty space of the house and porch. Cody walked through the kitchen, crowded with church members and neighbors. The counters and table were laden with food, the aromas all blending together in a buffet of food smells. A lady with dyed black hair and ivory skin offered him something to eat.

"No, thank you. I'm going to check on Bailey."

The woman took hold of his arm and led him to a stack of plates. "Oh, sweetie, she's fine. She's with friends. Now, you take a plate and eat something. She'll need you soon enough."

He took the plate she placed in his hand, and he dutifully walked the line of food, knowing he wouldn't eat and being careful not to take much. As he walked out of the kitchen, he smiled in her direction, showing her that he'd done his duty.

Bailey was in the living room, surrounded by quiet conversation and the hum of air conditioners. She looked up as he walked through the door, and her mouth lifted in a slight smile. He tried to get to her, but a hand on his arm stopped him, a man he didn't know who wanted to talk about bull riding.

It was as if these people were protecting Bailey from him. He didn't like that. He didn't like the invisible circle around her or the way Meg leaned against her as if the world were ending. He wanted to take them both away from this and make them smile again.

He kind of figured Jerry would have wanted the same thing. He also knew it wasn't going to happen.

He left the house because there were things he could do outside and obviously nothing he could do inside. On his way out the back door he started to toss the plate in the trash, but through the window he saw Blue. She could do with a treat.

He walked past the groups that had gathered on the porch and the lawn. A few he spoke to as he passed, but he didn't stop. He went to the barn because Jerry was gone and the animals needed to be fed, and he didn't know what else to do.

He did know how to take care of animals. He started with the cats, mainly because they were all around his feet. The momma cat ran ahead of him. The kittens chased his boots, not caring that the shoes were attached to feet.

Blue was sitting next to the feed room, as if she approved of what he had decided to do. "It isn't like I can do anything else."

Blue wagged her tail and belly crawled in his direction.

Deep breath—shake it off. Cowboy up, Cody. He leaned against the rough wood post at the corner of a stall. Jerry wasn't gone. He just wasn't this side of heaven anymore.

What should he do? Cody knew the obvious answer. Feed the animals. And then what? Go inside with Meg and Bailey and pretend they really needed him. He knew the answer to that because he could hear the cars rolling down the drive as more neighbors and friends showed up to do the job of comforting.

His phone rang. He sighed as he flipped it open. This was going to be another person he didn't have answers for, another person he didn't want to let down.

"Mac." He scooped grain into a five-gallon bucket as they talked. "I know why you're calling and I plan on being back on tour in two weeks. We have a funeral this week, so that's the soonest I can get away."

He listened to one of his biggest corporate sponsors read him the riot act about money invested. Colson Farm Supply had been easier to deal with because they had supported his decision to get clean. Mac Farmer had investors who wanted a return on their investment. Cody didn't blame them.

"I'll be on tour, Mac, and I'll be at the finals."

Mac finished the conversation by telling him that they wouldn't be sponsoring him in the coming season. Cody slipped the cell phone back into his pocket and turned around.

Meg was standing in the door, tears streaming down her cheeks. He set the bucket of grain down and took her into his arms.

"Hey, kiddo, don't cry." That wasn't fair. He remembered all too well the number of times he had wanted to cry and his mom had told him that tears wouldn't fix anything. "You know what, you go ahead and cry and I'll sit here and hold you."

He sat down on the bench he had put in the corner of the tack room and Meg sat down next to him. She leaned against his side, hiccupping and wiping her eyes.

"I don't want you to leave." She hiccupped again. "I thought you were going to stay with us. I wanted us to be a family."

"We are a family, Meg. You have a mom and a dad who love you, and we're going to be here for you."

She shook her head and looked up at him with dark blue eyes overflowing with tears. "You said you were going to leave."

"I have to go do my job, but I'll be back."

"To live?" She was putting him on the spot, and he didn't know the right answer. He didn't want to lie to her.

"I can't live here with you, because I'm not married to your mom, but I'll come and see you a lot."

She slid out of his arms. "I don't want to miss you, too."

"I know, Meg." He didn't want to miss her, either. The thought of leaving kept getting harder.

She shot out of the barn with Blue on her heels. Cody watched to make sure she got to the house, and then he went back to where he'd left the bucket of grain. And he felt like a failure. He didn't know how to make it all better. He didn't know how to bring back Meg's smile. He didn't know how to convince her that he would always be there for her.

He'd just have to show her. Hadn't his grandfather always said something about the proof is in the pudding? He didn't know what it meant, not really, but he imagined it meant something about actions speaking louder than words.

He tossed scoops of grain into the feeders for the horses and went back into the barn for the fifty-pound bag he would give to the cattle. He heaved it over his shoulder and walked out to the trough. The cows were waiting, bawling at him as if they thought he should understand.

"You girls are mooing up the wrong tree. I don't know a thing about making women happy."

A fifty-pound bag of grain did the trick for the cows.

After he finished feeding, he closed the doors to the barn and walked back to his RV. He considered going to the house, but the yard was full of cars. Half the town of Gibson was crowded into the Cross home.

He was a part of Meg's life but not really in Bailey's life. Wasn't that what they wanted? What he wanted? He had done what he could for her. He had kept his promise to Jerry.

Now he was on his own again.

He walked into the kitchen of his RV and flipped on the light over the sink. He had a good view of the back porch, where people had gathered to talk and to share food. Bailey walked out the door and stood with a small group. He convinced himself she scanned the area, maybe looking for him.

Probably not. She had people around her who knew her and whom she'd always known. He couldn't imagine a place for himself in that crowd.

He felt oddly outside the circle. But wasn't that what he wanted? Didn't he want to walk away without strings attaching him to her?

Meg—she was the thread that kept them connected, that would always connect them.

And he needed a drink. He needed an escape and a way to numb the pain. In the last eight months not once had it been such an overpowering need, sneaking up on him and taking hold.

He opened a cabinet door and rummaged through flashlights, cups and junk he should have thrown away a long time ago. Including the bottle at the back of the cabinet. He'd seen it a few weeks ago and had meant to pour it down the drain.

For some reason he hadn't.

He pulled it out, knocking over a flashlight and a few cups as he dragged it over the top of everything else. He hadn't emptied it because a part of him had probably wanted to keep it—just in case.

Perspiration beaded across his forehead, and he set the bottle down on the cabinet, setting a glass next to it. *Pour a drink, no one will know.* One drink wouldn't make him drunk or undo his sobriety. It would just be a drink to calm his nerves.

To numb the pain. He used to believe that. Now he realized it was a lie. The alcohol hadn't numbed his pain; it had made it worse. He hadn't dealt with problems back then; instead he had buried them.

He closed his eyes and when he opened them, he looked out the small window above the kitchen sink. Meg was on the swing, being pushed by a man Cody didn't know. The bottle gleamed amber and shimmering in the shaft of light peeking through the blinds that covered the window over the sofa.

Take a drink, give in. Or be strong. He remembered the lesson of Jesus fasting and the devil tempting Him to give up.

"God help me. I can't be strong on my own, but I have to be strong for Meg and Bailey." He took the lid off the bottle, lifted it and poured it down the sink.

"We are more than conquerors through Christ who strengthens us." He tossed the bottle in the trash and walked outside.

Meg looked up, her eyes rimmed with red from crying. She needed him sober. He needed that, too.

"Can I push my daughter?" He stepped behind the swing and the other man shrugged and walked away. Cody pulled the swing back and gave it a push. Meg laughed and asked him to push her higher.

"Anything for you, Meg."

Chapter Twelve

Three days later Bailey walked across the freshly mowed lawn of the cemetery. She could see the blue canvas shelter where others had already gathered, including an aunt and cousins she barely knew. At the church she had hugged them, shared words of sympathy, and somehow she had survived.

It didn't feel a lot like surviving.

Now, with Meg holding her hand and Cody walking on the other side, his hand close to hers, she tried to think about her dad, his life and what he would have thought of this solemn procession of people. He would have shook his head and told them to loosen up. He would have told them it was a beautiful fall day and they needed to watch the leaves change colors and hug their loved ones.

Jerry Cross would have loved the service at the church, when Gordy Johnson sang the good ole hymns and the congregation joined in. And after the message, Pastor John had allowed people to give short anecdotes about the Jerry Cross they'd known.

Meg had stood up and said that her grandpa always had hugs. Bailey had cried and Cody had held her hand. She hadn't thought about it then, about Cody still being there when he didn't have to be. Now that she did stop and think, she was thankful for his presence. She was thankful for the day he stopped to apologize and then stayed because staying had been the right thing to do.

She looked at him now, in his black pants, gray shirt and tie. He looked strong. He looked uncomfortable in the tie. Her dad would have laughed at them all for dressing up.

What would he have said to her? She longed to hear his voice again, and his words of wisdom. But she could imagine what he'd say. Probably something about pulling herself up by her bootstraps and carrying on. He would have told her to remember all that God had done and to be strong in the Lord and in the strength of His might.

She had to stay strong for Meg. She had to be the person for her daughter that her dad had been for her. He'd left footprints in this life, footprints to live by.

Cody's hand settled on her back, and he guided her to the front of the tent. Try as she might, she couldn't remember all of her pep talks to herself about being strong, not at that moment with Meg holding her hand and the pastor saying final words of goodbye to a man who had been a part of their community and church for fifty-eight years.

It was hard to put it together, that the man they were talking about, the man who wouldn't be coming back to them was her dad.

A final amen brought it all to a close. Bailey accepted hugs and offers of help. Lacey held her tightly for a long minute and then let her go and walked off. The crowds thinned. Bailey's mind numbly registered the words, the hugs and Cody at her side.

What would her dad have said about Cody? For a moment she closed her eyes, allowing herself to trust the strength of the man next to her. That's what her dad would have told her. He would have told her to forgive and move on and that she didn't always have to be so strong.

She held tight to Meg as Cody guided them back to his truck. Tears started to fall, the tears she had kept in check for the last few hours. Now they fell— after she had convinced herself she was in control.

Cody lifted Meg into the truck before turning to Bailey. She wiped at her eyes with a tissue that was disintegrating. As she tried to turn away, Cody caught her and pulled her close. She didn't want to be held close, not when tears were pouring and she really needed a tissue.

"Let me see if I have a tissue or a towel in the truck." Cody touched her cheek and then he was in the truck, digging around and talking to Meg. He came back empty-handed.

"I'm fine." She wiped at her eyes with her hand and tried to cover her face.

"No, you aren't." He shoved his hands into his pockets again. "Nothing."

"It's okay. I'm fine."

"A man should have a handkerchief for moments like this." He jiggled his tie, the way he'd been doing all day, and then he smiled. With long fingers, he loosed the knot and jerked the tie over his head.

He held it out to her with a wink and a smile. "Will this do?"

She took the tie, their fingers touching and then they moved apart. She held the tie to her face, and then she glanced up at him again.

"You realize it'll be ruined?"

"I won't wear it again. Ties are for funerals and weddings."

She sniffled and raised the tie to her eyes. His words, considering everything else that was going on, shouldn't have upset her. Who cared if he never planned on wearing a tie again?

Maybe she wouldn't even miss him when he left? The thoughts were those of a woman at the end of her rope. The man standing in front of her must have guessed that she was at the meltdown stage. Before she could voice an objection, he pulled her close.

She wasn't alone. Cody's hands held her close and Meg was in the truck. They would get through this. They would move on with their lives. Cody whispered those promises into her ear, and she wanted to believe, almost believed because his faith sounded strong.

"I'm not going anywhere, Bailey. I'll be here as long as you need me."

She nodded against his chest, feeling the dampness of her tears on his linen shirt. As long as she needed him meant that a day was coming when he would be gone.

"Bailey, I mean that."

I love you, Bailey. Those had been his words next to a campfire in Wyoming. And she had believed him.

She nodded again because she knew he meant it, but she couldn't say the words that were trying to wiggle free. He would stay as long she needed, but she knew there were limits to his terms.

What if she needed him forever? It was really starting to feel as if she might.

A week went by before Cody felt it was the right time to discuss his schedule with Bailey. It had to be done. He had obligations to his sponsors and to the sport that had given him so much.

He had obligations in Gibson. For a man who had escaped ties, he suddenly had a truckload. He had a daughter. He had land. He had a career and people depending on him.

After a light rap on the back door, he walked into the kitchen. He no longer waited for an answer. Somehow this old farmhouse had started to feel like home.

And two months ago a thought like that would have made him itchy to be on the road. He would have doubted his ability to be the person they needed.

"Where's your mom?" Cody squatted next to the chair Meg sat in.

She was putting together a puzzle at the kitchen table. Instead of answering, she pointed down the hall. He stood and kissed the top of her head. Before he walked away, he squatted again.

"You okay, sweetie?"

She nodded again, but she didn't look up. His heart ached to make it all better for her, to make her smile again and to take away the hole in her heart, the place where she missed her grandfather.

He missed Jerry, too.

"My grandpa died when I was little." He pulled a chair close and sat down. The conversation had to go somewhere, but he was still grasping. "And after a while, I wasn't as sad anymore."

Meg nodded and she didn't cry. She was his in so many ways. "I'm glad he went to heaven, but I wanted him to stay with us and take care of us."

"He knew I would take care of you for him." He couldn't let Jerry down—that was a new fear. Could he ever be a man like Jerry?

"But what about when you leave?" She knew how to get to the heart of things. She got that from her mom.

"I promise I'll always come back."

She glanced away from the puzzle and cast what had to be a dubious expression at him. Another thing she'd learned from her mom. She was five and she already doubted him.

"Meg, I promise."

She nodded and went back to her puzzle. "I believe you."

"I have to talk to your mom now." He stood and for a long moment he stared down at his daughter. "I won't let you down, Meg."

She held his gaze, her eyes wide and maybe wise beyond her years. "Do you love us?"

Did he love them? He closed his eyes and nodded his head. He loved them with all his heart. He smiled at his daughter and she smiled back.

He walked out of the kitchen. Now to face Bailey. He almost thought she'd be easier than Meg.

"Bailey?"

"In here." Her voice sounded choked. That had happened a lot since Jerry's death.

But there were also good days, when she laughed

and played with Meg. There were days she talked to him as if he was someone she wanted in her life.

He didn't know how to feel about that, or about how good or right it seemed to be that person. He could almost feel the roots digging in, wanting this to be the place where he landed for good.

Bailey was in her dad's room, sitting in front of the closet with boxes and bags. She looked up when he walked into the room. Today her eyes were dry. He didn't know how they could be, since seeing her surrounded by Jerry's belongings made him want to cry.

He sat down in the center of the piles of boxes and bags.

"I'm going through his things." She folded a shirt and stuck it in a garbage bag. "I keep talking to Meg about letting go and moving on. I think I need to lead by example."

He didn't want Meg to have to let go of anything. "I guess that's a good idea."

"It is." She folded another shirt, this time lifting it to her face for a moment before putting it in the bag with the other. "And what about you, Cody? You can leave, you know. We're fine now."

"I have land here, remember."

She nodded and continued to work through the pile of clothes. "I know and I've been thinking about that."

"Really?"

She moved to lean against the dresser, pushing aside a pile of things she'd been working on. "I thought that if I got things in order, I might be able to buy it back from you."

He rubbed the back of his neck as he tried to process that information. "Wow, I didn't expect that."

"Why? Look, we both know that this isn't what you want."

A year ago, six years ago, even two months ago, he might have agreed. Now he didn't know. Or maybe he did and he wasn't quite ready to process the information or what he was thinking and feeling. Good thing Bailey had it figured out.

"I guess neither of us knew me as well as we thought. I don't want to talk about this, because the conversation isn't going to go anywhere. The one thing I want to make perfectly clear, Bailey Cross, is that I'm in your life for a long, long time because I'm going to be a part of my daughter's life."

Tears pooled in her eyes and he regretted the sharpness of his words. When he tried to move close to her, she shook her head.

"No, I don't need that. You're right, and that was wrong of me."

"Not really. I've given you a lot of reason to doubt." He sat back again. "And the reason I came in to talk to you is because I have to leave. I have to make the next few events and the finals."

"I understand."

"Do you understand that I don't want to go?"

"Yes, I do, and I also understand why you're leaving. You've worked hard for this. You don't have to worry about us. We're used to taking care of things around here."

He worked this through his mind and wondered how much of it she meant and how much she was trying to convince him and herself that she didn't need him there.

"I might fly out Thursday to make the event in California. I might try to see my dad while I'm there."

Her face came up, her gaze meeting his. "You're going to see him?"

Of course it shocked her. It shocked him. How often did he mention his family? He spent more time trying to avoid that topic.

"Yes, I think it's time for us to work through some things."

She only nodded and he wondered if it would be selfish of him if he wanted her to be thinking about missing him. He shook free of that thought and the other that felt like missing her already. Lately he'd had a hard time remembering why he had been afraid of women who were looking for forever.

It seemed as if he might have been afraid of roots. Or afraid of being his father. In the last couple of months he'd proven to himself that he wasn't made in the image of Dalton Jacobs; he was made in the image of God, and the past no longer held him.

At least not in the way it once had. He was letting go. Bailey wasn't the only one learning that lesson.

"Wow, I didn't know he had these." Bailey held up pictures of her parents, obviously when they were newlyweds. Bailey looked like her mom.

It had been so many years since he'd seen his own mother, he couldn't remember what she looked like. He reached for a few of the pictures Bailey had already looked at. She watched him, but he could tell by the way she kept her face averted that she was pretending she wasn't.

"What about your family?" She finally asked. "I think there's more than you've told me."

What family? That wasn't really the answer she wanted. And he didn't want her sympathy. He had grown past that. Instead he moved from the floor to the edge of the bed, giving her back the pictures in his hands.

"My parents weren't—" He tried to think of the best way to explain. "They were divorced when I was little, and then they were busy living their own lives. No siblings and not a lot of extended family, especially once my grandparents were gone. We had a housekeeper named Maria."

Maria had cooked for him, taken care of him when he'd been sick and even gone to his school programs when his mother was out of town. When he turned eighteen and went to college, she went back to her family in California.

"I'm sorry." Bailey crossed her legs and leaned forward, nodding to let him know she wanted more.

"Bailey, it isn't a sad story of a little boy looking out the window, or whatever you're imagining. I stayed busy on the ranch and with the people who worked there."

"But it did affect you."

He could give her that. "Yes, it did. It made me worry that I couldn't be someone better than my dad."

"But you are."

"I hope." He softened his tone because he knew that Meg was a short distance down the hall. "And I hope you know that I won't let Meg down."

"I know that."

"And you." He didn't know why he said that or what he wanted from her.

"You don't have to worry about letting me down."
She placed the pictures into the open cedar trunk.

"I promised your dad."

"That you would take care of us, and you have.
You changed our lives and I'm so thankful for that.
But now you're off the hook as far as your obliga-
tion to me."

"I'm off the hook? Bailey, I'm the father of your
child. That's more than an obligation. That's something that ties us together."

"I don't want it to be a tie."

Shouldn't he feel relieved by that? He told himself
that was the case, but he didn't feel it. He couldn't
process what she was doing, but it felt as if she was
handing him his freedom. As he got up to walk out
of the room, he even told her a quiet "thank you."

Bailey waited until Cody was gone and she heard
the front door click shut before she breathed a sigh
of relief. In the last few days she had given this careful consideration, and she knew that the only way to
deal with Cody was to let him go. She wouldn't let
him lose the world championship over a promise he'd
made to her dad.

Hearing her daughter ask if he loved them had really brought it all home. He hadn't answered. She had
waited, breath held to hear what he had to say. And
the answer had been left to her imagination. Did he
love them? If he did, why hadn't he answered?

And why had she held her breath wanting to hear
him say that he did?

Since he hadn't answered Meg, she had done what
she thought best for them all. She had opened the door
for him to leave. She knew that this new Cody took

responsibility seriously, and she didn't want to be a responsibility in his life. Funny how in a matter of weeks, everything had changed.

At first she had worried that he would take Meg, and she had been jealous of his relationship with their daughter. She had worried that he would walk away and not come back. Now she didn't want to be the person he felt had held him back from what he wanted.

She didn't want to be the person he resented or felt obligated to.

At strange moments like this she remembered him hugging her close and telling her he'd stay as long as she needed him. And she had worried that her need for him might be "forever."

She needed to remember about letting go, and about a time to gain and a time to lose. Life had so many seasons and so many lessons to be learned. God was the ultimate teacher. She knew that in all of this He was teaching her to trust Him.

Ironically, she still seemed to be trying to control and make sure things worked out according to plan. As if God needed her help getting things done.

She stood and stretched. After two hours of working, she'd come a long way. She'd done a lot of letting go. Her dad's clothes were packed, old mementos were piled and photographs were tucked away in the cedar chest.

Cody was in the yard with Meg. Through the bedroom window she could see them at the swing. He didn't need to worry that he was the kind of dad who walked away.

As she walked out the back door, the rumble of thunder echoed overhead, clashing with the bark of the dog and the sound of a car engine on the highway. Bailey glanced toward the end of the drive and saw the car turning.

She recognized the long, blue sedan and knew that it belonged to an older couple from her church. She waited for them, wishing that they had called first. Exhausted emotionally, she really needed a break from condolences.

The car pulled to a stop. Bailey smiled and waved as the Bakers stepped out of the car to be greeted by Blue, who had managed to find a ball for them. They didn't smile back.

Dread tightened like a fist in Bailey's stomach.

Mr. Baker's stern gaze landed on Cody and Meg, and then it shifted back to Bailey with burning censure that placed an invisible scarlet letter on her chest.

"Ms. Cross, our pastor didn't feel a need to come and talk to you about your reputation, but we did."

Of course they did. Bailey didn't know if she should invite them into the house for tea or send them on their way. Cody had left Meg at the swing and was heading toward her with steady and meaningful steps.

This was a good time to show him she could take care of herself. She turned toward him, giving the Bakers her back for a moment while she grabbed hold of composure that was trying to flee under pressure.

"Cody, could you take Meg in for ice cream?"

He looked from her to the Bakers and back again to Mr. Baker. Cody didn't look like a man who wanted to back down. His mouth was set in a firm line, and his blue eyes flashed fire.

"Please." She made the word sound stronger than

she felt. It would have been so easy to melt, and to let Cody take over.

"Fine, I'll be inside if you need me."

Bailey turned back to Mr. Baker, somehow gathering a smile and some courage for the coming lecture. If Pastor John didn't feel the need to bring it up, it had to be good.

"Ms. Cross, there are people in town who are concerned by this situation."

"Situation?"

"The fact that Mr. Jacobs is living here is the source of a lot of speculation and rumor. It isn't a fit environment for your daughter, nor are you setting a good example for her or other young people."

"Of course." Bailey wilted on the inside. "But you do understand that he's staying in an RV."

"We know that his RV is here."

But they didn't believe he slept in the RV. Bailey wanted to cry. She wanted to ask them if they understood what it meant to gossip, and how hurtful a sin it could be. She wanted to ask them if they had ever needed someone to stand in the gap and help them the way Cody had helped her.

She wanted to ask them if they had ever thought of being alone. Instead she smiled.

"I'm so thankful that you came here to warn me. Your concern is touching. It's hard to handle gossip but I'm sure the two of you will clear this up and let people know that Cody is living in the RV and he's only here temporarily."

Mrs. Baker came to life. "Of course we know that, dear. And we don't hold to gossip, and we hate to make someone else's business our own. We only came out of concern."

Bailey wanted to believe them. She wanted to not be hurt, but she couldn't shake off the pain. This moment meant another change in her life, and another letting go for herself and Meg.

The Bakers had just fast-tracked that moment she had been dreading, the moment when Cody would leave. Because she knew that he wouldn't stay, not if he thought it would hurt Meg. And the gossip would hurt their daughter. If adults were talking, so were the children of those adults.

What if Meg went to school and one of the children in her class teased her? Bailey wanted to stop it all, to make it go away.

She wanted the Bakers to go away.

She smiled at them and thanked them for coming. They stood for a minute, staring at her as if they thought that continuing to stare might force her to come to her senses, or whatever they'd hoped to accomplish with their visit.

"I really do appreciate you coming out, and I will take what you've said into consideration."

"Goodbye then." Mr. Baker shook his head as he got into his car. His wife followed, her frown matching his.

Bailey breathed a sigh of relief as they started their car and backed out of the drive. And then she stood in the center of the yard not knowing what to do. She wanted to go to her dad for advice, but he wasn't there.

A soft whisper of a breeze, bringing the earthy scents of autumn swirled around her, reminding her of the source of strength she had that would never leave her. She closed her eyes, seeking peace.

"Did you straighten them out?" Cody touched her arm and she was tempted to lean back into his embrace. She wanted to let him handle it all and to know that he wouldn't leave.

She didn't want to be strong anymore. Not with Cody standing next to her.

Instead she turned to face him, finding it easier to smile than she would have imagined. His deep blue gaze traveled down the drive in the direction of the sedan just pulling onto the road.

"No, they set me straight about my tattered reputation and the way I'm going to ruin my daughter's life by having you here with us."

"What do you think we should do? I know that moving the RV is on the top of the list." He looked away from her, his jaw clenching the way it did when he was working through a serious problem. When he turned back, she could tell he thought he had the answer. "Marry me, Bailey. Meg needs for us to be a family."

That was *so* not the answer.

Not fifteen minutes ago she had told him goodbye in a way that she thought released him from his mind-set of being responsible for them, that he had to keep a promise to her dad.

Now he was proposing.

Marry him, for Meg's sake, not because he loved her. It sounded good, like the right move. And it sounded like an alternative to the mess they'd made of things. But it didn't sound like the right answer.

It didn't sound like love or forever. And as much as

she told herself it didn't matter, it did. In her heart, it mattered because right now she felt like that twenty-two-year-old young woman who had believed love could last forever and that Cody would be the one who made it happen.

"It would work, Bailey."

"No, I don't think so." Not without love, not if it was entered into as a solution to a problem or an answer to a promise he made to a dying man.

He brushed her hair back from her face and lifted her chin with his finger. The soft look in his eyes almost convinced her that maybe he wanted to marry her for the right reasons.

"It would solve everything." Wrong words if he meant to convince her.

"I'm not seventeen, Cody. I'm not a teenager who can't take care of herself. Remember, you already solved that problem by buying the farm. Your job here is done."

"No, my job has just begun because my daughter is here. Don't forget that important factor in this equation."

"I've been very aware of her for nearly six years."

"While I wasn't here." He brushed a kiss across her cheek and stepped away. "I guess if I was you, I'd have doubts, too."

Bailey nodded but she didn't answer. She didn't have to think about his proposal. She didn't want him to marry her just to solve a problem. The horses whinnied to her, a call for their evening meal. Bailey walked to the barn because that was easier than dealing with the mess she'd made of things. As she worked, she glanced in the direction of the RV.

Cody was loading the lawn furniture into the back of his truck and rolling in the awning of the RV. Meg followed behind him, seeming to fear he might never come back. At least Blue stayed next to Bailey. She still had the dog.

The cows had come up. Bailey walked out the back door of the barn into the bright sunlight, squinting as her eyes adjusted. Blue circled the cows, barking as Bailey pulled the string to open one end of the feed bag and emptied it into the trough.

She could hear banging as Cody readied the RV to leave. She didn't want to picture the look on her daughter's face. She remembered all too well what it had felt like to watch Cody Jacobs drive away.

After the RV was loaded and hooked to the truck, Cody came to say goodbye. He had changed into a clean polo shirt and had replaced his cowboy hat with a ball cap. He hadn't shaved.

"I'll be back in a week or so. Pastor John is going to let me park the RV at his place for the night."

"We'll be here." Bailey had hold of Meg's hand, but Meg pulled free and rushed into Cody's arms.

"I don't want you to go." She cried into his sleeve while he held her close.

"I know, sweetie, and I don't want to go. But remember, this is my job. Sometimes I have to go, but I'll always come back."

"Promise?"

"I promise." He kissed the top of her head and stood. His dark blue eyes sought Bailey's and he stepped close.

Bailey waited, not sure how their own goodbyes would go. They didn't hug, or even touch. He smiled and told her they'd probably talk before he left for California; and then he walked away, teaching her another lesson about letting go, this one feeling a lot like the one in Wyoming years ago.

Chapter Thirteen

"What's wrong with you today?"

Bailey turned at Lacey's question. They'd just worked through a seriously busy lunch shift, so there hadn't been a lot of time for talking. There definitely hadn't been a moment for Bailey to tell her friend about the previous day.

The proposal and the goodbye were still fresh on her mind. She didn't know how to mention it or what to say. Now Lacey was standing in front of her in the waitress station, effectively blocking any escape Bailey might have planned.

"What do you mean, what's wrong with me?"

Bailey could think of a list of things that were going wrong in her life, but she could think of more things right. At this moment she really needed to count her blessings.

"What's wrong with you? It's a simple question. I know you've had a rough few weeks, but this morning you came in with a snarl, and your eyes were puffy."

"Allergies."

"Yes, of course, allergies." Lacey fiddled with her apron, and when she looked up, there wasn't a smile. "How's Meg doing in school?"

"She's doing great. It took me a few days to adjust."

"How's Cody?"

Bailey poured herself a cup of coffee and stirred in a spoon of sugar, taking her time because she needed time. How was Cody? Gone? Out of her life? That was all way too melodramatic. Lacey moved from her post at the door and leaned on the counter next to Bailey.

"He's leaving." Bailey lifted her coffee and took a sip. "But from the look on your face, maybe you know more than I do."

"I do know about the trip the Bakers made to your house yesterday."

"That was a lovely time. Why didn't you just say that you knew?"

"I didn't want to force you to talk."

Bailey laughed at that, a real laugh that felt good. "Oh, so now you're tactful."

"I'm always tactful, and considerate." She smiled a sweet, too-sweet, smile. "And I guess that's why Cody's RV is at the pastor's house."

"Yes, it is." Bailey just wanted to sit with a cup of coffee. Preferably by herself. The bells on the door clanked, giving her a much-needed escape. "Oh, that's my customer."

"Chicken."

"You betcha."

Bailey shot a smile over her shoulder as she hurried to seat the customers and offer them menus. When she walked back to the waitress station, Lacey was filling ketchup bottles so the evening waitresses would have a stocked supply.

"Finish the story." Lacey didn't give her a break. "What happened?"

"He proposed." Bailey sort of enjoyed dropping that on her friend. She walked off with a carafe of coffee and two glasses of iced water.

"Hey, come back here."

Bailey shook her head as she walked across the diner to the corner booth that her customers had picked. She filled their coffee cups and set the water glasses in front of them as they scanned the menu.

They spent five minutes looking at the menu and then ordered the special. Bailey hurried back to the kitchen with the order, but then she took her time returning to where Lacey was waiting for her. She wasn't quite ready to talk about her very first proposal and why it had hurt so much to hear the words *marry me*.

"He proposed." Lacey didn't wait for her to walk to the waitress station.

Bailey cringed, wondering how many people had heard. She lifted a finger to her mouth to quiet her friend.

"A sympathy proposal, that's all."

"Sympathy. What does that mean? A gorgeous man proposed and you turned him down because you thought he felt sorry for you?"

"I turned him down because he offered it as a way to solve our problems. Marriage would give Meg a family unit and stop the gossip. End of story."

"You said no? Forgive me if I don't understand

turning down a man you're in love with and a man that is the father of your daughter."

"I can't base a marriage on what happened in Wyoming. I can't marry him because it would be the easy thing to do."

"But you love him."

The bells on the door were clanging again. Bailey and Lacey looked at one another; neither made a move toward the dining area.

"I won't be the person he resents, Lacey. I won't tie him to me that way."

"Why would he ever resent you?"

"Because he made a promise to my dad to take care of us. I don't want him to think that marriage is what my dad expected. Cody did what he had to. He bought the land. He's been here for us. He doesn't need to watch over me the rest of my life. I think it is time for us both to move on."

"Maybe he really wants a life with you?"

"That isn't what he wanted before, and I don't think it's what he wants now."

"How do you know that, Bay?"

Bailey opened the cooler door and pulled out two salads and a caddy with salad dressings. Lacey was ready with a tray, and a sympathetic smile.

Bailey shrugged. "Maybe I don't want to regret him again."

She regretted him.

Cody had stopped by the Hash-It-Out to say goodbye. He had gotten more than he'd bargained for. He'd gotten to hear what Bailey thought about him and their relationship. He was the person she regretted.

Of course he was. How could he not be on the list when he had been the person who had walked out on her and had left her to raise a daughter alone?

A daughter he hadn't known about, he reminded himself.

But that didn't undo what he'd heard her say. She didn't want to regret him. She meant the proposal and marriage. That had been a mistake, to propose spur of the moment as a way out for them both.

He should have known better. He should have told her that in the last few weeks, he'd been thinking of forever with her.

People were staring because he was standing in the dining room of the Hash-It-Out, holding his hat in his hands. He looked around the sparsely populated room, smiled at the few customers and shoved his hat back on his head.

He didn't want to be a regret in someone's life. He had enough regrets of his own.

He walked out of the diner and got back into his truck. For now he would drive over to the house and say goodbye to Meg. School had gotten out early and one of the ladies from church had picked her up and taken her home.

Telling Meg goodbye would be one of the hardest goodbyes of his life. Bailey probably wouldn't believe him, but saying goodbye to her in Wyoming had topped the list. Back then he hadn't wanted to get tangled up in something from which he couldn't escape.

Now he was tangled in more ways than one. And nothing had changed. He hit the steering wheel, looking for an out for his frustration and it didn't work. She didn't own the copyright on regret.

He wouldn't go where his mind wanted to go, to old habits and a way to numb himself against the emotions he didn't want to handle. His mind did go there, though, for a brief moment, trying to convince himself that he could deal with this if he drowned himself in alcohol.

Shaking off those thoughts, and the sharp edge of temptation, he gripped the steering wheel tightly and made a deep reach for strength.

The road to Bailey's took him past the land he'd bought. Land with green grass, gently rolling hills and a year-round spring. Bailey's land. Probably a good reason for resenting him. He had her land, the land she hadn't been able to save from foreclosure.

Cody took a deep breath and let it out. He wouldn't go backward, doubting himself and giving in to temptation. He felt it on the inside, a strength that didn't come from himself.

He hadn't let down Bailey or Meg.

And he wouldn't. He wouldn't marry Bailey. She was right: The proposal had been for the wrong reasons. He hadn't thought it through. He'd just been trying to do the right thing.

He'd been wrong on so many levels.

Pulling into the drive of the farm and seeing Meg on her swing, he knew one thing he wasn't wrong about. He wasn't wrong about wanting to be a part of his daughter's life. A big part.

She saw him coming and jumped off the swing mid-arc, landing on her bottom but laughing as she jumped and ran toward his truck. He slowed to a stop and opened the door.

"Hey, kiddo."

He climbed down and lifted her into the air. Blue barked and out of the corner of his eye he saw Elsbeth Jenkins watching from the porch. He waved.

"I miss you," Meg said as she leaned her head against his shoulder; he wondered how this had happened. Two months ago he had been on his way to the next event, and now he had this little girl and she missed him.

He didn't know if anyone before had ever missed him when he left. A few had been angry with him. He closed his eyes and held Meg close. And some had regretted him. Being missed and loved like this was a whole new feeling.

"I missed you, too."

"I don't want you to go away."

He put her down and took hold of her hand to lead her over to the swing. They walked side by side, and when he looked down, she was watching and trying to match her steps with his.

They sat down on the bench swing, and she leaned into his side, five years old and totally trusting. He hoped she would never lose that trust and that no man would ever come along to make her regret.

"Meg, I have to go, but I'll be back. Soon."

"Before school is out?"

"Before Thanksgiving."

"Is that when school is out?" She looked up, her eyes blue and large.

"It's less than six weeks." He lifted her hand and looked at her small fingers. "And I'll be here for Christmas."

She didn't respond. Her gaze shifted to the barn,

like she was trying to think of something. Blue had joined them and the dog's head rested on Meg's knees.

"Do you think my mom will be done being mad at you by then."

"I sure hope so."

Speaking of Meg's mom, there was Bailey, driving down the road in the new truck she'd bought the previous week. Cody stood and Meg joined him. He smiled down at her and then they walked across the yard together. This time he matched his steps to hers. She looked up and smiled before taking a giant step, which he pretended he couldn't match.

"I didn't expect to see you here." Bailey spoke to him but she leaned down to kiss Meg on the cheek. "Hey, sweetie, did you have a good day?"

Meg's eyes watered and she looked from Cody to Bailey and then back again, as if she expected him to do something. The problem with that was that he'd already tried something, and it hadn't worked.

Now he had to find a way to show her that he wanted her in his life for reasons that made sense—not to just fix a problem.

"I came to say goodbye."

Bailey stood up, nodding at his announcement. She probably didn't think he would come back.

"We'll be watching. And praying."

That he wouldn't be hurt. "I appreciate that."

He took in a deep breath and told himself this was for the best. Goodbyes didn't use to be so hard.

"Be careful." Bailey had hold of Meg's hand. "Meg, tell your dad goodbye."

Meg rushed into his arms and he held her tightly.

"This isn't goodbye, Meg. This is, *I'll see you soon.*"

He ignored Bailey because he knew that look in her eyes. He wanted to believe she was sorry he was leaving. Instead he told himself she was glad to see him go.

Bailey walked through the doors of the tiny Gibson post office. The building smelled like old paint and pine cleaner. It hadn't changed in years. And from behind the counter, Mary Walker was still watching the town like a hawk.

An easy, in-and-out operation wasn't going to happen; Bailey knew that the minute Mary spotted her. Bailey tried the avoidance maneuver: Keep eyes averted; pretend you haven't been seen. She put fifty cents into the stamp machine and pushed the button. Nothing came out.

A quick flick of her gaze in the direction of the counter and she could see Mary leaning, trying to get a good look at her. Bailey pulled her shirt down, flattening it. She was not pregnant.

That was the new rumor.

The door opened. Bailey kept her attention focused on the nonworking stamp machine. That thing had been in the Gibson post office since before her birth. No wonder it didn't work.

"Give it up, Bay. You're going to have to buy a stamp from Mary." Lacey nudged Bailey's shoulder and laughed.

"I'll cook you dinner if you'll buy it for me."

"No way—and ruin all of Mary's fun?" Lacey

glanced in Mary's direction and waved. "It'll all blow over."

"I've been saying that for two weeks." The rumors had started after Cody left.

"Yes, I know, and it really is starting to die down. You know that people love you and care about you. A few people needed something to talk about, and those few are getting straightened out by the rest of us."

"And I appreciate that."

"I'll buy your stamp. But I want shrimp on the grill and we'll watch bull riding together."

Bailey grabbed Lacey's arm. "I'll cook the shrimp and we'll watch a movie."

Lacey blocked Mary's view. "Why can't we watch bull riding?"

"Because I don't want to watch him get hurt." There, she'd said it, and nothing bad had happened. She had admitted that she cared.

Lacey should have been happy. She'd gotten her way. Instead there were tears in her eyes and a look of sympathy on her face.

"Bailey, I'm so sorry that I teased you." She wiped at her eyes. "I'm a horrible friend."

"You're a good friend. But I can't watch. I can't let Meg watch."

Hopefully Lacey would leave it at that and not ask her to explain why it mattered. Those were questions Bailey didn't want to answer, not even to herself.

She knew what she had to do. She had to move on. She wouldn't let herself spend a year moping. She was older and wiser; she was good at letting go.

"Then we'll have shrimp and play on the swing."

Lacey glanced in Mary's direction. "Let me get you a stamp and I'll be right back. I'll even buy the shrimp."

As much as it hurt to let go, Bailey realized how good it felt to have friends who cared. It felt good to know that she was strong enough to move on. Again.

She smiled at what had to be a reflection of her new strong self. "Shrimp and a stamp and no lectures?"

"Only twenty questions." Lacey smiled as she walked away.

"Fine, but I'm not answering." Bailey bit down on her lip and blinked away the tears that surfaced. She was strong enough to move on.

Chapter Fourteen

"What a bull." Cody whistled as he saw the animal run into the chute. The chute that meant the animal was meant for him to ride.

Jason laughed. He could laugh. He wasn't the one who would be riding that wild beast in five minutes. This one could make him or break him, literally. He didn't like the broken part. Not now, when he was riding healthy and heading for the finals next week.

It was the end of October. Missing Meg and Bailey had created a deep ache in his heart. He hadn't expected that. He hadn't expected his thoughts to drift to Gibson on a regular basis.

"Buddy, you'd better get your mind off Missouri and on that killer bull you've got in the short go."

The short go was the round that the highest scores for the event took part in. It determined the champion of the event and who took home the big check. He was in fourth overall and he could easily win. Riding this bull, not so easy.

"My mind *is* on riding." Cody slipped a glove on his riding hand.

"You left your heart in Gibson, Missouri."

"Stop with that."

Cody pushed past his friend, wanting to say a whole lot more than "stop." He'd taken so much from his friends; he had lost his reputation for being cool and untouchable.

The announcers were calling him Moony because they said he was mooning over a woman he'd left behind. They didn't know the half of it.

The farther he'd driven from Missouri, the more he'd realized his mistake. Mistakes, plural. He'd made more than one. And soon enough he'd have to go back and face them. He couldn't get out of it. He was going to be her neighbor.

"I'm going to ride this bull, and then I'm going to deal with you." He hoped Jason knew he meant it. Jason only laughed.

"I like this new side of your personality that isn't fuzzy with alcohol. You're a lot easier to goad. A lot edgier."

Cody managed a smile. He liked sober, too. He liked vibrant colors and being in control of his emotions. Even if the emotions were twisting inside him.

"Yeah, I'm glad I could make things more fun for you."

Jason grabbed Cody's bull rope, which wasn't cool, because it was time for him to head for the chute, and the bull that waited for him.

"Tell me something, Cody. Are you in love?"

"I love my daughter." His heart ached, remembering that last hug. And remembering the look in Bailey's eyes. "I'm the man that Bailey Cross regrets."

"Oh, come on, are you still holding on to that? Don't you know that women say one thing and mean something totally different?"

"I've heard that." He jerked the bull rope out of Jason's hand. "I have a bull to ride."

"You have a woman you need to make amends with."

"You're a good one to talk. Don't you have a woman in Oklahoma that you haven't talked to in a year?"

"Yeah, but that's different; she knows I love her."

Cody shot Jason a look and his friend only laughed. Cody didn't have time for laughing. He had to get on a big black bull that had a reputation for being mean.

The bull snorted, bucked and moved into the side of the chute as Cody slid onto his back. Jason helped by pulling the bull rope tight. That was the great part about the sport, the way competitors helped one another and prayed for one another. What other sport had men in direct competition cheering one another on?

Cody wrapped the bull rope around his hand. The bull, ready for the fight, jumped and tried to go out the end of the chute. Jason caught Cody by the back of his Kevlar vest and kept him from going headfirst into the bars of the chute.

"If I don't make it off this thing alive, make sure Bailey gets the deed to that land." He was half-joking as he made the comment to Jason. Jason didn't smile.

Cody nodded and the gate opened. The bull came out of the gate spinning, twisting and doing a belly roll that felt as if it was jerking Cody's spine out of his back. He tilted his head down and prayed he'd make it to the buzzer, and then out from under the bull's hooves.

The roar of the crowd combined with his heaving breath, and the bull's snorting breath. Slobber and dust swirled, the grime settling in his eyes.

The buzzer sounded and it was all over. Faintly, he heard people screaming. He caught a glimpse of Jason on the chute, waving and shouting, laughing as he cheered Cody on.

The ground swept around him in a blur, and there didn't seem to be a soft spot to land. One of the bull-fighters ran in front of the bull and yelled that he had it covered. That meant he'd distract the bull while Cody jumped. That's what bullfighters did; they took the hit so the rider could make a safe getaway.

Cody jumped, landing clear. Sigh of relief, and then a yank on his arm that delivered him from relief in less than one second. His hand was hung up and the bull was still running. He hated that he'd been here before—back in January, in the wreck that changed everything. He didn't want a flash of memory that felt a lot like panic as he tried to stay on his feet.

The bullfighters were there, telling him to stay on his feet. Like he didn't know that he needed to stay on his feet. He hopped and ran alongside the spinning, running fifteen-hundred-pound bull. The bullfighter clung to the other side of the bull, trying to loosen the rope, which was wrapped like a viper around his hand. He caught a glimpse of Jason and a few of the others, hats in hands, praying.

The bull turned, spinning back on him and kicking in the process. Cody's hand slid free as the bull gave him a hefty push with his mammoth head and rammed him into the ground.

And the only thing he could think about was why he loved Bailey and how he wanted to make things right. If only he knew what that meant.

Bailey had cleaned out almost the entire house, throwing away things they'd kept for years for no reason and boxing up other items she couldn't part with. Which was what had created the surplus of junk in the first place. Who kept stuff like this, ancient postcards from places they couldn't remember, and cards from birthdays twenty years in the past?

From the kitchen she could hear Meg and Lacey laughing at something they'd concocted, probably another batch of homemade dough to make silly creatures. The kitchen table was full of baked dogs, cats and horses. They'd have to clear it off soon, so they would have a place to eat lunch.

The homemade dough had been a way to distract Meg since last Friday night's bull ride, when Meg had watched the ride on TV and saw her father get injured.

Bailey still felt a thread of guilt because she and Lacey had been preoccupied with an out-of-control flame in the grill and hadn't realized that Meg had turned on bull riding. Or that she'd watched her daddy get hurt.

Cody had been unconscious when they carried him out of the arena on a stretcher. Meg had run from the house, crying because her daddy wasn't moving. Bailey and Lacey had hurried into the house in time for a replay of the ride. And a third replay, and then a

fourth. Each time they showed it, her heart clenched
with fear. Watching it, Bailey had realized just how
much she didn't want to see Cody hurt.

Together they had prayed, and Meg had refused to
leave Bailey's side for the rest of the night.

Fortunately a concussion had been his only injury.
It had been serious but not life threatening. And he
had called them from the hospital because he hadn't
wanted Meg to be upset.

Bailey pushed away other feelings because she
didn't want to deal with all of this, not right now.
She was packing up junk from the past. The past with
Cody didn't need to be unboxed for a second look.

Wyoming, like old postcards and letters, needed
to be boxed up and put away. For good. She hated
that she'd found a box of pictures from that summer.

With Meg safe in the kitchen with Lacey, Bailey
sifted through the pictures. She tried to remember
the names of people she'd forgotten. She stopped to
linger on a picture of herself with Cody.

Even now it looked like love. She reminded herself
of his goodbye, then, when he'd told her that cowgirls
always think they're in love. And this time when he'd
said goodbye with a makeshift proposal.

"Hey, the mailman just stopped. Want me to go out
and get it?" Lacey yelled from the kitchen.

"Sure."

Bailey knew that meant Meg joining her in a minute. She didn't want to explain the pictures and what
looked like a happy young couple. She tossed them in
the box and pulled the lid closed just as Meg jumped
through the door yelling "Boo."

Bailey put a hand to her heart and pretended to

scream. Meg laughed, and it was good for Bailey to see her laugh again. The hole in their lives was getting smaller. They still missed Jerry. They still felt the emptiness of the place he used to inhabit, but each day it got easier to go on.

And missing Cody was a thing of the past. Regret was in the past. Bailey hugged Meg and held her close. The screen door slammed shut and Lacey's sandaled feet clicked on the tile as she headed their way.

"Letter for you." Lacey tossed the real mail to Bailey. Lacey took the junk mail and Meg. "Looks like you might need a minute to look that over."

Bailey glanced down at the business envelope with the return address of a lawyer in Oklahoma. Her heart ka-thumped against her chest, and fear sent fingers of dread up her spine.

What had Cody done? She closed her eyes and said a prayer because she didn't want this to be about her original fears, that he'd take her daughter away. She slid her finger under the flap and pulled the letter out.

As she read, her eyes watered and her heart raced to keep up with her emotions. She read the papers again and then closed her eyes, trying to make sense of it all.

"What's up?" Lacey said from the doorway.

"Where's Meg?"

"Watching a movie. I told her to stay and I'd make cookies. The kind we can actually eat."

"Thank you." Bailey wiped her eyes.

"Gonna share?" Lacey sat on the floor next to her.

"It's a letter from Cody and from his lawyer. He doesn't want to be someone I'll regret." She blinked away tears but couldn't blink away her own regret. It stuck in her heart, forcing her to deal with what she'd been running from.

Her past. The part that couldn't be put in a box.

"Well?" Lacey reached for the letter and Bailey handed it over.

"He's signing the land back over to me, putting it in my name and Meg's."

"What's this about regret?" Lacey read over the letter, glancing up when she read the last line.

"I don't know."

"Do you regret loving him?"

Bailey shrugged, but she knew the answer. She resented being hurt. She regretted things they'd done, and said. She didn't regret having him in her life—except when it hurt and except when she had to get over him.

She didn't want him to walk away, and she didn't want him to be just the guy who picked up her daughter for weekends. Unfortunately that was the person he was in her life, and she needed to deal with it.

"I can't let him give that land back to me. It's his and he deserves it."

"And you want him close at hand. Why, Bailey? So he can be here for you in a way that is safe and comfortable?"

Bailey was reaching for the phone but Lacey's comment stopped her. "What does that mean?"

"It means you like safe. You like comfortable. You like to be in control. Cody undoes all of those things in you. He takes over. He makes you feel uncomfortable because you know you love him and you don't want to give in to that emotion. He definitely isn't safe."

"Thank you for that, Dr. Phil."

"Glad I could help. So this means you like a safe place to land, and your daughter needs a safe place to land. And Cody is it, but you don't want him to be."

"He proposed because he wanted to protect us, not because he loves me." She glanced over the letter again. "I don't want to be the person who trapped Cody Jacobs. I want to be the woman someone wants to love forever."

"Whatever."

"Whatever, what?"

"A man doesn't hand over a quarter of a million dollars if he doesn't love a woman."

"He loves his daughter and I'm giving the land back." She had the phone and she dug through a pile of magazines for the phone book, which she'd accidentally tossed into the throwaway pile.

"What are you doing now?"

"Calling the airport."

"Because?"

Bailey shot Lacey a look that did nothing but make her smile. "I'm going to Vegas to give this back to him and to tell him I don't regret him."

Lacey stood up. "I'm going to go play with Meg. At least she's honest about loving Cody."

Chapter Fifteen

Cody flipped his phone closed because it was obvious Bailey wasn't answering. He'd been trying all day. Time to put it away and let it go.

"What's up? Still can't get hold of her?" Jason had walked up behind him.

They were scheduled to sign autographs in the hotel lobby. He had thirty minutes to shower and get changed. Jason had fallen onto the bed and was kicked back like he planned to take a nap. Cody slapped his friend's boots off the bed.

"Get a room."

"I'm your roommate, remember? You have money and I'm this year's biggest loser."

"You don't try hard enough. You're not hungry."

"Okay, so my weekly allowance makes me weak. Think I should give it up?"

Cody laughed. "Nope, I think you should get a sweet wife and buy a farm of your own."

"Nope, not this cowboy. I'm going to leave settling down to guys like you. The more of you that I can get married off, the better my chances are going to be. Last week's knock on the head proves that romance takes the edge off the cowboy."

Cody rubbed his head. The bruise was still there, a dark spot on his forehead, right at his hairline. It could have been worse.

The bump on his head was the least of his concerns. Where was Bailey, and why did he feel panicked at the thought of not being able to reach her? He flipped his phone open again and dialed, again.

One ring, two; it was answered on the third. He sighed with relief until he realized it wasn't Bailey on the other end.

"Lacey?"

"You got it, cowboy."

He paused and she laughed, answering his unspoken question. "Caller ID—remember we live in the modern age of technology. Says right here, Love of Her Life. Oh, wait, no, it says Cody Jacobs. Sorry, she isn't here."

The woman talked nonstop. Cody smiled, for a second missing her. He missed Gibson. He closed his eyes, the biggest longing still hitting home, right in the region of his heart.

He missed Bailey. He missed her smile and the way she made him think about forever. He missed her in his arms.

"Where is she?" He turned his back on Jason's knowing grin. Jason should meet Lacey; that'd put a stop to his roaming. It would put a stop to his endless teasing of Dr. G.

"She's on a trip. She decided she and Meg needed a little time away from the farm."

"What about school?"

"Kindergarten, cowboy. They're not real strict with absenteeism at that age, and they let her take her work with her."

"Where are they?"

Long pause. He waited. "Lacey, are you still there?"

"Still here, but I'm creating a long pause, hoping you'll get off my case. She isn't here. She's on a trip. Let me see, yes, that's all she told me."

Cody flipped the phone shut and slid it into the front pocket of his jeans. Jason sat up and flipped off the television.

"Time to go, loverboy."

Cody picked up a magazine and gave it a good toss at his friend. "I hope you fall in love someday so I can give you a hard time."

The words slipped out and Cody couldn't move. Jason looked just as surprised, with his mouth hanging open and his eyes wide. Cody figured he probably looked just as shocked as Jason. He hadn't planned those words, and he hadn't thought about saying them until that moment.

No, that was a lie. He was lying to himself. He hadn't called it love, but he had thought about what he had been feeling and the way he missed Bailey. He had told himself he was just missing Meg, and Gibson.

He felt roots digging down deep, the kind that didn't choke the life out of a person. He'd been pruned for a reason, to make the roots stronger.

"Wow, you didn't expect that, did you?" Jason

threw a pillow and hit Cody in the face. He didn't even try to block it.

He sank onto the edge of the bed, gut-stomped worse than any bull had ever done. He loved Bailey Cross. And he had proposed to make things easier for her. What a lie that had been. He wanted to marry her because he loved her.

"I can't think about this right now. This is the last night of the finals. If I let myself get caught up in this, I won't be able to think."

"By *this* you mean love, right? Or are you too much of a man to say the word?"

Cody stood and reached for his hat, his favorite black hat. He pulled his jeans down over the tops of his boots and rolled the sleeves of his shirts down to button at his wrists.

"We need to go."

"So this is what love looks like."

Cody walked out the door, ignoring the guy who used to be his best friend laughing behind his back. Cody smiled as he pushed the down button on the elevator.

When he walked onto the floor of the lobby, there was a huge crowd already gathering. Tables had been set up to sell posters, hats and other souvenirs. People milled, waiting for autographs. There were women in high heels and high hair, wearing vests and cowboy hats. Kids wore leather vests and boots. Kids wore chaps and carried yellow-and-red lariats.

It was the same as every other year he'd been there. The air was charged with excitement, most of it coming from the riders who were ready to ride, not ready to sit and think or talk about riding.

The atmosphere was the same as every other year, and not. He was the man that Bailey Cross regretted, and she was the best thing that had ever happened to him.

Only he hadn't realized it until it was too late.

Meg had hold of a balloon and a poster of her very own daddy. And she wanted everyone to know it. There was only one problem: That meant that everyone was staring at Bailey, smiling and wondering who in the world she was and why she was here.

Here, as in Vegas. She was wondering the same thing. What in the world had she been thinking when she made that plane reservation and hopped on a flight across the country, far from home and safety?

Being this close to Cody, even if she hadn't seen him, didn't feel safe. It felt disconcerting because that's what she always felt around Cody.

"Mom, do you think he isn't here? What if he went home?"

By *home* Meg meant Gibson. Bailey didn't want to tell her daughter that Cody wasn't in Gibson. She didn't want to hurt Meg with the truth, that Cody was doing his best to detach from them. Why else would he send her a deed to that land?

He was tired of playing house. He was breaking the connection with them. If she had the land back, he wouldn't have to stay in Gibson, keeping a promise he'd made to her dad.

Bailey's heart broke for Meg. She told herself that it was for Meg that she'd cried and for Meg that she felt that emptiness all over again. It was as if she was holding her newborn daughter, wondering if she would always be raising her alone.

Why had she allowed her guard to drop and her heart to believe that Cody would be a real part of their lives? Meg's hand tightened on hers. A real part of Meg's life, she reminded herself. This wasn't about Bailey and Cody; it was about Cody and Meg.

"There's a man with a camera."

Meg pointed at the man heading in their direction. He wore a polo with the logo of a major sports publication and a gleam in his eye that said he thought he had a story.

Bailey turned, knowing now that Meg's announcement earlier that Cody was her daddy had been heard by the wrong people. That made everything more complicated. Bailey only wanted to give Cody back the deed or the intent letter that said he was signing the land over. Whatever it was, she wanted him to have it back. For Meg.

She wasn't about to let Cody Jacobs walk out of their lives, not without a fight. Not this time.

Now there were people staring and whispering. That seemed to be her lot in life. Someone touched her arm. Bailey jerked away, not wanting to be caught here like this.

"Bailey, come with me." Willow was at her side, a friendly smile in a crazy world far from Gibson, with its quiet streets and gentle pace.

"Where's Cody?" Bailey had hold of Meg's hand and Willow had hold of Bailey's arm. They were rushing through the crowd, away from the camera.

"We'll find him, but for now we have to get the two

of you out of the spotlight." Willow's pace slowed. "Unless you're okay with being interviewed."

"I'm not at all okay with that." She smiled down at her daughter. "Meg was excited. She didn't realize Cody had posters."

Willow laughed, the sound soft and friendly. "I heard. Everyone heard. She's proud of her daddy. Nothing wrong with that. The only problem is that Cody is a legend when it comes to relationships and his personality. You know what I mean."

"Yes, not everyone knows that he's changed. And no one knew about Meg until today."

"That's big news."

"Mom, where's my dad?" Meg's little legs were hurrying to keep up.

"Not here yet, sweetie."

Willow rushed them into an elevator. "You can hide out in my room until the dust settles. And later, I'll make sure you have good seats at the arena."

"Thank you." Bailey kept hold of Meg as they stepped onto the floor that housed the penthouse suites. Willow didn't travel inexpensively.

Willow inserted a card in the door and it clicked open. She motioned them inside. "Make yourselves at home. If you're hungry, order something. I'll let him know that you're here."

Bailey had thought about that, and maybe Willow's presence was an answer, a way to solve this without confrontation. She reached into her purse and pulled out the envelope.

"I don't need to see him. Could you give this to him? And if he'd like to see Meg, we can arrange that."

Willows eyes softened and she smiled. "Bailey, he wants to see Meg. He would want to see you, too."

Why did Bailey's heart react to that information, as if it was what she'd wanted to hear but been afraid to ask? She didn't want to be a sixteen-year-old, asking if a boy missed her. She bit down on her bottom lip and shook her head to clear her thoughts. She couldn't do this again. She couldn't handle letting him walk away a third time.

She didn't want to be an expert at letting go. And she didn't want Meg to learn lessons about letting go. In life it happened, but it didn't have to be the only lesson. Shouldn't there be a lesson about hanging on and making something work?

Cody obviously didn't want to be that person in Bailey's life, the one who made it work. His letter made that as clear as an April morning. And thinking it through, allowing herself to think about how much she really wanted that, made her heart ache.

"I'll give him your message." Willow stepped forward and gave her a stiff hug. "It'll all work out."

Bailey watched her unexpected friend walk away. As the door closed softly behind Willow, Bailey thought about what the other woman had said about everything working out. Didn't all things work together for good for those who trusted God?

The television came on, the theme music of a children's program breaking the silence of the room. Bailey smiled at Meg, who had curled up on the sofa with a box of cookies Willow had tossed her way. Willow didn't seem to know what to do with children.

With her daughter occupied, Bailey sat down in a chair next to the floor-to-ceiling window that looked out on the city of Las Vegas. Cody was out there somewhere, thinking he had worked everything out. He had rescued her, given her the land and made a promise to be a part of his daughter's life.

He didn't seem to have any trouble letting go.

Cody walked through the crowd toward the table that had been set up for autographs. People were staring, whispering; a crowd was forming. He didn't know what in the world was going on, but he sure wasn't comfortable with it.

"Big news." Jason had disappeared and reappeared now at his side, wearing one of his cheesiest smiles. Some people said he looked like England's Prince Harry. Cody preferred Opie, of *The Andy Griffith Show*.

"What's the big news? I'm going to win, but we all know that already."

Jason laughed and scooted out a folding chair to sit down. He pointed to the chair next to his for Cody.

"The big news is not you. The big news is the little girl who announced to everyone who would listen that you're her daddy. They say she had big blue eyes and dimples. Sound familiar?"

Cody jumped up, and the folding chair collapsed to the floor with a clang that drew more stares. Jason laughed and set the chair back up. He pointed for Cody to sit down.

"Calm down or you'll give it away. Look, here comes Willow and I think she's looking for you. She obviously isn't looking for me."

"She isn't looking for you because you welded her trailer gate closed."

"That was pretty funny."

"This isn't." Cody signed a poster that a little boy held out to him, and a hat that his dad held. "You all have a good day."

He smiled because that's what he was being paid for. His heart was chasing butterflies around his stomach. He rubbed a hand over his face and groaned.

"Cody, come with me."

"What?" He stared at Willow; she'd obviously gone crazy. He couldn't walk away right now.

She handed him an envelope and pushed Jason from his seat. Jason stood next to her, signing autographs and occasionally pushing something in front of Cody to sign.

Cody opened the envelope, knowing it was the one his lawyer had sent to Bailey. He read Bailey's note, that she didn't want his land and she wasn't letting him get away with walking out on Meg.

Walking out on Meg? He stood up, nearly knocking over the can of soda Jason had set on the table. "What does this mean?"

Willow shrugged. "I don't have the answer. I do have Bailey and Meg in my suite."

He looked across the room and made contact with one of the event organizers. Tad started and then shrugged. Cody stuffed the envelope into his pocket and followed Willow to the elevators.

"Why is she doing this?" he asked as the elevator doors closed them into the bronze-paneled box.

"She's protecting her heart." Willow pushed the top button.

Willow's pockets were deep, and Cody's respect for her had nothing to do with the dozen bulls she owned. He respected her because she was doing something for herself.

He pushed his hat down on his forehead and tried to regain some composure. He tried to find the answer he thought he'd already found, the one he'd been praying about.

When the door opened to the suite, Bailey looked up, surprise shining in her eyes. Meg ran across the room and threw herself into her dad's arms.

Bailey didn't.

"We've been looking for you," Meg warned in a whisper.

"I know. And I've been looking for you, too. For longer than I realized." He looked at Bailey as he said the words. "Do me a favor, Meg. Would you go with Willow and have ice cream so I can talk to your mom?"

"We'll go in the other room. I have fruit over there."

Meg nodded and slid to the ground. She looked from Cody to her mom and back to Cody again. Her little chin came up and she frowned. "I hope you two can be nice to each other."

Bailey covered her face with her hands. Cody thought she was crying. As the door closed behind Meg and Willow's departure, he realized she was laughing.

The laughter drew him to her, like a thirsty man to a well. She looked up, her eyes luminous in the dimly lit suite. Behind her the sky was a shimmering pink and the buildings were starting to light up.

It all dimmed in comparison with Bailey Cross and the way she made him feel, the way she'd always made him feel. What man in his right mind would run from a woman who completed him, who made him feel as if no matter what he was going through, if she was by his side, everything would be okay?

But what woman in her right mind would give a man like him a second chance to prove that she might possibly be everything to him?

He could start with two words and pray she gave him the opportunity to say the rest.

"Bailey, I'm sorry."

Bailey heard the words, but she couldn't get them straight in her mind, not yet. What exactly was Cody sorry for? And now that he was standing there in front of her, what was she going to do?

She'd spent the last two days memorizing what she'd say to him and how she'd set him straight. Now she could only stare at the cowboy in the red shirt and faded jeans, his white teeth flashing a hesitant smile in his suntanned face. She could think only about how right it felt when he was in her life and how wrong it felt when he walked away.

"So I guess we've been warned to play nice." His smile grew from hesitant to something that melted the ice.

"She learned that from her teacher. That's what Mrs. Parker says to Meg and her new friend Julie when they fight." Bailey explained.

He nodded, his jaw clenching and his gaze drifting from her to the window. He looked every inch a professional bull rider. And he looked like someone she wanted in her life.

He also looked a little bit upset. His blue eyes

looked like a spring storm on the horizon. So much for the warm feelings that had erupted when he took that first step forward. Now she was feeling more like a person who had misunderstood.

"I didn't come to fight." Not really.

"I can play nice if you can." He tossed the envelope on the table. "What's this about?"

"You go first. You tell me why you sent it."

"Because I didn't want to take it from you. I never meant for you to think that."

"I know you didn't mean to take it. But sending it back felt a lot like goodbye. I can't let you do that to Meg." She picked up the envelope but kept her gaze connected with his. "Taking this would mean giving you permission to be a temporary visitor in Meg's life."

"What about you?" He had moved while they talked, and now he was right in front of her.

He stood near enough to touch—if she had wanted to touch him. She could even walk into his arms and be held. She didn't want that. She was here because of Meg.

"I can let you go." She didn't want to. She no longer wanted to be good at letting go. She hadn't had a choice with her dad. She hadn't had a choice the first time Cody left.

"What if...?" He leaned close, his aftershave as cool as a spring morning. "What if I don't want to let you go?"

He leaned, his lips barely grazing hers, and then he took a step back. Bailey wasn't able to disengage so easily. Her breath was trapped painfully in her chest, and she wanted to step into his arms forever.

With eyes closed, she counted to ten, hoping she'd open them to find herself in control of the situation and her emotions. While she counted, her mind registered his words. She'd been so determined to set him straight that she hadn't really paid attention because she hadn't wanted to argue.

She opened her eyes, blinking to clear her vision. What she saw was Cody in front of her, looking as if he was waiting for an answer.

"Weren't we talking about you giving back the land, the only tie that you had to us?"

"We were talking about that, but I think we both know that the land isn't what ties me to Gibson, Missouri."

"Meg will always be there, and you'll always be in her life."

"And you?"

"What about me?"

"I don't want to be the person you regret."

Bailey covered her face with her hands, thinking of that day in the diner and the bell that had clanked over the door.

"You heard me say that?"

"I did. And I took it to heart."

Bailey rested her hand on his cheek and his eyes closed. "Cody, the only thing I regret is that you only wanted to marry me to give Meg a family. I regret mistakes I've made. I regret that I can't seem to let go of you."

"Why are you so determined to let go?"

"Because you're so determined to leave."

"I proposed."

She shook her head and walked away. Staring out

over the city skyline, she tried to figure out where the conversation was going and why it wasn't going the way she had rehearsed.

"You proposed to solve a problem."

From behind he reached for her hands and tucked his head close to hers, Bailey closed her eyes at his nearness and the feeling that this was right and that it should be forever. She tried to remember why it couldn't be.

"I wanted to marry you because I love you," he whispered, and then he brushed a soft kiss across her cheek. "I want forever. I just didn't realize it until it was too late."

"Is it too late?"

Bailey clasped his hands in hers and leaned back into his embrace. He turned her to face him. As he stared down at her, she waited with breath held and a heart full of hope. It seemed as if they were both good at racing off to say one thing and then finding out there was another plan.

"I don't think it's too late. I think it's just in time," he whispered. "Let me try this again, Bailey."

He held her hands and drew her close. "Marry me, because I love you and I want to be more than a father to Meg. I want to be your husband, the man you can count on."

A squeal interrupted the moment, and Bailey had to admit it had been a moment. Her legs were Jell-O and her heart was still trying to catch up with everything Cody had said. She hadn't even answered yet, because Meg was suddenly there and in his arms. And they looked like a family.

Willow stood at the door, her cheeks flushed. "Sorry, she escaped."

Meg leaned to whisper in Cody's ear. "We were listening at the door."

"Gotta run now. You all take your time in here." Willow said from the door. "Cody, I'll let them know you're on your way down."

"Well?" Meg was in Cody's arms, and they were both looking at Bailey, matching blue eyes and matching looks of determination.

"I'll think about it." She laughed and they didn't. "I thought about it."

"And?" Cody stepped close again, Meg's arms around his neck. She was obviously outnumbered.

"And I love you and I want forever with you."

"Forever won't be long enough."

"I wonder if they have a reservation at the Elvis Chapel?"

"Because when in Vegas…" Cody shook his head. "Sorry, honey, we're getting married in Gibson. After a nice long engagement of at least a month."

"A Christmas wedding?" Bailey closed her eyes, imagining the wedding and forever.

"Christmas is perfect." He hugged her again, a group hug with Meg in the middle. "And now I have to go win the world title. Because this is my last year to ride bulls."

She liked the sound of that, because it meant not letting go again.

* * * * *

Dear Reader,

I hope that you enjoyed reading Cody and Bailey's story, and I hope that you loved Meg, with her yellow sundress and pink boots. It is my deepest wish that reading this book took you on a journey, tugged your emotions and gave you something to think about when you reached *The End*.

How did this book come about? The characters started it all. They came to me one day, popping into my head as if they were meant to be. From the moment their story started to pour out on paper, it was obvious they had something special to teach us about forgiving others, forgiving ourselves and letting go—while holding on. It can all be summed up in Bailey's motto: Pull Yourself Up by the Bootstraps and Move On.

These characters were difficult for me to walk away from and I hope that you'll find yourself occasionally revisiting them, and Gibson, Missouri.

I love to hear from my readers. Please visit my website, www.brendaminton.net, and drop me an email.

Blessings,

Brenda Minton

Questions for Discussion

1. Cody Jacobs arrives in Gibson, Missouri, because he's on step 9 of a 12-step program. He's making amends for past actions, and seeking the forgiveness of people he had hurt. We've all made mistakes, done things we're ashamed of, or hurt people we care about. How important is it to make amends with those that we've hurt?

2. Bailey has her own secret—the child that she and Cody share. At first, keeping this secret from him seemed like the best option. Now she sees her mistake. Time and distance make it more difficult to go back and undo mistakes and wrong decisions. What are some repercussions of avoiding rather than dealing with a situation?

3. Cody struggles with alcoholism. He is now sober and he wants to stay that way. He's learning to acknowledge when he feels weak, and to withstand temptation. We all struggle with some type of temptation. What does the Bible say about temptation, and how to deal with it?

4. Bailey had to put aside self. Her first reaction is to push Cody from her life. But there are other people to think about. Her daughter, her father and Cody. How can considering the needs of others help us to put our own wants into perspective?

5. Bailey wants to do everything on her own. There is a thin line between being strong and being prideful. We all need help at some time in our lives. What does the Bible say about pride and humility?

6. When Bailey came home pregnant she found it hard to face the people in her community and her church. She felt judged. And she also judged herself for her mistake. What teaches a person: judging, pointing out their sin, or showing the love of Christ and forgiveness? For all have sinned and fallen short of the glory of God.

7. What could have happened to Bailey if there hadn't been people willing to love her and help her through her pregnancy? Is there someone in your life, your church or community that could use a word of encouragement or the reassurance that mistakes happen and can be overcome?

8. Bailey, like so many of us, was looking for answers and a way to get through a difficult time. She faced the loss of her father, the possibility of losing her farm and then the arrival of her daughter's father. There were moments when she went into self-preservation mode, looking for answers, but not really looking to God. And God did have a plan. It is easy to try and "fix" problems in our lives. How are situations changed when we seek God and His will?

9. If we believe that God has a purpose for our lives, shouldn't we also believe that He has a

plan, a direct way for bringing about that purpose? In Bailey's life, Cody was a part of God's plan.

10. People in Gibson, Missouri, were only too glad to have a little something extra to gossip about. Cody's presence at Bailey's provided the sourse of gossip. Some "sins" are obvious. We all know it is wrong to lie, to steal, to kill. Other sins, like gossip, are comfortable sins that fly around under the radar. Can a little "gossip" ever really be harmless?

11. Bailey's father left footprints of faith for his daughter and granddaughter. We all leave footprints as we walk through life. Have you examined your own footprints, the legacy you are leaving behind? Are there things you could change now that might make a difference in the lives of those who look up to you?

12. Cody sometimes doubted his ability to be the person he needed to be for Meg. But he made right choices—one decision at a time. He stayed in his daughter's life. He turned away from the temptation to drink. He gave Bailey space. We make one decision at a time, praying for the best. What steps do we take if we, or someone we're counting on, makes a wrong choice?

13. Communication 101: don't let misunderstanding remain between you and the people you love. Talk it out. Years ago Cody ignored Bai-

ley's phone calls. Now Bailey misunderstands the land that Cody bought and gave to her. When we walk away from a misunderstanding without resolving it, we walk away from something that might have been fixed with just a few words of explanation. Are there situations in your own life that could be fixed with a conversation and forgiveness?

A COWBOY'S HEART

The Lord is my strength and my song, He has become my salvation: He is my God, and I will praise Him. My father's God, and I will exalt Him.
—*Exodus* 15:2

To my sister Ellen Benham
and my brother-in-law Gary.
This is dedicated to you, for computers,
for weekends away and for friendship.

To Doug and the kids, because they love me,
even during a deadline crunch.

And of course to Melissa Endlich
and Janet Benrey. Without their encouragement
and belief in my stories, I'd still be piling unpublished
manuscripts in the closet.

To faithful and true friends, strong women all, without
whom my phone batteries would always be charged,
and I'd be a blob of insecurity. Thank you for listening,
for reading and for always being there for me.
Steph, Shirlee, Angela, Tonya, Dawn, Barbara,
Betty, Janice, Lori W and Keri.

For my number one fan, Denise Foster Dickens.
And Josie, for dinner, and for being the
most amazing neighbor ever.

To the girls at the Marionville, Missouri, library
for support and encouragement.

A deep debt of gratitude to Janet McCoy, for
answering questions and sharing stories.

To all of the women who struggle, hold on
to faith and never give up. Especially to
my new sister-in-Christ, Shirley.
You are strong and beautiful.

Chapter One

Country music crackled from aging PA speakers that hung from the announcer's stand next to the rodeo arena, and dozens of conversations buzzed around Willow Michaels. It was hard to discern one sound from another, and harder still to know if the queasy nervousness in her stomach was due to her bulls about to compete, or the way sounds faded in and out.

A hand touched her arm. She smiled at her aunt Janie, who had insisted on attending with her, because it was a short drive from home, and well, because Aunt Janie went nearly everywhere that Willow went.

"Didn't you hear me?" Janie asked.

"Of course I did."

"No, you didn't. I've asked you the same thing three times."

"I'm sorry, I'm just distracted." Willow slid her finger up the back of her ear. The hearing aid was at its maximum. And Janie was waiting for an answer that Willow didn't have.

"I said, I have a friend I want you to meet." Janie

searched Willow's face, her growing concern evident in her eyes.

"Don't, Janie, please don't give me that look. It's the batteries, nothing more."

"Make an appointment with your doctor."

"Who's the friend?" Willow went back to the previous conversation. At that moment, even if it meant meeting a man, Willow wanted to avoid discussing the fact that she hadn't heard her aunt. Discussing it would only make her deteriorating hearing more real.

"My old neighbor, Clint Cameron, is here."

"Clint?" Not a stranger, but a forgotten crush. Willow remembered now, and she didn't want to remember.

She was too old for high-school crushes, and she had experienced too much heartache to go back to being that girl who dreamed of forever.

Her marriage to Brad Michaels had been a hard lesson in reality. Willow was still forgiving him and still letting go of her own forever-dreams that had ended five years ago, with divorce.

She was still forgetting, and still healing.

She was still finding faith, a faith that had been a whisper of something intangible for most of her life. Now it was real and sustaining. Somewhere along the road she had realized that she wasn't flawed, and she didn't have to be perfect.

Janie touched her arm again. "Are you with me?"

"I'm with you."

"It won't hurt, Willow."

"You think?"

Janie laughed, "It won't hurt, I promise."

"Of course it won't. I'm just amazed that I unloaded the bulls, fed them, and you found a friend."

"The Lord works…"

"In mysterious ways." Willow wanted to sigh. Instead she smiled for her aunt. "Okay, let me make sure my bulls have water, and I'll come find you."

"Good." Janie smiled a little too big. "He's parked on the other side of the pens."

Willow waited until Janie walked away and then started toward the pens that held her bulls. If she had any sense at all, she would hide and avoid meeting Clint Cameron for a second time. The first meeting had been a pretty big disaster.

The bulls milled around their pen, big animals with flies swarming their thick hides. They stomped in an effort to rid themselves of the flying pests, big hooves sloshing in the mud left behind after last night's rain.

Willow leaned against the metal gate, needing that moment to pull it together, to let go of fear. The water trough was full—taking her last option for avoiding Janie and her friend.

She had accomplished a lot in the last few years. She'd made it in a man's world, raising some of the best bucking bulls in the country and supplying stock for some of the biggest bull-riding events in the world.

She had survived Brad's rejection. His rejection had hurt worse than the ones that came before him. She'd really thought that he meant their marriage vows.

He hadn't. He hadn't meant it when he repeated "in sickness and in health," or "till death do us part."

He hadn't meant it when he said she was the only woman for him.

Willow watched her bulls for a few more minutes, and then she turned to go in search of her aunt and Clint Cameron.

She remembered the first time she'd met him, a cowboy in faded jeans, torn at the knees. She remembered a smile that had put her teenage dreams of forever into overdrive. She'd spent the next year wrapped in daydreams of a guy that she'd been afraid to talk to.

In search of Janie, she made her way through the crowd, greeting a few people who called out or waved. Bulls were being run through the gates of the nearest pens to the chutes where the riders would climb on for the ride of their lives. A few men were getting bull ropes ready for their rides.

She finally spotted her aunt. Janie stood at the edge of the crowd. Next to her was a man Willow didn't recognize. He looked nothing like the blurred memory of a gangly teen with faded jeans and a stained T-shirt. This man wore a bent-up cowboy hat with the faded imprint of a hoof. The strong angles of his jaw proved he was no longer a kid.

His Kevlar vest, worn to protect his torso from the horns—or hooves—of an angry bull, was open, exposing a pale-blue paisley shirt. Tan leather chaps covered his jean-clad legs, brushing the tops of his boots. As Willow approached, he bent to catch something her aunt was saying.

Janie waved, motioning her forward. Willow waved back, reminding herself that she was stronger now than she'd ever been. But feeling strong when faced with a childhood dream wasn't as easy as she'd thought it would be. Especially when the dream was now a flesh-and-blood man with a wide smile and his arm wrapped protectively around her aunt.

Willow reached down deep and found strength, reminding herself that her new dream wasn't about happy-ever-after with a man. Her goals were now being achieved with a truck-load of bulls and success in the sport of bull riding.

But she wondered if he remembered her. Did he remember how she had said hello some sixteen years earlier, and then disappeared into Janie's house to watch from the window? He had spotted her there, waving when no one was watching. Even now the memory brought a flush of heat to her cheeks.

Willow took the last ten steps, joining her aunt and Clint Cameron. He took off his hat, revealing sandy blond hair that looked like it had been cut with electric clippers. Probably in front of a hotel mirror.

He should have used the clippers on his face. His five o'clock shadow was a day old, covering his sun-tanned cheeks and highlighting a mouth that turned in a slow, easy grin. Gray eyes, laugh lines crinkling at the corners, connected with hers.

On his off days he probably modeled for a cologne company with a typical western name—something like *Prairie Wind* or *Naughty Pine*. She smiled, try-ing hard not to look at the names of his sponsors, for fear she'd actually see *Naughty Pine* emblazoned on his sleeve or collar.

He wasn't a gangly teen anymore. And her heart still did that funny dance when he smiled at her. As a girl, not quite fourteen, she hadn't known what to do with that reaction. Now she carefully stomped it down, because she didn't need complications.

"Willow, this is my old neighbor, Clint Cameron."

He held out a hand and Willow let him take hers in a handshake that meant his fingers clasping around hers, holding tight for just a moment before releasing.

"Nice to meet you, Clint." Maybe he wouldn't remember her, the awkward kid who had stumbled through a greeting and then hurried back to the house.

He did, though. She could see it in his eyes. He smiled, revealing a tiny dimple in his left cheek that could have been a scar.

"Nice to meet you again, Willow."

"Clint's moving home. He's going to remodel his old farm house." Janie's eyes went liquid for a moment, and Willow knew what this meant to her aunt, to have someone back who had meant so much to her. "And he's made the points to ride in bigger events."

"Congratulations." Willow smiled, and then took a step back. "I'm sure we'll be seeing you around."

Janie caught her arm, stopping the perfectly planned escape. "I told Clint we might have some work for him to do. You know, I'm not getting any younger. It wouldn't hurt to have an extra pair of hands around the place."

"We can talk about that, Janie." Willow smiled at Clint Cameron. His gray eyes twinkled, and he saluted her with a tip of his hat as he put it back on his head, pushing it into place.

"If you don't have a lot for me to do, that's fine." He shrugged, like he really meant it. "I'm going to be working on our old farm down the road from you, getting it fit to live in."

"We'll work something out."

Clint Cameron smiled again, and Willow felt a twinge of regret, because she no longer believed in happy-ever-after with a cowboy.

Those dreams had faded a long time ago, victims of rejection and reality.

As Willow Michaels walked away, Clint drew in a deep breath and did his best not to whistle in surprise. He'd heard all about the tall stock contractor with the long, honey-blond hair and eyes the color of a clear spring sky.

Meeting her changed everything, though. He hadn't been prepared for a woman as cool and detached as a barn cat, the kind that didn't care if you paid attention to it or not.

He hadn't been prepared for the girl he'd met years ago, now a woman. What a woman.

"Don't let her scare you off, Clint. She's had a tough time of it, but she's coming around."

He smiled down at Janie. She'd been about the closest thing he'd ever had to a mother. His own mother had died when he was barely eleven and his sister was seven. He'd been left to raise Jenna by himself, and to deal with their drunken father.

Janie had been there to keep the pieces together.

She'd done the most important thing of all: she'd taught him to have faith. She'd also taught him to believe in himself. If it hadn't been for her he wouldn't have gone to college. He might have ended up just like his dad.

Janie had a new project. She was fixing her niece,

Willow. Will for short, or so he'd heard. He couldn't imagine calling her Will.

"I should go. I'm one of the first riders up." He shifted away from Janie, but she caught hold of his arm.

"Think about what I asked you, Clint."

"Have you even told Willow that you want to move to Florida?"

Janie shook her head. "No, not yet. This business means so much to her. I've been putting off my decision because I was afraid Willow would give it up on my account. I don't want her to think she has to sell her bulls. If she had someone else she could comfortably rely on, the transition would be easier."

"I don't think she'd appreciate you trying to arrange her life this way. And I'm not going to push myself off on her, Janie. She's proven herself in this business, and I think she'll handle making this decision on her own."

He softened the words with a smile, because he didn't want to hurt Janie, the woman who had fixed a broken teenager, helping him to believe in himself. She wanted to do the same thing for her niece.

But Clint didn't plan on pushing his way into a life that had more Do Not Enter signs than a minefield.

Relationships weren't his strong suit. A long time ago he'd realized that he had a habit of choosing girls, and then women, who needed to be fixed in some way. Not that he thought Willow Michaels needed to be fixed. He just wasn't taking chances.

Not only that, but she was way out of his league. Another aspect in relationships that clearly didn't work.

He scanned the crowd and spotted Willow in a line

for the hamburger stand that was a fundraiser for the National Future Farmers of America Organization. The aroma of grilled burgers drifted, and had lured a long line of people. Willow stood next to another stock contractor, her expression animated as they carried on a conversation.

He couldn't help but smile.

"You know, Janie, I have a feeling that Willow is a stronger person than you think."

"Of course she is, but she can't drive these bulls all over the country without some help."

"Seems to me that she can."

Janie smiled, her soft brown eyes twinkling. "Clint Cameron, if I didn't know better, I'd say you were trying to put me in my place."

"I'm only saying that I don't know your niece, but I have a feeling she can handle things." He fastened his Kevlar vest as he spoke. "If you want to move, Janie, you just need to tell her."

Janie laughed, "You should have come home more often. I've missed having someone around who wasn't afraid of me."

"I had a job."

"Working down there on those oil rigs in the Gulf. What kind of job is that for a country boy who wants to ride bulls and raise cows?"

"It paid the bills. It put money in the bank." Money meant for repairs on a farm that had gone downhill.

"Well, I know it was good honest work. I'm only saying that I missed you."

Clint leaned and kissed her powdery soft cheek. "I missed you, too."

"You go ride that bull. But be careful. We need you in one piece."

Clint laughed as he walked away. He laughed because Miss Janie had always had a knack for drama. It was a strange trait for a sensible woman.

As he threaded his way through the men standing near the chutes where the first few bulls were penned up and ready for their rides, he caught sight of Willow. She stood near a small group of people, her gaze concentrating on their faces as she read their lips. She nodded at something one of the men said and then she shifted her attention, focusing on Clint. As if she'd felt him staring. And for that moment, he couldn't look away.

He nearly ran into one of the event judges. The guy grabbed his arm and shot him a look.

"Sorry about that," Clint mumbled as he lifted his bull rope and continued moving through the crowd.

"You're up, Cameron." One of the men motioned him forward.

The MC in the announcer's stand gave the name of the next bull and followed that with Clint's name and a little information on his career. Of course they just *had* to mention that he was thirty-one, a late bloomer for bull riding.

He'd been at the sport for as long as he could remember. He just hadn't had the time to invest into making it a career. That didn't interest the crowd. They wanted to think about the old guy, the newcomer. Even in bull riding the fans wanted a Cinderella story.

Clint slid onto the back of a big old bull, one that

he'd come up against before. Part Brahma and part Angus, the bull had a mean streak a mile wide.

A warm night in May didn't make the bull any nicer. The animal slid to his knees and then back up again, leaning to the left and pushing Clint's leg against the side of the chute.

One of the other riders, a guy named Mike, pulled the bull rope and handed it to Clint. Clint rubbed rosin up and down the rope and then wrapped it around his gloved riding hand. The bull lurched forward and someone grabbed the back of Clint's shirt, keeping his head from bashing into the metal gate in front of him. The animal shook its head and flung white foam across Clint's face.

Clint leaned forward, the heaving, fifteen-hundred-pound animal moving beneath him. Fear in the guise of adrenaline shot through his veins, pumping his heart into overdrive. The bull calmed down for a brief moment, and Clint nodded.

The gate opened, and the bull made a spinning jump out of the chute, knocking his back end against the corner and sending Clint headfirst toward the animal's horns. With his free arm in the air, whipping back for control, Clint moved himself back to center.

Eight seconds, and he felt every twist, every jump, every lurch. As the buzzer rang, Clint dived off for safety, not expecting the last-minute direction change that the bull added in for fun. Clint hit the ground, and the impact felt like hitting a truck. A loud pop echoed in his ears, and pain shot from his shoulder down his arm.

The bull turned and charged at him. He rolled away, but he couldn't escape the rampaging animal, its hot breath in Clint's face and the hammering of its hooves against solid-packed dirt.

That big old bull was face-to-face with him, pawing and twisting. Clint rolled away from the hooves and then felt a hard tug as someone jerked him backward, away from danger.

The bullfighter yelled at him to move. Clint did his best to oblige, but his left arm hung at his side, useless. The pop he'd heard when he hit the ground must have been his shoulder dislocating.

A blur of blue in front of him, and the bull changed direction to go after the bullfighter. Those guys were bodyguards and stuntmen, all in one package. Clint hurried to the side of the arena and the fence.

As he held on to the fence, watching the bullfighters play with the overzealous bull, he caught a flash of blond. He turned and saw Willow Michaels watching from the corner gate.

When he limped out of the arena, his eyes met hers for a split second and then she walked away. She wasn't the first princess to turn her back on him. She probably wouldn't be the last.

Telling himself it didn't matter didn't feel as good as it usually did. Fortunately he had the throbbing pain in his arm to keep his mind off the blow to his ego.

Medics were waiting for him as he walked out the gate. They offered help walking that he didn't need. He'd dislocated his shoulder before, so he knew the drill. He just didn't feel like talking about it.

"Want some help getting in?" One of the paramedics motioned inside the back of the vehicle.

"I'll just sit on the tailgate." He had no desire to climb, with or without help.

"Suit yourself."

He leaned back and just as he started to close his eyes, Janie was there. She wore that "mother hen" look that he remembered from his childhood.

It was a shame she'd never had kids of her own. But then he might have missed out on having her in his life.

"Is it dislocated?" She nearly pushed the paramedics aside.

"I imagine it is." He managed a smile that he hoped wasn't too much of a grimace.

"Do you need to go to the hospital?"

"I think the paramedics can manage."

Janie didn't look convinced. She was five-foot-nothing but a force to be reckoned with. Funny how she hadn't really aged.

Not like his dad. His dad was barely sixty-five, but already an old, old man. His liver was shot, and his mind was going. Janie would always have her wits about her.

"Don't let him sit there and suffer." She stepped back, and motioned the paramedics forward.

She had no idea about suffering. The pain he had felt just sitting there was nothing compared to that moment when they yanked his arm and pushed it back into its socket. Working through it meant a serious "cowboy up" moment. He took a few deep breaths that didn't really help.

"There, nothing to it." One paramedic smiled as he said the words.

"Yeah, nothing to it." Clint shrugged to loosen the

muscle, but the pain shot down his arm and across his back.

"It'll be sore, and I'm afraid there might be more damage than just the dislocation. Best get it checked out with the sports medicine team. Until then—" he held out a sling "—pain meds, and you might want to get a ride home tonight."

A ride home? For the first time in a dozen years a "ride home" meant a ride to Grove, Oklahoma. And now it meant Willow Michaels living just down the road. He couldn't quite picture her as the "girl next door."

Chapter Two

In the midnight-black of the truck, lit only with the red-and-orange glow from the dash, Willow nudged at the cowboy sleeping in the seat next to her. They'd driven the two hours from Tulsa and were getting close to the ranch. Janie hadn't helped. She had fallen asleep shortly after they'd taken off.

"Wake up." She nudged Clint again, careful to hit his ribs, not the arm held against his chest with a sling. "Do you have a key to get into this place?"

He stirred, brushed a hand through hair that wasn't long enough to get messy and then yawned. He blinked a few times and looked at her as if he couldn't quite remember who she was.

"Willow Michaels, remember? We offered you a ride home?"

He nodded and then he shook his head. "I don't know."

She didn't hear the rest because he yawned and covered his mouth. Moments like this were not easy for her, not in the dark cab of a truck, not with someone she didn't really know.

He said something else that she didn't catch. Willow sighed because it wasn't fair, and she didn't want to have this conversation with him.

This kind of insecurity belonged to a ten-year-old girl saying goodbye to her parents and wondering why they no longer wanted her with them. And always assuming that it was because her hearing loss embarrassed them.

He said something else that she didn't catch.

"Clint, you have to talk more clearly. I can't see you, and I don't know what you're saying."

There, it was said, and she'd survived. But it ached deep down, where her confidence should have been but wasn't.

He looked at her, his smile apologetic as he reached to turn on the overhead light. The dim glow undid her calm, because the look in his eyes touched something deep inside. Wow, she really wanted to believe in fairy tales.

Sorry.

And when he signed the word, his hand a fist circling over his chest, she didn't know how to react. But she recognized what she felt—unnerved and taken by surprise. When was the last time a cowboy had taken her by surprise?

She cleared her throat and nodded. And then she answered, because he was waiting.

"It isn't your fault. It's dark, and you didn't know."

How did he know sign language, and how did he know that it made hearing him so much easier? Even with hearing aids, being in the dark made understanding a muffled voice difficult—especially with the diesel engine of the truck.

"I know it isn't my fault, but I should have thought." He shifted in the seat, turning to face her as he spoke. "I'm sorry, I'm not quite awake."

"About the house?"

"I don't need a key to the house."

"Aunt Janie, you should wake up now." Willow downshifted as they drove through the small almost-town that they lived near. Grove was another fifteen miles farther down the road, but it was easier to say they were from Grove than to give the name of a town with no population and no dot on the map. Dawson, population 10, on a good day. The town boasted a feed store and, well, nothing else.

"Janie, wake up." Willow leaned to look at her aunt.

Janie snorted but then started to snore again. The vibration of Clint's laughter shook the seat. Willow shot him a look, and then she smiled. He had used sign language—that meant she had to give him a break.

She was still trying to wrap her mind around that fact. It had been a long time since someone had done something like that for her. Something unexpected.

"Where did you learn sign language?"

He shrugged. "I picked it up in college. I have a teaching degree, and I thought sign language would be a great second language. Everyone else was studying Spanish, French or German."

He signed as he spoke, and Willow nodded. She reached to shift again as the speed limit decreased.

"I'm rusty, so you'll have to excuse me if I say the wrong thing."

"You're fine." And the sooner she dropped him off at the little house surrounded by weeds and rusted-out trucks, the sooner she could get back to her world and to thoughts that were less confusing.

The driveway to his place was barely discernable, just a dirt path mixed in with weeds and one broken reflector to show where it was safe to turn. She slowed, not sure what to do. The trailer hooked to her truck jolted a little as the vehicle decelerated and the bulls shifted, restless for home.

"Don't pull in. You won't be able to turn the truck."

She agreed with him on that. She didn't have a desire to get stuck or to have a flat tire. Not with a load of homesick bulls in a stock trailer hooked to the back of her truck.

"But what are you going to do about tonight? Do you even have electricity?"

"I dropped off flashlights and a few other necessities this morning. Don't worry, I'll be fine." In the light of the cab he had stopped signing, but he spoke facing her.

The snoring from the far side of the cab had stopped. Aunt Janie sat up, yawning. "Clint, don't tell me you plan on staying here tonight?"

"There isn't that much night left, Janie. I'll be fine. Take Willow home, and get some rest. She's got to be tired after the day you two put in."

"You've had a long day, too." Willow pushed aside something that felt like anger, but maybe came from leftover feelings of inadequacy.

It had more to do with the past than with the present. It had to do with Brad telling their limo driver to take her home while he went into town, to a party that would have been too stressful for her to attend.

Alone. She'd always been at home alone. And she'd been sent away when she failed to meet expectations. The past, she reminded herself. It was all in the past and God had restored her life, showing her that she didn't belong in a corner alone.

She mattered to God. He had given her an inner peace and the ability to believe in herself.

"You're right about that." He stood in the open door, holding Janie's hand as she got back into the truck. "You two have a good night. See you tomorrow."

Tomorrow. When he would invade her life. Willow couldn't really thank him for that, not if he was going to be another person who found it easy to believe her hearing loss meant she couldn't take care of herself.

Clint woke up after a short few hours of sleep, stiff and sore, his arm throbbing against his chest. He rolled over on the sleeping bag and stared out the cobweb-covered window, so dirty that it might as well have had a curtain covering it. His savings account had seemed more than enough until he got a good look at this place.

Six months since his last visit home and two years since he'd been in this house. It looked like the dust had been there since then, or before. Not to mention his dad's old truck, tires flat and the frame rusting, growing weeds at the side of the house.

His dad had moved to a house in town two years earlier, and then to the nursing home. It hadn't been easy, putting him there, knowing he needed full-time care.

Clint's phone rang, and he reached for it, dragging it to his ear as he flipped it open. His sister said a soft hello.

"You sound bad. Do you look bad?" She laughed when he groaned an answer.

"Other than a dislocated shoulder, I had a great night."

"Sounds like fun. I'm sorry I missed it."

"Wait until you come down for a visit. Janie is still Janie. And her niece is living here."

"The one that used to visit in the summer?"

"The one and only."

"Is she still beautiful?" She was determined to see him married off.

"If you like tall, blond and gorgeous, she's okay." He rubbed his hand across his face, trying to rub the sleep away. "She isn't my type."

"Have you ever found your type?"

"Nope. I'm happily single."

"I don't think so, brother dear. I think you need a woman to soften your rough edges. You need someone who will take care of you, the way you've taken care of everyone else."

"I don't have rough edges. So, what's up, Sis?"

He knew there was more to this call. He thought he might need to sit up, because the tone of her voice, even with the laughter, hinted at bad news. Holding the phone with his ear, he pushed himself up with his right hand and then slid back against the box of supplies he'd left here yesterday.

"What's up, Jen?"

A long pause and he thought he heard her sob. He didn't hear the boys, his twin nephews, in the background. His stomach tightened.

"Time to put our Family Action Plan into place. I'm going to Iraq."

Not that. He could have prepared himself for almost anything, but not the thought of his kid sister in Iraq. And the boys, just four years old, without a mom. He couldn't think about that, either. They had discussed it some. He had just convinced himself it wouldn't come to this—to her leaving and the boys in his care.

"Clint, I need for you to take the boys."

"You know I will. But there has to be someone better for them than me, an uncle who rides bulls for a living and who's camping in a house without electricity." For the moment.

"You're it. You're my only family, their only family. You knew this could happen."

"I want to make sure this is the best thing for them, that I'm the best thing."

"You were the best for me."

He closed his eyes, wishing he had been the best for her, and that he'd been able to give her more. He'd done his best. They both knew that.

"When?"

"I have to leave for Texas in five days. I've known for a while, but I guess I was hoping that something would happen and I wouldn't have to leave them." She sobbed into the phone. "Clint, they're my babies."

"I know, Jen. And you know I'll take care of them."

"If something happens…"

"We're not going to discuss that. But you know I

love them and I'm going to take care of them until you get home."

She was crying, hundreds of miles away at a base in Missouri. She was crying, and he couldn't make it better. Sleeping under this roof, in this room, he remembered the other nights she had cried, when they had been kids, and he'd sneaked in to comfort her, to promise he'd make it better.

He had prayed, and she had doubted God even existed.

"I can't make this better, Jen."

"You do make it better." She sniffled, her tears obviously over. "Clint, the Army has been good for me, you know that. And I'm ready to go. I know that I have to go."

"But it won't be easy."

"It's easier knowing that you'll have Timmy and David."

"Do you want to bring them here, or should I come to you?"

A long pause, and he heard the sob she tried to swallow. "I want to see Dad before I go."

He looked out the dirt-covered window at the tree branch scraping against the glass, forced into movement by the wind. "Yes, you should see him. And it would probably be better for them if you got them settled here."

"I'll be down in two days," she whispered, and he knew she was crying. And he felt a lot like he might cry, too.

How was he going to let his little sister go to war, and how was he going to take care of two four-year-old boys? And then there was Willow, added by Janie to the list of people who needed his help.

Covered with dust and bits of hay, Willow walked to the door of the barn to see what the dog, Bell, was barking at. Of course it was Clint Cameron walking down the drive, a tall figure in faded jeans and a blue-gray T-shirt. A baseball cap shaded his face and his arm was still in a sling. She shook her head. Cowboys.

She brushed her hands through her hair and shook the hem of her shirt to rid herself of the hay that had dropped down her neck. Clint didn't spot her. As he walked up the steps to the house, Willow turned back into the barn.

She tossed a few more bales of hay into the back of her truck and cut the wires that held them together. A quick glance at the sky confirmed her suspicions that a spring storm was heading their way. The temperature had dropped ten degrees, dark clouds loomed on the horizon and the leaves of the trees had turned, exposing the underside. A sure sign of rain.

Before the rain hit, she needed to feed her animals. Cattle and horses were waiting and the bulls were bellowing from their pens because they knew it was breakfast time. She opened the feed-room door and stepped inside. The tabby cat that lived in the barn scooted inside and sniffed around in the corners of the room, looking for mice.

Willow grabbed a fifty-pound bag of grain off the pile and carried it out of the room. As she lifted, preparing to drop it into the back of the truck, Clint stepped through the open double doors of the barn and walked toward her.

She dropped the bag of grain into the back and returned to the feed room. When she stepped out with another bag, he was leaning against the side of her truck.

"Need some help?"

Willow tossed the second bag of grain. "I've got it. And I think it's probably better if you give your shoulder a couple of weeks to heal."

"Yeah, probably." He moved away from her truck. "Willow, I'm not trying to take over or anything. Janie told me you might need some help around here, and I'm a pretty good hand. If you don't need help…"

He tilted his head to one side, a soft look in eyes that were more the color of the ocean—gray with a hint of green—rather than just a shade of gray.

She shrugged. "A kid from down the road helps out sometimes. There are times when I can use more help."

"Hey, that's cool. I need to get work done on my own place, so I don't want full-time work right now." He moved away from her truck. "I wanted to see if you had some tools I could borrow."

"Tools."

He nodded. "To borrow."

"Yes, I know, I heard." She sighed, pushing down the insecurity his presence brought out in her. "Tell me what you need and I'll find them for you."

"It looks like rain, so I thought I'd pull a tarp over a section of the roof of my place. There are a couple of spots that look like they might leak."

"How are you going to climb a ladder?"

"I can handle it."

"I can give you a ride to your place." Willow

pointed to a toolbox in the corner of the feed room. "See if I have what you need."

As he dug through the tools, she finished loading the grain. He stepped back out of the feed room and set the metal box in the back of her truck with a brown-paper bag of nails left over from one of her own repair jobs.

"You've done a lot with this place. When did you build this barn?" He leaned against the side of her truck, his baseball cap pushed back, giving her full view of his eyes. Eyes that flashed with a smile that for a moment put her at ease.

"I had the barn built two years ago. The fences—" white vinyl that always looked clean "—we put up last year."

"It looks good." He was smiling, and then he laughed a little. "Just seems like an odd choice."

"White vinyl fences?" She smiled, because she knew what he meant. Some men had a problem, a hang-up, with a woman raising bucking bulls.

"No, you, here, raising bulls. I seem to remember that you grew up in Europe."

That was part of the story. She didn't feel the need to tell him everything. She closed the door to the feed room and turned to face him.

"I did, other than a few summer visits to see Janie, but I love living in the country. And I love raising these bulls."

"I can help you feed before you run me over to my place."

"If you want, you can help." She walked to the driver's side of the truck. When she got in, he was opening the door on the passenger's side. "Did one of those guys drive your truck home this morning?"

"My neighbor, Jason Bradshaw's sister, drove it home."

She nodded, her gaze settling on his shoulder. "Do you need to see a doctor?"

"No, I know the drill. It'll be sore a few days, and then it won't."

She shifted into first gear and eased away from the barn. Her bulls were in the field behind the building. She had smaller pens for her "problem children" and a pen for calves that were being weaned. The cows that were expecting she kept in the main pasture with her horses.

Brad had done one thing for her in their divorce that she hadn't had in their marriage. He'd given her freedom in the form of a hefty divorce settlement. For the first time in her life she was her own person. Other than Janie's motherly advice, no one told her what to do. Not anymore. No one made decisions for her.

There was no one to walk out on her.

"I'm impressed with what you've done here, but I guess I still don't get it. You could have raised horses."

"I could have done something safe?" She smiled at the hint of red coloring his cheeks. "Years ago I went to a bull ride with Aunt Janie. I've been hooked ever since. It just seemed like the right choice."

It made her feel strong.

"It seems to fit you."

She smiled at the compliment.

"Thank you." She eased the truck through the gate of the first pen and stopped. "I'll get in the back of the truck and feed, if you can drive? Just ease down this lane next to the fence and stop at the feeders."

"I can do that."

As she slid out of the truck, he moved across the seat behind the wheel. She climbed into the back of the truck and used a pocketknife to slit the top of a bag of grain. As the truck slowed and pulled close to the feeder, she dumped the grain and the cows trotted forward, ready for breakfast.

The rain started to fall just as they were finishing. Willow jumped down from the back of the truck and climbed into the passenger side. Rain dripped from her hat and she rubbed her arms to chase away the chill. Clint reached for the heater and turned it up a few degrees.

"Wow, this is going to be bad." She looked up at the dark clouds rolling across the Oklahoma sky. "And you have a leaky roof."

"I do at that."

So softly spoken, she barely caught the words. For the past few months she'd been telling herself it was her imagination. But now she needed to face the truth. Words were fuzzy, and there were times that she couldn't hear a conversation on her cell phone, or even a person at her side.

Progressive hearing loss, the doctor had told them so many years ago. In the beginning it had been so mild, no one noticed, not really. Sometimes kids don't listen, that's how they had interpreted her behavior.

Progressive, but for years the change had been gradual, nearly unnoticeable. Now the changes to her hearing were very noticeable.

Why now?

She closed her eyes, and when she opened them, he was watching. Willow managed a smile and nodded in the direction of the house.

"We'll go in and have a cup of tea with Janie. Maybe the rain will stop."

"Sounds good." He pulled the truck to a stop in front of the long, log-sided ranch house.

Rain poured down, drenching them as they hurried up the steps to the covered front porch. Janie opened the door, handing them each a towel.

"Dry your hair."

Willow took off her hat and wiped her face and then ran the towel through her hair. "We were on our way to fix Clint's roof."

Thunder crashed and the rain shifted, blowing onto the porch. Janie opened the door and motioned them inside. With the rain hitting the metal roof of the porch, it was impossible to hear.

Inside the rain was muffled, and ceiling fans brushed cooler air through the room. Willow shivered again.

"Clint will have to stay in the foreman's house." Janie pointed for them to wipe their feet on the rug. "When it stops raining, Willow can take you over to get your stuff."

"I have a house, Janie."

"You can't live in that place. The roof leaks, the porch is falling in and it'll be weeks before the power company gets out to run new lines." Janie shot Willow a look, one that made her wish she could glance away and not hear what her aunt was about to say. "Tell him to stay, Willow. You need the help, and he can't live in that house."

Willow sat down on the old church pew Janie had bought from an antique store. She kicked off her boots and slid them under the seat. Standing across from her, Clint held on to the door frame and pulled off his boots.

"The foreman's house is in good shape. Janie even keeps it clean. The furniture isn't the best..."

"I'm not worried about the furniture."

Janie smiled. "There, it's all settled."

"Right." Willow smiled, hoping that was a good enough answer. But it changed everything. It put Clint Cameron firmly in her life.

She followed her aunt into the kitchen, lured by the smell of coffee and something baking in the oven. Clint followed.

Janie continued to talk as she washed a few dishes. Willow poured herself a cup of coffee and listened, but she knew she was missing pieces of the conversation. The plan included Clint at the ranch in the foreman's house, and Willow letting him help with the bulls, and with the driving when they went out of town.

Clint, his stance casual as he leaned against the kitchen counter, shot Willow an apologetic smile. When Janie turned away for a brief moment, he signed that he was sorry. And she didn't know what to do with that gesture, that moment.

It wasn't easy, to smile, to let it go. After all of this time, building a new life, his presence made her feel vulnerable, weak.

Weak in a way that settled in her knees and made her want to tell him secrets on a summer night. She sighed and walked out of the room, away from gray eyes that distracted and away from the memories of long-forgotten dreams.

Clint set his tea glass on the table. He didn't want to follow Willow Michaels out the door, but he couldn't let her walk away. This was the pattern of his life. There had been the cheerleader in high school who had been hiding abuse with a smile, and he'd found her crying. The girl down the road who had been planning to run away from home when she found out she was pregnant.

He followed Willow to the hall where she was putting her boots back on. She looked up, mascara smeared from the rain and her hair hanging over her shoulders, still damp. She smiled as he sat down next to her.

"I'm not trying to hijack your life." He signed as he whispered, because he didn't want Janie to overhear and misinterpret.

"I know." She pulled on her second boot and sat back. "I just need for you to know that I'm not incapable of doing this by myself. I don't mind you living here, or even helping out."

"I know that." He glanced at his watch. "I have to visit my dad. But I need to talk to you about something."

"Follow me out to the barn. I need to check on a young bull that I have there. He has a cut on his leg. I think he got into some old barbed wire."

He nodded and reached for his boots. As he put them on, Willow walked into the kitchen. He could hear her telling Janie that she was going to check on a bull, and then she'd drive him back to his place to get his truck.

A few minutes later they walked out the door. The sun was peeking out from behind clouds, and the rain had slowed to a mist. The breeze caught the sweet scent of wild roses, and it felt good to be home.

The dog, Bell, ran from the barn and circled them, stopping right in front of Willow before rolling over to have her belly rubbed. Willow leaned to pet the animal and then she turned her attention back to him.

"So, what did you need to talk about?"

"My nephews."

"You have nephews?"

"Twins, they're four years old." He stopped, rubbing a shoulder that hurt like crazy, thanks to the rain and sleeping on the floor. "My sister is being sent to Iraq."

"Clint, I'm sorry." Her voice was soft, her accent something indiscernible with only a hint of Oklahoma.

"She wants me to take them while she's gone."

Her gaze drifted away from him, and she nodded. Shadows flickered in her eyes and he wondered what put them there? Him? The boys? Something from her own life? What made a woman like her give up everything and move to Oklahoma?

Maybe she'd found what she was looking for here, with Janie, and cattle? He could understand that. He'd lived in cities, small towns, and here, on land that had been in his family for nearly one hundred years. He preferred this place to any other.

"It won't be easy," she spoke in quiet tones, "for any of you."

"No, it won't. But I wanted to make sure it's okay with you. Now there will be me *and* two little boys underfoot."

She smiled. "Of course it's okay. We'll do whatever we can to help you out."

"I appreciate that." He headed for the barn, following her, and still wondering what had put the shadows in her eyes.

But he didn't have time to think about it, to worry about it. He had to think about his dad, and now about Jenna and the boys.

Chapter Three

Clint walked through the halls of the nursing home, not at all soothed by the green walls that were probably meant to keep people calm. Even with his dad here and in bad health, Clint still felt like the kid that never knew what to expect. That came from years of conditioning. His dad had been the kind of drunk that could be happy and boisterous one minute, and angry enough to hurt someone the next.

As much as he wanted to convince himself that the past didn't matter, it did. And forgiving mattered, too. Forgiving was something a person decided to do.

He'd made his decision a long time ago. He'd made his decision on his knees at the front of the little country church he'd gone to as a kid. He'd found faith, grabbing hold of promises that made sense when nothing else had.

But being back here brought back a ton of feelings, memories of being the kid in school who never had a new pair of jeans or a pair of shoes without holes.

He'd always been the kid whose parents didn't show up for programs or games.

He reminded himself that he wasn't that kid. Not now. He had moved on. He had finished college. He had worked his way up in the sport of bull riding. He hadn't made a lot of money, but at least he had something to show for his life.

His attention returned to the halls of the nursing home, sweet old people sitting in chairs next to the doors to their rooms, hoping that someone would stop and say hello. A few of them spoke, remembering him from a long time ago, or from his visit last week.

His own father sometimes remembered him, and sometimes didn't.

"Well, there you are." Today was a day his dad remembered.

"Dad, how are you?" Clint grabbed the handles of the wheelchair and pushed his dad into the room.

"I didn't say I wanted to come in here."

"I don't want to stand in the hall." Clint sat on the bed with the quilted bedspread and raggedy stuffed elephant that one of Jenna's boys had left for their granddad, even though their granddad rarely acknowledged their presence.

"So, did you find a job?" his dad quizzed as his trembling hand reached for a glass of water.

Clint picked up the glass and filled it from the pitcher on the table. He eased it into his dad's hand. It was full and a little sloshed out. Clint wiped it up with a napkin and sat back down on the bed.

"I have a job. I'm a bull rider. And I'm going to work for Janie."

"That old woman? Why would you work for her?"

Clint glanced out the small window that let in dim afternoon light shadowed by the dark clouds of another storm. He had to shrug off his dad's comments, the same comments he'd always made about Janie.

There were questions Clint would like to ask now. Did his dad really dislike Janie, or was he just embarrassed that her money had put food on their table and clothes on their backs? He breathed deep and let go of the anger.

Too many years had gone by to remind his father of that time, and to hurt him with the truth that would have sounded like accusations. He stood and walked to the window. Behind him his dad coughed.

"I could use a drink."

Clint shrugged but didn't turn away from the window, and the view of someone's hayfield. A tractor sat abandoned in the middle of the field, half the hay cut and the other half still standing. Something must have broken on the tractor. Not that it mattered. But for a moment he needed to think about something other than the past, and his dad still needing a drink, even with his liver failing.

"Where's your sister? Is she home from school yet?"

His dad had slipped into the past, too.

Clint turned, shaking his head as he sat down on the bed. It was easy to forgive a man who was broken. The surprising thing was that he even felt compassion.

"Dad, Jenna is in Missouri. She's going to Iraq."

"Why would she do that?"

"She's in the Army." He took the water glass from

his dad and set it on the table. "Dad, do you remember? Jenna is twenty-seven. She has two little boys."

"She shouldn't have had them without a father. She should have married that boy."

"He didn't ask." Clint had to fight back a remaining shard of anger over that situation. The ramblings of an old man he could overlook. The past could be forgiven. His sister being hurt, that was something he still had to work on.

"What's your sister going to do with those boys?"

"I'm going to take care of them."

His dad laughed. "You? How are you going to take care of two little boys? Do you even have a job, other than working for Janie?"

"I'm helping her niece with the bucking bulls she raises."

His dad's eyes widened at that and then narrowed as he smiled. "Are you in love with her? I imagine she's way out of your league."

How could one conversation reduce him from grown man to a sixteen-year-old kid teaching the judge's daughter to ride the horse she'd gotten for her birthday? *Way out of your league* must have been the statement that took him back.

"No, Dad, I'm not in love with Willow Michaels. She needs help, and I need a job."

"I need to take a nap, and you need to find out why Jenna didn't come home on the bus. She hasn't even fed the chickens."

"Okay, Dad, I'll go check on her." Clint stood, towering over his dad's frail body. Before he left, he leaned and hugged the old man who had hurt them all so much.

Forgiving had been taken care of. Forgetting was getting easier.

Now he had to go home, to the foreman's house and get it ready for the boys. He tried not to think about that house not being his, or about the home he'd grown up in not being a fit place for two boys.

As he climbed into his truck, he tried, but couldn't quite block the thoughts returning, thoughts of Jenna leaving the boys. He tried not to think about her being gone for a year, and what could happen in that time. And he tried not to think about living a dirt trail away from Willow Michaels—*who was way out of his league.*

Six in the morning, Willow was barely awake, and as she glanced out the kitchen window she saw two little boys run across the lawn, heading toward the barn. Two days ago Clint had asked her if she would be okay with the twins living on the farm, and now they were here. She hadn't thought about them being here so soon.

The bigger problem now was that the boys were running for the pen that held her big old bull, Dolly. She set her glass of water down on the counter and hurried for the front door. Janie, sitting in the living room, looked up from her Bible, brows raised over the top of her reading glasses.

"Is there a fire?"

"No, but there are two little boys heading for Dolly's pen."

Dolly was her first bull. At bull-riding events they called him Skewer, because it was easier on a cowboy's ego to get thrown from a "Skewer" than a

"Dolly." Gentle or not, she didn't want the two little boys in that pen.

As she ran across the lawn, she glanced toward the foreman's house. A small sedan was parked out front, the same one she'd seen easing down the driveway yesterday. No one was outside. The boys, silvery-blond hair glinting in the sun, weren't slowing down. They obviously had a plan they wanted to carry out before the adults realized they'd escaped.

Willow hurried after them, rocks biting into her bare feet. If she didn't catch them in time… She shook off that thought, that image. She would get to them in time.

"Don't go in there," she shouted, cupping her mouth with her hands, hoping the words would carry and not get swept away on the early morning breeze.

The boys stopped, turning sun-browned faces in her direction, sweet faces with matching Kool-Aid mustaches. They were armed with paper airplanes and toy soldiers.

Willow's heart ka-thumped against her ribs. Fear and remnants of loss got tangled inside her. She had to stop, take a deep breath, and move forward. The way she'd been moving forward for the last five years, one step at a time. Rebuilding her life.

The boys were watching her, waiting.

She reached them and they stared up at her. Their eyes were wide and gray, familiar because up close they looked a lot like Clint Cameron.

Their gazes shot past her. She turned as Clint and a young woman walked out of the foreman's house. The two, brother and sister, paused on the front porch and then headed in her direction.

"Uh-oh," one of the boys mumbled and his thumb went to his mouth.

"Don't suck your thumb," the other shoved him with his elbow, pushing him hard enough to knock the slighter-built of the two off-balance.

"You two do know that it isn't safe to go in the barn or around the bulls, right?" Willow knelt in front of them, her heart catching.

They nodded. The smaller boy tried to hide the thumb in his mouth by covering it with his other hand. Their twin gazes slid from her face to something behind her. *Clint?*

She stood and turned, ready to greet him and his sister. The little boys scurried to the side of their mother, their hands reaching for hers.

"Clint." Willow didn't know what else to say. She didn't know that she wanted to say more.

"Willow, these two rowdy guys are my nephews. This is my sister, Jenna."

Jenna, brown hair streaked with blond highlights and petite frame clothed in shorts and a T-shirt, held out her hand. "Nice to meet you. And I'm really thankful to you for giving Clint a place to keep the boys."

"You're welcome, Jenna. We're glad we can do it."

Willow squatted to put herself at eye level with the two little boys, matching bookends with identical looks of sadness and fear. Their mother was leaving. Willow fought the urge to pull them close, to promise that everything would be okay.

She thought about her own fears, her own longings. It all paled in comparison to what this family was going through.

"My name is Willow. What are your names?"

"Timmy," the bigger of the two pushed at his brother again, "and this is Davie."

"David," the boy mumbled, looking down at the ground.

Insecure? She understood insecure, and how it felt to not know where she was supposed to be, or what she should do.

Janie had joined them, and she was hugging Clint's sister, holding her tight for a long minute while the boys held tight to their mother. When Janie turned back around, tears shimmered on the surface of her eyes.

"Jenna doesn't have a thing to worry about, does she, Willow? We'll be here to help Clint with the boys until she can make it home."

Willow smiled at the boys again. Just little boys, and they were going to have to say goodbye to their mother. She'd been ten when her parents sent her away, forcing her to leave their home in Europe and attend a special school in the States.

She knew how hard it was to let go of what was familiar. She also knew that Jenna's heart had to be breaking, because nothing hurt a mother worse than letting go of a child.

"Of course we'll help." Willow ignored Clint, because she couldn't look into his eyes. She couldn't acknowledge, not even to herself, how hard this was going to be.

Janie smiled, her brown eyes soft. Janie knew.

Time to escape. Willow ruffled the blond hair of the smaller boy, and he looked up at her, gray eyes seeking something, probably answers. She didn't have any. She could pray, but a child didn't want to hear that, because he wouldn't understand what God could do. At his age, the little guy just wanted his mom to stay with him.

"I need to get my shoes and get some work done." Willow smiled at Jenna, who seemed unsure and probably needed reassurance. "Don't worry about the boys, or Clint. We have plenty of room here."

"Thank you." And then Jenna hugged her.

"I'm sure we'll see you before you go." Willow pulled away, from Jenna and the situation. "Boys, remember, stay out of the pens."

Clint started to follow her, but she stopped him. "I can handle this. You spend time with your sister."

"You're sure?"

Positive. What she needed was time alone, to think about how her life had just changed. What she didn't need was Clint Cameron invading space she had carved out for herself. And what she couldn't do was look into his gray eyes, eyes like those of his nephews, but seeing so much more.

A few hours later Jenna drove down the road, and Clint could only pray that God would keep her safe. Janie had the boys, feeding them cookies and drying their tears. He was going in search of Willow to see if she needed help with anything, and knowing she would probably say that she didn't. She had a way of handling things.

Country music blared from the office at the end of the barn. Clint peeked around the corner of the office door. She wasn't there. An empty soda can sat on her desk, along with the wrapper from a chocolate bar, more than one. He smiled, thinking of her sitting there with music blaring, eating chocolate. What did that do for women?

So much for the calm, cool facade that she'd fooled them with in the bull-riding world. He now knew her weakness. Ms. Calm-Cool-and-Collected ate chocolate and didn't like to share her personal space.

That knowledge didn't help him out a bit. He was definitely in her personal space, and with no way out.

He found her in the arena, standing on a platform above a bull and strapping a training dummy to his back while she talked into the headset of her cell phone. Her brows drew together, and her lips tightened into a frown.

Obviously bad news.

He approached from her side, making sure she knew he was heading her way. She nodded and turned away, maybe to open the chute for the bull, maybe to avoid him. The gate on the chute opened, and the bull turned to face out, encouraged by the woman above his chute. A teenager, slight, and quick on his feet, stood in the arena, keeping the bull in a spin.

"Looks good. How old?" Clint leaned against the post next to Willow.

Her hand slid up her ear.

"I'm sorry?" She smiled.

"The bull looks good. How old is he?"

"He's two. I'm not sure if he's going to make it. He doesn't like to buck."

"Do you need my help? I can open the gate, strap on the dummy?"

A pointed look at his shoulder. "I don't think you should."

"Got it." Help not needed. He had to find his place here. He had to apologize. "I'm sorry about the boys this morning."

"They were being boys, Clint. They're fine." She leaned against the rail of the scaffolding next to the chute where the next bull was waiting. Her expression softened, because it was about two little boys. "How are they, though?"

"They're okay." He remembered their tears when Jenna left, and his own. They were all fine. And scared. "At least they're here with me. We'll get through."

"If I can help…"

"You have."

Another one of those looks he didn't understand, and shadows in her blue eyes that could probably convince a man that she needed to be held. But he knew better than to step into her life. There was a world of difference between them.

She was designer clothes and gourmet meals. He was fast food and the clearance rack at Wal-Mart. And he liked his life. For the moment he looked a lot happier with this discount life than she looked with her top-drawer existence.

She turned away from him to watch the bull come out of the chute and then she shook her head. "Brian, run him through the gate, and we'll get him something to eat. Bring Wooly in next."

"Willow, if I'm going to live here, I really want to help out."

"Have you been to the doctor yet?" She shot a pointed look at his shoulder, his arm still in a sling.

"Not yet. It's an injury I've had before, and I know what to do."

"So, you'll be ready to ride bulls at the next event. Or are you going to call and let them know that you'll be a no-show."

"You know I can't do that and stay on tour."

"Then go to the doctor. If you can't afford…"

"I can afford it."

He sure didn't need insults and charity.

"I'm sorry." She picked up the training dummy that Brian had tossed onto the platform and leaned to put it on the new bull. "We'll work together. I don't know specific jobs to give you. I know each day what I need to get done. And if something unexpected comes up, I fit it into my schedule. I guess we start with you helping us with feeding time."

Her phone rang and she smiled an apology and stepped away from him. At least now he knew how he stood, at the ranch, and in her world. He was one of the unexpected things she was fitting into her life.

"I'm sorry, I can't hear you." Willow walked away, knowing that Clint wasn't the kind of guy to purposely listen in on a conversation, but knowing that if he heard, he would have questions.

The caller on the other end apologized for the bad connection. She closed her eyes, wishing it really was a problem with the phone. But the bad connection had nothing to do with cell service.

She glanced in Clint's direction and saw him talking to Brian. Distracted, she had to gather her thoughts and listen to the caller as he told her something about a bull she had for sale.

"Sir, could you call me back on my home phone? Or perhaps e-mail." She held her breath, praying he'd say yes and wondering if God heard such selfish prayers.

It wasn't selfish, not really. Because God did understand her fear. She'd talked to Him about it quite a bit lately.

"I'll e-mail." The caller came through clearly for a moment, and she thanked him. She needed a break, a real break, the kind that meant things going smoothly for a few days.

Just a few days, time to gather herself and figure out her next move. She turned, facing Brian and Clint with a smile that felt strong. But eye contact with Clint wasn't helping her feel strong. It was the way his lips quirked in a half grin and lines crinkled around his eyes.

He had a toothpaste-commercial smile that could make a girl dream of moonlit nights and roses. She no longer had those dreams.

"Where are the boys?" Neutral ground that felt safe, safer than holding his gaze.

"Janie is fixing them grilled cheese for supper, after she's already filled them up with cookies." He leaned to hold the dummy for Brian. "We're going to the chili supper and carnival at church tonight."

"Yes, she told me. That's a good way to distract the boys. The next few days are going to be hard for them."

"She told me you're not going."

She wondered if he understood what it meant to invade someone's personal space. It wasn't always done physically. Sometimes it was done emotionally, with nosy questions and interference. Maybe he didn't care?

"No, I'm not going."

"Because…"

She stepped away from him. "Because I don't like chili."

Because she didn't like crowded places with too many conversations, explanations for people who talked in quiet tones, and curious glances from those who saw the hearing aids.

She loved bull riding, where people respected her and curiosity didn't matter, because she had proven herself. She loved her non-hearing friends in Tulsa, because with them she could be herself.

He didn't appear to be giving up. He had stepped closer and wore a persuasive half grin. She remembered him smiling like that when she'd been thirteen and he'd only been a year or so older. She had dreamed of that smile for a long, long time, wondering what it would be like to fall in love with a cowboy.

She shook off the old memories and listened to what he was saying now. Now, sixteen years and several rejections later, her heart had been broken so many times it was held together with duct tape.

"Everyone likes chili. Or at least they like it when they know there will be dozens of desserts, and the money is going to help the church youth group."

Willow liked arguing less than she liked chili. Worse than that, she disliked the feeling that someone was trying to make plans for her. "I'm not going, Clint. I'll give you a check for the youth group."

"Willow, I wasn't trying…"

She sighed, because she knew that he wasn't trying, that he hadn't intended to take over. "I know you weren't. Have a good time tonight. Make sure you guys close up and turn off the lights when you're done in here."

Clint reached for her arm, and she knew he wanted to say more. He didn't. Instead he smiled and let his hand drop to his side, as if he understood.

As she walked across the drive to the house she saw the boys through the window. They were so young, and so brave. Their mother was brave.

The warm smell of grilled cheese and fresh coffee greeted her as she walked through the door of the house. She kicked off her boots and headed for the kitchen, stockinged feet on hardwood.

The boys looked up from cups of tomato soup, red liquid dripping from their chins. She smiled, but she wanted to hug them tight. The little one, David, not Davie, gave her a tremulous smile that threaded its way into her heart. The bigger of the two, Timmy, just frowned.

"I heard that the two of you had cookies. Were they good?" Willow kneeled next to the table, putting herself at eye level with the two children.

They nodded and both took another bite of their sandwiches, dripping cheese as they pulled the bread away. Grilled cheese and tomato soup, Aunt Janie's cure for everything, including broken hearts.

"Want something…" Janie's words faded out as she moved away.

Willow turned, shooting her aunt a questioning gaze. The words had blended with the radio and the dishwasher's low rumble.

"I'm sorry, Willow. Do you want to eat, or are you going with us?"

"I'll eat with the boys." Willow smiled at the two and stood up, her legs protesting her squatting next to the table.

"The boys are going with us." Janie smiled. "But they don't like chili."

"I don't blame them."

Janie frowned. "It isn't chili you're avoiding, it's people."

"And lectures."

Janie wiped wet hands on a kitchen towel, her frown growing. "Willow, are you okay?"

"Of course I am."

The house vibrated with footsteps, heavy steps. Willow turned as Clint walked into the room, his wide smile directed at the boys.

Janie handed her a bowl, and Willow turned toward the table. Clint had taken a seat with the boys. He had a glass of iced tea and a cookie.

"You have a cow that's about to have a calf," he said after taking a drink of his tea.

"I know. I've been checking on her every few hours."

"Is this her first calf?"

"Second."

"She's young."

Willow exhaled and pretended she didn't have an answer for that. He set his glass down and she looked up, knowing he wasn't going to let it go.

"Yes, she's young. The first time she got into the wrong pen." She wouldn't go further, not with two little boys at the table.

"Maybe I should stay home, in case she gets down on you. You might have to pull the calf."

Like she didn't know that. She gave him a pointed look and lifted a spoon of soup to her mouth. After taking a bite she set the spoon down.

"I can handle it, Clint. I know how to pull a calf. I know how to take care of my cows."

"I was just offering."

"If I can't handle it, I have a good vet." She took in a breath and smiled. "You need to take the boys to the carnival at church. I can handle this."

He raised his hand and smiled. "Got it."

Timmy laughed and David looked worried.

"Guys, don't ever argue with a woman who has her mind made up." Clint picked up a napkin and wiped grilled cheese crumbs off David's chin.

Willow smiled, because how could she not? And when she looked up, he winked. Just like that, he undid everything.

Chapter Four

Clint threw another plastic ring around another soda bottle and took the two-liter cola that the girl handed him. The low rumble of a diesel engine caught his attention. He turned and watched as Willow pulled into the parking lot of the church. She backed the red extended cab into a space and cut the engine.

And he smiled. Unexpected. She was obviously a woman who always did the unexpected. He liked that about her. And he liked the fact that she was here, and she had made it pretty clear that this was the last place she wanted to be.

But she was getting out of her truck, and she was smiling. At him. That smile made him want to win big stuffed bears for her and carry cotton candy. It made him want to…

Rescue a woman who didn't want or need to be rescued.

"Uncle Clint, isn't that Miss Willow?" Timmy tugged on the sling and Clint grimaced.

"Yeah, buddy, that's her. You boys stay with Janie, and I'll bring her over here."

Because he wanted just a few minutes alone with her. A smile shouldn't do that to a guy. It shouldn't make him want to take her off by the creek, alone, for a walk in the dim glow of early evening. A smile shouldn't do that to a man, but it did.

That smile made him want to forget that she was a princess and he had nothing to offer but a crumbled old farm and a lot of dreams.

She stopped at the edge of the parking lot and waited for him. She was tall and gorgeous, in jeans and a peasant top, her hair in a ponytail.

"Imagine seeing you here." He grinned and hoped that she would smile again. She did.

"I decided that if the boys could do this, so could I." She glanced past him to the boys. "They're really brave."

"They are." He started to offer his hand and reconsidered. "Stick with me, it won't be that bad."

Had he just said that? From the amused look on her face, he knew he had. He pushed his hat down on his head a little and laughed.

"Stick with you, huh?"

"Something like that. I'll even hold your hand."

"I'm a big girl. I won't get lost." She looked past him again, and she didn't take his hand. "The boys are heading this way. I'm really here for them, not you."

"Ouch, that hurts a guy's ego."

She turned to face him, and he knew she hadn't heard. He repeated and she smiled.

"I think your ego will be fine."

"You're probably right." And on the chance that she would hold his hand, he held it out again, palm up. She took it, her fingers grasping his and he felt like he might be her lifeline.

When they reached the twins, she let go of his hand and reached for the boys. They moved to her, and for a minute it made him really believe they might be okay. He hadn't expected that she'd be the one to make him feel that way.

"What is there to do around here?" she asked David, always the quiet twin, always seeking assurance.

"I like the pony ride and…"

"The big bouncing castle." Timmy grabbed her hand.

"Pony ride first." She put an arm around each and smiled at her aunt. Watching her with the boys, Clint wanted to be four again and small enough for ponies and the moonwalk.

"What about me?" he asked, hurrying to catch up. Willow glanced back at him.

"You're too big for the moonwalk."

"I'm not too big."

"Uh-huh." Timmy had hold of Willow's hand. "And you promised us cotton candy."

"Cotton candy, of course. And I have a pile of prizes I need to put in the truck."

Willow stopped, still holding on to the boys. "I'll take them on the pony ride."

"Sounds good." He didn't really want to walk away. He wanted to stay with her, with the boys, because she was easy to be around.

But he had been dismissed, and the boys got to

hang out with Willow. He felt a little cheated as he walked off with nothing but stuffed animals and bottles of cola.

Willow lifted David onto the back of a brown-and-white spotted pony. He leaned toward her, his gray eyes big. "I'm afraid of horses."

She smiled and wanted to tell him that it was okay, that fear sometimes pushed a person to be strong. He was too little to understand. He only knew that he was afraid.

"I'll stay next to you."

He nodded and then the horse moved a jolting step forward. Little hands grabbed the saddle horn and his mouth tightened into a serious line. Willow patted his arm and winked.

"Pretend he's one of those purple horses in front of the grocery store. They bounce, but they don't move." She kept hold of his arm. "He can't go anywhere but in a circle. And if he tries, I'll grab you."

"Promise." His voice was soft and she read his lips.

"Promise." She wouldn't let him go.

She searched the crowd for Janie and Clint. Janie had found a group of friends, and they were all sitting under a canopy. She spotted Clint walking in their direction, three sticks of pink cotton candy in his hands.

Even without the cotton candy, he stood out in the crowd. He was a cowboy in faded jeans and a dark-blue polo. His hat shaded his face but didn't hide the smile that she somehow imagined was just for her.

For a moment she was like David on his pony, not afraid, just enjoying the ride.

But what about tomorrow? What about reality?

How long could she go on, pretending everything was fine? How long could she convince herself that she wasn't afraid? Who would catch her?

She knew the answer to that. She would catch herself.

"Could we ride again?" Timmy yelled from his horse.

"One more time." She pulled tickets from her pocket and handed them to John, a neighbor who was donating his time and his ponies for the youth group to raise money for a mission trip.

He took the tickets and said something to each of the boys about being cowboys like their uncle.

Clint walked along the outside of the portable fence that circled the ponies. "Cotton candy?"

He held one out to her. The pony turned his head and nipped, wanting the sugar more than Willow wanted it. David laughed, a real laugh. He hunched, and his shoulders shook. Willow laughed, too, and then Timmy was laughing. The pony didn't care; she wanted the sugar and the bar that kept her going in her circle clanked as she stretched out her neck.

The boys continued to laugh, and Willow wiped tears from her eyes. When she looked up, Clint was watching, his dimpled grin now familiar.

The ride ended. She helped David down. Timmy hopped to the ground, a little cowboy in his jeans, boots and a plaid shirt. Janie and Clint were waiting for them at the gate. The boys took their cotton candy.

"I'd like to take the boys in to have their pictures taken," Janie announced. "Sandy is in there with her camera."

"Sounds like a great idea." Clint held out the last

cotton candy and Willow took it, surprised that it was for her. "Do you mind if I take Willow for a buggy ride?"

Willow swallowed a sticky-sweet bite of cotton candy, remembering why she liked it so much, and also why she hadn't eaten it in years. "Clint, I have to leave. I wanted to spend a little time with the boys, but I have to get home to that cow."

Under the wide brim of his white cowboy hat, his brows arched in question. He didn't believe her. Of course he didn't. For a moment, she didn't believe herself. She had come down here for the boys, and then for other reasons. Maybe because she wanted to walk with a cowboy and eat cotton candy?

"I really do have to go. She's close to having that calf, and I don't want to lose either of them."

"Of course." He smiled and she remembered that his smile was the reason she'd jumped in her truck and driven down to the church.

She averted her eyes and glanced down at the boys, each holding cotton candy that was nearly gone. "You two have fun."

They nodded but took another bite of spun sugar. They wouldn't sleep for a week. She laughed a little and turned to face Janie and Clint.

"I'll see you all later." She made her escape. It was definitely an escape, she realized that. She was running from someone who made her feel too much.

And she had more reasons for running than he could possibly know.

Clint woke up at daybreak, the sun just peeking over the flat, Oklahoma horizon. He looked in at the boys, still sound asleep. They'd stayed late at the church, where the boys had played games, throwing rings around soda bottles and darts at balloons. They now had a cabinet full of root beer, and a bag of cheap toys and stuffed animals, all prizes from the games they'd played after Willow left.

At least the cow had been more than just an excuse. The proof was the spindly-legged calf standing next to her momma in the corral next to the barn.

Sometimes he wondered if she gave anyone a chance to really know her. Or was it just about him? He could still remember her peeking through the curtains all those years ago, hiding. Embarrassed?

He put on a pot of coffee and then went to wake the boys. David was already stirring, his eyes blinking open a few times and then catching with Clint's.

How did he do this? How could he be a parent when he didn't have any experience, other than having been an older brother? Doubts hung out in the pit of his stomach when he thought about it.

Clint kneeled next to the twin bed and smiled at the little boy, a child with his sister's dimples. Clint closed his eyes, praying for them to get through the next year, and praying for Jenna to stay safe.

She had to come home to the boys. They all needed her. He included. David leaned on one scraped elbow, his eyes sad. Clint mussed the kid's hair and tried to pretend they were all okay, and that he knew how to be the parent they needed.

"How about cereal for breakfast?" Clint asked as David sat up, rubbing sleep-filled eyes.

"We like pancakes," Timmy's groggy voice said from the other bed.

Clint turned, smiling at the other twin. "I don't think I have stuff for pancakes, Timmy."

"Aunt Janie does. She said so. Last night she said—" and he cleared his throat to make the point ""—you boys come over in the morning, and I'll whip you up some homemade pancakes.'"

Four years old and a mimic. Clint laughed at the fair imitation.

"Okay, we'll go to Janie's for pancakes." He stood, stiff from squatting, and from too many times landing on a hard-packed dirt arena. "Get dressed, okay?"

"I don't want pancakes." David covered his head with the blanket. "I want my mom."

The words were muffled, but the emotion wasn't, or the slight sob that followed.

Clint stood at the door, his heart squeezing. "I know, buddy. But she'll be home as soon as she can get here."

In a year. One year of her children's lives, lost. One year of missing milestones. One year of him worrying, and praying she'd be safe.

He smiled at Timmy. "Help your brother get ready."

One year of life on hold for all of them.

A short time later, he walked out of Janie's and across the road to the barn. The boys were eating pancakes, and Janie was hugging them, pretending the tears in her eyes were from dust.

He walked through the large double doors at the front of the barn and was greeted by silence. Light poured out from the open door of Willow's office.

He stopped at the entrance. She stood at the window, looking out over the field. Her forehead rested on the glass of the window and her hands were shoved into the front pockets of her jeans.

After a few minutes, he said her name. She didn't turn, didn't even start. There was no indication that she'd noticed his arrival.

So how did he make his presence known, and keep from scaring her? He stepped up into the room and reached for her, but then pulled back. When she turned, she saw him there. She jumped a little and then exhaled.

"How long have you been here?" Her voice was husky, soft.

"A few minutes. I said your name."

She looked away. He noticed then that the hearing aids she normally wore weren't in sight. That was the reason for the silence, for the lack of music, and why she hadn't heard.

Willow, are you okay? He signed the words, stepping to block her from walking away.

She smiled. "I'm fine."

She sat down on the edge of her desk. "Are you okay?"

And that's how she changed it, making it about him, not her. It wasn't just deflection on her part. He could see in her eyes that she cared, that she wanted to know that he was okay. He was. It was the boys he wasn't so sure about.

"I'm fine."

"I don't think so."

How do they live for a year without their mom? He sat down next to her, signing the words. "Will there come a time when it doesn't hurt so much, when they don't cry because they miss her?"

"I don't know. She's their mom. I can't imagine them not missing her all the time."

Her voice broke and she brushed away a few tears, and he didn't know what to do. He couldn't fix them all. He was barely holding it together for his nephews, barely making life okay for his dad. He knew that they had to be his priority.

He had a bad habit of trying to take care of people, maybe because he'd been taking care of people his whole life.

Willow didn't want or need that from him. He had to remember that, and not get confused about what he was feeling for a woman who was a strange mixture of strength and vulnerability.

The boys. He shook his head. "I can't get David to eat."

"He's heartsick. Maybe ice cream? It's good for fixing a broken heart."

The low rumble of a truck pulling up out front interrupted his thoughts and stopped him from asking about her broken heart. *Are you expecting company?* he signed.

She glanced out the window and groaned. "No, not really."

"Looks like someone is here bright and early. Do you know who it is?" He spoke as he signed because he knew she read lips.

"Not a clue."

She ran a hand through long, blond hair. Tall and slim, she looked strong. In faded jeans and a long-sleeve shirt tucked in, she looked like every other cowgirl that he knew.

And then again, she looked a lot like someone trying to pretend.

"It's probably the man interested in that gray bull. He e-mailed." She admitted as she rummaged through papers on her desk, "I don't remember his name."

"He called yesterday?"

"I asked him to e-mail." She turned off the coffee pot on the desk. "Can you bring the bull up?"

"Do you need for me to talk to him?"

She bit down on her bottom lip and he hated that he had asked. But when she nodded, he no longer regretted. Sometimes accepting help made a person stronger. He wanted to tell her that, but she was walking away, and he couldn't say anything.

Chapter Five

Willow walked out of the house, ready to face the man with the truck, and whatever questions he had for her. Janie had smiled as she left, but she'd been too busy with Timmy and David to ask questions.

At the door to the barn, she paused, giving herself a minute to regain her strength and to feel composed. The shadowy interior of the barn, with the smell of hay and animals blending together, did that for her. She loved hiding here, and praying here.

She loved Oklahoma and its wide openness. Growing up in Frankfurt, Germany, where her father had worked for the government, she had been surrounded by buildings, concrete and the smell of exhaust. Cities were exciting and had an energy all their own.

But living here gave Willow energy. This was her home, and it had always felt like it was where she belonged.

Here she could be the person she wanted to be, not the person others expected her to be. This place wasn't about black-tie dinners, pearls and putting on a smile for society.

At the end of the barn she saw Clint and the owner of the truck. Their stances were casual, but the movement of their hands, the way they faced one another, warned of something less than casual.

Willow approached cautiously, trying to hear their conversation, but the words were lost. Clint turned in her direction, his eyes relayed a warning she didn't get.

"Hello, I'm Willow Michaels." She held her hand out to the man who wasn't a rancher, not in his dark slacks and white button-down shirt.

"Ms. Michaels, I'm with the *Midwest Informer*. We're doing a feature on bulls used in bull riding. We're interested in a woman's point of view."

"I'm not sure…" She shot a look in Clint's direction. His lips had narrowed, and he gave a short shake of his head.

"The article is going to run whether you talk to us or not. We just wanted to give you a fair opportunity to talk about your bulls, and the abuse these animals suffer."

"Abuse?" She glanced again at Clint. His fingers signed for her to be careful.

And the reporter caught the gesture. She saw the light spark in his eyes and he smiled. "Ms. Michaels, you could be the feature of our article. A woman who raises bucking bulls. A disabled woman."

"I'm *not* disabled. And I'm not a feature, Mr.…"

"James Duncan."

"Mr. Duncan, my bulls are not abused. My bulls receive excellent care, the best food and a home where they are prized for their abilities. I have nearly twenty animals that are actively used in bull riding, some in the top arenas, and some in smaller rodeos. Each month they work approximately ten minutes, ten minutes total, and yet they receive the best care. How can that be cruel?"

"They're forced to buck."

"No, they're not forced. If I have a bull that doesn't buck, then I sell him, because bulls either buck or they don't. And my bulls are protected from abuse." She ground out the words, no longer being careful. "The bull-riding community protects their animals, even at the events."

Her hands were shaking, and she knew that her voice had reached a higher octave. The man in front of her continued to smile, and out of the corner of her eye she saw Clint straighten from his relaxed pose, leaning against the barn.

Willow shook her head at him, not wanting him to intervene. He backed up, but he remained tense, like a guard dog about to do damage, and her heart reacted. She nearly smiled at the reporter.

"Mr. Duncan, I believe this interview is over. If you really want the truth, and not a sensationalized spin on my sport, then attend an event with us. Watch how my bulls are treated, and then write the article."

"That's a nice offer, Ms. Michaels, but I have my story."

He walked away, his steps light, as if what he had done didn't matter, as if he was happy with the way things had gone. And Willow was shaking, unable to stop because it did matter. It mattered when someone took away your strength or made you feel like less than a whole person.

She closed her eyes and took a deep breath. Strong arms pulled her close. She stiffened, but he didn't let go. And she didn't want to pull free. She wanted to melt into his embrace, and for just a minute, let herself be protected.

He bent and his cheek, rough and unshaved, brushed hers. His scent, mountain air and pine, teased her senses as his hands rubbed her arms and then slipped down to hold her hands.

"You were amazing."

No, amazing was how it felt to be held by someone who thought she had been strong, when she had really felt like walking away.

Slowly, regrettably, she backed out of his arms. "Now what happens? What story does he think he has that is better than the story of my bulls?"

"The story of you. The story of bulls. Or maybe of us."

"Us?"

He smiled, those gray eyes twinkling with amusement that she didn't get. "Us, because he thought there was an us."

"There is no us. There is no story. He's going to target a sport that I love, and my personal life. And there's nothing I can do about it, or about the rumors that will fly once that magazine comes out."

"No, Willow, there's nothing you can do about it." He shook his head. "I have work to do."

He walked away. A cowboy in faded jeans, scuffed boots, and callused hands that had held her close. His expression as he turned from her had reflected his own pain, and something in his eyes she hadn't understood.

Willow walked into her office and closed the door. She yanked off her hearing aids and threw them in the box, because there were days when it didn't pay to hear.

And days when she feared she would lose her hearing completely.

She sat down in the leather office chair that swallowed her, wrapping around her, but feeling nothing like the arms of a cowboy.

Cowboys didn't understand how weakness felt, or fear. Maybe that wasn't fair. Clint had watched his sister leave for Iraq, leaving behind two little boys. He understood fear.

She bowed her head because God understood her fear. He understood forsaken. She whispered the words of Jesus on the cross, "My God, My God, why hast thou forsaken me."

Forsaken was how she had felt when her parents put her on a plane to Chicago. She had been ten years old, and frightened, but they had decided she needed to attend a private school for hearing-impaired children.

Forsaken was how she felt when her husband told her she couldn't be the wife he needed. He had ended it by telling her he needed a wife that would help his career. A wife who liked to socialize. A wife who didn't embarrass him.

He had picked her best friend to replace her.

Forsaken. But not. Even when she had felt alone, pushed aside, and rejected, God had been there, a prayer away. God hadn't forgotten her. He had a plan. Maybe not her plan, but His plan. And maybe it wouldn't be easy, but she had to convince herself there would be moments of beauty that would make all the pain worth it.

She reached into the box and withdrew the hearing aids, her life since age ten. It had started with meningitis she'd caught as a preschooler, and slowly progressed to severe hearing loss.

And now, now the slow progression was increasing. She slipped the pieces of plastic behind her ears and found the number of her doctor in Tulsa. The way to deal with fear was to confront it, head on.

When she walked out of the barn a short time later she had an appointment with her doctor. His nurse had told her that it was probably nothing.

Laughter carried across the lawn, soft and fluttery. Willow glanced in the direction of the driveway in front of the house. Clint was helping the boys into the truck. They were "three-of-a-kind," and that brought a smile she hadn't felt five minutes ago.

Little David turned and waved his tiny, sun-browned hand. His smile was timid and sweet. Timmy's wave was big, and his smile consumed his face. Sunlight glinted from their silvery-blond hair, and she knew that someday they would be carbon copies of their uncle.

Their uncle, Clint. He turned, a grimace on his face as he tried to smile with Timmy tugging on his left arm, still held to his side in a sling. Two weeks, the doctor had told him. Maybe longer. Not good news for a guy that made his living on the back of a bull.

She walked in their direction, drawn by the boys.

She wanted to hug them. She wanted to promise them that their mother would come home. She wanted to apologize to Clint, but she didn't know what to say.

"Where are you three off to?" She smiled at the boys.

"We've gotta get in some kind of school." Timmy answered as he always did, mimicking the last adult to give him information.

She laughed, knowing that his words were an echo of something Clint had said to them. He had mentioned to her that the twins needed to enroll now for kindergarten in the fall.

"That sounds like fun." Her gaze lingered on David, because the look on his face told her he didn't agree that it would be fun.

"It will be fun." Clint chucked David under the chin, smiling at the child. "And after we enroll, we're going to get ice cream. Want to go with us?"

Willow hadn't expected that. She hadn't expected to be included, and hadn't thought she would want to say yes. The boys were watching her with twin gazes that said they wanted her to go. She looked up, connecting with Clint, and not sure if he really felt the same as the boys.

But the boys wanted her to go. And David needed to eat. She smiled at the twins.

"I could probably use your help." Clint shrugged the shoulder that was still healing. "Sometimes they're hard to hold on to."

Did he really need her help? Maybe not as much as she needed to spend time with Timmy and David, eating ice cream and laughing over silly jokes that children told.

"I'd love to go. Let me tell Janie."

"She isn't here. Her bridge group is meeting."

"Okay, then let me get my purse. If you need me to drive, it might help if I have my license."

"I can drive."

No more arguments or excuses. Willow climbed into the passenger seat of the truck. The boys climbed into the backseat. And then Clint was in the seat next to her, and she looked away. It was easier to glance in the backseat and smile at the boys, both jabbering about ice cream and school, childhood things that were easy and light.

Clint had watched Willow's smile disappear. He had seen the tears shimmering in her eyes. There could have been several reasons. The boys, maybe, or the reporter. Possibly the call he'd overheard her make. He hadn't listened to the entire conversation. He knew she'd called a doctor's office.

Seeing that soft shimmer of tears, and knowing her fear, helped him to push aside his anger with her, or whatever he had felt when she pulled away from him, saying things that made him think that she had her own thoughts about being out of his league. She didn't want rumors spread about the two of them.

"My aunt isn't really meeting with her bridge group." She smiled now. He took his attention off the road for just a second, long enough to see that she'd pulled herself together.

"Really?" He didn't want to get in the middle of this mess.

"She wants to move to Florida with her friends." Willow fiddled with a ring on her right hand. "She thinks I don't know. But a friend of hers was excited about the plan and let it slip."

"Willow, she doesn't want to hurt you."

"And I don't want to hurt her by keeping her here."

He wanted to ignore this side of her that cared about the happiness of others. He had already learned too much about Willow Michaels. He had learned that she was easy to like, and easy to care about. And he had a dad in a nursing home, and two boys to raise for the next year. He didn't need more complications.

She could be that and more.

"I'll miss her, Clint. But she isn't hurting me by doing what she has always wanted to do. When I was a teenager, she talked about retiring to Florida someday. She wants to go with friends. She wants to learn to play golf, and figure out what shuffleboard is all about."

"Does anyone really understand shuffleboard?"

"Someone must."

The day had started with a reporter ambushing her, and now they were talking about shuffleboard. She was a survivor. They had that in common.

"She's afraid you'll sell the bulls if she leaves."

He glanced away from the road, to see how she took that news. She was smiling.

"She's always looking out for me. When my parents shipped me off to Chicago, Janie met me at the airport. They didn't ask her to. She found out what they'd done, and she showed up without telling them. She didn't want a little girl to get off the plane alone, in a strange city, to be met by strangers."

"She bought our Christmas presents and put us through college." Clint smiled at the memory. "She didn't believe in storing up, for herself, 'treasure on earth, when there were little treasures down the road, needing so much.'"

"I will miss her if she goes." She was looking out the truck window. "But I won't sell the bulls. I'll figure out a way to make it work."

"Tell her that."

"I'll tell her." A short pause, and then she laughed. "That's why she wants you working on the ranch. She's making sure I have someone to help me. I was afraid it was all about matchmaking."

"She's always trying to protect the people she cares about." But he had sort of thought it might be about matchmaking, too.

They drove toward Grove and past the house that Clint still planned to remodel. Soon. Clint's mind switched in that direction, and away from Willow, thinking about that house and what needed to be done. He thought about the cattle he wanted to raise on a farm that had been neglected for more years than he could count.

And then his thoughts returned to a part of their conversation that he had heard, but hadn't really thought about.

"Your parents sent you to the States alone? Why?"

She shrugged. "They had a busy schedule, school was starting. That summer they realized how bad my hearing was. I hadn't really noticed. Or maybe I had adjusted without realizing. As it got worse, I paid more attention to lips when people spoke, and I asked a lot of questions. But that summer my hearing got progressively worse."

The information poured out of her, surprising him.

She was so matter-of-fact, so accepting. But he was imagining how it changed a person's life, to be unable to hear conversations, or to be left out of what was going on.

"But they sent you across the world, alone. That couldn't have been easy."

She shrugged as if it didn't matter, but he wondered if that was the truth. "Who has a perfect story, Clint? Not you, not me. Some have stories that are a little sweeter, with less pain. But almost everyone has a story. My parents love me, but they were busy with their careers. And frankly, I was a little embarrassing. I was a clunky kid with thick glasses, hearing aids and a penchant for hiding in corners."

"You were a clunky kid?"

"Tall, scrawny, and clunky."

She had more stories, he knew that. What had sent her running to Oklahoma and Aunt Janie? What kept her hiding in that corner and pushing people out of her life? Did it all go back to a little girl who thought she'd embarrassed her parents?

But she was right, everyone had a story. And he wouldn't push for hers. His story sat in the backseat of his truck, two little boys that needed him to focus on their lives, and their well-being. And he had a history of poor choices in the romance department that made him more than a little gun-shy.

As if she understood, Willow glanced over her shoulder, her smile real, and not meant for him. "You know what, guys? I think we should eat pizza before we have ice cream."

It was that easy for her to shift the conversation away from her, to make it about two little boys. He thought she'd had a lifetime of experience, deflecting attention from herself. She knew how to build walls.

He had built a few himself.

Willow walked through the door that Clint held open for her and the boys. A wall of cold air greeted them: someone wasn't afraid to turn their air conditioner on before June. Willow shivered and the boys reached for her hands, one on either side.

She smiled at the hostess who mumbled something about seating them. A hand waved from across the restaurant. A farmer that had sold her a few cows. She nodded a greeting and then he noticed Clint.

"Great." Clint spoke close to her ear. "Here we go again."

"What?" Willow pulled out a chair at the table the hostess had led them to.

Before Clint could answer, the farmer, Dale Gordon, stood next to their table. He was a big guy, with striped overalls and a wide smile.

"Clint Cameron. I'd heard you were back in town. Don't tell me you're going to try and make something of that old farm."

"Sure am, Dale."

"Might as well sell it to me."

Now Willow understood. She pretended to help the two boys with their napkins as she listened to bits and pieces of conversation.

"I'm not going to sell something that's been in my family for over a hundred years, Dale."

"It was in my family first."

"Your granddaddy lost it in a poker game. Tough luck, but I'm not selling."

Dale laughed. "You've always been hardheaded."

"Sure have and so have you. I think we're cousins, at least six or seven removed."

"Something like that." Dale patted Clint on the back. "Let me know if you change your mind about the old place."

"Will do, Dale."

Willow smiled up at the waitress who had arrived to take their order. She was a cute girl with blond hair in a ponytail and pale blue eyes that sparkled with sunshine when she smiled at the boys.

"Can I take your order?"

Clint looked at Willow, waiting for her to order. Now would be the time to tell him she really didn't like pizza. She smiled and ordered a salad. Clint ordered a large pepperoni pizza.

"Has he always wanted that land?" Willow turned her coffee cup over for the waitress to fill it.

"For as long as I can remember. There were a few times I was afraid my dad would sell. He always sobered up and came to his senses."

She tried to picture Clint as a kid, holding his family together, the same way he was holding it together now.

"It couldn't have been easy."

His brows arched at that. "What couldn't have been?"

"Your dad."

"It wasn't all bad."

She waited for him to tell her more. But he didn't share. Instead he moved aside their drinks and the napkin holder as the waitress arrived with their pizza. The boys lifted their plates for a slice, and for the first time in a long time, Willow was tempted by pizza. The crust was soft, and cheese dripped.

Clint laughed. "You can have a slice. Surely you're not on a diet."

She shook her head. "Nothing like that. I'm not much of a pizza person."

Both boys were staring, eyes wide. She felt like she'd just announced something scandalous. Clint laughed again.

"Have a slice, Willow."

Pizza, a day with Clint and the boys, and her heart tripping all over itself. Willow didn't know how much more she could handle.

"Okay, one slice." She took the plate with the pizza. Clint handed her a fork.

"You'll like it better if you just pick it up and eat it. But I have a feeling you're a knife-and-fork girl."

She didn't take the fork. "Don't make assumptions, Clint Cameron."

The pizza was hot, but she picked it up and took a bite. And she wasn't sorry that she had. She smiled at the boys as she pulled the slice away, cheese stringing along behind it.

"Okay, I admit it, pizza is good."

Clint put another slice on her plate and moved her salad aside. "Some things grow on a person."

Yes, some things did.

They were finishing lunch when Clint stood and pulled his phone out of the pocket of his jeans. Willow moved David's cup away from the edge of the table and shot a glance in the direction of the man walking away from them, the phone to his ear and his conversation lost to her.

"What kind of ice cream would you all like when we get to the ice cream parlor?" Willow smiled at Timmy, who licked sauce off his fingers and then reached for his soda. She handed him a napkin.

"I like bubble-gum-flavored." Timmy blew bubbles into his soda with his straw and spoke out of one corner of his mouth.

Willow couldn't have heard correctly. "Bubble gum?"

He nodded, "Ice cream."

It sounded disgusting. David didn't answer. His gaze held hers and she saw the tears form. "Oh, sweetie, what's wrong?"

"I like chocolate, and my mom puts stuff on it," he whispered, and his thumb went to his mouth. A look from Timmy, and he pulled it back.

Willow pulled him close and wanted to hold him forever, because she understood how it felt to lose something important. And she couldn't begin to know how a four-year-old could cope with that loss. Even if it was only temporary. He was a baby who needed his mommy to tuck him in, to tell him stories and sing to him.

Willow had always wanted to be someone's mommy.

How did she tell a child that God understood, and that time really did heal? How could she promise him that God would bring his mom home safe?

David's sun-browned arms wrapped around her neck. A hand fell on her shoulder, and she pulled back. Clint stood next to her, his concerned gaze on her, and then on his nephew.

"That was the nursing home. They're having problems with my dad. I need to see if I can help them calm him down. Or give permission for them to take him to the hospital."

"Do you want me to stay with the boys? I could take them home."

He shook his head and his gaze lingered on Timmy first and then David. He was carrying the weight of the world on broad shoulders, but were they broad enough? His sister gone, his dad sick, and two boys who needed him.

How did he manage to take care of everyone, and himself?

"You could drop us off at the ice cream parlor," she suggested, hoping to make it easier for him, hoping he would see that she could handle two boys and ice cream.

He shook his head again at first, but then he smiled. "Okay, I'll drop you off. This shouldn't take long. And if it does, I'll text you."

Text, not call. She smiled. "Okay, it's a plan."

When she walked through the doors of the ice cream parlor with two little boys, each holding a hand, she felt a funny leap in her heart. For a short time, she could fill this role in their life. She could be the soft touch.

It was easy, dealing with them, loving them. They were safe.

Clint's dad had dementia. They'd explained it to him before, about small strokes and alcohol. But he didn't always grasp the reality of it until days like today, when his dad was angry at the world. He had thrown apple cake at a nurse's aide, made rude comments to one of the other residents and then fought with his nurse.

It didn't feel good, having to send him to the hospital. And now, it was hard to smile as he walked into the ice cream parlor. But he did smile.

He smiled because it was easy when he saw the boys scraping the bottoms of their bowls, and Willow licking around the edges of a cone.

David had finally eaten enough to make Clint feel like the kid might survive. The boy had even eaten a couple of slices of pizza.

"Hey, how did it go?" Willow asked, after a bite of cone.

"Good. He's fine." Okay, not fine. But Clint could take care of this on his own. He was used to taking care of his family.

He looked at the boys and realized just how much Willow and Janie had helped since Jenna left. With his arm still in a sling, and sore from the exercises the doctor had given him, keeping up with two boys was a chore.

Willow smiled and pointed to the seat next to hers.

"Thanks." He sat down, aware that she was six inches away and smelled like springtime.

"Want ice cream?" she offered, taking another bite of hers.

"No, I'm full from pizza." He patted his gut. "Got to stay in shape."

She laughed. "Oh, of course. I forgot."

"What, you don't think we take our sport seriously?"

"I know you do. I also know enough about bull

riding to know you aren't sitting on the back of a bull for another couple of weeks."

"I think I have something to say about that."

"I think Dr. G does, too. She'll be back, and you'll be in big trouble."

"Well, I can't stay off tour for long."

Her smile faded. "I know."

"Thank you for doing this with the boys."

"I'm the one who's thankful. I've had a great afternoon."

Clint glanced at his watch. "I hate to ruin it. We should probably head home."

Home. He ran the word through his mind again. It had been easy, saying it like that. His home was really a run-down farm a half mile from hers. But her farm had become his home.

And she looked pretty uncomfortable with that.

Chapter Six

Clint ran the bull into the chute, glad for the roof of Willow's indoor arena. The rain had started yesterday, after they got home from having ice cream, and it didn't look like it would let up any time soon. He really needed to practice before the next event. He needed to know that his shoulder would stand up to the pressure of riding.

Clint climbed on the back of the bull, remembering the first time he'd ridden one, and how that experience had made him feel. He'd loved the sport from the beginning—the challenge, the friendships, and even then, working out frustrations with his dad.

The bull, young and inexperienced, went to his knees in the chute. Clint nudged, hoping to convince the animal to stand. Brian, the kid who helped Willow part-time, reached through the gate and gave the bull a push.

"He ain't comin' out, Clint." The kid, sixteen and already missing a tooth from a bad bull wreck, grinned.

"Go ahead and open the gate." Clint leaned, tentatively preparing to lift his left arm, his free arm. It ached, but nothing he couldn't handle. He had to grit his teeth and get through it.

The gate opened, the bull stayed on his knees. Brian took his hat off and shook it at the animal. Like a bottle rocket, the bull exploded out of the gate, taking them both by surprise. Clint hunched, his shoulder protesting the sudden movement.

"Keep your chin tucked." The feminine voice carried, combining with the rush, the pounding of his heart and Brian whooping at the side of the arena. "Watch your free arm. He'll switch and spin left if he thinks he can't get you off to the right."

He heard, and listened. She knew the sport, and she knew what it took to stay on her bulls. But he had to think fast on a ride that could last seconds.

No buzzer. He finally took the leap, hoping to land on his feet, not his shoulder. He tripped as he went down and held his breath for contact with the ground. When he landed, he rolled, and the bull ran off. Good bull, giving a guy a break.

He stood, stiff, and afraid to test his shoulder. It hurt. That was all he needed to know at the moment. But he could move his arm. That was a plus.

"I don't know why you guys do it." Willow shook her head as she approached, picking her way across the arena in high heels that made her taller than ever, nearly as tall as he was.

He was tall for a bull rider. He liked that she didn't have to look up to him. He liked that he could hug her and she'd be at eye level.

He wanted to hug her. But he smelled like bull,

and she had walls. He didn't want to confuse the two possibilities—attraction, or just his stubborn need to protect. He didn't know which fit his feelings for her, and didn't want to analyze. And she was dressed to go out. He let his gaze slide over the black pants and black-and-white top with sheer, gauzy black sleeves. She smelled like something expensive and floral.

She cleared her throat. "Clint, should you be riding?"

"I needed some practice if I'm going to make that next event." He reminded her of the event she'd already questioned him about. "I can't afford to lose my sponsors."

"You can't afford a serious injury to your shoulder."

"I'm used to dealing with it, Willow. I know what I can take and what I can't." He glanced back at Brian. "Go ahead and put him up for the night."

"It was a good ride." Willow spoke, but she looked off toward the gate, not at him.

"Thanks. Where are you going?" None of his business, and he should have kept it that way.

"Tulsa. I'm meeting friends. I won't be home until tomorrow. Maybe late."

"What do I need to do around here?"

"If you can feed. And keep an eye on Janie."

He laughed at that. "Janie doesn't want a keeper any more than you do. The two of you are more alike than you realize."

"We know how to take care of ourselves, Janie and me."

She smiled, and his mouth went dry. He almost gave in to the urge to hug her, to hold her tight. He wanted to taste lips that smelled like strawberry lip gloss and bury his face in hair that smelled like citrus.

And those thoughts should have been enough to convince him that he was losing control, and forgetting his priorities. Two little boys, a sister in Iraq, and a dad slowly drifting away from reality.

His reality. No time for relationships, and no time for pursuing a woman that didn't want to be pursued.

"Well then, I guess I'll go." She took a step back, and he moved with her.

She looked vulnerable, and a little lost. He couldn't let her leave like that, no matter what his convictions, or hers. And he didn't plan on confusing his need to fix with love.

"Willow, are you okay?"

"Of course I am." She glanced away, and he wasn't convinced.

He touched her cheek to turn her, and her eyes closed. Before she could move away, he leaned, not pulling her to him but keeping his fingers on her cheek. He kissed the strawberry gloss, and she kissed him back.

When she stepped away, he saw regret. He hadn't wanted to make her regret. He didn't want to regret either. But maybe she was right. It was the wrong time, the wrong place.

She had walls that he didn't have time to climb or break down.

"See you in a couple of days." She touched his lips, wiping away the gloss. "We shouldn't do that again."

He didn't agree, but then again, he did.

* * *

The restaurant was dark and the conversation at the table was quiet, hands moving, sometimes words, and with the curious stares of people around them. Willow watched the lips of a friend, but her mind wasn't on conversation or friendship.

She was thinking about Clint, and the kiss. She was thinking about regret. She was thinking about tomorrow.

Where are you, Willow? Angel signed. Angel had been profoundly deaf since birth and didn't like to speak orally in public.

Willow smiled when Angel nudged her. "I'm sorry, I have a lot on my mind."

The doctor's appointment? Angel signed.

"And the man my aunt hired to help me."

Is he cute?

"He's cute. He's likes to take care of people."

The waiter approached with plates of food. Willow waited until they were served before continuing. She sprinkled salt on her vegetables and passed the shaker to Angel.

Cute and *sensitive*, Angel signed and shuddered. *That's bad.*

"I'm not saying it's bad."

Your ex-husband hurt you, Will, but that doesn't mean another guy would.

"I'm not going to let him, because I'm not looking for a relationship. I have a life now, the life I want."

Your life isn't reality, a life with no one telling you what to do. What's that all about? Angel's eyes sparkled with humor.

"It's safe."

Angel took a bite of pasta and spoke as she chewed, her hands signing with passion. *"Safe" isn't living. "Safe" is a cocoon that shuts the world out.*

Big words from Angel, who lived in the deaf culture, her world of choice. Willow lifted her brows, the only response needed to bring a smile from her friend. And then Angel signed, *I'm dating someone.*

"Hearing?"

Yes, hearing. Angel flushed a light pink. *And he loves me.*

"Where did you meet?"

You're not going to believe it.

"Try me."

Angel smiled. *At the grocery store. My cart hit his, and he accused me of doing it on purpose.*

Willow laughed. "Did you?"

She couldn't imagine her shy friend doing anything to draw attention to herself, but the pink in Angel's cheeks flushed a deeper shade.

"You didn't!" And then everyone was staring, people at their table, and at other tables.

Do you have to announce it to the world? Angel reached for her glass of water and smiled at the curious friends, all waiting for an explanation.

I'm sorry, Willow signed, and then explained to the others that she was happy for Angel, she had a new man in her life.

The first man in my life. Angel's pink cheeks remained flushed. *I'm twenty-seven, and for the first time in my life, I think I might be in love.*

"I'm happy for you."

Angel shook her head. *No, you're worried. You*

think he'll hurt me. The way Brad hurt you. You think he won't be able to accept my deafness.

"That isn't what I think." But didn't she feel that way? Hadn't she always believed her parents had sent her away out of embarrassment and Brad had divorced her for the same reason?

There had been other relationships. She didn't want to go down that path tonight, thinking about past hurts.

Yes, you do, Willow. You think he'll reject me. Angel smiled to soften the words. *But he loves me. And when someone loves you, they accept everything about you. He's even learning sign language.*

"You're right, and I'm sorry."

Where's your trust?

"Trust?" Willow thought maybe she'd heard wrong, in the shadowy light of the restaurant, maybe Angel had signed something other than the word "trust."

Trust God. You never know what He can do if you open yourself up.

"You're right, Angel. And I'm so glad you've found someone."

Willow hugged her friend and let the conversation end, because Angel deserved to be happy, and not all relationships ended in pain.

The words of the doctor the next day undid any feelings of strength she had imagined the previous night with Angel and her other friends. Sitting alone in his office, just a nurse for company, Willow listened as he explained that her hearing might continue to decline. To what degree, he couldn't be sure until the test results came in, but he wanted her to be prepared.

Prepared for profound hearing loss. A hearing loss that would make her hearing aids virtually useless.

For weeks she'd convinced herself that it wasn't happening. It was just her imagination. Now she had to face reality. If she couldn't hear, how would she manage at bull riding events? How would she keep her business going?

The doctor apologized, and then he handed her the card of a psychologist, because she might want to talk to someone. She numbly took the card and shoved it into her purse.

My God, my God, why hast thou forsaken me? Tears burned her eyes as she walked out of his office and down the hall, but she wouldn't let them fall. She wouldn't cry. Not yet. She would process this information and deal with it.

She would survive.

She would do more than survive. God hadn't brought her this far to forsake her. She hadn't started this new life to give it up. And there was a chance that the test results would come back and show that this was temporary. Or that the progression wouldn't continue.

She took a deep breath and tucked her purse under her arm, feeling stronger for having convinced herself to have faith. Sometimes it took a little convincing when things looked dark.

She saw him in the lobby, a figure in faded jeans and a polo shirt, leaning against the wall near the water fountain. He was wearing his tired-looking straw hat, and a toothpick stuck out of the corner of his mouth. He straightened as she approached, his smile quick and sure. She hadn't been forsaken.

God had sent a friend.

And she really needed a friend. He held her gaze as she walked toward him. She remembered her regret yesterday, when he'd kissed her. She remembered the confusion she'd seen in his eyes.

But he was here now. That had to mean something.

How many times in life had she gone through moments like this alone, without someone to talk to? Too many to count. She had always handled things. She handled being a child and knowing the other students could hear the teacher. She had handled boarding school. She had handled her husband's rejection.

How would it feel to share her feelings with this man? She drew in a deep breath, because today wasn't the day. He was standing in front of her, but she couldn't let herself open up. She had to deal with it, figure it out, before she could share with someone else.

She couldn't get through this, trying to make sense of it, and worrying about how he would handle it.

"What are you doing here?"

"I couldn't let you do this alone."

"How did you know?"

"I overheard your conversation."

"Eavesdropping?" It was easier to smile than she would have imagined.

"Yeah, I guess. I meant to ignore it, to let it go. But I couldn't. I thought about it all day, about how you wanted to do everything alone, including this. But I couldn't let you."

"The boys?"

"With Janie."

Willow pushed the down button on the elevator. "Did you tell her where I am?"

"No, I didn't even tell her why I needed to come to Tulsa. I snooped and found the address in your office. Sorry about that."

He held out a handkerchief. She took it and brushed at her eyes, wiping away tears that hadn't fallen. She even smiled, because she could picture him in her office, peeking through papers.

"Sorry for which, for eavesdropping, snooping or following me?" She looked up at him.

He took the handkerchief and gently wiped under her eyes before handing it back to her. She held it, staring at the mascara stains, and wishing her heart wasn't melting. The duct tape she'd used to put it back together was coming apart at the seams, and she wanted to give a little of herself to a man who carried handkerchiefs and took the time to snoop through her papers.

"Should I apologize for trying to be a friend?"

She shook her head, but she couldn't answer, not without crying. She didn't want to cry. A few tears had leaked out, but she could hold it together. She didn't want to be the woman he pitied.

He touched her back and guided her through the open doors of the elevator. Once inside they stood at the back, shoulders touching. She had needed a friend, God had sent one, and the one He had sent was willing to wait, to not push for answers

"Do you want to talk?" Clint looked straight ahead, that straw hat pulled down over his eyes.

Her hand slid into his. "I can't talk about it right now. But I'm glad you're here."

She wasn't alone. Clint's hand squeezed lightly, and she didn't pull away. His hand holding hers convinced her that maybe, just maybe, he was someone she could let into her life.

The elevators touched the ground floor, and the doors slid open. They walked out together, no longer touching, and fingers no longer interlocked. Reality, a nice guy who knew she needed a friend.

"Would you like lunch before we drive home?" Clint asked as he walked by her side, into bright sunshine.

"I'm not hungry."

He nodded and led her across the parking lot to her truck. As they stood at the door she realized he had asked her another question, more words she hadn't heard.

"I'm sorry, what?" She couldn't make eye contact, so she stared down at her purse and the handkerchief.

"Are you going to be able to drive?"

She nodded and looked up. "Of course. I'm fine."

Always fine. But Clint didn't look like he believed her. As much as she wanted to tell him what the doctor had said, she couldn't, not yet. She wanted to hold on to hope for as long as possible.

She stood on tiptoe and kissed his cheek. "Thank you for being here."

"I haven't done much."

"You were here, and you didn't have to be." She filed that thought and knew she had to return to it later.

"I'll follow you." He pulled his keys out of his

pocket and stood, waiting, like he wanted her to say more.

She shook her head. "You go on. I have to pick up a few things here."

As he started to turn, she caught hold of his arm. "Clint, thank you."

He smiled and walked away. She hoped he believed her. She had needed him. Now she needed to be alone for a while.

Clint walked out of the barn the next morning, hearing laughter and Willow's husky, alto voice. She had both boys on the swing that hung from an old oak in Janie's front yard. It was the kind of swing kids used to love, just a board strung on thick rope and tied to a sturdy branch. It was the kind of swing that made a kid think he was flying.

It was wide enough for both boys. They were leaning back, legs out, as they soared into the air. Willow caught them as they came down and gave them another push.

"Swing your legs out." She laughed as she coached them. "Make it go higher."

Had she ever been a child like that, carefree, swinging into the air, pretending she was flying? He hadn't been that kid. Most of the time he'd spent worrying about his parents, or his sister.

Now he worried about the boys. And Jenna. Because when she called, just before leaving Missouri, she had sounded scared, but she hadn't admitted to fear. Willow and his sister were a lot alike.

He crossed the lawn, Willow's dog nipping at his boots, asking for attention. He took a minute to toss the stick the dog had picked up and then he moved on. The boys called out to him, waving as they made another trip heavenward. Willow stepped back, smiling, but not at him.

She wasn't ready to talk about yesterday. He knew better than to push. Better to talk about the trip they were taking next week.

"When do we leave for Kansas City?" He leaned against the tree, out of the way of the swing.

"Next Thursday. I want to be there early enough for the bulls to settle in and settle down."

"The boys?" He didn't want to ask that of her, didn't want to ask in front of them. "I can drive my own truck."

"Nonsense, we can all ride together." She nodded toward the big old diesel that she drove to larger events. How many women would drive a truck like that? "I have a DVD player in my truck. We can bring movies."

"That sounds good. We can take turns driving." He knew better than to tell her he would drive.

Her gaze remained on him as he spoke, and she didn't turn away until she thought the conversation was over. She nodded, and even smiled a little, because she had to know that he was being careful not to step on her toes.

For her sake he wanted to believe everything was okay, as she insisted. He didn't believe it, though, not with shadows lingering in her eyes and her smile melting away when she thought no one was watching.

She smiled at the boys as they came back to ground. The twins jumped off the swing and walked unsteadily as they adjusted to being on land again.

She didn't hear them talking to her. Clint touched her arm, and signed, repeating their question about the pony in the field.

He wondered why she had a pony, but didn't ask, because her eyes narrowed, and she bit down on her bottom lip as her gaze studied the two little boys. They had turned and were waiting for an answer.

She should have kids, he thought. She should have five or six, and someone in her life taking care of her. He smiled at that, because he knew she didn't want to be taken care of, not in a coddling sort of way.

She was strong enough to hook a stock trailer to a truck and drive cross-country with a load of bulls. She was strong enough to start over after a marriage that had obviously hurt her.

What had happened yesterday at the doctor?

If he asked, she'd shut him out, so he didn't ask. And she was answering the boys, telling them they could ride the pony.

"Where did you get a pony?" He followed the woman and two boys to the barn.

"I bought him at an auction, half-starved and pitiful."

"And you needed a pony?"

She headed for the tack room, next to her office. Music played, and a horse in one of the stalls whinnied a greeting to them. This was the kind of barn a cowboy dreamed about, the kind he dreamed of.

Willow, unaware of his mental wanderings, opened the door to the tack room and flipped on the light. Inside were several saddles, halters and bridles hung on the walls, and saddle blankets were lined up along a board that had been nailed along one side of the room.

She turned back to face him. He realized she hadn't heard the pony question.

"You needed a pony?"

"I couldn't let him be sold to the…" She smiled at the boys and didn't finish her explanation for why she bought the pony. But he knew why companies bought sick old ponies at auctions, and he would have done the same thing she had.

It was one more thing he knew about her. She rescued sad animals. And cowboys who had no place to go. He glanced down at his nephews. And she rescued little boys who had to say goodbye to their mother.

"Who rescues you, Willow?" The words were out before he could stop them. And she had heard.

She turned, her head tilted to the side. She had just pulled a tiny saddle out of the tack room and she set it on a rail, a miniature bridle hooked over the saddle horn.

"What does *that* mean?"

He shrugged and resisted the urge to be a coward and run. Instead he picked denial. "Nothing."

"It meant something."

"Okay, it meant something. I guess I don't want to talk about it any more than you want to talk about your doctor's appointment yesterday."

She smiled, a little sad and a little proud.

"I rescue myself, Clint."

The answer he had expected from her. "Fair enough."

"Come on, guys. Let's go ride Tiny Boy. And then we can brush him and give him grain."

Because riding was about learning responsibility. He smiled as he followed her to the end of the barn and through the double doors that led to the field. She carried the saddle and ignored him, sending an obvious message that he didn't fail to understand. He knew the most important thing about her.

She rescued herself.

Chapter Seven

The Kansas City event was one that Willow loved. It was huge. It was close to home. And people knew her. She had friends here. As she walked through the wide halls toward the arena and the area where the bulls were penned and waiting, she managed to push aside the fear that had reared its ugly head when her doctor left a message the previous day that she needed to call him.

She hadn't called. She'd do that when she got home. This weekend she would take care of business. She would watch her bulls perform, and she'd visit with friends. What she wouldn't do was let her peace be stolen away.

Next week she'd deal with reality.

Tonight's reality was a pen holding her bulls, bulls she'd raised and trained herself. She had earned the right to supply these animals to some of the biggest bull-riding and rodeo events in the country.

She wouldn't feel bad about her life and her accomplishments. She wouldn't lose faith.

Arms crossed over the top rail of the pen, she watched the bulls, thinking about the animals, her life here, and the life she'd left behind. It felt good to be happy, to be content. It felt good to be in control. No matter what.

"Feels good, doesn't it." Clint was at her side. "You've done a great job with these bulls."

"It does feel good. It's something I've done for myself. I'm not doing it for my dad, or for Brad. It hasn't been given to me." She turned, smiling because she had given more of an answer than she'd planned to give. He was good at disarming her. "No one can take it away from me."

"No one can."

No one could take it away from her. But she could lose it all if her hearing loss continued to escalate. Eventually she would have to tell the people in her life. She would have to admit that she couldn't always hear the announcer calling the names of the bulls, or the riders. She couldn't hear when her name was called because her bull had won certain challenges.

She would have to admit to herself that she needed help. And then she would admit it to Janie, and to Clint.

"I'm going to talk to Bailey. Have you seen Janie?" She unhooked her arm from the fence and turned, facing him.

"She's with the boys. Cody Jacobs brought a horse with him, and they're taking turns riding."

"Okay, then I'll catch up with you in a little while."

He nodded and she walked away. Bailey was easy

to find. She was at the edge of the arena, watching her husband give the twins a ride on his big buckskin gelding. His daughter, Meg, stood at his side. Willow approached her friend, remembering how they met and how hard it was for Bailey and Cody to let go of the past and find a future together.

And Willow had helped to bring them together. She had helped in their happy-ever-after, even though she hadn't believed in one for herself.

"Willow, you look gorgeous." Bailey moved toward her, hands coming out to take Willow's.

And Bailey glowed. Willow's gaze lingered on the other woman's belly. The rumors were true. "Oh, Bailey, you should have told me."

"I wanted to wait until I saw you. I wanted to tell you in person." Bailey's smile was soft. "Willow, I…"

"Please don't, Bailey. This is your moment. I'm your friend, and I want this for you."

Willow hugged her, holding her tight. When they stepped away from one another, Willow smiled, wanting to prove her words. It wouldn't hurt.

"When are you due?"

"Six months."

"I guess it's too soon to know if it's a boy or girl."

Bailey laughed, "Yes, way too soon."

"How is Meg taking this? Is she excited?"

"She's excited, and then she starts thinking about sharing her parents, and sharing her puppy. As quickly as she thinks of those things, she starts thinking of plans for what she's going to teach the baby."

"Do you have names picked?"

Bailey laughed at that, a real laugh, the kind that made people turn to look at them. "Meg likes the name Dolly, after your bull. She thinks we should name her brother, if the baby's a boy, *Dolly*. Thank you for that."

Willow laughed with her friend, and when the laughter ended, Bailey reached for her hand. "How did your doctor's appointment go? I wish you would have said something sooner. I would have gone with you."

"I know you would have. But really, I'm used to it." Used to being alone. She shook the thought from her mind.

A movement caught Willow's attention. She glanced up, making eye contact with Clint, standing near the gate. He smiled, and she felt it, almost as if he had reached out and touched her.

His fingers moved, asking if she was okay. And she was, of course she was. Why would he ask that? She ignored the question and he walked toward them, his walk a casual, cowboy swagger.

"Is there something going on that I should know about?" Bailey smiled, her eyes shifting from Clint to Willow.

"You know there isn't. He's helping me, and we're helping him with the boys."

"He got hurt a couple of weeks ago, didn't he?" Bailey smiled at Clint, who was nearly to them.

"Yes, he dislocated his shoulder."

Clint stopped in front of them. He smiled at Bailey and held out his hand. "Clint Cameron."

"Bailey Jacobs. Nice to meet you, Clint."

"Willow, that young bull is a little droopy, and he isn't drinking water."

"He likes bottled water. I think the chlorine in city water makes him sick. I should have told you." She stepped away, giving Bailey an apologetic smile. "I need to check on him. But we'll have dinner tomorrow night?"

"Of course."

"Okay, then, I'd better go." Willow walked away, knowing that Clint was on her heels. She felt him there, his arm brushing hers as he caught up.

"You okay?"

"Of course I'm okay. Why did you think I wasn't okay? And that bull had better be sick." Not that she wanted the bull to be sick. "I mean, I hope you didn't make that up."

He laughed and shook his head. "The bull is sick, and your face was pale. You looked like you were trying to be happy."

"I *was* trying to be happy. Is there something wrong with trying to be happy for a friend?"

"Nothing at all. I just thought you looked upset."

Willow sighed and turned to face him. It was crowded, and he moved her to the side. "Do you think she thought I was upset? I would never want her to think that I wasn't happy for her."

"She didn't notice."

Willow bit down on her bottom lip. "Bailey and Cody deserve to be happy."

Willow's phone rang a few times as she approached

the bull pen. It vibrated in her pocket, and she pulled it out and flipped it open. Her attention was on the sick bull, and the caller's voice faded in and out.

"I'm sorry, I didn't catch that." She held the phone tight and blocked the sounds of the arena, where people milled, checking on bulls and talking about the event.

The caller repeated the question, but she only caught that he wanted information. Clint moved in front of her, signing that he could take the call.

Because she couldn't. And she knew it. She shouldn't be angry with him, it wasn't his fault. She didn't want him to think she needed him or anyone else to take over because she couldn't handle it. She didn't want to give up. Would he understand that she had to keep trying, and hoping it would work?

With Clint watching, she gave the caller her e-mail address and explained that her connection was bad and there was too much noise in the arena.

She hung up and slipped the phone back into her pocket.

"I could have taken that call for you." Clint rested one foot on the bottom rail of the pen that held her bulls.

"Yes, you could have, but I didn't want you to. I handled it."

"Yes, you handled it."

She looked at the young bull, only his second time at an event this size. He didn't look good. She didn't like to think that he could really be sick.

"We should call the vet."

"Do you want to do that?" Clint continued to stare at the bull. His hands moved deftly, and she nodded in answer.

Sign language was just easier sometimes. Signs didn't have to compete with the commotion of the arena. Signs weren't overheard. And he knew that. He couldn't know that there were times she couldn't hear him.

Or maybe he did.

"Willow, what's up?"

She closed her eyes and leaned her forehead against the top rail of the pen. "I'm sorry. There's so much going on, and you're here, and you don't deserve to catch the brunt of it all."

"I can handle it."

She didn't know if *she* could handle it. "Thanks. I would appreciate it if you would call the vet. I need to see what Janie is up to. And I'll take the boys with me. If you want?"

"That would be great."

Yes, it would. For the next few hours, until the event started, she could be distracted by Janie and the boys. She could keep her mind off babies, sick bulls and the competition.

Later tonight she would be alone, and then, in the privacy of her room, she could fall apart.

After Willow walked away, Clint went to the locker room to call the vet, and to get ready. He had wanted a last-minute prayer, a quick check of his equipment, and what he'd gotten instead was a conversation with Cody Jacobs.

Clint left the locker room and walked through the narrow hall leading to the arena, his bull rope dragging behind him with the bell clanking against the concrete floor. He needed his mind on the ride against a bull that should be a sure thing, and not on the magazine article that Cody had shown him, an article about a deaf woman raising bulls, and the abuse of the animals.

Cody had, for some reason, seen Clint as the person who needed to know, the person to handle the problem. Like Willow was his to handle, or protect. Clint had wanted to explain to Cody about his dad, his sister in Iraq and the twins. He had almost asked Cody Jacobs if he understood what it meant to have a full plate.

Instead he had agreed that someone needed to break the news to Willow. And he was the guy. The guy who was going to have to hurt her, and he knew she was already hurting. He didn't look forward to telling her.

At least she had the good news that her bull wasn't sick, just cranky and in a bad mood. He sort of understood how that bull felt. He was a little cranky himself.

When his bull was in the chute and ready, someone called out to him. It was Jason Bradshaw. The two had never run in the same circles. But Bradshaw was a good guy and a good neighbor.

"I'll pull your rope, Clint." Jason stood on the outside of the chute, ready to help.

They were in the same circle now. Bull riding had a way of breaking down social barriers. On the back of a bull, it wasn't about where you grew up or what your savings account looked like. The bull didn't care.

The crowd cheering from the stands didn't care.

"Thanks, Bradshaw." Clint fastened his Kevlar vest and pulled his hat down tight. He climbed over the gate and settled on the broad back of the bull.

"Mammas Don't Let Your Babies Grow Up to Be Cowboys" was the song blasting from the speakers, and over the snort of the bull and the steady stream of conversation around him, he could hear the crowds singing the chorus of the song. He could hear the heavy breathing of the bull and the clang of metal as the animal pushed into the gate.

A glance to the side, and he saw Willow talking to Bailey but watching him. Funny how life had thrown them together, the princess and the pauper. He smiled as he slid his hand into the bull rope, because he knew they weren't a fairy tale, just two people who would have something in common for a short time.

Bull riding smudged lines and brought people together. But that didn't mean they were in each other's lives.

He found his seat on the back of the bull, distracted, and he knew better. The bull was steady, calm, he'd done this before. Clint bowed his head and said a quick prayer, wound the bull rope around his gloved riding hand and nodded for the gate to open.

A bull that was a sure thing, an easy ninety-point ride. Clint made all the right moves, doing his best to make a good ride even better. He used his free arm to keep in the center. He kept his gaze focused forward, on the bull's head, and he kept his toes pointing out. As the buzzer sounded the end of eight seconds, he jumped, but miscalculated and hit the gate, his head connecting first, and then his shoulder. Or maybe it was simultaneous.

Fire shot through his shoulder, and he slumped to the ground, not even caring that the bull raced past him. Jim Dandy wasn't a mean bull, had never been mean.

A bullfighter held a hand out, and Clint took it.

"Thanks." Clint rubbed the back of his head.

"You okay?" One of the sports medicine team had joined them.

Clint nodded, and it hurt. All over.

"I think he hit his head on the gate and scattered his chickens." The bull-fighter pounded Clint on the back, chuckled and walked away.

Clint cringed because it had done more than scatter his chickens. He could almost imagine the questions people would ask, about why a cowboy kept trying to ride the bull. He didn't have an answer, but he knew that it was about competing with something wild. Man against beast, a battle as old as time.

Some men chased tornadoes, others jumped from planes. He rode bulls, sometimes for eight seconds, and sometimes not.

He stood and tipped his hat to the cheering crowd

as the medics followed him out of the arena and through the building to their temporary examining room—heavy curtains hung on bars to give the riders a little privacy.

"Have a seat, Clint." The physician, a man in his sixties, pointed to a table covered with sheets of white paper.

"Do I have to? I'm sure it's fine." Sore, but fine. He had to be fine.

"How about if you let me be the doctor, and you be the bull rider. We'll both be better off for it." Doc Clemens smiled as he lifted Clint's arm at an angle that didn't feel too good. "Hmm."

"What's 'hmm' mean?"

"It means that I don't think you should ride, but I also don't think you're going to listen to me. It means that I can't be sure until further examination, but I think you're finally going to need surgery."

"Hmm." Clint smiled and then grimaced when one of the medics placed a bag of ice on his shoulder. "That's cold."

"I think you should call it a weekend."

"I can't. If I can win…"

"Yes, *if* you can win. There's always that elusive *if.*" The older doctor was a little less than pleasant when it came to bedside manner. "If you want, we can try tying it down. Sometimes it works."

His elbow tied to his waist to keep him from moving his arm straight up. He'd be able to move it just enough to keep it in the air, away from the bull and the automatic disqualification if he touched the animal. He shook his head, not sure if he liked the idea.

A commotion outside and men clearing a path interrupted the conversation. Willow kept her gaze on him as she walked through the room.

"Don't be stupid, Clint." She smiled at the doctor, who went a little red in the face. "If you can't ride, you can't ride."

"I can ride. It's my free arm."

"Which you need for balance."

He shot a look over her shoulder in time to see a few of the guys laugh and shake their heads. This he didn't need. And if she'd been thinking, she would know she didn't need it, either. She had just added to the rumor that had been started by the magazine article. Not that she had any way of knowing about the magazine.

But after the interview she'd made it pretty clear she didn't want her name linked with his.

"Willow, I'm going to make the right decision for me."

And for his family. The weekend had a big purse at stake, and that money would go a long way in building his dream. It was money that would put up fences and buy cattle.

"What about the boys?" She looked around a little nervously, as if she had just realized where she was and who all was watching. Calm, cool and detached crumbled across her face, and she bit down on her bottom lip, suddenly vulnerable.

He wanted to pull her close and tell her it would all work out. But he couldn't make those promises to her.

"Everything I do is for my family." He spoke a little softer and started to reach for her hand. Instead he winked as if he didn't feel a need to convince her he was okay. "Don't worry, I've been hurt a lot worse than this."

"Okay, well then, I guess I'm going back out there. Janie has the boys already tucked in, so you can crash and not worry about them."

She nodded and walked away, not giving him time to respond, to argue, or to even ask her how her bulls had done. And since Doc Clemens was about to stick a huge needle in his shoulder, it didn't seem to matter.

Chapter Eight

Willow left Clint and walked down the hall, back to the crowds gathered behind the chutes. Several stock contractors smiled, a few riders nodded in her direction. They all seemed to be whispering. And she seemed to be the center of attention.

The center of attention was exactly where she didn't want to be. She avoided that place, the place where people stared and whispered.

It could be about anything. It could be that they were already discussing the fact that she stomped into the examining room and confronted Clint as if she had a right.

She tried to tell herself that she was used to people staring and talking about her in quiet whispers. Not here, though, in this sport where she'd been accepted. One of the contractors left his group of friends and headed in her direction.

"How ya doin', Willow?" Dan slapped a rolled-up magazine against his thigh and sighed.

"I thought I was fine, Dan. But from the look on your face, maybe I'm not?"

"Willow, I'm not going to beat around the bush. There's a pretty nasty article in this magazine. I have a feeling you haven't seen it."

She shook her head. No, she hadn't seen it. He handed it to her, and she unrolled it. Willow glanced at the cover, and then she understood the whispers, the curious glances. She flipped to the page of the article.

"I'm sorry, Willow."

She nodded as she skimmed the article, a story about a woman with a disability, and bulls being mistreated. She glanced at the bull in the chute and the cowboy sliding onto his back. The judge was there, making sure it didn't take too long for the cowboy to get settled and out the gate. That rule was meant to protect the animals and keep them safe from stress or injury.

And her own bulls, drinking bottled water and eating the best hay and grain available. She skimmed the article, stopping when she saw Clint's name. She groaned and shook her head.

"Great."

"It isn't the end of the world." Dan chuckled. "Shoot, Willow, there are plenty of couples around here that met at a bull ride. And Clint's a good guy."

"But it isn't true."

"Of course it isn't. But you're okay. You have good bulls, and nothing to be ashamed of. This isn't the first article written about bull riding, won't be the last. This guy took his story to a personal level that wasn't really necessary."

She thanked Dan, smiling and shaking her head when he tried to give words of encouragement. As she walked away his words were indiscernible, but she caught something about it not being a big deal.

For her, it was a big deal. This was about her reputation. It was about people respecting her as a professional, not thinking of her as someone weak, someone who needed sympathy or help.

Ignoring Bailey, who waved from the sidelines, wanting to talk, Willow walked back to the area where temporary pens had been set up for the bulls. Her bulls were there, fed, cared for and healthy.

She ripped the pages out of the magazine and dropped them in a nearby trash barrel. The article was trash. And it felt good to watch the pages flutter down, finding a resting place with soda cans, wrappers from burgers, and popcorn.

"What are you doing?" Clint stood next to her, glancing into the trash barrel. She hadn't heard him walk up.

She shrugged and ripped more pages, feeling better already. "I'm not a victim. I'm not disabled. I'm a woman of faith. I'm strong. I take care of my animals."

"Okay."

She glanced up at him, smiling when he smiled, because she knew that she wasn't making sense. "Did you know about the magazine?"

"I did, and I was going to tell you."

"Were you working up the courage?"

He pointed to the bag of ice under his shirt. It had been taped to his shoulder with duct tape. "No, I was getting a shot in the arm."

"Do I really act like this person he portrayed me to be?" She hoped not.

She didn't want to discuss the money that had been the consolation prize at the end of a marriage. Or the husband who had used her father's name to build his own career in Washington.

Worse, what he'd said about her relationship with Clint. She had traded a privileged life in Washington for a cowboy with a fading dream of being a pro bull rider.

The article hadn't been kind to him, either.

Clint smiled, reassuring, calm. "You're not the person in that article. The divorce is behind you. It's a part of your past."

Heat crawled up her cheeks. "I was dumped for someone I thought was my best friend."

"I know." He shrugged his right shoulder. "And I have fading dreams of making it big."

"Your dreams aren't fading."

"No, they're not fading, just changing. I'm getting too old for this sport. But I'm going to rebuild that farm that's seen better days. And I could think of worse things than having my name connected to yours. Even if it is just a rumor."

She looked down, glancing at the few pages of the magazine still intact, including a recipe for some midwestern-style casserole.

"Oh, wow, I want this recipe." She folded it up and put it in the pocket of her jeans.

"Changing the subject?"

"Maybe. I don't want to talk about this. I don't want to talk about what this says about us, or about my bulls or how I lucked into success."

Clint leaned close. He didn't touch her, and she wanted to be touched. "You didn't luck into it. You did this on your own. You're incredible."

She nodded, and then she backed away, because they were in a public place and they didn't need to feed the gossip that had already started.

"Thank you. I'm sorry for what the article says about you. It isn't true."

"I know."

She took a few more steps back. "I have to go."

Because there had to be lines, somewhere between them, lines they didn't cross. Because if they crossed the lines, and he became someone she counted on, how could she go back to not having him in her life?

She would handle it, because that's what she did. She had learned to handle things as a kid, moving from place to place, trying to make new friends, and losing good ones along the way. She handled life, and being alone. She handled men walking away.

She smiled, and he smiled back. "See you in the morning."

He reached for her hand. "Let's grab a cup of coffee and unwind. I won this round, and I'd like to celebrate."

A cup of coffee. Friendship. A man who understood that she was strong and she could survive. But he was also a rescuer. So was the coffee a lifeline, or friendship?

"Not tonight."

Tonight was a good night not to be rescued. Tonight she needed to keep her distance because there was a soft, vulnerable spot in her heart, and an ache to be held. She said goodbye and walked away. But behind her Clint was still standing by her bulls, and her heart was remembering how it felt to have lines crossed with a kiss.

Sunday morning, Willow walked down the steps to the small area of the stadium where church was being held. It was quiet—no bulls bellowed from the chutes and cowboys didn't line the platform, waiting to ride. Maybe a hundred people had gathered to worship. There were bull riders, stock contractors, family, and even a few spectators.

One of the guys played the guitar, signaling a start to the service. Willow sat at the back, not wanting to be a part of conversation or greetings. Today she wanted to be alone, to think about the future and why she was suddenly dreaming about a cowboy.

Janie had taken the boys to a local church, and then they were going to the zoo. They would make a real day of it, and the twins needed that. Clint had planned to sleep in, because pain meds did that to him, he'd explained.

Willow didn't feel abandoned. She needed time with God, to worship and to feel His presence. She had work to do on her heart that morning, and it had to do with anger toward the reporter. She'd lain in bed last night reliving the interview and what she should have said. And then moving on to what she'd say if she ever saw that guy again.

Real anger, real emotion, the kind that if it wasn't controlled could get a person in real trouble. She smiled at the thought but then reminded herself again how wrong it would be to say the things she wanted to say.

The song service started. Willow stood, closing her eyes to listen because the guitar was soft and the voices were strong. She sang along, enjoying that moment when the world slipped away and she was alone with God. And since God was the only one close enough to hear, she didn't mind singing out loud.

Alone with God, and then a soft breeze and mountain pine cologne. A shoulder touched hers. She opened her eyes, and Clint smiled down at her. She closed her eyes again, not wanting to be distracted, and knowing how easily it could happen.

The music ended, and they sat down together. The speaker for the day was one of the bull riders. He opened his Bible and announced a passage of scripture. Willow flipped through her Bible, looking, but missing the chapters. She had sat too far back to read lips, and too far to catch everything he said.

And it was her own fault, for being stubborn, for wanting to be alone. Two months ago it wouldn't have been an issue. Now, now everything was different.

Clint reached for her Bible and pointed to the correct passage. *And the peace of God, which passeth all understanding, shall keep your hearts and minds through Christ Jesus.*

She read the verses above and the ones that came after, and then she lingered again on *peace. Not* as the world gives it, but peace that is real. Not found in things, not found in circumstances, or in perfect moments, but peace found in God.

The speaker's hushed tones didn't quite reach, but Willow didn't care, God had already spoken to her heart in those verses.

Clint touched her arm as she strained to hear, and

then his hands moved, signing the sermon, deftly, quietly, just for her. And he didn't know what the doctor had told her, or the uncertainty of the future. She blinked against the sting of tears, and her eyes blurred as she watched his hands.

Hands that rode bulls, hugged little boys, fixed fences, and now, spoke the words of God for her.

When the sermon ended, Willow signed *thank you*, just for him, between the two of them. And then she reached for his hand and pulled it to her lips. A brief kiss, something to let him know how his kindness touched her.

"I have to go now." She slid past him, not wanting to wait, to explain, or to have him tell her he understood. He wouldn't be able to understand what she couldn't begin to fathom about herself, her life or her feelings.

He reached for her hand as she started up the steps, and she stopped.

"Willow, we both have to eat lunch."

Simple, nonintrusive lunch.

She had a list of reasons why she had to walk away, and for a moment they seemed meaningless. To be honest, she couldn't remember a single one of those reasons.

"Okay, lunch is good."

He stood up, grinning, and then he winked. "Say it like you mean it."

"I mean it." And suddenly she did, because his hand reached for hers, warm, callused and strong, and he was a friend.

"I'm buying."

"I can buy my own lunch."

"You go first." She smiled, not looking at him, but wondering what was in his mind, and what face he was making.

"First?" He was pulling the keys to the truck out of his pocket.

"Secret sharing, remember?"

"Okay, I'll go first."

Curious, she looked up, and he smiled, his eyes crinkling at the corners. He had pushed his hands into his pockets, and he pulled them out, signing as he spoke.

"I sucked my thumb until I was four."

And she could picture that, because she knew that he must have looked like David. An insecure little boy with silver-blond hair and gray eyes. And now, insecure? She didn't think so.

"That isn't embarrassing." She opened the passenger-side door, even though he was there. "That's cute."

"Cute, huh?" He laughed. "So you think I'm cute?"

"Four-year-old Clint, with blond hair and torn jeans, his thumb in his mouth, was cute. You're…"

His brows arched, waiting.

"You're too full of yourself."

"You still think I'm cute."

"For a dirty ole bull rider, who limps a lot and creaks when he stands up, I guess you're okay."

"So, now it's your turn." He was leaning in, one hand on the door to keep it from blowing shut. Up close she could see the crinkles at the corners of his eyes and a tiny cut on his forehead from the fall last night.

"I don't think so. You gave me thumb sucking, which isn't private or embarrassing."

His smile faded and he looked at her, a long look that made her doubt whether she should push him for personal information.

"Never mind."

No, I'll give you something. He signed, slower now, more thoughtful. She stopped his hands, holding them in hers.

"I can hear you."

"Okay. I've never really been in love. A couple of times I thought I might be, but it never worked out." He shrugged.

And Willow had been right; she was sorry that she'd pushed him to reveal his stories. It was too much information, and in his eyes she could still see that boy who had been hurt too many times.

Sharing secrets was dangerous. It had opened a door that shouldn't have been opened.

"Too much information?" He smiled and when he climbed in behind the wheel, he shot her a look. "Your turn."

"I'm not sure if I made that deal." She clicked her seatbelt and reached to turn the radio down.

"I think we did." He started the truck and shifted into Reverse. "Come on, if I can share that I'm a dropout in the school of love, surely you can give me something."

"You want me to share something miserable about my life, so you can feel better about yours?" She couldn't help but smile.

"Something like that."

"Okay, I won't go into detail, but I, too, am a—what did you call it?"

"Dropout in the school of love."

"Catchy, in a tongue-tying sort of way. Okay, I'm the girl most likely to be standing alone at any social function because people think I can't communicate. And I'm the most likely to be dumped." She could have told him the many different ways she'd been dumped or stood up. But that was a little too much reality for a beautiful summer day.

He winked. "At least we have each other."

"Of course. Now, if you think we've sufficiently humiliated ourselves, I would really like pizza."

His eyebrows arched. "Pizza it is."

Step one in developing a new life— Try new things.

She smiled at Clint and he smiled back. And it felt a lot like trying something new.

Clint's phone rang just as he was paying the waitress for their lunch. He answered and listened as Janie explained that David had fallen asleep on the way back to the hotel from church, and he was crying for his mom. They hadn't made it to the zoo.

When they walked through the door of Willow's suite at the hotel, Clint saw David sitting in a corner of the couch, tears still streaming down his face. Willow made a noise, and he turned. Her eyes shimmered with tears and she gave him a watery smile.

"I'll take Timmy downstairs for ice cream," she offered.

"No, don't. I'm not sure what to say to him, Willow. I don't know how to get him through this."

"Pray with him, Clint. That's the only answer. He's a little boy, but a child's faith is stronger than you think." She smiled past him, at the child on the couch, hugging knees to his chest. "And hug him."

He nodded, but it took him back more than twenty years, to his own mother sitting on his bed praying for him to make wise decisions. He had forgotten. How had he forgotten something so important?

He also remembered how it had felt when she didn't come home that first night after the accident. His world had shattered, and he'd had to pick up his own pieces, and Jenna's, too, because their father hadn't been able.

He did have an idea of how Timmy and David felt. They were younger than he had been, but he had experienced those empty nights of waiting for someone to come home. Jenna would come back.

Willow touched his back and when he turned, she smiled. "Do you want me to stay?"

He did. But he shook his head. "No, I should handle this one. I'll take both boys to my room. And then they should probably take a nap before tonight."

"Are you riding tonight?"

He shook his head. "No, I'm not going to take that chance."

"I'm sorry."

He shrugged, and he was sorry, too. It was his dream slipping away. He had a feeling she understood.

"I'll catch up with you later." He gathered the boys and headed for the doors. "I'll help you with the bulls tonight, since I won't have anything else to do."

The boys leaned against him, a little weepy and a

little tired. Just boys in need of one-on-one time. He held them close and walked them to the door. Willow stood to the side, and he remembered what she'd told him about herself, that a lot of her life she had stood by herself in a hearing world, feeling different.

Chapter Nine

Tuesday morning, Willow fed her animals early and headed for the house to talk to Janie. On the drive home from Kansas City she had prayed about talking to her aunt. She wanted Janie to keep her dream of moving to Florida. First Willow had to convince Janie that she'd be able to run the ranch without her aunt to help.

When she walked into the kitchen, Janie turned from taking the newly baked biscuits from the baking sheet. She didn't smile. Not good.

"What's up?" Willow leaned against the counter, watching her aunt.

"I have a message from your doctor for you. He wants you to call." Janie frowned again. "You went to the doctor?"

"I did, and he did tests."

"And?"

"And, I don't know. I haven't talked to him yet." Willow poured herself a cup of coffee that smelled old, but she didn't really want to drink it. She wanted something to distract herself. "Janie, I don't want to talk about it. I'll call him, and I'll find out what the test results were."

Big sigh from Janie. "Okay, but you have to let me know what he says."

"I will." Willow smiled, and then she wrapped her aunt in a loose hug. "Janie, I know you want to move to Florida, and I want you to sell me the ranch. Or at least let me lease it."

Janie pulled loose from the hug. "Don't butter me up with hugs, Willow. I'm worried, and you want to sidetrack me with this conversation."

"I'm not buttering you up. I put it off, and now seems like a good time to talk. You want to move. And I don't want you to stay here, believing you have to take care of me."

Janie shook her head. "You know that I don't think that."

Willow sipped the burnt coffee and then poured it down the sink. It was past disgusting. "You would stay for that reason. I can hire Clint. And I have Brian."

"I know you do. But you're my girl, and I don't want to leave you alone."

"If you don't go, you'll regret it, and I'll feel guilty."

Janie nodded. "I'll think about it. The girls are flying down to Florida in two weeks. I might just go with them. If you think you'll be okay."

"I'll be okay. And now, I need to go talk to Clint. I need to make sure he's willing to help. If not, I'll put the word out that I'm looking for a foreman."

"Clint would be a great choice. The two of you…"

Willow raised a hand. "Don't go there, Janie. Clint is a friend, and that's all. I'm not looking for anything more than friendship. I've learned my lesson."

"We all have lessons to learn. We never stop learning, and we should never stop growing. But we should also keep the doors open so that God can do what He wants to do in our lives."

"I'll remember that." Willow grabbed a biscuit off the baking sheet and blew a kiss to her aunt. "I'll be back."

As Willow walked toward the foreman's house, she tossed the last bite of biscuit to Bell, who trotted along behind her, stubby tail wagging. Willow could smell bacon frying.

As Willow walked up the stairs to the front porch of the house, she heard Clint singing along to the radio. The boys were laughing. She stopped, not wanting to interrupt.

She leaned against the side of the house, listening to something beautiful. The laughter of the children, the love in Clint's voice when he told Timmy to get ready for a great breakfast, and country music filtering out the screen door. She hugged herself, wishing for something she couldn't have and knowing that soon she might not be able to hear moments like this.

"Oh man, this isn't good," Clint shouted. The boys screamed. She couldn't make out all of their words.

Time to interrupt. Willow knocked on the door, and he yelled for her to come in. She walked into the kitchen and into chaos. The skillet was on fire. Clint was slapping it with a wet towel. The boys were standing against the far wall, hands over their mouths.

"The lid, Clint." Willow walked across the room,

searching the counter. No lid. She grabbed a baking sheet out of the dish drainer and slid it over the top of the pan, smothering the flames.

Clint dropped the singed towel in the sink, and then he rubbed his shoulder. "I'm not a cook."

"Obviously. But what have you done all these years, because you're definitely not starving?"

"Drive-thru, what else?" He smiled. "What has you down here so bright and early?"

"I guess I'm here to tell the boys that I can make decent scrambled eggs." She looked into the pan. "But the bacon is a lost cause."

"I can help." Clint grinned, and the boys groaned.

"I think that's a response you can't ignore. Timmy and David have vetoed your offer." She grabbed the carton of eggs and a bowl out of the dish drainer. "Do you have milk?"

Clint pulled a half-full jug out of the fridge. "Milk. What else?"

"Cheese?"

He found cheese and tossed the bag next to the milk. "What are you doing here so early, other than making breakfast for three starving guys?"

"Did I say I would make you breakfast? I think I just offered to make breakfast for the boys."

"You wouldn't let me starve."

"No, I wouldn't." She cracked eggs into the bowl. "I came down to talk to you about working for me. Permanently. Janie and I discussed her move to Florida. I don't want her to feel like she has to stay here and take care of me."

"You know that I want to work on my farm."

"I know. And I really can put out the word that I need to hire someone. It's just that you…"

She sighed, because it was a lot to tell him. He made her feel comfortable. And he knew sign language. The comfort part was easy to admit. But if she admitted the part about sign language it meant admitting something more about herself and her future.

"Willow, I do want to work for you. I only mean to say that I can work here, and I can work on my place. I can do both."

"I don't want to take you away from something that's important to you."

"You won't be taking me away." He took the lid off the milk and handed it to her. "We work well together. I don't think you're going to find anyone else quite like me."

She smiled up at him. "I can't imagine that I would."

Timmy and David gathered at her side, watching as she cracked eggs into the bowl. They were still wearing pajamas, and they hadn't brushed their hair. Their uncle had the same hadn't-been-up-long look. She glanced sideways at the man next to her in sweats cut off at the knees, bare feet and a white T-shirt.

"Can we help?" Timmy looked into the bowl.

Distracted, she nodded, and then she had to admit she hadn't really heard his question. He gave her a look and repeated it.

"You can." Willow handed him the whisk. "Can you mix this up for me?"

The little boy stirred and stirred until the eggs were foamy and splattering on the counter.

"I think that's good." Clint took the whisk and handed it to David. "Your turn."

David stirred, more gently. He kept hold of his bottom lip with his teeth, concentrating. Willow leaned and kissed the top of his head. She prayed for their mom, that Jenna would come home soon.

And she prayed for herself, because she had to call the doctor and face her own future. They were all facing changes. She wrapped an arm around Timmy and he cuddled into her side.

She wouldn't have traded that morning with them for anything.

After breakfast Clint watched Willow heading for the barn, the twins walking with her. She had a surprise for them. He knew that it was a calf from a local dairy farm. She'd bought it for the boys to bottle-feed.

He cleaned the kitchen, washing the skillet the eggs had been cooked in and leaving the bacon pan to soak. As he walked down toward the barn, Bell joined him, carrying the ever-present stick in her mouth. He tossed it and kept walking.

Squeals of delight echoed in the early morning, and somewhere a rooster crowed, a little late. Clint walked around the side of the barn and saw the boys standing in front of the corral, both holding tight to the giant-sized bottle that they held through the fence for the calf.

The calf pushed again, like he would have done to his mom's udder, trying to get more milk. The boys laughed, real belly laughs. The calf pushed the bottle, and they dropped it on the ground. Timmy held out his hand, and the calf slid a long tongue over the boy's fingers.

Clint leaned against the corner of the barn and watched Willow. She was leaning against the fence, gazing at the boys. Her hair was pulled back in a ponytail, and her blue eyes shimmered. When she saw him, she smiled, a smile that didn't hold back, that didn't have shadows.

David had picked up the bottle, and the calf sucked again, just getting air. The boys groaned because they didn't want to stop feeding the calf. And the calf wasn't ready for them to stop.

"We'll give him grain, guys. He won't be hungry." Willow took the slobbery bottle and held it loosely in one hand. Clint laughed, because she owned bucking bulls, and she was holding that bottle like it was a bug.

"Want me to take that?" he offered.

She tossed it, and he had to catch it or get hit. His hand slid down the side, and the calf slobber slimed him. Okay, it wasn't pleasant. He looked up, and she was giving him a look, brows raised and a little quirk to her lips.

"What's the matter, is it disgusting?" she asked as she handed the feed bucket to the boys. Timmy held the handle and climbed the fence to dump it into the feeder.

David grabbed the water hose.

Clint shrugged. "Doesn't bother me at all. What did you name the calf?"

"Sir Loin," the boys shouted in unison.

"Nice." Clint shook his head. "I'm not going to ask."

"It was a tough choice." Willow grinned. "Sir Loin, or T Bone."

"Cute." He didn't mean the name of the cow, but she didn't have to know. "Do you mind if the boys stay here with you while I work on my place?"

She shook her head. "Not at all. We're going to drive down the road to look at the neighbor's new puppies."

"New puppies?" He had a bad feeling about this.

"Don't look so worried. They won't be weaned for a few weeks."

"I'm not worried." But he was. Not about the puppies, but about his sister, his nephews and Willow. "I'll see you later. I'll be at the farm if you need me."

He walked away from Willow and realized that was what bothered him. He was having a hard time walking away from her. How could he let himself be that person in her life when he had twin nephews counting on him for bedtime stories, the right brand of pudding and promises that their mother would come home soon?

As he drove up the drive of the old farmhouse, a shiny new truck pulled in behind him. He parked and the truck parked next to him.

Jason Bradshaw stepped out of the other truck, his grin wide and a pair of work gloves in his hands. Clint met him at the front of his truck, surprised to see the bull rider at his place. Jason, with his strawberry-blond hair and sheepish grin, had lived down the road all of Clint's life, but the younger man had never really been a friend of his.

"Jason, how are you?"

"Better than you." Jason shot a pointed look at

Clint's shoulder. "I heard you're going to need surgery. That's a tough break."

"Yeah, but it'll work itself out. What are you up to today?"

"I called up to Willow's and she said you were down here working. I thought I could help."

"You don't have to."

"That's what neighbors do for each other. I just bought the fifty acres next to you. Never know, I might need some help over there someday."

"Okay, then. I guess the first thing I'm going to do is fix that porch."

His phone rang as he was pulling the toolbox out of the back of the truck. He flipped it open, smiling when he heard his sister's voice for the first time in too long. Jason sat down on the tailgate, waiting.

"Sis. How are you?"

A long pause. He wondered if they'd lost their connection. "Jenna?"

"I'm here, sorry, but things are loud. Clint, are the boys okay?"

"Of course they are. They're with Willow, and Janie is taking them to vacation Bible school tonight. They miss you." He heard her sob.

"I miss them, too. But I know if I talk to them, it'll make it worse for them and for me."

"Jenna, is everything okay?"

"Good as it can be."

"And you're eating your vegetables?" He waited for her laughter. This time it was soft, not like her laughter used to be, when she'd been off at college and homesick. That question had always worked on her, a lifetime ago.

"I'm eating my vegetables, but they're dehydrated, and worse than yours. Are the boys eating?"

"Are Oreos a breakfast food?"

"No, Clint, Oreos aren't a breakfast food. Buy them instant oatmeal."

Instant oatmeal. Why hadn't he thought of that? "Okay, I can do that."

"Clint, I have to leave now. I won't be able to call again for a while."

"Why?"

"Gotta run. I love you." And then she was gone and he was holding a phone and he didn't have any way of knowing if she was safe.

"That's tough." Jason held his gloves in his hands and didn't say more. Clint looked at the other man, wondering about his appearance here, and about the past.

Jason had always been the one smiling, the one joking. And Clint knew his life hadn't been easy. It had just looked easy from the outside.

"Yeah, it's tough," Clint said as he slipped on his gloves. "It's hard to take. I've always been able to protect her."

"Yeah, I know."

"Really?"

Jason Bradshaw, whose smile was as famous as his bull riding, shrugged. But he didn't smile. "She used to sneak out to meet me. I guess you didn't know that."

Clint's fist drew back, and Jason raised a hand, stopping him. "We didn't do anything, Clint. I never did more than hold her hand."

"But she snuck out to meet you?" Anger still simmered as he waited for an explanation.

Jason slipped on the leather work gloves. "Clint, life isn't always pretty, and it's good to have friends who understand and who listen. We were never in love. We were just friends, and we talked."

Clint backed away, no longer wanting to hit the guy. He knew how it felt, to need a friend. Willow flashed to the front of his mind, a friend. Just a friend.

"Well, let's get to work." Jason carried the toolbox.

Clint followed, still thinking about his sister, and about misconceptions. He needed more of an explanation from Jason. "When did the two of you meet?"

"At the hospital—years ago. She was there to see a friend. I was there—" he didn't look at Clint "—to see my mom."

"I'm sorry, I heard she passed away."

"She'd been sick a long time."

"It couldn't have been easy."

Jason smiled. "No, it was never easy." He set the toolbox on the porch. "After meeting Jenna, and realizing we lived pretty close to each other, we started talking. She was only seventeen, and I knew we weren't going to date, but she was a good friend. We'd sit down there—" he pointed to a tree at the edge of the property, near the pond "—and talk for hours."

"And I thought she had mono, because she was tired all the time." Clint laughed and let it go.

It wasn't as easy to let go of the phone call with Jenna. Pounding nails into wood helped.

Jason Bradshaw handed him more nails, smiling like everything was okay. They were doing all the right things, making life as normal as possible. They were rebuilding a house, and he was taking the boys to vacation Bible school. Normal things that filled normal summer days.

But Jenna was thousands of miles away in Iraq, and her boys were with him. And on top of that, nothing had prepared Clint for the way Willow Michaels would change his life.

It took him by surprise, the need to see her, to talk to her. It had happened a lot lately, that she was the person he thought about when he needed a friend.

At that event in Tulsa, when Janie had reintroduced them, he'd been afraid that Willow would be one of those people he felt a need to fix. And she wasn't. Maybe he was the one in need.

Bell jumped up from where she'd been sleeping next to the dining room table. She'd crawled into the spot before the boys left with Janie for vacation Bible school. Willow thought that it was because the boys dropped a lot of food when they ate and so Bell received limitless treats off the floor.

Now Bell was jumping and turning in circles, her own way of alerting Willow to a visitor. Willow finished washing the last of the pans from dinner and followed the dog to the door. She watched as Clint's truck pulled to a stop and he got out. He held his left arm to his side, releasing it when he saw her watching. He rolled his shoulders a few times, and then headed for the house, moving slowly.

Willow opened the door and met him on the porch. He carried a plastic bag from the store. From the look on his face, he'd had a long day. He looked haggard, and his shirt was stained. Dust coated his jeans. She motioned him inside.

"Did you get a lot done?" She sat next to him as he struggled to get his boots unlaced.

"Let me." She leaned and untied the laces and then pulled his boots off. When she looked up, he was leaning against the back of the bench, his eyes closed.

"Jenna called," he whispered, not opening his eyes.

"And?"

"She had to go and said she couldn't call for a while. I tried e-mailing her and didn't get an answer."

"There's a logical explanation. She had work to do and just wanted to touch base."

"That's what I've been trying to tell myself all day, but it doesn't feel right. Her conversation didn't feel right."

"You have every right to be worried, Clint."

He opened his eyes. His smile was soft, concerned, tired.

Willow reached, wanting to touch him, but knowing it was the wrong move at the wrong time. They were alone and both lonely. She could see it reflected in his eyes, that he needed to be near someone in the same way she did.

"I have this huge thing of chocolate–peanut butter ice cream." He held up the bag from the local ice cream parlor. "I thought we could share it."

"You just *happen* to have ice cream?"

"I might have driven into town just to buy it, maybe to tempt you into spending time with me."

"It worked." She stood, and then she reached for his hand and pulled him to his feet. They were standing face-to-face, and the room suddenly seemed too small and too warm. "I'll get the bowls."

"I'll help."

He followed her into the kitchen, helping by being in the way each time she turned around. She slid past him to the fridge where she had a nearly full jar of fudge topping. She lifted it, and he nodded.

"We can sit on the porch." He dug a spoon out of the drawer after she twisted the top off the fudge. "It's cool, like it might rain."

"It isn't going to rain, but the porch would be nice." She wanted to say something about the worried look in his eyes. She wanted to tell him that she'd sat on the porch after dinner, and she couldn't hear the crickets.

Instead she handed him a bowl of ice cream and led the way outside. They sat down side by side on the porch swing.

"I wish I could do something to help." She glanced sideways, and he nodded, but he didn't answer.

"Good ice cream," he finally said. But she couldn't tell that he'd even taken a bite.

He leaned back in the seat and stared off into the night. The sun had set, and the security light flickered on. His face was in shadows, smooth planes and stubble on his cheeks. His chest heaved, and she felt, but didn't hear, his sigh.

Willow set her bowl down and reached for his hand, his fingers warm and strong. "I'm praying for Jenna, and for you. I know this isn't easy. But Clint, you're doing a great job with the boys. And Jenna is going to come home real soon and be their mom again."

"Thanks, Willow." He squeezed her hand and

"I know you can, but I'm not going to let you."

And that made it feel too much like a date, too much like a line crossed. But a strong person could let a man buy her lunch and not be frightened by tomorrow, or next week, or even next year.

It's just lunch, Willow. He had pulled his hand free and signed the words, keeping it between them and not the people walking up behind them.

"I know."

"Tell me one really embarrassing thing about yourself. Something really private."

Willow pulled away, ready to think up an excuse, a reason she needed out of this lunch date, and then she saw his smile. He winked and pulled her close again.

"Kidding, Willow. Nothing embarrassing or private, not today."

"No, I like that idea. But today, you have to tell me something about yourself, too."

They were walking down a hallway lit by fluorescent lights, toward the exit at the back of the building, and somehow they had lost the others from the church service. Or maybe they'd gone a different way. Willow hadn't really been paying attention. Instead she felt a little lost in the lighthearted moment between herself and a cowboy in new jeans and a white button-down shirt, the sleeves rolled up to expose blond hair on suntanned arms.

He was the kind of cowboy a girl could lose her heart to. The kind dreams were made of.

He pushed the doors open and motioned for her to go through. They walked across the parking lot, not talking. It reminded her of the day at the doctor's office when he hadn't pushed for her secrets.

smiled. "You've been a big help with the boys. I would have burned more than breakfast if you hadn't showed up when you did."

"I was happy to help."

"You'll be a great mom someday." He smiled, like the compliment meant everything, and he didn't know how much it hurt.

She looked away, not wanting to deal with his words, an innocent statement that shouldn't have hurt so much, not after so many years. Clint leaned forward, his hand still holding hers.

"Willow, are you okay?"

She turned, trying to smile, trying not to cry. "I'm fine."

"No, you're not." He stroked her fingers. "I'm not sure what I said…"

She couldn't stop the tears or the flash of memories that flickered through her mind. She couldn't stop the images of the accident, and the memory of the pain that followed.

"Willow?" He pulled her close, and she couldn't stop the tears, the aching emptiness that shouldn't still hurt so much.

She would never be anyone's mom. She shook her head, trying to clear her thoughts, trying to undo the moment.

"Willow, I'm sorry." He held her tight, his hands on her back. "Tell me what's wrong."

Tell Clint. Let him into her life, and take the chance that someday this decision to share would bring more pain. More pain and someone else walking away.

He was holding her close. And he had never

walked away from her in embarrassment. He had used sign language for a Sunday sermon on peace.

"Clint, I can't have children." She whispered the words into his neck. He hugged her closer, and his hands stroked her hair.

"I'm sorry." And this time she knew he was sorry because she couldn't have children, not because he'd said the wrong thing.

And she was sorry, too.

She had wanted to hold her baby girl, to give her a name, to raise her and love her. And now, because of one moment, one missed traffic signal, a car horn she hadn't heard, she would never have children.

"Do you want to talk?" He pulled back a little to ask the question and she shook her head, because she wasn't ready to talk. She wanted to stay in his arms for a few more minutes, before realization hit and he put it all together.

She couldn't have children. She would never go through the normal process of falling in love, getting married and having babies.

Her husband had walked away from her the day after their daughter was buried. She couldn't tell Clint, because she didn't want his pity. She didn't want to watch another man walk away.

She brushed away the last remnants of her grief, the tears that still trickled out. She had really thought she'd cried her last. But sometimes the grief sneaked up on her, taking her by surprise. And then came the guilt. It ached deep down inside her heart, where God was still helping her to forgive herself.

Clint was waiting for an explanation. After all of those tears, he deserved one.

"I had a car accident when I was six months pregnant." She rubbed a hand over her eyes and tried to piece it all together again for the man who had held her while she cried. His shirt was still damp from her tears. "When I woke up, my baby was gone, so was my ability to have children, and my marriage was over."

His eyes closed, and she wondered about his thoughts. She remembered Brad closing his eyes, and then opening them, lashing out in anger and blaming the accident on her hearing. When Clint's eyes opened she saw that he was sharing her grief, not condemning her.

Her own emotions did something they rarely did; they took her by surprise. She had a sudden need to keep him in her life, to hold on to his friendship.

I'm sorry, he signed. That one gesture had never meant so much.

Clint reached for Willow's hand and held it for a long time, not knowing what to say. He knew he couldn't take away her pain. He didn't think she was asking that of him. She had shared because…because why?

A weak moment? Or because they were friends? In that moment it felt like more than friendship. It felt like something he had never experienced. It took him back to that moment when Jenna had called, and he could think only of seeing Willow, talking to Willow.

She was strong. He had never met a stronger woman. He thought of her losing her child, and her husband. He thought of her that day at the doctor's office, stoic, facing whatever was in store for her.

He thought of her prayers for him, for Jenna and for two little boys that missed their mom.

"You're strong, Willow, stronger than you think."

"It's an illusion. At any moment, I could lose it. I could be weak."

"We're all weak at some time or other."

"Maybe so." She stood, gathering their bowls and not speaking further.

"You're okay?" He stood next to her, trying to figure out the next step in this process, and not sure if he should take another step.

"I'm fine." She smiled to prove it. "And you're strong, too."

She kissed his cheek. He had to be strong, because he wanted to pull her against him and make promises he probably couldn't keep. He wanted to kiss her senseless.

He had to leave. He backed away from her, taking the scent of her with him, and remembering the taste of strawberry lip gloss.

She had shared her heartache with him. Now wasn't the time to share other emotions, or ask her if he was imagining something between them that might not exist.

Now wasn't the time. Maybe there wouldn't be a time, because he could see in her eyes that fear of being hurt again.

"I'll see you in the morning." He took another step back. "Do you want me to help you do the dishes?"

She held up the two bowls and smiled, like she knew that he was stalling. "Two bowls, Clint. I think I can manage."

He nodded. "Okay, I'll go then."

"Don't forget, the boys are spending the night with us."

"Of course." And it was time for him to go. He backed off the porch, holding the rail and smiling as he turned to leave.

"See you tomorrow?" she called out after him.

He turned at his truck, surprised to see her still standing on the porch, and looking like a girl who really did want to know if the guy was coming back.

"Of course."

Chapter Ten

Clint followed Willow out of the house after lunch the next day. The boys were still with Janie, because after a night of movies and popcorn, they weren't ready for the fun to end. Willow was nearly to the barn when he caught up to her. A hand on her arm, and she turned.

"I'm going to visit my dad, and I'm going to pick up a few things for our next trip. Did you need anything in town, or do you want to ride along?"

"Trip?"

"Austin?" Bull riding, like she didn't know what he meant.

"Yes, I know what Austin is. You're not riding."

"I am riding because this is the last event before the summer break. I know that I need surgery. I also know that I can ride. I've been on a few practice bulls."

She shook her head. "You could do more damage."

"I could, but I don't plan on letting that happen. Do you need anything from town?"

"Oh, so you can tell me what to do, but if I try to say anything about your riding, you change the subject."

He pushed his hat down on his head and dug his heels into the firm dirt, and reality. Willow was staring at him, waiting for a response, and he didn't have one. He smiled, because she looked about fit to be tied.

"I'll see you later, Willow."

"I'm going with you."

"Really?"

"You offered." She shifted on booted feet and bit down on her bottom lip. "I do have a few things I could pick up at the store."

"You don't mind running by the nursing home with me?" Willow, going with him, to see his dad. What kind of move into his life was that?

"I don't mind at all."

But did he mind her going? A long time ago, but not that long ago, he'd been a lanky teen with dirty jeans, and girls like Willow wouldn't have climbed into his truck if his had been the last truck out of a burning town. That kid was still inside him, still fighting acne, and dreaming about someday having a wife and a family, maybe a ranch with some cattle and a nice truck.

He hadn't had a lot of time for fun back then, not with farm work, his dad drunk most of the time and Jenna relying on him. He still had that list of priorities, things that had to come first, had to come ahead of his own dreams.

Willow had shifted everything, and now he had to figure out where to put her in his life.

"Where to first?" Willow was talking to him as she pulled her hair back and tied it with a thin scarf. Strawberry lip gloss tinted her lips, and he was having the hardest time of his life remembering his responsibilities.

"The nursing home." He opened the passenger door of his truck for her, and she climbed up, reaching to pull the door closed. He shut it from the outside and took his time getting to the driver's side.

"Why are you acting like I've invaded your personal space?" Willow spoke as soon as he climbed into his truck. "You've been invading *my* space since the day I met you."

He reached to turn down the radio. He didn't need a country song about a stupid boy. Not even if that's what he thought about her ex-husband walking out on her.

"You're not invading my space. I have a lot on my mind."

She was on his mind. Great, all of his thoughts were starting to sound like a country song. If this day ended with the dog getting run over or someone going to prison, he'd switch to rock music.

Intent on letting the conversation drop, he reached to turn up the radio. She turned it up more, smiling. "I like this song."

Of course she did.

They were a mile from the nursing home. "Willow, I need to warn you about my dad."

"Okay."

"He's hard to handle. Sometimes he's in the past, sometimes not. And he says things, sometimes hard things."

"I can handle it."

He knew she could, but he didn't want her to be on the receiving end of one of his father's verbal assaults. "Maybe you should…"

"Wait in the car?"

"I'm sorry."

"If you want me to wait in the car, I will. I'd rather go in with you."

He pulled into the parking lot of the nursing home. "No, I don't want you to wait."

He'd always been the one who was there for others. He'd been there for his dad, and for his sister. Other than Janie, he'd never really thought about having someone "there" for him. But that's what this was about. It was about Willow trying to be there for him. It felt like a new pair of boots, not quite right.

He had put her in the category of another woman he was drawn to who probably needed to be fixed in some way. That had been his track record in the past.

He parked, and she got out of the truck. Willow, tall and beautiful, from a world far removed from his. And she was the one who was going to be there for him as he faced a father who was sinking into a world they couldn't understand.

Her hand slipped into his, and the earlier discussion about riding bulls and being in each other's space faded from his mind. It was no longer important.

At the front desk they signed in as visitors. Willow signed her name next to his. As they walked down the hall, their shoulders brushed, and his hand touched hers. He felt her fingers on his, but they didn't clasp hands. He didn't explain to her about his dad, and about the times the older Cameron had gotten drunk and hit his children because he'd been positive their mother died in that car accident because of them, because she'd been on her way to school to pick them up.

Clint inhaled deeply at the memory of the patrol car pulling up at the school and the social worker helping them into the vehicle.

Willow's fingers slid through his. She knew how his mother had died. She'd explained that Janie told her and she was sorry.

"How long has he been here?"

"A few months. I moved him in here before I moved home."

"That couldn't have been easy. I'm sorry."

She had lost a child and her husband had walked out on her. He kissed the side of her head, his lips brushing her hair. "Thank you."

"Is that you, Clint?" The raspy voice from inside the room carried into the hall.

"It's me, Dad."

"Is Jenna with you?"

Clint led Willow into the room, felt her hesitate at the door, but then she stepped close to his side again.

"No, it's my friend, Willow."

"Where's Jenna?"

Clint sat on the edge of the bed, next to the frail form of his dad. Willow walked to the window. He wondered if the broken-down tractor was still in the field out there and if she was wondering why the farmer had left it that way.

"Dad, Jenna's in Iraq. Remember?"

"Why's the judge's daughter with you?" His dad made a noise in his throat. "You know she's out of your league."

Out of his league. He brushed off old insecurities.

"She isn't the judge's daughter. Willow is Janie's niece."

"The one that can't hear? What's she doing here?"

"Dad, she can hear." He shot Willow an apologetic look, but she was smiling, not at all upset.

"I don't care if she can. Get me some oatmeal that isn't runny. They always bring me runny oatmeal."

"I'll bring some oatmeal later." He poured water instead. "Dad, I'm going to be gone a few days. We're going to Austin."

"Eloping?"

"No, we're going to a bull ride."

"Does she have money? That aunt of hers has money."

"Now you're embarrassing me. And I have my own money."

"Then maybe you ought to get me out of this roach motel."

Willow's laughter was soft, and Clint's dad looked at her. He smiled.

"Dad, when I get home, I'll take you to dinner. How does that sound? Maybe we could go to church together."

"You aren't going to take me to church. I don't have any use for religious people."

And that hurt. Clint couldn't think about this part of his father's life, the part without faith. He closed his eyes, repeating a prayer that he'd repeated numerous times over the years. He wanted his dad to have faith.

"Dad, when I get back, we'll go to church and then we'll go to lunch. We'll get a good steak." Steak for church.

"Fine, we'll go to church if you'll buy me steak. Don't bring those boys or that old woman."

"We'll all go together." He leaned and kissed his dad's thinning gray hair. "We'll go together, Dad. I'll see you next week."

"Goodbye, Mr. Cameron." Willow touched his father's arm as she walked by his bed. "I'll see you at church."

Clint waited at the door for her, and they walked out together. His dad yelled something about not wanting them to elope.

"I'm sorry about that. I did try to warn you."

Willow laughed, soft and easy. "He's something else."

"He's always been something else. He was charming, funny, drunk and mean. The best of all worlds."

"It had to be hard on you, and on Jenna."

"It wasn't easy, but we survived." He pushed the door open and held it for her. "As a teenager life was about faith and surviving, about believing that God really would deliver us from that situation. And as hard as it was, I loved him, and I still love him. He taught me to ride. He taught me to fish. He had his moments."

"Janie said you were a hard worker and everyone loved you."

He grinned, winking as he opened the truck door for her. "Yeah, everyone loved me."

Everyone really did love Clint. Willow watched him walk through the small grocery store in Grove, being greeted by older women and people closer to his own age. Willow walked along behind him, pushing the cart and tossing in items that weren't really on her list. Clint paused at the end of the aisle, talking to a woman with a beehive hairdo and cotton dress. He motioned Willow forward.

"Do you know Janie's niece, Willow Michaels?" he asked the woman, who was giving Willow a look that clearly measured her against Clint and drew a lot of conclusions.

"I don't believe I've met her." The woman smiled.

"Willow, this is Addie Johns. She was my high-school math teacher." He laughed an easy laugh. "And she somehow taught me calculus."

"It wasn't easy." Addie Johns shook her head. "The boy had horses and cows on the brain. And girls."

Clint flushed a light shade of red. "Now, Addie, you know that isn't true."

The older woman laughed and patted his hand. "No, it wasn't true, was it. As a matter of fact, I don't think I've seen you in love before."

Willow choked because Addie Johns meant only one thing by that statement. She was putting them together as a couple. And that couldn't happen.

"Oh, Miss Johns, we're not…"

"Ready to tell everyone." Clint finished Willow's objection and then reached for her hand. "We can trust you to keep it a secret, though."

"Oh, of course." Addie Johns grabbed her cart. "Well, I should get my shopping done. You two have a wonderful day. And don't forget to send me an invitation."

Willow waited until the lady disappeared before punching Clint on the arm. "Why did you do that?"

"To see who would be more surprised, you or Addie. I think you win."

"She'll tell everyone in town."

"More like the entire county." He laughed. "I can hear it now. Phones ringing up and down the line, ladies at home, washing dishes and speculating on a wedding date, and if we'll last, or…"

"Stop." Willow pushed the cart away from him, tossing a few packages of cookies in with a bag of Reese's.

"I was joking, Willow."

"I don't want to be a joke."

He pulled the cart to a stop and stepped close to her side. Willow backed away, feeling the cold of the frozen-food coolers behind her. Clint leaned in, smiling, his gum cinnamon and his cologne a soft hint of pine.

She glared, hoping to put him in his place.

"Okay, it wasn't a joke."

She looked away, even more confused. "Clint, stop."

"Make up your mind, Willow. Do I stop, or do we take a few steps forward to see how this works out?"

Everyone loved Clint. Willow couldn't let herself

think those thoughts, or how it felt when he cared about her. He didn't understand the difficulties a relationship with her would include.

"Clint, I have so many things going on in my life right now."

"So do I."

"So, we don't have time for this conversation. Not now. Not here."

"When *do* we have time?" He smiled at a lady pushing her cart past them, a baby in the seat.

"Clint, I can't have children." Her voice broke as she whispered what he already knew, but he hadn't realized that it meant something more.

He was looking at the baby, waving, and Willow was looking at him. Her words registered, and he remembered last night, when he'd held her and it had felt like her heart was breaking, and that a breaking heart was familiar ground to her.

"I know, Willow."

"I can't have children. I can't have a marriage with children." She looked away, but not before he saw the broken look in her eyes.

"You have something that does come with a relationship. Yourself. Willow, when a man falls in love with you, it is about loving *you*."

"What man doesn't want a child with his name, his eyes, his pitching arm or whatever it is that's important to men."

"You're right, I guess, that's something a man does think about. But…"

She reached for the cart. "I can't talk about this."

"You're running from what we both know isn't going to go away." He walked next to her as she headed for the check-out with a cart full of junk food.

Would his feelings for her go away? He wanted to fold her in his arms and hold her forever. He'd never felt that before, not once in his life. It had nothing to do with fixing her.

"There are a lot of things that aren't going away, Clint."

He didn't have a clue what she meant by that, but she was piling groceries on the belt and talking to the cashier. He sighed, because he knew this wasn't the time or place. What had started as a little teasing had gone way wrong.

"Okay, we'll play this your way, Willow. We'll talk later."

She nodded, but he wasn't sure if she heard. And he wondered if later would ever come around.

Willow sat in her office, thinking about the previous day with Clint—visiting his father, and then the incident at the store. Heat crawled up her cheeks when she thought about Addie Johns calling friends to inform them that Clint had finally found a woman.

Those women had probably been praying for years that Clint would find a nice girl, settle down and have a few kids. Willow finished her candy bar and tossed the wrapper in the trash can.

Why *hadn't* he found a nice girl and gotten married? She thought she'd ask him. Maybe it had to do with chasing his dreams of being a bull rider, and having family obligations.

The phone rang, and she ignored it. She wasn't in the mood to deal with calls or not being able to hear the caller. She buried her face in her hands and waited until the ringing stopped and the answering machine picked up. The words were fuzzy.

Fuzzier than last week. Even fuzzier than a month ago. And she hadn't returned the call to her doctor because she didn't want to know the test results. Not yet. She didn't want to tell Janie, who was busy making arrangements for a trip to Florida with her friends.

She didn't want to tell Clint, because it felt good to have him in her life, treating her like someone who could take care of herself.

The door to her office opened, and Clint peeked in, smiling as he knocked on the side of the door frame. The boys jumped in ahead of him. They were wearing shorts, T-shirts and rubber boots.

"What are you guys up to?"

"Going fishing." Timmy held up his fishing pool. "Wanna come with us?"

David smiled, his fishing pole held tight in his fist. But he wasn't asking her to go. This morning he had told her he really just wanted his mom's hugs.

"Where are you going fishing?" she asked, looking up to meet Clint's questioning gaze.

"The creek, down by the church." He wore bright-red swim trunks and canvas sneakers. "Come on, be a sport."

"A sport?"

"Yep, the opposite of 'not a sport.' As in, we really want you to come with us."

Timmy shook his head. "We think you have the best snacks."

"Oh, so you have ulterior motives for inviting me?"

"To get you out of this dusty office." Timmy did a deep-voiced imitation of Clint, and Willow laughed.

"Okay, I'll come along. And I'll bring good snacks. We wouldn't want Uncle Clint to burn the house down."

Clint ruffled Timmy's hair. "Good job, buddy. Now you guys run down to the house and get that white cooler for drinks."

Willow watched the boys leave and then she stood, walking around to the front of the desk. Clint was still watching the empty door.

"You okay?" She touched his arm and he turned, his smile a halfway attempt.

"I'm not great. I'm pretty sure I'm failing at this whole guardian thing. David is throwing fits, and Timmy is trying to take over as the 'head of the house.'"

"You're doing fine, Clint. They're just sad little guys right now, and you all have a lot of adjusting to do."

"I guess so, but I sure hope I don't mess them up before she gets back."

"You won't mess them up. I won't let you."

He smiled, and then his expression softened. He touched her hair, and she shivered as his fingers slid down the strand, twirling it around and then letting it drop.

When had she stopped telling him that they couldn't do this, couldn't cross the line? When had his presence in her life started to feel like a forever-dream again?

When would the bottom drop out and leave her heart broken again?

"Having you here was pretty good planning on God's part." He glanced at the door and stepped away from her.

The boys rushed back into the room.

"Ready to go?" Clint asked, like nothing had happened. And Willow decided that nothing had, not really.

Except that Timmy was laughing, and David looked suspicious. Timmy spoke up. "Were you gonna kiss her, Uncle Clint?"

"Now, Timmy, what gentleman asks a question like that?"

"I just wanted to know." The boy dragged his feet a little and looked up, kind of sheepish. Willow didn't buy it because she saw the mischievous glint in his eyes.

"Right." Clint took the cooler. "Come on, let's get good snacks and go fishing."

"I need to check on one of my bulls." Willow grabbed her keys off the desk. "Can I meet you at the house?"

"Do you want me to do something?"

"No, I can do it." She followed them out of the barn, and as they headed across the gravel road to the house, she walked down the side of the fence and climbed over at the padlocked gate.

Dolly had been bullying a younger bull earlier in the day. She wanted to make sure the bigger animal hadn't done any damage. First she had to find him. She saw Dolly. He was standing at the watering trough, looking innocent. The other bull wasn't in sight.

Chapter Eleven

Clint turned when he heard a bull bellow. He shouted, but Willow didn't turn. She kept walking, as if she had no idea. He yelled again, and the boys screamed. The black bull that had been standing along the far fence was running toward her as she walked in the opposite direction.

"Willow!"

He left the boys standing in the yard and ran. He knew he wouldn't make it in time. He could only pray that he made it in time to keep the bull from killing her. He prayed she would hear him and turn around.

The bull hit her from behind, pushing her to the ground and wallowing her into the dirt. She did what a bull rider would do, curled into a ball and tried to roll out from under the pounding hooves.

Clint climbed the fence and jumped to the ground, yelling at the bull and waving his arms. Willow lay motionless on the ground. The bull changed directions as Bell came running across the field. The dog charged at the bull's legs, leading the animal away.

"Willow?" He dropped to his knees next to her, brushing a hand across her face. "Willow, wake up."

Her eyes opened briefly and then closed again. Clint pulled her close and stood up, holding her limp form in his arms.

"Honey, you sure aren't light." He kissed her forehead. Her eyes fluttered again. "Wake up, okay?"

She blinked again and groaned, her hand going to her head. He watched, helplessly, as blood oozed from the cut. When he was almost to the truck, he shouted for Timmy to open the door.

David stood to the side, his teeth worrying his lip and his eyes wide in fear. He smiled at the boy, hoping to ease his fears.

"She's okay, guys." He prayed he wasn't lying. He slid her into the truck and then rummaged for napkins he'd stored in the console between the seats. "Climb in the back."

He turned and the boys were scurrying to the driver's side to do what he'd asked. He held the napkins to her forehead, and she moaned and opened her eyes again.

"Hold on, we're going to the hospital."

She didn't say anything, and her eyes closed.

Silence and cold were the two things she noticed first. But a warm hand touched her cheek. Willow blinked, and it hurt. Her head ached, and the light hit right behind her eyes. She blinked again and then managed to keep her eyes open. Clint stood in front of her, his expression full of concern.

Welcome back, he signed, his lips moving. No sound.

What had happened? Panic hit, she moved, trying to get up. Pain shot through her head and down her back. She groaned and let firm hands push her back to the mattress.

The nurse smiled, her lips moved. "Calm down."

Willow closed her eyes, trying to remember. She opened them again when Clint's hand touched her arm. His hand, because it was rough, strong, and warm. A doctor stood next to him, asking questions.

Do you remember what day it is? Clint signed.

"Thursday." She moved her hand to her ears. "Where are the hearing aids?"

Broken. Do you remember what happened?

"I think a truck got loose and ran over me."

Close, it was a bull. He was smiling, but the lines around his mouth were tight, and humor didn't light his gray eyes.

"It felt like a truck." She wanted to smile, but everything hurt. And she shuddered, remembering. She remembered the ground vibrating, and being hit from behind. That big head had pushed her down, and her forehead had hit something hard.

You remember what happened? Clint's hands moved, asking the question.

"Yes, I remember. I think the bull knocked me down. I was going to check on him."

Clint sat down on the stool next to her bed. *Willow, you didn't hear me.*

She looked away, smiling when Janie walked through the door. "I'm fine. I'm not sure why the two of you look so worried."

We're worried because we… He looked away. *Because we care about you.*

She touched her head, wincing because the pain was sharp. She hadn't heard Clint. Tears squeezed between closed eyes, warm on her cheeks. She shivered, and a blanket slid over her.

When she opened her eyes, Clint was there, no one else. "Thank you for being here."

"That's what friends do. They help each other. You've helped me with the boys. You've given us a place to stay, and you make them feel safe." He signed the words and his lips moved.

"They're easy to love." She covered his hand that rested on her arm. "Where did Janie go?"

"She left so that I could talk to you."

"Oh." An intervention. Great.

"You didn't hear me."

"Maybe you weren't shouting loud enough."

"Willow, you have to tell us what's going on. We care about you." His hands moved as he spoke, showing his anger in a way that she clearly understood. "I guess you don't have to tell me, but I do think you owe Janie an explanation."

She looked away, not ready for this, for finding out the truth about his friendship. Would it last when he learned the truth? He touched her arm, and she couldn't ignore him, or the truth, any longer.

And she reminded herself how few hearing people had ever taken the time to sign for her. She'd always relied on reading lips. Clint had bridged that gap. He didn't have to.

"I know that I owe you both an explanation. But I didn't want this to keep Janie from moving."

"This."

"My hearing is going to get progressively worse."

Explain, he signed.

"Profound hearing loss. The hearing aids will be practically or totally useless. It's hard to tell at this point."

He sighed, and his hand went to his chest, his fist circling his heart. *I'm sorry*.

She nodded, because what else could he say, or she say? This was it, the truth, the inevitable. This was where she learned how strong a friendship they had.

This is where she found out if he stayed in her life or walked.

"It isn't the end of the world." She'd had a few days to deal with the news. She could see shock all over his face.

"Of course it isn't." He smiled as he said the words.

Reality was easy to think about, until a person was face-to-face with it. Complete hearing loss—a huge change in how she lived, and how the people around her lived their lives.

It changed everything.

"Where are the boys?" she asked.

In the waiting room with Janie, he signed, and she nodded.

"We should go. They're probably hungry. And I ruined their day at the creek.

"The boys are fine with Janie. She's going to take them home, and she's going to call your folks to let them know what happened."

"No, don't call my parents. They'll just worry, and I don't want them to worry."

They're your parents, Clint signed, and then he stood up, like he meant to leave. She didn't want him to go. "And they'll be hurt if they find out later."

"I have a concussion, and my head hurts. I need to sleep."

No sleeping. A new doctor entered the room, a woman with short brown hair and fingers adept at signing. *You'll have to stay awake for a while. And I would really like it if you would spend the night.*

Willow groaned and closed her eyes. "No, please don't make me spend the night."

It felt like five years ago, when everyone made the decisions for her. But it wasn't. This time she had Janie and Clint. And she had faith. Five years ago she had really and truly been on her own, with God as an afterthought, filed somewhere at the back of her mind like so many other childhood memories.

"Does she have to spend the night?" Clint signed and spoke to the doctor, not leaving Willow out of the conversation. "We can keep an eye on her."

The doctor looked from Willow to Clint. "I want her to stay for a few hours, and then we'll discuss her going home."

Clint patted her arm to get her attention. "I'll go talk to Janie about taking the boys home. Or I can take them home, and Janie can stay with you. Either way, one of us will be here."

Willow closed her eyes and nodded. When she opened them, Clint was gone. He was talking to Janie. Or had he left? She couldn't find a clock on the wall and had no way of knowing what time it was or how long she'd been there. She closed her eyes again, wanting to escape the pain, because it wasn't just the bumps and bruises from the bull that hurt.

* * *

Willow was asleep when Clint walked through the curtain partition that separated her from other patients. He didn't want to wake her, but knew he had to. She looked peaceful in sleep, as if it was rest that she needed.

He touched her arm, and her eyes flickered and opened. His smile brought one from her, and then her hand touched the place on her forehead where they'd given her a few stitches.

"Ouch," she whispered. "That's going to leave a mark."

He smiled and laughed a little. "Yes, it's going to leave a mark."

"Does it look bad?"

You look better than you did, he signed, and then laughed. "Not that you ever look bad. I mean, you usually look great."

"I'm not sure if I feel hurt or complimented." She pushed the button and lifted the bed to a sitting position. "I do know that I'm ready to get out of here."

"You have to stay until the doctor releases you. And I wouldn't push her. She isn't in favor of you leaving today."

"The boys…"

"Are fine with Janie." He scooted the stool closer to her side. "Willow, this is serious. We need to come up with a plan."

"Clint."

He lifted his hands and shook his head. "You're right, none of my business."

"No, it isn't your business." She smiled past him,

and he turned in time to see a nurse walk away. Willow's hands began a quick firing of words. *I don't want to have to come up with a plan.*

Why?

Avoidance. I know what's happening to my own body. I also know that if Janie knows, she'll put off moving.

You think you're only strong if you hold on and don't let people help you.

I've let you help. She smiled like it all made perfect sense. "Now, I really want to get out of here, Clint. I want to sleep in my own room. I want to have breakfast with Janie and the boys."

"For a price I could see if it could be arranged."

"For a price?"

"You have to let friends face this with you. You're not alone, so stop acting like you are." He smiled, to soften the words. "Trust your friends."

"I know, and I do trust you. But you have your hands full with the boys. And if this is going to happen, I have to deal with it and learn how to keep going."

"I know, but just remember, you can trust me."

Trust. An easy little word but with so many complications.

It was easy to commit to someone when things were going well, when there were no obstacles in the way. But obstacles could damage any relationship, even something as simple as friendship.

She was going to lose her hearing. End of story. That was a big complication.

Clint touched her hand, drawing her attention back to him. "It's going to be okay. And I'm going to be here to help."

"I know. And I do trust you."

"You're saying what you think I want to hear because you want something. You want to go home."

She shrugged. "Is it working?"

"No."

Of course not. He wasn't easy to dissuade. He wasn't prone to chasing rabbits or getting off track.

"Okay, fine, we'll talk. I've been dealing with this, trying to get through it and adjust."

"But you're doing this alone, and we could have helped."

"You won't always be here." She shifted her gaze toward the window, away from his sympathy. "Janie won't always be here. What am I going to do with my business when I can't hear a caller on the telephone, or announcers at events?"

"I get it." He stood but he didn't move away. "But I don't get why you think you're doing this alone."

"I know that I'm not. I'm just trying to prepare."

"We can help you with that."

She shook her head. "No, you can't. You can't help me face how people will react."

"Which means?"

"There are three different ways people can react. One. Let me keep living my life, and keep treating me the way I've been treated. Second. Some people will walk away, because it's just too difficult to deal with. Or the third option, start treating me like I can't take care of myself."

He nodded, not answering right away. And she wondered which option he would choose.

"One day at a time, Willow. That's how we'll deal with this."

He kept saying "we" like he meant to stay in her life. Each time he said it her heart battled between wanting to believe and being afraid to believe.

"Yes, one day at a time."

I'm not going anywhere. He signed it with force.

"I know you aren't. Now go see if you can break me out of here. I promise to be good."

He nodded. "I'll see if I can make a deal."

"Thank you."

He walked out the door and after he left she sighed and leaned back against the bed. Clint wanted to make sure she survived whatever might happen to her in the future.

Thirty minutes later he lifted her off her feet and carried her the short distance from the doors of the hospital to his waiting truck. Her arms were around his neck, and when she argued that she could walk, he shook his head.

She'd correctly guessed his type. He was a rescuer. He couldn't help himself. It was as much a part of him as his eye color, as his faith, as his sense of loyalty. And it wasn't a bad thing, his need to rescue.

Maybe he needed rescuing, too? That thought brought a smile that she hid in the soft curve of his shoulder. She could rescue him.

He opened the truck door and leaned in to set her on the seat. His arms were around her, and hers were still wrapped around his neck. His breath, minty and warm, touched her cheek as he drew back, and he paused, his hands resting lightly on her arms.

As they stared at one another, Willow tried to think of something to say. Words failed her. Clint's hand brushed hair back from her face and lingered at the nape of her neck.

"I'm going to kiss you." His hands also signed the words, soft and beautiful, like a whisper.

"We'll regret this tomorrow." The words edged past the tightness in her throat.

"Maybe."

As he leaned closer, Willow held her breath, waiting for that moment when Clint's lips touched hers. It wasn't a fleeting kiss, not a promise of something more to come. The kiss *was* the promise. It felt like forever, warm and firm, touching places forgotten, or places she'd never known.

She slid her hands through his hair and waited for reality to return as his soft curls wrapped around her fingers. The kiss went deeper, and her emotions took flight as his hands rested on her back, holding her close.

A long moment, and they pulled apart. Willow couldn't talk, she nearly couldn't breathe. That kiss had felt different, it had felt dangerously close to falling in love. Clint leaned against the door of the truck, looking like he'd been run over by the same bull that hit her. He pushed a hand through his hair and whistled.

Who was rescuing whom?

"That was either the best thing I've ever done, or the biggest mistake of my life."

Willow's mouth opened and she shook her head. Reading lips could sometimes be a problem. Surely she'd misunderstood. "Big mistake?"

His fingers moved, slow and a little shaky. *How do we go back to friendship?*

Lines drawn and now smudged. Badly smudged. She'd drawn those lines herself, knowing she had to find the place where he fit comfortably into her world, where he wasn't a threat, and where he was least likely to hurt her.

What now?

"I'm not sure, Clint. But I'd like to go home." Because suddenly—maybe because of the head injury, or maybe because of a kiss—she couldn't remember why it had been so important to her that he be only a friend.

And now *he* seemed to think they could only be friends.

He started to say something, and Willow looked away, avoiding his words. He touched her shoulder, and she shook her head. She wasn't going to listen. She signed the words, and he turned her so that they were facing each other.

Not fair, he signed.

"Kissing me like that and calling it a mistake wasn't fair." She lifted her chin a notch, more for confidence than a statement of defiance. "I need time to think, and I really don't want to listen to what you have to say. If I have to, I'll close my eyes."

He laughed. "That's about the most juvenile thing I've ever heard from a grown woman."

"Yes, it is, isn't it? Juvenile, but effective."

She couldn't stay mad at him when she'd been thinking what he'd had the nerve to say. A great kiss, or a big mistake. She thought maybe it fit into both categories.

Chapter Twelve

Clint left Willow in Janie's capable hands that first night, and the next day she spent resting. Janie insisted. He waited until the second day after the accident to face her again, and to let the boys visit.

The boys had demanded it. A whole day without Willow had been too much for them. He followed them into the house, warning them to take it easy because she might not feel like having company. Especially rowdy four-year-old company.

But he figured his company would be the least welcome, because he had stepped a little too far into her life. As much as it had felt as if she enjoyed being in his arms, as much as he enjoyed having her there, it had definitely done something. It had put distance between them.

Maybe because they both had a lot to think about. He sure hadn't been expecting this when he met her. He hadn't been looking for these feelings.

As he walked down the hall, he heard Janie in the back room, talking to the boys. Willow was silent.

He walked into the sitting room where the boys were chattering to Janie, and Willow was trying to follow along. As he walked through the door, he signed their excited words for her.

Willow smiled over their heads, and the boys continued to jabber about the kittens crawling around in the barn and Bell chasing a mouse.

"Guys, get off Willow. Give her a break." He signed as he spoke to the boys, making sure she didn't get left out.

"They're fine. They're just excited about their new trucks."

"They're going to play, and then we're going to try the creek again." He sat down on the couch next to Willow.

"Sounds like fun. I think I'll not go this time."

"You didn't make it last time."

"And because of me, the boys missed out on fishing and the rope swing." She hugged both boys and kissed the tops of their heads. Clint told himself it was silly to be jealous of little boys.

"I think they understood." He pulled the boys to his side and gave them each a bear hug. "I'm going to get some work done this morning. We'll do the creek this afternoon, guys. For now, the two of you can play outside where I can see you."

Willow followed him to the front door. As the boys grabbed their cars and ran off for a dirt patch that they were itching to dig around in, Willow caught hold of his arm.

"Clint, don't do this."

"Do what?"

"Don't treat me different. Don't let my hearing,

a kiss, whatever has happened, don't let it change things between us." She bit down on her bottom lip and shrugged, "I don't want to lose your friendship."

"You haven't lost me, Willow."

"Haven't I?"

"No, you haven't. I have a lot on my mind. Yes, I'm worried about you. I'm worried about what this all means to your future here. I'm worried because I haven't had an e-mail from Jenna. I'm worried because the boys miss their mom. I'm about exhausted from worry."

"Then don't let me be one of the things you worry about. I'm fine. I've been taking care of myself for a long time now, and I'm going to keep taking care of myself. I'm not giving up on this farm, or raising bulls. I'll figure something out. And I'm still very capable of helping with the boys. Don't take that away from me."

"I'm sorry, Willow." He brushed a hand through his hair. "This isn't about you. It's me. I'm just tired, and I have work to do in the barn."

"Okay, go work in the barn. I have an appointment in town." She pulled him back. "Hey, that's my barn. Is there something going on that I should know about?"

Well, he really hadn't wanted to deal with this right now. But from the look on her face, he wasn't going to have the chance to walk away without telling her everything.

"Nothing important, just going to clean the stalls and meet James McKinney later. He wants to look at that little cow you were talking about selling, the Hereford."

"James McKinney is coming to look at one of my cows? James doesn't like my cows."

"They're cows like everyone else's."

"No, not in James's mind they're not." She frowned, and it was cute. "I think in his mind my cows are city cows."

"Well, he must have changed his mind. I saw him at the feed store, and he mentioned buying a cow for his granddaughter. She's joined 4-H."

"And you offered to sell him my cow."

"You told me you wanted to sell her." He shook his head. "Willow, I'm just about confused now. If you don't want to sell that heifer, I'll call him and tell him not to come over."

"Go ahead and sell her." She turned and walked back inside the house. Bell sat on the porch staring at Clint and then looking at the door.

"She even has you confused, doesn't she?" He patted his leg, and the dog followed him out to the barn.

After cleaning out a few stalls Clint fixed a bottle for the calf and held it over the fence. The black-and-white animal nudged the bottle and then latched on and drank down the milk in a matter of minutes. Clint pulled the bottle away and dumped grain into the trough.

"That's it, buddy." He dropped the bottle in the bucket, sat it inside the barn and then walked through the dry, dusty lot. He glanced up, hoping for a sign of rain. Not a cloud in the sky. It was near the end of June, and they could use a good soaking before the grass dried up and they had to start hauling in hay from somewhere else.

The cow he was going to show James McKinney was in the corral. He'd brought her up last night, separating her from the rest of the herd to make it easier to show her today. When she saw him coming she mooed a pitiful sound, asking for her companions and some grain. He lifted the bucket of grain he'd carried out for her. That'd have to be enough to keep her happy.

A deep red with brown eyes in a white face, she lumbered to the feed and shoved her nose into the molasses-covered corn and oats, snorting and blowing it across the metal trough. He reached through and rubbed the top of her head. She jerked away, grain slobbering from her mouth as her tongue licked to draw it back in.

"Yeah, you're not the only female mad at me." He lifted his leg and hooked his boot on the lower rail of the fence. "I'm a pretty unpopular guy this morning."

"Talking to yourself, Clint?"

He turned and smiled at Janie. She wore polyester pants, a loose top and rubber work boots. He smiled, remembering her fifteen years before, out in a storm trying to save one of her prize cows, which had been having difficulty giving birth. She'd pulled out the calf that had refused to exit the birth canal, and then she'd pushed on that mama cow until she got to her feet. She had saved them all, including Jenna and him.

"Yeah, I guess I am."

"You're going to have to stop trying to be such a hero." Janie reached through and rubbed her hand along the floppy ear of the cow.

"What do you mean by that?"

"I mean that all of her life Willow has had people making decisions for her. This ranch was the one thing she did on her own. Now, more than ever, she needs to feel like she's still in control."

"I'm helping."

"You *were* helping. But this accident and the test results changed things." Janie's eyes watered. "Oh, Clint, we don't want to think of Willow going through something like this. But she's facing it, and she's determined. Don't treat her any differently."

"I'm not." He sighed. "I sure don't mean to."

"Did you mean to fall in love with her?"

He laughed at that. "Janie, one thing I'm not is in love. I'm here to help Willow for as long as she needs me. But I don't have time for relationships. I've got two little boys to raise and a farm to rebuild."

Janie patted his arm, the way she'd been doing since he was a twelve-year-old kid, asking for odd jobs. "You're a little too convinced you're the only one who can take care of everyone, but you've got a good heart."

"It isn't bad to take care of people that you care about." The rumble of a truck coming down the drive sounded like an escape.

"No, it isn't bad, unless you are so busy taking care of everyone that you forget to let them into your life." She glanced in the direction of the old, blue farm truck pulling up to the barn. "That's old McKinney. I'm leaving before he can ask me to have coffee at the café."

"Maybe I'm not the only one so busy taking care of everyone that I forget to let people into my life." He shot the comment at her retreating back.

Janie turned, smiling. "I guess you learned it from me. Is that a good thing, Clint?"

He shrugged. "I don't know, Janie. You've always seemed pretty content."

"Think about what I've said. I'm going to check on the boys. They're playing out front. Willow went to get new hearing aids."

"See you in a bit."

She continued on, her boots scuffing in the dusty dirt. Clint sighed and leaned his back against the fence. Janie, in her sixties and alone all of these years. He couldn't remember one time that she ever went out with someone, other than her friends from church.

He wondered if she ever got lonely. And if someday he would look back on his life, a life without someone to share it with, and regret. His entire life he'd spent taking care of Jenna and his dad, and later, the boys. And love had seemed like something that didn't really last.

James McKinney walked through the gate and headed in his direction. The old farmer's eyes were on the cow, and he was nodding. Clint fought back a smile. James McKinney had more money than most banks. He actually owned part of a bank or two. But like so many of the older farmers, you couldn't tell by looking at him. He drove a twenty-year-old truck that he didn't see a need to replace. He lived in a house that hadn't seen a new roof in thirty years and was still being heated with wood and cooled with fans.

James McKinney was the old guard of farming, the guys who didn't go into unnecessary debt and raised cows for meat, not show. He didn't have no use, he would say, in pedigrees. He wanted a cow that would produce good calves.

Until now. And Clint knew that girls changed everything. Even a crusty old farmer.

"She looks good, Clint. Why's Willow getting rid of her?"

"She has to cull a few, James."

"You wouldn't try to pull one over on an old guy, would you, Clint? Your daddy pulled a few good ones on me." The older farmer laughed. "He sold me a horse one time, told me she was a champion of some kind. That horse was nothing but the champion of running her rider through barn doors."

"I remember that horse." Clint smiled. "Sorry about that. And no, I don't deal like my dad did."

"That's good to know." James walked around the cow, looking from all angles. "I hate to even admit this, but my granddaughter wants a cow to show in community fairs."

Clint nodded. He understood. A man would do strange things for a woman. "Well, things change, James. And I bet grandkids change a man even more."

"You wouldn't believe it if I told you." He scratched his chin and nodded, slow, thoughtful. "She looks like a good little heifer. Gentle, too."

"She likes most people." Everyone but him.

"You couldn't get a better heifer for your granddaughter, James." Willow's voice. She walked toward them, smiling and dismissing Clint with a look. He backed away, because he knew that territorial look on her face. He'd seen barn cats like her, circling their territory, backs arched.

"Will she lead?" James asked Clint. Clint looked at Willow. Nope, she wouldn't lead, and she sure couldn't be pushed.

He wasn't sure what to do, but Willow was looking at him, so he signed the other man's inquiry because the questioning look on her face said she hadn't heard.

"Yes, she'll lead," Willow answered.

James McKinney looked from Willow to Clint, as if he wasn't sure which one of them he should be talking to. Clint pointed to Willow, it was her cow. He was just the unlucky guy that was trying to help.

"Do you think she'd make a show cow?" James McKinney muttered and shook his head as he glanced over the heifer, his back to Willow. Clint signed the question and Willow adjusted the new hearing aids she had obviously gone to Grove to pick up.

"She will, James." Willow had a lead rope, and she walked through the gate and snapped it onto the halter the cow wore. "Stand aside, gentlemen."

She led the cow out of the pen and closed the gate behind her. She walked up to James McKinney and handed him the corded rope. "Take her home with you, James. I'm sure Clint already gave you a price."

Ouch. But she was right, he had given the farmer a price, the one Willow had quoted him earlier. He pretty much knew at that moment that he was in serious, very serious, trouble.

Willow left Clint with James McKinney and walked across the lawn to the swing where the boys were sitting, the two of them together. They were always together.

She shot a look in the direction of the barn and Clint saying goodbye to James McKinney. Ignoring him was the only way for her to take back her space.

She'd lived through this before, with her parents, and with other men.

She had wanted Clint to be different. She had wanted him to not be her dad, with a protective streak and that need to make decisions for her, as if she couldn't. She had hoped he wouldn't be the man that couldn't handle her deafness.

Her heart leaped to his defense. He had signed for her, allowing her to be included in the conversation with James.

She pulled back on the ropes of the swing and gave the boys a little push. They looked back, smiling, but not laughing.

Each week that passed, missing their mother got harder, not easier for them. With her trip to Austin canceled—thanks to her accident—they wouldn't have to travel for a few weeks. They could all use a break and a little stability.

She pushed the boys a little harder, a little higher. They were still quiet, still not themselves. She brought them back to earth, holding tight to the ropes until the swing came to a halt.

"Do you guys want ice cream?" She moved to the front of the swing and squatted in front of them.

They nodded, their little faces dirty and their hair sticking out in all directions. They needed a bath. Men didn't notice those things.

"Hey, I have an idea. Why don't the two of you put on swim trunks, and we'll turn on the hose. You can play in the water, cool off, and I'll even get some soap for you to bubble up with."

They looked on board with her plan until she mentioned soap. But they needed it. She knew they'd been playing in the driveway, making miniature roads through the dirt and gravel for their toy cars.

"Come on, ice cream and a shower in the garden hose." She smiled, making it sound like a great idea.

Timmy finally nodded and slid off the swing, a hand on David's arm pulling the smaller twin along with him. "Come on, David, you're starting to stink."

Willow smiled, because she knew Timmy had heard that from someone. Probably from Clint. The boys ran ahead of her, in a hurry for the ice cream, not the baths.

"You boys need to find swim trunks for the hose."

They were running away from her, and if they answered, she didn't hear them. But they would know where to find what they needed. While they got ready and picked ice cream, she'd drag out the hose.

A shadow near the barn. Clint. He waved and walked back into the shadows. She saw him tug out his cell phone, and then a dark sedan pulled down the drive. Willow stopped to watch, her heart hurting as the men stepped out of the car and walked up to Clint.

The boys were running into the garage where the extra freezer held the boxes of ice cream bars. She followed along at a slower pace. She laughed as she walked into the dark room, but she didn't feel like laughing. The boys were stripping, and under their clothes they had on swim trunks.

"You guys are ready to go?"

"We wanted to go to the creek today," Timmy explained. "Uncle Clint said he'd take us later."

"Okay, grab a fudge bar or ice cream sandwich. Oh, and there are orange Push-Ups."

The two of them were rummaging, looking for

their favorites. Willow smiled as she walked out the back door. The hose was on a caddy. She pulled it loose and hooked it to the sprinkler. When the boys walked out, ice cream dripping down their chins, she was ready for them. She turned on the water and pointed.

"There you go. Finish your ice cream and then jump in. I'll get towels and soap."

"No soap!" David looked at her and said the words with a disgusted face that left no room for doubt.

"Sweetie, you have to get clean."

"'Cause you stink." Timmy was nodding, like he was the expert on stinking. "You smell worse than my dirty socks."

Pleasant. Willow wrinkled her nose at them. "Dirty socks is a bad smell, David. I'll be right back."

She glanced at the barn as she walked through the garage. Clint was standing near the barn door, his hat in his hands and his face pointed away from her. The car was gone. The boys were laughing and jumping through the sprinkler. She wanted them to stay young and innocent. She didn't want their hearts to be broken.

Chapter Thirteen

Clint watched the car drive away and then he looked across the drive to see Willow with the boys. He couldn't go over there, not yet. The boys disappeared around the side of the house, carrying ice cream. Clint smiled at that, at the sight of them being little boys, and Willow being herself with them. He could hear the boys shouting something about cold and then squeals combined with laughter. Willow's laughter melted with theirs.

He wanted to laugh with them, to tell them everything would be okay. But he couldn't. He headed their way. At the corner of the house he stopped and watched. They were running under the cold spray of the sprinkler. They had soap, and they would step out of the water, scrub and run back under the water. A creative way to get them clean. He wanted to smile, and he wanted to cry.

Willow turned, smiling when she saw him. She was sitting in a lawn chair, blond and perfect, jean shorts and a T-shirt, her hair pulled back. He must have revealed something because her smile dissolved and she stood up. As she crossed the yard, slipping past the boys and the spray from the hose, he prayed for strength.

He prayed that God would do something huge. He prayed his sister would come back home alive.

That she would come back.

His eyes burned and his chest felt tight.

It all looked so normal. It looked like any other day. The boys were playing, splashing on a summer afternoon, with the blue Oklahoma sky a backdrop for their fun, and bees buzzing over the flowers on a nearby bush.

How could it look like everything was okay, when it was anything but?

"Clint?"

He looked up. Willow stood in front of him, nearly as tall as he was. Her blue eyes met his and held his gaze, looking deep, like she could see into his heart. He hoped she couldn't, because the thoughts in there were pretty scrambled right about then.

"I can't talk about it." He touched her shoulder as he passed. He couldn't talk yet. Not because he didn't want to, but because he couldn't get the words past the tight lump in his throat.

"Aunt Janie?" Willow rushed past him, opening the screen door on the back of the house. "Could you come out here and watch the boys?"

Janie walked out, smiling, wiping her hands on a kitchen towel. She glanced from him to Willow and then to the boys. Her eyes narrowed, and he looked away, not able to tell her, not yet. He needed a few minutes to get it together, for everyone's sake. For the boys' sake.

"Clint?"

He shook his head and walked past her, into the air-conditioned dining room of her house. Willow followed him inside, her hand rested on his shoulder while he gathered his thoughts and fought back the wave of fear that got tangled with faith, as he tried to tell himself God could take care of Jenna.

"She's missing." He whispered the words and then turned and said them again. "Jenna is missing."

"Oh, Clint." Her only words as she stepped close and her arms wrapped around his waist, holding him tight.

One harsh sob escaped the lump in his throat and Willow's tears were hot on his neck. He had to hang on, to be strong. If he looked outside he would see the boys, playing in the mist of the sprinkler. A summer day, blue skies, and people relying on him. For just a few minutes he wanted to not be that person.

"What happened?" Willow whispered against his neck.

He moved back a step and closed his eyes as he took a deep breath. Willow's hand remained on his arm. When he opened his eyes she moved her hand to his cheek and a soft, tremulous smile curved her lips.

"Her unit was moving and it was attacked. They can't find her anywhere."

"They'll find her."

"What if…"

"We're not going to give up, Clint. We're going to keep praying and keep having faith."

"I know. I know." But his heart ached and faith was in short supply at the moment.

"I'm going to pray, Clint. I'm going to have enough faith for both of us right now."

He closed his eyes and breathed in, nodding his agreement. Right now that's what he needed.

He glanced out the window and saw Janie with his nephews. The boys needed him. As much as he wanted to stay in Willow's arms, he knew that his priority was outside, with two little boys who were about to learn that their mother was missing.

"Don't tell them." Willow grabbed his arm. "Not yet, Clint. Give the military time to find her. Give the boys this day to play."

Before he took away their sunshine.

How would they recover from this? Would they? He brushed a hand through his hair and watched as the boys played, splashing fine mists of water at Janie. She raised the towel and laughed. But he could see that her laughter was strained, because she knew.

As he watched, Janie looked his way, her smile fading. Willow's hand still held his arm, like she thought her hold on him would keep the inevitable from happening.

"I have to tell them. I can't keep this from them."

"They're babies."

He sighed, wishing the huge breath he took would relieve the tightness in his chest. It didn't. The truth was still there, heavy on his heart. He smiled down at Willow. Her gaze had left his face, and she was looking out the window, at his nephews. He lifted the hand she'd placed on his arm and kissed her palm.

Her gaze shifted back to his face. "Don't tell them,

Clint. Don't make them carry this weight. We can carry it for them until we know something definite."

Definite. The word hit like an arrow. Until he knew for sure if his sister was coming back to them. He held on to Willow's hand, knowing she would let go of her anger with him for this time, while he needed her.

And he did need her.

He'd never needed anyone before, not the way he needed her. All of his life he'd taken care of things, of people, and he'd been just fine with that.

He couldn't even think about when it had started, this needing her. And now more than ever, the boys needed him. They needed him strong.

"You're right. We won't tell them. Not yet."

She nodded and walked out the door ahead of him, already wearing a smile for the boys to see. But he had seen the look in her eyes before she turned away. Her eyes reflected her sorrow, for him, for the boys and for Jenna.

He pasted on a smile of his own as he walked out to join the boys under the sprinkler, not caring that his clothes got soaked.

Life had just taken a sudden turn, and now, everything was about Timmy and David and getting through the days and weeks to come. His gaze connected with Willow's. She stood just at the edge of the spray of water, letting it hit her arms and face. He could see the tears still trickling out of her eyes as she watched the boys play.

The boys wouldn't let him remain in his stupor. Timmy splashed him, and when Clint smiled, the child stood for a moment studying him. Like he knew something was wrong. Clint forced a bigger smile and splashed back.

"Why don't you guys finish up and we'll go back to our house for a little while. You can put on dry clothes, and then we'll cook hot dogs."

"Could we make a fire?" David edged out of the water and his thumb went to his mouth.

"We can build a fire, yes."

"Do you have marshmallows?" Timmy stood under the spray of water, and he still didn't look convinced that everything was okay.

"I don't have marshmallows."

"We have some," Janie offered.

Clint backed out of the water, still unable to really make eye contact with Janie or Willow. "Thanks. The two of you can join us."

"I can't tonight, Clint." Janie pushed herself out of the lawn chair she'd been sitting in. "Willow can come down. We have all of the fixings for s'mores."

Timmy grabbed Willow's hand. She looked at Clint, and he knew she'd lost part of the conversation. He signed the plan for her. She smiled down at Timmy and nodded. "I'll be down, sweetie. We can sing and make s'mores. It'll be fun."

Timmy and David, soaked and shivering from the cold well water, grabbed his hands.

"Let's go." Timmy pulled on him, and Clint smiled goodbye to Willow and Janie.

At six-thirty Willow walked down the drive to the foreman's house. Clint was at the edge of the drive, making a circle with rocks for the fire. The garden hose was out, because the grass was dry for so early in the summer. Willow smiled because the boys were dragging huge limbs they'd found at the edge of the yard to the fire pit.

Timmy walked backwards, pulling on a limb that had to be ten feet long. David dropped his and brushed his hands off on his denim shorts. He picked it up again and heaved to set it in motion. An offer to help would have crushed him, so she watched, praying he wouldn't get hurt.

"They're having fun." Clint spoke when she was close. He placed the last rock and sat back on his heels.

"They're definitely having fun." She pulled up one of the lawn chairs he had set out and lowered herself, still aching from the run-in with the bull.

"You okay?" Clint stood, dusting his hands off on his jeans and then pulling up a chair for himself.

"I'm good. It's you I'm worried about. And the boys."

We'll get through this, he signed, *and Jenna will come home.*

She will, Clint. I know she will, she signed back, rather than speaking. This protected the boys from overhearing. She didn't want them to hear this conversation.

He nodded and glanced in the direction of the boys. They were still dragging too-large limbs, huffing and puffing as they made their way across the yard. "I should help them."

"They're fine. But we should probably find some smaller pieces of wood."

He grinned at that. "You're a campfire girl?"

"I happen to know a few things about camping."

She stood up and reached for his hand. "Come on, let's help the boys."

You're helping me, Willow. He spoke the words with his hands, and she silently thanked God for good friends. "Thank you for coming down here tonight."

"I wouldn't have left you on your own."

"Yes, you would have."

"No, Clint, I wouldn't have. This is no longer about us. It's about two little boys." She lifted his hand and kissed his knuckles. "It's about you, too. Friends help each other."

As they crossed the yard to trees at the back of the house, Clint didn't comment.

"Janie talked to our pastor." Willow reached for a few twigs for kindling. "He wants to have a prayer service tomorrow night."

"What about the boys?"

"We'll take them to the nursery and let them play."

"Okay." He touched her arm and pointed back to the house. "They want to eat."

Willow turned and smiled at the boys. They were standing at the corner of the house, side by side.

"I think we're being summoned." Clint grabbed a few more small limbs. "Coming, guys."

Willow followed Clint back to the front of the house and dumped her wood next to the pile the boys had dragged up. With that amount of wood, they'd have a fire until late into the night. And maybe that's what Timmy and David planned.

She sat down in the lawn chair and watched as Clint piled kindling and paper. He struck a match, and a little flame burst into life, catching the paper and the smallest twigs.

And then it went out.

He tried again. Willow snickered and the boys laughed. Clint gave her a look and shook his head, but his lips turned into a little smile. A sheepish smile that flickered and then dissolved as he bent to concentrate on the fire, and worry. She knew he was worried.

"I can do this." He struck another match.

"Of course you can." Willow agreed, but she shook her head, and the boys laughed again.

Clint sat back on his heels and tossed her the matches. "Go ahead, smarty pants, you get it started."

Willow stood. "Okay, I'll make you a deal. I'll get the fire started, and you have to roast my hot dogs."

"Done." He held out his hand. "Shake on it."

She didn't want to shake on it. His gaze challenged her, and she took his hand. But he didn't play fair. He held her hand, his thumb brushing hers a few times.

"Thank you for making me smile," he whispered, and then he kissed her cheek.

The boys covered their mouths. Willow laughed and walked away, but her insides were shaking because he kept switching things around on her, making her want him in her life.

She opened the cabinet on the carport and pulled out a bag of charcoal and starter fluid. As she walked back, Clint called her a cheater.

"I'm not cheating. Did I not say that I could build a fire?" She piled charcoal under a few twigs of wood and one larger piece. After dousing them with starter fluid she waited a few seconds and struck a match. The charcoal blazed, and the wood sparked, crackled and caught fire.

"Tah-dah."

"You win." Clint stood next to her. "I still say you cheated, but you win."

Willow handed him her stick. "I like mine well-done. And my marshmallows light brown, so that they're just hot enough to melt the chocolate."

"Yes, ma'am." Clint hugged her waist, one arm around her, and his shoulder brushing hers. When he let her go she backed into her chair to watch.

The boys sat one on each side of him and he helped them skewer the hot dogs. Willow's heart ached for the three of them. Their faint conversation drifted back to her and she strained to hear, wiping away tears that trickled down her cheeks.

"Can't we have marshmallows first?" David asked.

"Nope, buddy, we have to eat something good for us."

"Hot dogs aren't good for us," Timmy informed him with a slight shake of his head. "They're full of servatives."

"*Pre*servatives," Clint corrected.

"Yes, those." Timmy lifted his nearly black hot dog out of the fire.

"Here, Timmy, let me help you get that on a bun." Willow walked to the table that held their condiments, chips and bottled water. "Do you want ketchup?"

Timmy shook his head. He looked up at her, eyes watery. "I want my mom, 'cause she knows that I don't like buns, and I just like mustard."

Willow actually felt her heart break. It cracked into a million pieces and flooded her eyes with tears she couldn't blink back fast enough. Timmy was staring at her with a thousand questions in his little eyes, and what could she do?

"Tim, buddy, that isn't fair." Clint's face was a mask of control that Willow knew he couldn't be feeling.

"It's okay." Willow smiled and brushed Timmy's hair back, patting him on the back rather than giving him the hug that she wanted to give, but knew that he didn't want at that moment. She could see it in his stiff little shoulders and the challenge in his eyes.

"Come on, guys, let's eat fast so we can have s'mores. I love s'mores." Willow squirted mustard on a plate and let Timmy push his hotdog next to it. He reached for a small bag of chips and walked off, still hurting.

David inched closer to her side. He tugged on her hand and she looked down, smiling because he was smiling. "I like my hot dog on a bun."

"Do you like mustard or ketchup?"

He pointed to the ketchup. Willow fixed his plate, and he picked the seat next to hers.

Clint was still facing the fire. Willow wanted to tell him it would be okay. She couldn't. How could she make that promise? Especially when his back was to her, and his shoulders were as stiff as Timmy's, a sign that he was trying too hard to be strong.

The fire flickered, orange and blue flames dancing in the light breeze and shooting sparks into the air that fluttered and died out. It kept Clint in a trance for a few minutes, thinking, praying. The boys were behind him, talking to Willow in soft tones about the sound of the crickets that she couldn't hear, and why they loved s'mores the best, but hot dogs were okay, too.

Kid talk, like everything was okay. And they had

no idea that their world hinged on a group of guys thousands of miles away searching for their mother. He sighed and closed his eyes, feeling the heat from the fire blending with the warm summer night and a light breeze.

"Do you want one, Uncle Clint?" Timmy tugged at his hand, looking up at him with eyes that still questioned.

"Yes, I do want a s'more." He wrapped an arm around his nephew's shoulder and thought back to his own childhood, before his mother died.

A lump of emotion rose from his heart to his throat, and he swallowed it down because he had to make this work for the boys, for their sake. Timmy leaned in close, his hand tighter on Clint's.

"Can we call my mom?" The little boy asked.

"Let's sit down and pray for her instead." Clint sat down in the lawn chair and pulled Timmy onto his lap. "We can't call her right now, but we can say a prayer for her."

"Do you think she will know that we're praying?" Timmy whispered.

"I think she will. And she definitely knows we love her." Clint's silent prayer was that his sister would find faith. Now more than ever.

Timmy nodded against his shoulder, leaning in close and wrapping sticky-marshmallow arms around his neck. Clint couldn't look at Willow. He knew that in the dark there would be tears in her eyes.

He wanted to hold them all. He wanted to hold Jenna, too. A hand touched his arm. Willow. She smiled at him and nodded. He was doing okay.

He prayed, and David climbed onto his lap with

Timmy. Willow pulled her chair closer. As the fire burned down to coals, they sat together, singing "Jesus Loves Me."

Clint prayed his own prayers, silent prayers for wisdom. He hadn't hurt this bad since his mother's death. He remembered that day, and the following year, dealing with the pain and no one to really lean on. He hadn't known how to tell anyone how bad it hurt. Willow was sitting next to him, her hand on his arm, and he didn't know how to let her in.

Chapter Fourteen

Sunday evening the church parking lot was full of people. Willow stopped her truck, parking at the edge of the road, the only space left. The tiny community church, far from town and any real housing development, didn't have need of a big parking area, not on a normal Sunday.

Today wasn't just any Sunday. Today was the day after they had learned that Jenna Cameron was MIA. Today was a day of prayer that she would come home to her sons and her family.

Clint had come early with Janie and the boys. The boys would be in the nursery, far from the service and prayer. Clint had taken Willow's and Janie's advice. The boys didn't need to know.

How would the boys survive this, if Jenna didn't come home? And Clint? Last night sitting next to that fire with the boys, she had watched him struggle. Even after the boys had gone to bed he had insisted that everything was okay. He was fine.

He wasn't fine. He was hanging on to pride, using

it as a lifeline. She recognized it because she knew that it had been her stumbling block from time to time.

Janie stood on the steps of the church, waiting for her. Willow smiled at her aunt, who had put off her trip to Florida. Indefinitely. She couldn't go anywhere with Jenna missing.

And then there was Mr. Cameron in the nursing home. He thought Jenna had run away again, like she did every time she didn't like the rules. Willow wiped at her eyes and smiled for her aunt.

"I'm glad you're here. Clint needs you." Janie slipped an arm through Willow's as they walked up the steps.

Willow wanted to disagree about Clint needing her. Clint was so used to being needed, he had a difficult time letting others be strong for him. He was still trying to protect and rescue. This morning she had caught him returning phone calls for her.

For now it didn't matter. He needed the distraction. He couldn't go to Iraq and find his sister. He couldn't make things right. So he was walking around in a stupor, rescuing everyone in sight.

She saw him at the front of the church, no longer himself. He wore khaki pants and a white button-down shirt. She compared him to that cowboy she had met back in May, with the toothpaste smile and eyes that crinkled at the corners.

Today he had the weight of the world on his shoulders. It was a burden he needed to give to God. She knew it was easier said than done.

"She's coming home, Clint." Willow squeezed his hand and let it go.

He touched his lips with his fingers and lowered his hand. *Thank you*. His gray eyes watered, and he looked away.

The pastor walked through a door at the side of the sanctuary, a kind man in his sixties who loved his congregation and treated them all like family. His family. And the compassion in his eyes said that he hurt when they hurt.

Pastor Gray smiled out at the gathering. Willow turned, seeing people she'd never seen before. The pews were crowded. People were lining the walls.

As the pastor spoke, Clint signed the words for Willow. And she let him, because she had to accept what was happening to her hearing. She was learning to let go of pride.

"When we pray, we're to pray believing that God in heaven hears our prayers, and answers our prayers. Sometimes we say we're 'just going to pray about it.' And we make 'just' sound like a last resort. But the word *just* means something very different. It means 'immediately.' It means 'now.'

"'I'm just going to pray' is sometimes our way of saying, 'well, nothing else has worked, I'm just going to pray.' But add the word *immediately* in place of *just*. 'I'm immediately going to pray.' That's what we should do in every situation. Every time we stumble, doubt, or fear, we should 'just pray.'" He paused and smiled. Clint continued to sign, catching up. "And that's what we're going to do now for Jenna Cameron. We're just going to pray."

He stepped out from behind the pulpit. "And we're going to pray, believing our God in heaven hears and answers. We're not going to pray thinking that God might or might not answer. We're going to be the woman who touched the hem of Jesus's garment, knowing in faith that to touch Him would bring healing."

"Amen." Clint whispered the word.

Amen.

Clint stood and Willow walked with him to the altar, aware that others were pushing in around them to pray. It was warm and close. Willow knelt next to Clint, aware that someone had knelt next to her.

I'm trying to have faith, Clint signed.

Willow swallowed, nodding, because she understood "trying to have faith." She understood moving forward one day at a time, waiting for that moment when a person realized the meaning, the purpose of a situation and knew they could make it.

We have to ask for more faith. She moved her fingers, silently, words for Clint alone.

More faith. Clint bowed his head and nodded.

Walking out of the church with the boys, Clint saw Willow standing off to the side waiting for him, her expression soft as her gaze settled on them.

"Do you want to eat dinner with us?" Willow asked as they walked across the lawn to the parking lot. He noticed her truck at the edge of the road. Janie had ridden with him.

Janie rounded up the boys, smiling and talking like everything was normal and that tomorrow would be a fun day. She told them they would even get out the garden hose again. If it didn't rain.

Willow had asked him about dinner. "No, not tonight."

"Clint, you should come to the house. There's no reason to be alone."

"I'm not alone." He looked away.

"There are ways of being alone without being alone." She smiled, but the gesture was weak. "I know from experience. And I know all about using pride to close out the world. I know…"

"I know you do." He wanted to hold her, because she knew how it felt to lose things important to her. Someone important to her. He couldn't imagine her pain in that hospital, alone. He couldn't imagine complete silence.

He felt pretty weak compared to her.

"Don't shut us out, then." That determined lift of her chin.

"I won't shut you out. But I'm going to get the boys to bed early. I'll see you in the morning."

"Okay."

"Willow, I'm fine."

"Of course you are. We women are the only ones who need someone to lean on, right?"

"Something like that," he teased, hoping she'd smile and let it go.

"I'm here if you need me." She let it go, that easily.

"I know you're here."

He watched her walk away, and he was sorry that he'd spent a lifetime hiding his own pain and handling things alone. Janie had always just known, without him telling her.

From the looks of things, her niece didn't think he was a closed book, either. He'd sure never thought of himself as transparent.

On Thursday afternoon the military chaplain called with news. Clint listened to the man on the other end, faceless and practically nameless, telling him that they had leads. They were hopefully optimistic that they would recover Jenna Cameron.

Hopefully optimistic and *recover.* Clint tried to push the terms aside, to not think too deeply about what they meant. He was pretty sure the military had meant to give him hope. He reached down deep for faith, because it felt buried by the emotion of the last few days.

Sunday and the prayer meeting felt like a lifetime ago.

The boys were in the barn with Willow. Clint walked through the double doors and headed in the direction of the office. He could hear the boys laughing and Willow talking to them.

He stopped short of entering the office. He couldn't go in there like this, because he knew the boys would see it in his eyes. If they didn't, Willow would.

Deep breath, and he ran a hand through his hair. The smile he plastered on was for the boys, to keep them smiling. They looked up when he stepped into the room.

They were on the floor, coloring pictures of Black

Beauty. Willow was sitting at her desk, a catalogue in front of her.

"What's going on in here?" He sat down opposite Willow.

"The boys are coloring." She smiled at Timmy and David. "I'm picking an Arabian mare from this catalogue."

"You know the guys at the feed store are going to tease you."

She smiled. "They tease me about everything. The feed I buy, the vitamins I give my animals, and I think they make fun of my truck."

He laughed because they did make fun of her truck. "You drive a purple diesel around the country. And then there's your Ford. You have fuzzy dice hanging from the mirror."

"A little girl gave me those dice."

"Tell that to the guys, not me."

"Nope, let them talk." She opened the catalogue and pushed it across the desk. "I like this mare." Eye contact. "Have you heard anything?"

"Yes."

She looked down at her hands, the mood slipping from easy laughter to serious. She glanced at the boys, and he followed the look.

They have leads and are "hopefully optimistic." Clint signed, *I don't know what that means. But last night David asked when his mom will call.* Willow's eyes filled with tears. *What do I say to a question like that?*

She shook her head and her hands moved in silent communication. *I don't know. I'm sorry.*

They need normal. They need church and the park. I need to take them to the zoo or the lake.

Then do it. Keep them busy. She smiled. *Keep yourself busy. Take them back to church.*

Clint glanced back at the boys. They were still coloring, ignoring the silent communication between adults. They had accepted that sometimes signs were used for words.

I'm afraid that they'll hear something at church.

I know. But, Clint, you can't hide them away here. Hiding is just that, hiding. It's fear and lack of trust.

She was right, he signed. He didn't tell her the rest. If he couldn't handle this situation, how would he handle the next fifteen or so years, trying to raise them alone, trying to make the right choices?

We're having faith that she's coming home. Willow signed with determination. Determined, the way she approached everything in life.

She was facing profound deafness, and yet she didn't seem to waver in her convictions, in her determination and her faith.

"You're right." He stood up, but another catalogue caught his attention. "What's that?"

"Independence." She smiled, her eyes bright, maybe with tears. "I'm facing my future and letting go of pride. There are ways I can help myself to be independent. New phones. Answering machines that change a voice message to a typed message, and a few other gizmos."

"I think that's great. And don't forget, you have friends."

"I won't forget." She smiled up at him, winking in a way that made him want to forget everything. "And don't you forget either."

"Hey guys, let's go riding." He turned back to Willow. "Want to go?"

She did. Smiling, she stood and held a hand out to David. Clint didn't know what he would do without her.

And that thought brought a lot of other questions he wasn't ready to deal with. Questions like—where did she fit into the rest of his life? Did she even want to be there, or were they just friends?

He pushed those questions aside and walked to the tack room to pull out bridles and saddles.

After a long ride, Willow slid to the ground and pulled a groggy David down. He wrapped his arms around her neck and she held him for a minute. When he didn't move, she glanced down and he smiled up, his eyes heavy.

"You need a nap." She pulled him close and held him for another minute before setting him down.

Timmy seemed a little more alert, but not much. Willow smiled at Clint, and he winked. Her heart couldn't take much more of his charm. Cowboys either didn't know their power over women, or else used it so effectively that it came off as innocent and unknowing.

She'd met hundreds over the last five years. And

she'd always managed to keep her distance and not be touched by that charm.

Until now.

"I'm going to take these boys home for a nap." Clint was unsaddling the horse he'd ridden and Timmy and David were sitting on the ground, leaning against a stall door.

Willow cross-tied the mare in the center aisle for a good brushing. "Do you want me to brush your horse?"

"No, I can take care of him. What about dinner tonight?"

"What about it?"

He glanced over the bare back of the big old buckskin he'd bought. The horse was faded gold with a black mane and tail. Showy, but solid. A cowboy's horse.

"Dinner. What are you doing? Janie is gone, isn't she?"

"She's with her friends." Willow tossed the currycomb in a bucket and led her horse into the stall. Clint walked up behind her with a scoop of grain. He leaned in past her and filled the bucket.

"Do you want to run into Grove with us?"

"For dinner?" She shrugged.

"You have to eat."

"Yes, I have to. Okay, sure."

"If you don't want to…"

She glanced at the boys, now leaning against each other, eyes closing. "Take them home. And yes, I'll go with you. They have great fried chicken at the new diner."

"Fried chicken it is."

He led his horse away, out the back door to the gate. Willow watched. She glanced back at the boys and Timmy was awake. He gave her a look and then shifted away. When Clint returned, the boys jumped up, grabbing his hands and mumbling goodbye to her.

Willow watched from the barn as Clint headed down the road to the foreman's house, a boy on either side, both leaning against him.

It was a picture she'd like to have hanging on the wall of her office, the cowboy in his faded jeans, T-shirt and white cowboy hat, and two little miniatures walking next to him down a dusty country road. For a minute it almost felt like they belonged in her life in a forever kind of way.

She allowed herself to have that dream, of being loved forever. She thought it might feel like this, like a summer afternoon in the country and a man who was always there. It had been a long, long time since she'd daydreamed of cowboys and forever. Sixteen years to be exact.

It could only be a dream.

She walked across the road to the house, Bell following at her heels, a stick in the dog's mouth. Bell was an optimist, always believing someone would take the hint and throw the stick. Willow leaned and grabbed it from the slobbering dog, regretting it immediately. She tossed the stick and wiped her hands on her jeans. The dog ran across the yard. Rather than bringing the stick back, she took it to a hole she'd dug and lay down with it.

Willow walked up the front steps of the house, listening to quiet country sounds that were even now fading. She sighed, because she didn't want to think about it all being gone.

Silence. She'd spent two days in a world of complete silence until she got new hearing aids. And soon it would be permanent.

She would survive. Because God was with her, always. Even in the silence.

And if there was a miracle, she prayed it was for Jenna, bringing her home to her boys.

Janie wasn't at home. Willow walked through the empty house, thinking about the time when Janie would move. She hadn't allowed herself to really contemplate that day, and what it would mean to her.

Now she did. As she sat in the living room under the gentle push of air from the ceiling fan, she thought about living in this house, in silence. Alone.

She closed her eyes and thought about the business she'd built, and holding on to independence. And for a minute, just a minute, confidence faded and she felt afraid.

She wouldn't be able to hear the telephone or the radio. She wouldn't be able to hear the announcer at bull-riding events.

Everything she'd lost, and would lose, coiled around her heart. Brad. The baby. Now her hearing, and maybe her business. She'd thought Brad would love her forever. She had believed they would have children and a family that laughed together. She had never dreamed she would lose her hearing completely.

Her mind snaked back to thirty minutes ago, thinking about Clint in her life forever. She had let go of those dreams until he walked into her life again. And now, how did she go back to being content with this life she had chosen, living on this ranch, raising bulls and being single?

"God, get me through this," she whispered and closed her eyes. "Give me peace that surpasses all understanding, and show me Your will for my life, so that I don't feel so alone."

The fan continued to swish cool air from the air conditioner, and Willow drifted off.

Clint dozed off in the recliner, feet up, two boys on his lap. When he woke up one arm was asleep. The other was empty. He blinked and sat up, sort of. He moved his head and then his arm, the arm Timmy had slept on. Stiff.

He moved it a few times, bending and clenching his fist. David slept on the other arm. He moved the little boy, who moaned and curled up as Clint got out of the chair. He reached for a blanket on the couch and draped it over David.

Timmy. He peeked in the kitchen. No sign of the missing twin. On the way down the hall, toward the bedrooms, he turned the temperature up on the thermostat.

No sign of Timmy in the bedroom. No need to panic. He could picture his nephew sneaking outside to play with Bell, or with toy cars. He couldn't see him wandering too far from the house.

He walked out the front door and stood on the porch. No sign of the missing twin. The yard was dusty from lack of rain, and humidity hung in the air like a wet rug, weighing down the atmosphere. Clint wiped a hand across his already-perspiring brow.

"Timmy!" He cupped his mouth with his hands and shouted into late afternoon silence. "Timmy!"

No answer.

He walked back into the house, the screen door banging behind him. David was sitting in the recliner, holding on to the blanket like it was a lifeline.

"David, do you know where Timmy went?"

David shook his head, but his eyes were big, and Clint wondered.

"David, buddy, this is dangerous. If you know, you have to tell me."

The little boy shook his head again, and tears rolled down his cheeks. Clint didn't blame him. He felt a lot like crying, too. But someone had to be the grown-up. And that seemed to fall on him.

"Come on, let's go to Willow's." Clint picked up David's shoes, and the little boy slid them on. And then he raised his arms to be carried.

Clint walked down the road to Willow's, searching the fields on either side for the figure of a little boy. David clung to his neck, wiry legs wrapped around his waist. The boy sucked his thumb, and Clint didn't stop him.

Timmy could be anywhere. He could be in the barn, or with Willow. He could have gone in with the bulls. Clint told himself Timmy wouldn't do that.

But then again, an hour ago, he wouldn't have thought Timmy would take off while everyone else was sleeping. So where did that put Clint on the parenting scale? Not too high, he figured.

He pounded on Willow's front door, and she didn't answer. That gave him hope. Maybe Timmy had gone to her and the two were together. He knocked again. Still no answer. He pushed the door open and looked in.

Willow was asleep in the living room, stretched out in a chair with her feet on the ottoman. He stepped into the room and hesitated above her, looking down at a face peaceful in sleep and every bit as beautiful as when she was awake.

He knelt, setting David on the edge of the ottoman and reached for Willow's hand. She shifted and then jumped a little. Her smile was sleepy, unguarded.

"Waking me like that could get you hurt." She sat up, pulling her knees to her so that David had more room.

"I can't find Timmy. I woke up from a nap and he was gone."

Willow moved, reaching for the shoes next to her chair. "We'll find him."

"I'm going to head down the road on foot. Could you check the barn?"

She slid on her shoes. "Of course I can. I'll take my cell phone so you can call if you find him."

Willow walked out the barn, David tagging along behind her. She surveyed the fields, and the pens that held bulls. She prayed she wouldn't see him anywhere near the bulls. He knew better. Of course he did.

"David, did your brother say anything about leaving or doing something?"

"No." The child reached for her hand. "He just wants Mom to come home. So do I."

"I know, honey. But did he say something about playing outside, or doing something without telling any of us?"

David shook his head. "No, he just wonders how far away Iraq is."

"It's a long way."

Bell ran out of the barn. Willow reached down to pat the dog. If anyone knew where Timmy was, it was probably Bell. And that didn't do them a lot of good.

She flipped on lights as they walked through the doors of the barn. Something moved, catching her attention. She squinted as her eyes adjusted from bright sunlight to the dim recesses of the barn.

It might have been her imagination, or not. She thought a door closed on one of the stalls, just barely. David's hand was still in hers, and they hurried toward the stall that held her mare.

The horse whinnied, and she heard a thump. Willow let go of David's hand and ran to the stall. She peeked in, afraid of what she might see, afraid that the horse had hurt the child.

The noise had been caused by an overturned bucket. Willow smiled down at Timmy, who was trying to steady the upside-down bucket. The mare had a bridle on her head, the bit under her mouth, not in. No saddle.

"Timmy, what are you doing?"

Timmy frowned at her. "I'm going to find my mom. Uncle Clint is just going to leave her over there lost, and she isn't going to come home if someone doesn't go get her."

Big, brave words and a child's broken heart. How had he found out? Willow opened the door and spoke quietly, reassuring the horse who was trembling and holding steady as the little boy leaned against the mare's side, obviously thinking he could ride her bareback.

Willow picked him up and scooted the bucket out the door. She pulled the bridle off the horse, slid a hand over the mare's neck and then backed out of the stall with the sobbing four-year-old in her arms.

"Shhh, sweetie, it's okay."

Timmy shook his head against her neck, and tears soaked her skin. "I want my mom."

"I know you do." And it was Clint's place to tell the boys everything. Willow reached into her pocket for her phone and speed-dialed Clint's number. When he answered she choked back a sympathetic sob. "He's here, in the barn. He isn't hurt, but he's hurting."

Because somehow he had overheard that his mother was missing.

Clint ran from the main road back to the barn. When he walked through the doors, he took a deep breath and slowed down. He walked toward Willow and the boys.

Timmy and David sat on the bench next to Willow. The boys didn't look at him. Willow shrugged, and her smile wavered. He grabbed the five-gallon bucket next to the bench, turned it over and sat down facing the boys.

"What's up, guys?"

Timmy looked up, his eyes and nose red from crying. He swiped a hand across his face. "I want you to go find my mom."

Clint swallowed and nodded, taking a few minutes to process the comment. "Well, kiddo, I can't do that. I can't go to Iraq. And your mom wouldn't want me to leave you alone."

Clint would have liked nothing better than to hop on a plane and go to Iraq to look for his sister. He couldn't tell that to the boys, or tell them how worried he was.

"We're fine here with Willow." A four-almost-five-year-old's logic. It sounded like it made perfect sense.

"I can't leave you here, partner. And there are real soldiers looking for your mom." How had the boys found out? "Timmy, you have to tell me what's going on. How do you know your mom is lost?"

"Missing. She's missing. I heard the word at church and then when you were talking on the phone. You said she's still missing. And I think guys shouldn't leave sisters alone."

"And I agree. But when guys make a promise, like the one I made to your mom, we have to keep those promises."

David didn't comment.

"David, buddy, do you understand that?"

David shook his head.

"Timmy, do you understand?"

Timmy shook his head. "No. I just want my mom."

"I know, buddy, I know. And I want her to come

home. I think we should pray. That's the most important thing we can do, pray."

He held his arms out, and Timmy climbed onto his lap.

They prayed. And Timmy and David added their own prayers to the end, asking God to bring their mom home safe.

As Clint listened, he felt his own faith grow. Kids did that. They made everything seem possible. They had faith…until adults came along and cast seeds of doubt.

It was easy to think of all the negatives, the bad things that could happen, the worst possible outcome.

Clint closed his eyes, refusing to undo the faith with which the boys prayed. And he couldn't look at Willow, because he had prayers of his own that seemed selfish at the moment.

Chapter Fifteen

Clint walked through the wide double doors at the end of the barn. The shadowy interior was familiar and comforting. Ten days, and Jenna hadn't been found. There had been calls to tell him they were searching, but nothing to give them hope. Nothing to give the boys hope. It wasn't easy for two little boys to go to bed each night, knowing their mom was missing.

A movement at the far end of the barn. Willow pushing a wheelbarrow of grain. She was up early. And she was angry with him. That had been pretty obvious the day before, when he'd heard her struggling with a call and he'd taken over.

He shouldn't have.

He should give her space, because she knew how to take care of herself.

She turned and saw him. She set the wheelbarrow down and stood, waiting. A cowgirl in shorts and a T-shirt. He walked toward her.

"Good morning."

She nodded. "I have coffee in the office."

"I had some." He looked in the stall next to him, at the Arab filly she'd bought. An Arabian. He shook his head, still wondering why she'd done that.

"Stop looking at her like that." Willow walked up next to him. She still smelled like soap and herbal shampoo. Her hair was a little damp.

"Sorry, I'm just not sure what you're going to do with her."

"I think she's pretty." She smiled at him. "It's about endurance, Clint. She can go for hours, and she has a pretty face."

"It's all about a pretty face?"

"She's sweet." She rested her hand on the horse's red-gold neck, and the animal moved closer, nuzzling her shoulder. "See what I mean?"

"Yes, she's sweet."

Not a cow horse.

"You're too set in your ways." She said it and walked off, and he thought she probably meant it in more ways than one.

He opened his mouth to say something, but a shrill ring interrupted.

"Telephone." He nodded toward the office. "The phone is ringing."

She hurried in that direction and he followed. She had picked it up and was talking when he walked into the room. Instead of finishing the conversation, she handed it to him.

"It's someone from the military," she whispered with her hand over the receiver.

He took it, but he didn't lift the phone to his ear. He didn't want to hear. Not this way. Shouldn't they come to his house and tell him in person. Shouldn't there be something more to it than this?

Willow sat on the edge of her desk. She touched his arm. "Answer it, Clint."

He did. "Clint Cameron here."

"Clint, it's me."

He cried. And all his life he'd been taught that only sissies cried. He could hear his dad telling him to stop that bawling. But real men cried when they heard the voice of their sister for the first time in weeks. Real men cried when prayers were answered.

"Clint?" Her voice sounded weak.

"Jenna. Where are you?"

"I'm on my way to a hospital in Germany."

"Where? I'm coming over there."

She laughed, a soft, fluttery and weak sound. "No, you're not. You're not dragging the boys over here. Not here, Clint. Give me time."

"What happened?"

"It's a long story, but I was safe."

"Where have you been?"

"Safe. I'll tell you more when I see you."

"You're okay?" He sat down on the desk next to Willow. He was shaking, and Willow's hand was on his arm. The long pause, static on the line, and the sound of chopper blades, all felt like chaos in his stomach.

"I'm going to be okay. It's going to take time." She sobbed, and he couldn't stand it. "They're not sure about my leg, Clint."

He didn't cry this time. He had to be strong. He had to be able to take care of her. "I'm coming over there."

"No, you're not. You're going to take care of the boys until I can come home. When I get to the States you can come and see me."

"I don't know."

"You have to agree." She paused, a long pause. "If you come over here, I'll give up and let you take care of me."

"I love you, Jen."

"I love you, too. I've been praying for you."

She was praying for him. She was lost, far from home, and she'd prayed for him. How long had he prayed for her to find faith?

"We prayed for you, too."

"You didn't tell the boys, did you?"

He looked at Willow, remembering that she wouldn't let him. "No, I didn't tell the boys."

The boys found out on their own. He would tell her later, not now when she needed to think of herself and getting better.

"Good. I'll call again later, and I want to talk to them."

"They've missed you. We've all missed you."

"Are you in love yet?" He could hear her smile when she asked the question.

"You've got to let it go."

"So, you are." She breathed deep and he heard engines rumbling and people talking. "I'm praying you'll let someone love you."

He glanced away from Willow. "I love you, Jenna."

"Chicken."

She said goodbye, and he set the phone down on the desk. She was safe. She was going to need him more than ever.

"This is definitely a good day." Willow hopped down from the desk, her smile radiant.

"She said her leg is bad. What does that mean?"

The smile she'd worn faded, and she shrugged, her eyes shadowing for a minute.

"Whatever it means, I know she'll get through it with your help. She's alive, and she's coming home to her boys." She hesitated. "And from my end of that conversation, it sounds like she's strong."

"She is." He remained on the edge of the desk. "She's stronger than I am."

"You're human. She knew she was alive. You didn't."

He nodded, because he hadn't thought about it that way. "I'm going to work those two-year-old bulls."

"Not today, Clint. Take time with the boys. Let them know that their mom is coming home to them."

"You'll need help."

"No, actually, I can take care of things around here." Her smile this time was a little tense. "Remember, I've been doing that for a while."

"There are a few messages on the answering machine, calls that need to be returned." He knew that Janie used to make those calls, but Willow had been pushing Janie back, reminding her that she had to do this on her own.

"Clint, I can do this."

"I know you can."

She frowned and pointed to the door, pointing him to the exit. "Try saying it like you mean it."

"I don't want to fight with you."

"I'm not fighting. I'm taking care of my business. I'm holding on to my life and my future. And I'm going to tell you now, when Jenna comes home, you're going to have to let her do things for herself."

"I know that, Willow."

She shook her head, and by then he was angry with her. But from the snarly look on her face, she was pretty mad herself.

"No, you don't. You take over. Whether you mean to or not, you do. From the moment you learned about my hearing, you changed. You started treating me like I'm a different person. And I'm not."

"I'm going to spend that time with the boys. I'll talk to you later."

"Clint?"

He lifted a hand as he walked out of the room. He didn't have time to work this out with her, not when he had the boys—and Jenna coming home wounded. If he'd been taking over, now was the time to back out and let her have the reins back.

He could do that, no problem.

Clint was avoiding her, had been avoiding her since the phone call from Jenna. Three days, and they'd barely talked. She could think of reasons why. He was mad at her, maybe for telling him to give his sister room. Or maybe he'd realized, after returning calls for Willow, and having to repeat things when he spoke to her, that even a friendship with her required too much work.

He wouldn't be the first person to make that decision. And now she had additional baggage that came with a relationship. Her worsening condition. And no children. She touched her stomach because today was the anniversary of the accident.

It didn't hurt the way it had once hurt, thinking of her baby, and knowing that she would never again experience that thrill of life growing inside her belly.

God was helping her to move forward, and giving her new joys. The twins counted as a joy. They were a blessing she didn't want to miss out on.

Willow poured food in the cat's bowl and walked out of the barn. She stood outside the building, enjoying a cool breeze and the sweet smell of rain in the air.

They needed rain, desperately. Her gaze traveled to the foreman's house. Clint was running around the yard, shooting the boys with a water gun. She smiled at the sight of them together, happy again.

Yesterday he'd brought them over for some of Janie's homemade ice cream. It had been a celebration, with sparklers for the Fourth of July, and because Jenna would be coming home.

Prayers answered. Willow walked across the road and stopped near the swing. Not forsaken.

She looked up, amazed by the dark clouds eating up the blue. They hadn't had rain for three weeks. They needed moisture, not a gully washer that would hit the ground and run off before it could soak in.

Rather than going inside, she sat down on the swing to watch the storm approach. The breeze stirred the leaves in the tree. A piece of paper someone had dropped bounced across the lawn. The temperature dropped a good ten degrees.

Willow looked up, watching the stirring in the clouds with interest. With the temperature dropping this fast, it could get bad. And she had animals in the field. She got up and hurried back to the barn, remembering a cow that hadn't come up for feeding time.

Knowing this cow, Willow knew without a doubt that she'd gone off somewhere alone to have her calf. Of course the cow would do that with a storm coming.

She hurried through the barn, eager to get to the other end, and a clear view of the southern sky. If tornadoes were forming, they would form in the southwest and move northeast. The pattern was nearly a given.

When tornado season hit, she always tried to remind herself that the storms seemed to hit the same areas over and over again. It was a phenomenon she didn't understand. But she also knew that nothing in life was for certain.

Her Arab filly poked a nose over the stall door and whinnied as Willow passed. "Hey, sweetheart, it'll be okay."

The wind whipped, blowing a door, banging it so hard that Willow heard and jumped. The horse skittered to the back of the stall. Willow turned in the direction of the noise. Nothing but the wind.

Her old farm truck was parked out back. She pushed a hat on to her head, grabbed a horse blanket, and rope and ran for the truck. Rain was starting to fall and she didn't want to think of the cow out there alone, laboring with a calf that might be too big to be delivered.

Huge drops of rain pelted the windshield as she drove through the gate and down into the field. She had to get out and close the gate behind her. When she got back into the truck, she was soaked. She shifted from Neutral to First gear and let the truck coast through the field as she searched for the cow.

A few minutes later she spotted the animal in a

small stand of trees, obviously laboring to have a calf that wasn't going to be easy to deliver. Willow parked and jumped out of the truck. The heifer gave her a pitiful look that begged for help.

"Oh honey, we're in big trouble." The feet of the calf were showing. The cow looked exhausted with her sides heaving, like she'd been at this for awhile.

And the rain began to fall in earnest.

Willow wrapped the rope around the hooves of the calf as the cow went to her knees, exhausted from labor. "Poor baby, you're just not going to be able to get this one out yourself."

It wasn't the first calf that Willow had needed to pull. It wouldn't be the last. Every year there were several that needed her help, and sometimes the help of a veterinarian.

Now to get the baby out and back to the dry barn.

A movement a short distance away caught her attention. She turned as Clint ran toward her, hunkering down in the rain, his hat tilted.

"What are you doing out here?" he shouted as he moved in closer, his gaze landing on the cow.

"I had to check on her, and I found her like this."

"You could have asked for help."

"Where are the boys?" Willow continued to work, and Clint moved in close, kneeling on the soggy ground next to her.

"They're with Janie. She got home a few minutes ago." He grabbed the rope and made an adjustment on the knot she had tied. "It'll slip loose."

"I've done this before."

"I know you have, but it's pouring down rain, and I'm here. You could get in the truck and wait."

"Get in the truck?" She blinked a few times, and then wiped the rain from her face. "You're telling me to get in my truck? This is my cow, and I know how to do this. She isn't the first cow that I've had down, and not the first one that I've dealt with alone."

"It's pouring, you're soaked and that lightning is getting close."

"I'm not leaving." She pushed in next to him to prove her point.

"Fine, be stubborn." He grabbed the hooves of the calf and slipped his hands down. "Pull when I say to pull."

"I've done this before." She shouted over the wind and the crash of thunder. He shot a look back and shook his head.

Twenty minutes later the calf was on the ground, and the mother, exhausted but alive, turned to nudge her offspring. Birth. Willow always cried after a birth, whether it was a cow, horse or a litter of kittens in the barn. The miracle of birth moved her. It deepened a longing that she tried to ignore.

"We need to get them to the barn." Clint ran to the truck and grabbed another length of rope. The rain had slowed to a steady mist, but they were both soaked, and their feet sloshed through the soppy mud under the stand of trees where the cow had taken shelter. It hadn't proved to really be a shelter, but the cow didn't know better.

"I'll lead her to the barn." Willow took the rope from his hands. "You drive the calf on up in the truck."

Clint stood in front of her, his gaze holding hers. "Why do you keep pushing me away?"

"I'm not. I'm doing what I've been doing for five years. I'm taking care of my animals, and I'm not letting you take over."

"You're pushing me away."

"I'm sorry you feel that way. I feel like I'm standing my ground and holding on to something that is important to me." She bit down on her lip, waiting for him to say something. She was waiting for him to understand how afraid she was. But she couldn't say it out loud.

She couldn't tell him about her fears. She was afraid of the eventual silence. And she was afraid of losing him. What would he think if she told him that? Especially now, with Jenna coming home and needing him.

She just looked at him, wanting him to get it. And wanting him to make walking away easy.

He didn't say anything. Instead he leaned forward, keeping his hands at his side, and he kissed her. His lips were wet from rain and cool air. Willow closed her eyes, realizing that the storm had nothing on this, on whatever connected them. She wanted to explore it, figure it out.

And she wanted to run from it, before it consumed her and then left her empty.

He pulled back, leaving her cold and uncertain, shivering in rain-soaked clothes. "I'm sorry that you are so determined to push me away," he whispered. She didn't hear, but she read his lips.

"I'll meet you back at the barn." She slipped the rope around the cow's neck.

"Willow, I'm trying to say something here. Are you going to walk away?"

"I'm not sure what I'm doing, Clint. I didn't want you to know about my hearing because I didn't want you to change. I didn't want you to start treating me differently." She held tight to the rope and blinked as she focused on his face. "But things have changed."

She waited for him to answer, to tell her that he would let her be herself. She wanted him to do something to show her things hadn't changed.

And as she waited, she saw their friendship melting away because he didn't understand. For him, being strong seemed as natural as breathing. And for her, it was like struggling for every breath.

I can't do this anymore, he signed. *I can't.*

"Can't what?"

"Never mind, we need to get back to the house." Clint gave her his jacket. "Since you insist on being the one to walk her to the barn."

Willow nodded, but she didn't know what to say.

He said something she didn't catch.

"What?" She faced him, faced the gray eyes that sometimes flashed with humor, or simmered with some indiscernible emotion. This time the look simmered.

"Willow, whether you want to admit it or not, things are going to change. For all of us. So you find faith, and you learn how to deal with it, but you can't keep it from happening." He exhaled and shook his head. "My sister had part of her leg amputated. She's a single mom with twin boys. Everything is changing. And what you're going through isn't fair, either. If I could fix you all…"

"Clint, you don't have to fix us."

"That isn't what I meant."

She nodded, but she didn't know what to say. And her mind went back to his comment about not being able to take this, and it reminded her of someone about to walk away. He thought she needed to be fixed.

And all she really needed was to be loved for who she was.

"Willow?"

"We should go." She glanced over her shoulder, at more black clouds rolling their way. "Looks like we're about to get hit by more rain."

"You're running from me."

She wished it wasn't true, but it probably was. His eyes reflected the storm, and his smile had disappeared. He deserved some kind of explanation.

"I want you for a friend, not a caretaker."

"Sometimes we're stronger when we let someone help us."

"But you're taking over. You see me as someone you need to fix."

She waited for him to tell her he'd give her space and that he could be in her life without taking over. But instead he took a step back, a step away from her. She saw it in his eyes, realization. He knew that she was right. He sighed and turned away.

The rain started to fall again, this time a gentle, soaking rain. Willow pulled her jacket collar up as he walked away.

He got into the truck and she started up the hill, the cow walking behind her and the truck just ahead. She could see Clint's reflection in the rearview mirror as he kept an eye on them. And she knew that everything changed today.

She had pushed someone from her life, someone who had become maybe her best friend, and it hurt. It hurt worse than that moment when Brad told her their marriage was over. It hurt worse than the plane ride when she was ten years old.

This hurt deep in her heart, like an ache that might linger for a long, long time. And all she had wanted was for him to say he could be in her life without taking over.

Maybe he couldn't.

Chapter Sixteen

"Why aren't you talking to Clint?" Janie asked after two days of silence. Willow had wondered when her aunt would bring it up.

"I'm not *not* talking to him."

"Okay, then what is this? He came back from helping you with that cow, and since then the two of you have been circling like wasps that have had their nests messed with."

Willow sort of chuckled and smiled. "That's a nice visual image."

"Okay, so, tell me what is going on."

"He's a macho cowboy who likes to fix people. I don't need to be fixed, and I told him that."

"Tell him you love him."

Willow picked up her purse. "I'm not going to tell him I love him. Years ago I had a crush. Now I don't know what I have. I do know that I need to run into town."

"You're stubborn."

Willow nodded. "Yep, I am. Need anything from the store?"

Janie shook her head and walked off. Willow walked out to her truck, patting her leg as an invitation for Bell to ride along.

When she pulled into the feed store in town, an older farmer waved and headed in her direction. Bart Jenson. She took in a deep gulp of air and mentally prepared herself for a man who just couldn't handle the idea that she raised bulls. It wasn't proper he had said, more than once.

"Mr. Jenson." She closed the door of her truck and smiled. He didn't smile back.

"I want to talk to you about the fence of yours that borders my property."

"Didn't we already settle this?"

A truck pulled into the parking lot. Clint's truck. Oh, she so didn't need this. She needed to handle Bart and pay for her grain so it could be delivered on Monday. She didn't need to settle an old dispute all over again.

Clint was getting out of his truck. The windows were down, and the boys waved from the back seat.

"I settled it with that stubborn aunt of yours, but now you own the place." Bart's voice was as growly as his personality. He hitched his thumbs in the straps of his bib overalls and put on his benevolent face, the one he used when talking down to a woman.

Clint was heading their way. To take over. She knew that look on his face. He thought she needed to be rescued.

"I'm sticking with the agreement, Bart. I'm paying

for one thousand feet of fence. I'll have it finished by the end of August."

Bart turned away from her. "I'll just talk to Clint about it."

Willow wanted to stomp. She wanted to demand that the older farmer talk to her. And he was ignoring her, waiting for Clint. Willow waited, too, ready to be angry and to tell Clint that he didn't need to fix this for her.

"Clint, I want to discuss this fence situation with you."

"It isn't my fence, Bart."

"Yes, but you know as well as I do that this woman don't know a thing about how this should be done."

"Sounds to me like she does."

Clint smiled and then he tipped his hat and walked away. Willow tried to thank him, but he kept going, and she knew that meant more than words. Bart Gordon was red in the face and looked like a man about to blow. Willow faced the problem, her problem, but her gaze shifted back to Clint, walking through the door of the feed store.

"Bart, I'm sticking with the deal. I keep my word, and I'm asking you to keep yours."

"My word is good, young lady. But I'll have you know, this is the last time we'll do a deal like this."

"Have it your way." She smiled. "But we're going to be neighbors, and we're going to have to work through problems from time to time."

"You won't last on that ranch by yourself, not without Clint or Janie to take care of things."

He stormed off, and Willow wanted to remind him that she'd taken care of herself for five years before Clint Cameron showed up. She could still handle things on her own.

But the thought wilted inside her, because she was having a hard time believing. She knew, without a doubt, that she was going to need help running the ranch.

She knew that she would miss Clint. And he had just proved that he could let her handle things alone. She would have told him, but when he walked out to his truck, he passed by without speaking to her.

And tomorrow he was leaving the boys with them so that he could visit Jenna in the hospital. He planned on being gone for close to a week. Willow started her truck and backed out of the parking space without going in for feed.

Clint walked down the hallway of the hospital, the antiseptic smell so strong he could nearly taste it. He glanced down at the number on a piece of paper the lady at the information desk had given him.

He neared room 512 and his heart ka-thumped in his chest. He could count on one hand the times in his life that he'd been afraid. This one counted.

He paused at the door, giving himself a minute to breathe and to be the older brother Jenna needed. Funny that Willow was pushing him away because she thought he was strong, and because he had a habit of taking over. He felt anything but strong. He shoved the paper into his pocket, practiced a smile and walked into the room.

Jenna was awake and looking at the door, like she'd known he was there. She smiled, a little weary, kind of sad. He took a few steps, aware that they were both on the verge of tears.

"Hey, Sis." He leaned, pulling her to him in a hug that was awkward for them both.

"Let me go now, Clint, you're suffocating me."

He let go and backed up. He was suffocating everyone he cared about. Suffocating the people he loved. He took off his hat and sat down in the seat next to hers.

"Are you okay?" Jenna reached for his hand.

"I've had better days. But I'm here for you."

She laughed, shaky and weak from painkillers. "Clint, are you always going to be there for everyone?"

"I'm sure gonna try."

A light squeeze on his hand. "I'm glad you've always been there for me."

He nodded, and his gaze shifted down to her leg, the amputation a success, they had said. He didn't know how losing part of her leg could be a successful surgery. He was just glad she was alive. And she had faith. Both were answers to prayer.

"I'm going to be okay." She made it sound like a fact.

"I know you are."

"I think I probably feel better than you do."

"I don't know." He leaned forward, resting his hat on his knee. "What happened?"

"I don't remember a lot, but I woke up in sort of a house. An older lady, she'd been a nurse a long time ago, had watched the attack on our convoy. When she saw me, alive, she sent her nephew to drag me to her house. She wanted to save me."

"She did, didn't she?"

"I think so." Tears slid down her cheeks. "I don't like to think about what could have happened."

"Then we won't. Instead let's talk about getting you back home, back to the boys and the farm."

"It's going to be a little while before that happens."

"I know." He touched her brow, brushing back dark hair that fell into her eyes. "But we have you. That's what matters."

"How are my boys?" Tears flooded her eyes. "Can you bring them soon?"

"I will. And they're fine. They're with Janie and Willow. They're probably eating too much ice cream and running the house." He pulled folded pages from a coloring book out of his pocket, along with snapshots of the boys. "They sent these for you."

She took the papers and opened them, tears trickling down her cheeks as she stared at her boys, smiling from the photographs that he hadn't thought to take. The pictures had been Willow's idea.

"They're doing great, Jenna. They miss you, but they're good."

"Thank you for taking care of them for me." She wiped at her eyes with a tissue she pulled from a box on the table. "Are they okay, Clint? Do they know what happened?"

"They're doing great. And they've taken care of me most of the time." He sat forward in the chair. "They do know. They have a lot of questions and suggestions."

They both smiled at that.

"I miss them so much."

"They miss you." And he told her about Timmy's near-escape when he went to look for her.

She smiled, a little bigger, a little more genuine. "Now, I want to talk about you and Willow."

Of course his misery was what she needed to cheer herself up. He nearly laughed, yet he didn't feel like laughing. He definitely didn't want to talk about Willow, who was barely speaking to him.

He had a problem with relationships. He'd known it since high school. He'd had a habit of dating girls who needed to be fixed. The worst mistake had been the judge's daughter. She'd been angry with her parents, and he'd been a good way to get back at them.

After it was over he realized he hadn't loved her after all, because he hadn't really missed her. She'd hurt his pride more than anything.

He missed Willow. Even though he saw her daily at the farm, he missed her.

"Come on, Clint, give it a chance." Jenna tugged at his hand.

"Do you really need to go in that direction to be happy?" He smiled and she laughed.

"Yes, I do. Tell me all about it."

"She thinks I have a habit of taking over."

Jenna laughed. "And you think you don't? Clint, you always take over. It's a big part of your macho personality."

"Fine, I take over. But I can't change who I am, and I don't have time for a relationship."

"Did you want a relationship?" Her laughter was gone, and she looked too serious. "When are you going to let yourself have time?"

"Jenna, I can't think about that right now. I need to think about you and the boys."

She struggled to sit up, and when he reached to help, she put a hand out to stop them. "Hold it right there, cowboy. See, that's your problem. I can get up by myself. I have to learn to do this on my own. And you can't take over."

"I wasn't."

"You were. You've always taken care of me. And I let you. Now you're trying to take care of Willow. You're a pretty hard guy to fight off, and maybe she's afraid she'll lose."

"I was just trying to help."

"Help by letting us be strong. Help me by realizing that I'm a grown woman with two boys that I have to take care of. Willow has built a business without your help."

"Her hearing is getting worse."

"So, help her to be strong. You can do that. And you have to build your own life. A life that doesn't include taking care of me, the boys or Dad."

It took a minute for that to sink in, and when it did, it hurt. He'd always taken care of Jenna. And now, when she needed him more than ever, she was telling him to back off. She was his little sister. He didn't think he could.

"Clint, let me take care of myself, and I promise, when I need help, I'll ask." She handed him a piece of paper. "And I bet if you ask Willow, she'll tell you that she's willing to ask when she needs help."

"It isn't easy." Changes, they were all facing changes. And if he wanted to keep Willow in his life, he had to be willing to change.

"You're right, it isn't easy. You're a great brother, a great person, but your relationships have always been about taking care of someone. That isn't really love." She pointed to the paper she'd handed him. "That's my life, right there on that paper. I wrote up a one-year plan, a five-year plan and a fifteen-year plan. That's where I want to be and what I want to do. I have goals. I have dreams of my own."

He looked at the list. It included being a mom, taking care of herself and her children and raising horses. Taking care of herself. She had underlined that goal.

He nodded, but it sure wasn't easy. "Good plans."

"Yes, they are. And you need to make a few plans of your own." She smiled, his little sister, strong and a force to be reckoned with. "Plans that don't include taking care of me."

"I'm being lectured." He shook his head at this fact.

"Yes, you are. I think that I have to give you a push so that you'll let me take the steps I need to in my own life. And when you go home, make nice with Willow and let her love you back. Give her room to breathe."

He sat back, realizing what she was telling him. He had been acting like everyone else in Willow's life, taking over and making decisions for her. He should have concentrated on the one thing he realized he really wanted to do.

He wanted to love her.

But he didn't know if she'd be willing to let him. She had walls, and because of him, the walls were now a little higher, and harder to climb.

* * *

The phone rang. Willow didn't want to mess with it so she let it go to voice mail. She ignored Janie's questioning look.

"Don't you want to take that?"

Willow shook her head and walked over to the table where the boys were coloring horse pictures that she had printed off the computer. Clint had been gone for four days.

She didn't want to think about missing him or why she missed him. The boys missed him. They had cried last night, and she had come close to crying with them.

This was tougher than being thirteen and falling in love with an image, someone she didn't really know. That had been a crush, built around a fictional cowboy with Clint's face.

This was different. This went deeper, because now she knew the cowboy. She had held his hand. He had held her.

Letting go of the real thing would be harder than letting go of the dream she'd built all those years ago.

But she had other things to think about. She had an event in a week. She had young bulls that needed to be sold.

Her heart was breaking. That was the hardest thing to come to terms with. She hadn't expected it to happen this way, with her missing Clint and feeling as if she had missed out on something.

"Willow, why are you doing this to yourself?" Janie's question was soft. Willow didn't know if her aunt was whispering, or if it was a bad day.

She turned, smiling for her aunt. "I don't know what you mean."

"You're ignoring phone calls. You're ignoring my questions about what happened between you and…"

Willow raised a hand to stop her aunt. The boys were coloring, but she knew they heard and paid attention to everything. They were smart little guys.

"Let's go outside," Janie suggested, motioning to the front door.

Willow followed, telling the boys to keep coloring, and to not forget their juice. She moved the juice boxes closer and ruffled the hair of each boy as she walked out.

Janie was waiting for her. Waiting, and Willow knew that everything she'd thought about over the last week had to be said.

"Janie, it's time for you to let go. You need to move to Florida. You can't let that condo sit there empty."

"I'll go when I'm ready. But right now, you need me, and Jenna is going to need me."

"We'll both be fine, I bet. And if we need you, we'll call. But you have to go, or you'll regret letting this pass you by."

"Do you regret, Willow?"

"I don't know what that means." She sat down on the porch swing and kicked to make it rock. Janie took the seat opposite. "Do I regret what?"

"Do you regret that you pushed Clint away?"

Willow kicked the swing again to keep it moving. Janie reached out and stopped the momentum. "Don't ignore me."

"I'm not. I need time to think. I don't believe I pushed him away. I made a decision. Janie, when he learned about my hearing, he changed. He started treating me like an invalid."

"Then talk to him."

"I did. He can't help himself. He takes over. That's who he is. And I'm me. I can't stop being the person that I am, just to let him be the tough guy."

"What are you going to do with this place if you don't have help? You're going to have to have someone, so why not Clint?"

"Because that isn't how I want him in my life, taking over, making decisions for me. Taking care of me."

She wanted him to love her. She had gained so much in the last few years. She had gained faith, and friends. She had confidence in herself, and in her abilities. She had a business that she loved.

And Clint. He had to be included in the things she had gained. And lost.

"Janie, it isn't unusual for me to have people in my life who can't handle my deafness. Maybe Clint can't handle it. It does mean a whole different kind of relationship."

"Some people can't handle it, Willow. But when God brings the right person that person will be able to handle it."

Clint. That's the person Janie meant. And Willow wanted it to be so. But she blocked the thought because she didn't want to be hurt again. Another broken heart, and the world would run out of duct tape.

"I've considered selling the bulls," Willow admitted, and it hurt to say it out loud for the first time. It didn't feel right.

"Oh, Willow, you stubborn girl. You'd rather sell the bulls than ask for help."

"I don't know."

Janie moved to the swing and patted Willow's knee. "Will you pray about this? Don't rush into something and then have more regrets."

"I've been praying."

"And you think this is the right choice, the right direction to take?"

"I don't know yet." She had to take each day as it came. "I'm not sure how to feel or what to do."

A delivery van rumbled down the road, interrupting their conversation. Willow stood as the van stopped and the driver got out. He hurried up the walk, and she held on to Bell, who had a distaste for men in brown uniforms.

"Willow Michaels?" he asked, looking at the package to read her name. Her regular driver knew that without asking.

"Yes."

"Package. Sign here." He held up the electronic clipboard, she signed and he handed over a box.

"What is it?" Janie asked as Willow walked back across the porch.

"No idea."

"Open it."

"I am." Willow slid her fingernail down the side of the box, loosening the tape. She pulled out a box and realized it was from the catalogue she'd been looking at days ago.

She opened the box and looked at the phone, the very phone she had circled in her catalogue. Her eyes watered as she read over the typed gift card inside the box. "Because you can do all things through Christ who strengthens you. This is a step forward."

"Clint did this," she whispered.

Janie patted her arm. And Willow didn't know what to say. It had always felt as if he was taking over. But now he was giving her freedom. He was giving her room to breathe, to be strong.

"He's a good man, Willow."

"I know he is."

"Okay, we'll both make hard choices. I'm going to plan on leaving for Florida at the end of August, after I go to Texas and spend a week or so with Jenna. That's the date I'm giving myself. Now, your turn."

Willow laughed, Janie made it seem so easy. "I don't know which to tackle first, the bulls or Clint."

"Both." Janie smiled. "Follow the old saying, 'take the bull by the horns.'"

"That's dangerous."

"What are you afraid of?"

"Loving him and losing myself. Or loving him and not being able to give him everything."

"That isn't love, Willow. You find yourself when you fall in love. But you won't know if you don't give it a chance."

Willow nodded but she wondered how she could give love a chance when she knew what her future held and what she wouldn't be able to give to a relationship.

No one was at home. Clint opened the door after knocking a few times and peeked inside. Silent. He walked out to the garage. Janie's Cadillac was gone.

Willow's truck was there. Janie must have taken the boys somewhere. So where was Willow?

On the way home from Texas he had felt his insides tensing, but in a way he hadn't experienced before. He'd had that keyed-up feeling on bulls, just before the gate opened. But this was different. This feeling felt a lot like going home to someone that he missed. And hadn't expected to miss, not like this.

She was in the corral with her new mare. She stood in the center of the arena, the horse on a lunge line, trotting in a wide circle. He watched the two work, the woman and the horse. Willow whistled, and the mare changed from a trot to slow gallop. She must have sensed him watching her, because she turned and smiled. The smile was reserved, as if she had questions.

He had questions, too.

She spoke to the horse, and the mare stopped, standing still, legs square and ears alert. He had to admit she'd made a good choice with the Arabian. Willow walked up to the horse, spoke softly, petting the mare's neck, and then she turned and walked up to the fence. The horse walked at her side.

"Welcome home." She acted as if she didn't know what to expect from him. "Janie took the boys to Tulsa to shop for school clothes."

"I see."

"How is Jenna?"

"Strong. Like you." He hoped that would thaw the ice. It helped a little. She smiled.

Funny, he had thought he was rescuing her. But she had rescued him. She had introduced him to what it felt like to fall in love. And now he had to wonder if she was going to let him tell her.

"Thank you for the phone." She leaned against the fence. He opened the gate and walked through to join her.

"Is it the one you wanted?"

"It is. You were snooping in my office again."

"I confess, I snooped." Distracted, he rubbed the mare's velvety face. "Willow, I want you to know that I'm not trying to take over."

She laughed and he looked up, meeting blue eyes that melted his heart. "You were."

"Yeah, maybe I was. I'm kind of used to taking care of people."

"Being taken care of isn't the problem. You taking over like you think I can't take care of myself, that's the problem."

"I know, and I'm working on that. I've always been a fixer. But you don't need to be fixed." He ducked under the head of the horse and stood next to Willow. The mare pushed at him, so he took the lead rope and tied her to a post.

"No, I don't. But I'm working on letting people help me." She smiled up at him, and he felt his world coming undone. Maybe, just maybe, he could be the cowboy who took care of her forever.

If he asked, would she say yes?

Willow slipped her hands into his and waited, expectantly, for him to give her a hint that maybe, just maybe this could last. She had prayed for this moment, for God to show her if this man would be the one who wouldn't walk away.

She hadn't realized how much she wanted that,

not until the phone arrived and she realized that as much as he had seemed to be taking over, he did know when to back away.

He had listened to her. And he knew to let her be strong.

"I'm sorry, Willow. I didn't give you the credit you deserve. You're smart and beautiful and strong, and you don't need me to rescue you."

"Sometimes I do, Clint." She enjoyed saying it, enjoyed the widening of his gray eyes and the tender smile that chased away his frown, and dissolved the worry lines that had gathered at the corners of his mouth.

"How often?"

"How often do I need you to rescue me?" She smiled. "Maybe more often than I realized. Clint, sometimes I'm really afraid of what is happening. I'm afraid of the silence. And I'm afraid of being alone."

He took off his hat and dropped it over a post. His gray eyes were intense, holding her gaze. He smiled a little.

"That's honest," he said. "Thank you for that."

"I guess it's time for honesty. Right?"

"Right. I'm glad you might need to be rescued, because I have something on my mind." He tangled his fingers in the hair at the back of her neck and pulled her close, his touch gentle and her heart teetering on the edge.

"Really? What?"

"I have forever on my mind." He signed the words as he spoke.

"Okay, we can talk about forever," she whispered, her hand on his arm, pulling him even closer, needing him closer. She liked that his scent was as familiar to her as rain on a summer morning. "Why do you have forever on your mind?"

And she was afraid, because there needed to be more honesty between them.

"Because I can't think of forever without you."

All the right words, but she'd heard those words before. "Clint, have you really thought about this, about my hearing, about babies?"

She choked on those words, and he pulled her closer, holding her so that her cheek was against the warmth of his neck and his arms were strong around her waist.

"I've thought about everything, Willow. And I can't think of anything but loving you." He pulled back, but his hands remained on her waist. "Willow, would you consider loving a cowboy who has a bad habit of rescuing the women in his life?"

"Do you rescue a lot of women?"

He leaned, his forehead touching hers. Willow closed her eyes as his hands moved up her arms to rest on her shoulders. His touch was gentle, his hands calloused but familiar.

"I'd like to think about having only one woman to rescue for the rest of my life, and hers."

"Do you have a certain woman in mind?" Her eyes were still closed.

His lips touched hers, gentle, persuasive, letting her know in no uncertain terms what woman he wanted to rescue for the rest of his life.

And she wanted to be rescued.

He kissed her one last time, and then he pulled

away. Willow opened her eyes, still dazed, still trying to think about forever with this man.

"I do have a woman in mind." He kissed her again, at the corner of her mouth and then on her temple. "And I want to make a promise that I'll only rescue you when you need to be rescued." He smiled. "And maybe sometimes when you need it, but don't think so. But I promise to listen when you tell me I'm taking over, and I promise to back off and give you space to be strong."

"I like that idea. If you'll agree to let me rescue you every now and then."

He smiled and pulled her close again. "You already rescued me."

"I like the idea of forever." With a cowboy whose heart was true, and who loved her completely. "We can rescue each other."

And it was just like her dream sixteen years earlier. She had a forever-cowboy, one whose heart was true, and who didn't walk away.

* * * * *

Dear Reader,

When I think of Willow Michaels, I think of all the strong women who I know, or have known. I want to be one of those women, someone who trusts God and overcomes. I want to be Peter, willing to step out of the boat and walk on water, even if I do sink from time to time. To be that strong woman, we need to learn to trust God, believing He is, and that He is able. We also need to trust ourselves, the decisions we make and our ability to handle difficult times or situations. Sometimes we let ourselves down, or we even feel as if God has let us down. At times the people we counted on, or trusted, knowingly or unknowingly let us down. That doesn't mean the end of the road. It's merely a starting place, a detour, a new route that we hadn't expected.

We move on. We forgive. We rebuild. In the process, we grow. In *A Cowboy's Heart,* Willow is like so many of us: she's walking that walk of faith, stumbling, but getting back up again.

Pray hard, stand strong.

Brenda Minton

Questions for Discussion

1. Willow Michaels lost a child, her husband, and now she's facing complete and profound deafness. Situations that we encounter cement our faith, making it personal. What milestone in your life created that moment when your faith became real and tangible for the first time?

2. Willow is embarrassed when Aunt Janie reintroduces her to Clint Cameron at the rodeo, because she'd had a crush on him when they were younger. Have you ever been faced with a person from your past? How did you handle it? Was it easy? Awkward?

3. Willow tries to avoid discussing her hearing loss. But avoiding a situation won't make it go away. How do you think Willow felt, knowing that her hearing was getting worse?

4. Willow, like us, could face problems with faith, or with her own strength. Like most of us, she flounders before she finds solid ground. When does Willow seem to let go and let God take over?

5. Clint returns home to take care of his ailing father, a man who has been abusive and neglectful. He realizes that although he's forgiven his father, forgetting takes longer. How do we separate the two?

6. Clint's faith is strong, but he tries to take care of everyone in his life, and forgets that God is more than able to carry that burden. Have you ever found yourself in a similar situation? How did you handle it?

7. Clint's nephews spend a lot of time with Willow and Aunt Janie on their ranch. Do you think this was hard for Willow to handle, considering all she'd lost in her life? Why or why not?

8. Willow realizes that peace comes from God. The world, on the other hand, finds peace in possessions and in circumstances that go the way we want. How could Willow have dealt with her situation, other than seeking God? How did seeking God's peace change Willow's attitude toward her situation?

9. Clint sometimes confuses his need to "fix" people with love. What motivates that need to "fix" others? Are you guilty of trying to "fix" people? How?

10. Willow takes a chance and trusts Clint with her biggest secret, that she can't have children. How hard is it to open up in a relationship and let people know those things about ourselves that we could keep hidden?

11. When Clint learns that his sister has gone missing, he feels helpless, dependent on the strength of others, and dependent on God. Willow as-

sures him that she can be strong for both of them. When have you been strong for others? How did the situation turn out?

12. When the church prays for Clint's sister, Jenna, to come home, the pastor teaches that prayer should be our first response, not an afterthought. "Just pray" takes on a new meaning when we realize that one definition of the word *just* is "immediately." If we realize the power of prayer, does it change our lives?

13. Willow prays for God to show her if Clint was the man who would love her forever. Did God show her Clint was the man for her? How? Have you ever asked for a sign from God? Was it answered? How?

Love Inspired
CLASSICS

Six sweet, heartfelt stories from fan-favorite
Love Inspired® Books authors!

**HOME TO CROSSROADS RANCH and
THE BABY BOND**

by Linda Goodnight

**HIS SMALL-TOWN GIRL and
HER SMALL-TOWN HERO**

by Arlene James

**THE GUARDIAN'S MISSION and
THE PROTECTOR'S PROMISE**

by Shirlee McCoy

*Available March 18, 2013,
wherever books are sold.*

REQUEST YOUR FREE BOOKS!

2 FREE INSPIRATIONAL NOVELS
PLUS 2
FREE
MYSTERY GIFTS

Love Inspired

YES! Please send me 2 FREE Love Inspired® novels and my 2 FREE mystery gifts (gifts are worth about $10). After receiving them, if I don't wish to receive any more books, I can return the shipping statement marked "cancel." If I don't cancel, I will receive 6 brand-new novels every month and be billed just $4.74 per book in the U.S. or $5.24 per book in Canada. That's a saving of at least 21% off the cover price. It's quite a bargain! Shipping and handling is just 50¢ per book in the U.S. and 75¢ per book in Canada.* I understand that accepting the 2 free books and gifts places me under no obligation to buy anything. I can always return a shipment and cancel at any time. Even if I never buy another book, the two free books and gifts are mine to keep forever.

105/305 IDN F47Y

Name _____ (PLEASE PRINT) _____

Address _____ Apt. # _____

City _____ State/Prov. _____ Zip/Postal Code _____

Signature (if under 18, a parent or guardian must sign) _____

Mail to the **Harlequin® Reader Service:**
IN U.S.A.: P.O. Box 1867, Buffalo, NY 14240-1867
IN CANADA: P.O. Box 609, Fort Erie, Ontario L2A 5X3

**Are you a subscriber to Love Inspired books
and want to receive the larger-print edition?
Call 1-800-873-8635 or visit www.ReaderService.com.**

* Terms and prices subject to change without notice. Prices do not include applicable taxes. Sales tax applicable in N.Y. Canadian residents will be charged applicable taxes. Offer not valid in Quebec. This offer is limited to one order per household. Not valid for current subscribers to Love Inspired books. All orders subject to credit approval. Credit or debit balances in a customer's account(s) may be offset by any other outstanding balance owed by or to the customer. Please allow 4 to 6 weeks for delivery. Offer available while quantities last.

Your Privacy—The Harlequin® Reader Service is committed to protecting your privacy. Our Privacy Policy is available online at www.ReaderService.com or upon request from the Harlequin Reader Service.

We make a portion of our mailing list available to reputable third parties that offer products we believe may interest you. If you prefer that we not exchange your name with third parties, or if you wish to clarify or modify your communication preferences, please visit us at www.ReaderService.com/consumerchoice or write to us at Harlequin Reader Service Preference Service, P.O. Box 9062, Buffalo, NY 14269. Include your complete name and address.

LI13R

"I can't undo what I did." She leaned back against the wall and with her fingers pinched the bridge of her nose. Soft blond hair framed her face.

"No, you can't." He guessed he didn't need to tell her what an understatement that was. She'd robbed him. She'd robbed Lindsey. Come to think of it, she'd robbed his entire family. Lindsey's family.

Jana's shoulder started to shake. Her body sagged against the wall and her knees buckled. He grabbed her, holding her close as she sobbed into his shoulder. She still fit perfectly and he didn't want that. He didn't want to remember how it had been when they were young. He didn't want her scent to be familiar or her touch to be the touch he missed.

It all came back to him, holding her. He pushed it away by remembering coming home to an empty house and a note.

He held her until her sobs became quieter, her body ceased shaking. He held her and he tried hard not to think about the years he'd spent searching, wishing things could have been different for them, wishing she'd come back.

"Mrs. Cooper?"

He realized he was still holding Jana, his hands stroking her hair, comforting her. His hands dropped to his sides and she stepped back, visibly trying to regain her composure. She managed a shaky smile.

"She'll be fine," he assured the woman in the white lab coat, who was walking toward them, her gaze lingering on Jana.

"I'm Nurse Bonnie Palmer. If you could join me in the conference room, we'll discuss what needs to happen next for your daughter."

Jana shook her head. "I'm going to stay with Lindsey."

Blake gave her a strong look and pushed back a truckload of suspicion. She wasn't going anywhere with Lindsey. Not now. He knew that and he'd fight through the doubts about Jana and her motives. He'd do what he had to do to make sure Lindsey got the care she needed.

He'd deal with his ex-wife later.

He's committed to helping his daughter, but can Blake Cooper ever trust the wife who broke his heart?

Pick up THE COWBOY'S REUNITED FAMILY *to find out. Available February 2014 wherever Love Inspired® Books are sold.*

SPECIAL EXCERPT FROM

Love Inspired.
SUSPENSE

A U.S. marshal must work with an FBI agent to save a child's life. Read on for a preview of the next exciting book in the WITNESS PROTECTION series, THE BABY RESCUE by Margaret Daley, available February 2014

FBI agent Lisette Sutton entered supervisory U.S. marshal Tyler Benson's office in Denver, and two men rose. In front of the oak desk, the larger one of the pair was probably Deputy Marshal Colton Phillips, the person she would be teamed with in this case involving child smuggling and baby brokering across state lines.

As she took a seat, she slid a glance toward U.S. marshal Phillips. He swung his gaze toward her. His startlingly blue eyes fringed in long lashes caught hold of her, and for a moment she couldn't look away. Intense. Focused. Assessing, as she had. Her stomach fluttered. Slowly one corner of his mouth tilted up, and he glanced away—turning his attention to his supervisor, who was talking.

"From what Don Saunders has given us so far, we're dealing with a black market baby adoption ring that covers a good part of the United States," Benson said.

Benson cleared his throat. "Now that Saunders is here in Denver and settled into a safe house, we need more. He has additional information he'd promised the marshals in St. Louis once he was out of the area. Time to question the man, and if he's bluffing, call him on it if he wants to remain in WitSec."

"From my boss I heard there was an incident yesterday in St. Louis. What happened?"

"A couple of guys interrupted our transport to the airport," Colton said. "I talked with Marshal McCall in St. Louis this morning. They have interrogated the three men involved in the wreck and run background checks. There doesn't appear to be any connection to the criminal elements in St. Louis."

"Could Don Saunders have orchestrated an escape somehow?"

"Not likely. It's not like he had access to a phone at the safe house, or that he left the place."

"But if he has been compromised in any way, our chance to find out more about this organization and catch others involved will vanish. A smuggling ring like this can't exist. Children are involved."

Phillips sat forward, closer to her. "I know exactly what's at stake with this case."

To find out if Colton and Lisette can work through their differences and solve their case, pick up
THE BABY RESCUE, available February 2014
wherever Love Inspired® Suspense books are sold.